ALL

MEAT

A Redneck Meets
LSD-25

A Novel Set in The Sixties

by

John Aalborg

ALL MEAT
A Redneck Meets LSD-25

First Edition, paperback print
ISBN: 978-0-9849365-6-4
Bleep-Free Press
http://www.bleepfreepress.com

Transcribed and vetted by Alberta Pedrick from the original (ca 1970) typescript manuscript.
Final digital draft vetted by "Cheater".

This is a work of fiction including all the characters. The "Sixties Cultural Revolution" was real, however, and many who partici-pated in this transformation of society walk among us today.

Author's Rating: "All Ages"
Publisher's Rating: PG-14 (mild erotica)
Home Schooler Rating: MA (USA)

Parents are responsible for child's book choices.

Acknowledgments:

Special thanks to:

John Schaffner, Victor Chapin, and Barney Karpfinger — New York literary agents whose early encouragements went unheeded for so long.

Perry Gamsby, founder and CEO of StreetWise Publications, Sydney AU, who supplies most of my get-off-your-ass encouragement, and Owsley Stanley who was responsible for most of the LSD.

Alberta Pedrick, who took to her home the recently discovered typewritten manuscript (in a raggedy old box), a book I do not remember writing, and transcribed the 556 pages to a digital format while maintaining the original by accompanying the text with her suggestions in a red font.

And to Gene Smith, Houston writer extraordinaire, who emailed the following after my discovery of the lost novel: "Allow me to make a suggestion. Before you rewrite everything to your current, 'mature' point of view, just read the damn thing. You've probably got a 60's era time machine on your hands. Allow yourself to be who you were."

CHAPTER 1
Miami — The Magic City
Near the end of "The Sixties"

Harry's home was in an older section of the City of Miami — Alapattah — a funky enclave of quaint — and often grand — frame, coral rock, and stucco houses shaded by tropical vegetation and towering poinciana trees — a white neighborhood in the path of an overwhelming black invasion. On this morning after Thanksgiving, hours yet before dawn, Harry Schaffner was sitting in his lovingly-rebuilt Ford F-100 pickup truck and splitting the darkness with the roar of the big engine. It was a 351 Cleveland V-8 with a stick shift he would proudly announce to anyone who cared.

Vrrrrrrrrrrrooooooooooooooooooom pop pop pop... He was blipping the throttle of the pickup, warming it up, while he rammed his arms and bent his shoulders through a set of isometric exercises.

Vvvvvvrrrroooooooooom pop...

Soon to be the last white man on the block, he could not care less, he told himself, about the noise. The bow of his twin-engine power boat loomed over the back of the truck bed, and it was glistening with dew and sparkling red through the darkness from the truck's tail lights. The boat and the truck were Harry's pride, despite the fact he owed money on them. "Twin modified Renaults, Merc outdrives!" Just thinking about his rig would bring smiles to his face but not to his family. Or his nearest neighbor.

Vrrrrrrrrrrrrrrrrrrrrrrrrrrrrooooooooooooooooom pop pop pop...

Over in the next house, old John Neeley reached for the alarm clock and turned its face toward the night-light, which was in the shape of a glowing, phosphorescent crucifix. 3:00 AM! Harry's truck and boat trailer were between the two houses, right next to Neeley's bedroom window. Forgetting the night-light cross of Jesus, Neeley cursed Harry silently. And he cursed Harry for the morning his ailing wife, Mavis, died in this very room, complaining (as she often did) about the noise Harry was making next door.

"If your old lady is so sick, why doesn't God fix her!" Harry had yelled at him once, pushing away the zippered Bible which Neeley was waving in his face.

Well, Neeley smiled to himself, today is moving day and Harry will soon be begging to have his nice, God-fearing, white neighbors back.

Annie pulled her head out from under her pillow as soon as Harry's rig rolled out of the yard. She had gone back to bed after getting Harry up and making his breakfast and packing the plastic cooler with all the things he liked to take along. She was exhausted from being up half the night with little Perry, who was sick; and then having to get up again to get Harry ready for his boat trip. It was almost too much to keep awake but it was time to give Perry his medicine. Then, if he was okay she could go back to sleep — sleep all morning maybe — if Janey didn't bother her. Janey, Perry's sister. A little older but trouble in her own way.

The floor of the large, frame house was cold, but Annie was glad that the long, hot Florida summer was finally over. And it had been a relief to hear the pickup pulling down the street through the gears. The boat trips lasted all day — often all weekend — and Harry always returned home beat but happy, his energies calmed, his spirits up from another successful bout with the sea, happy to be home safe and warm and hungry with hot food on the table — even happy and comfortable enough to listen to the children for a while, the only time he seemed to enjoy talking with them. And he always came home horny.

She padded into little Perry's room and covered him. Only six years old but he looked so long now, his feet nearly touching the end of his little bed. He will need a big bed soon, she thought, bending over him and listening. His breathing seemed a bit better, though Perry's bony chest was still heaving rapidly. She hated to wake him up for the medicine, but it was time. His eyelids fluttered and he coughed. First a gurgley cough and then a spasm, a real fight for air. Perry struggled to sit up and then began to cry. "Mommy, why did you wake me up? It took so long to fall asleep! I never get any sleep! I'm going to die if I don't get any sleep!"

Annie was shaking the medicine bottle.

"And you brought the wrong spoon again!" Perry yelled. The effort brought on another coughing spell.

"Perry, you have to take this or your cold won't go away. The doctor said that if..."

"It's not going away, Mommy! And my teacher said if I keep on missing school I have to take First Grade over!" After coughing up again he added: "And Doctor Shane is no good and he doesn't care about me because he can't make me better!"

Annie had the cap off the bottle and was about to pour the medicine into the spoon.

"Ohhhhhh!" Perry moaned. "Antibiotic again! And with Janey's spoon!"

"Janey's spoon isn't going to poison you," Annie said, but she didn't pour the medicine.

"What if it has her germs on it, Mommy?"

"It's a clean spoon. I washed it first."

"Washed it! Washed it! Does washing kill germs? Huh? Did Daddy say that washing kills germs?"

But Annie had already gotten up from the edge of his bed and was heading for the kitchen for Perry's special spoon. It was true, the doctor did say that Perry had little resistance to disease at this point and that his cold, which had dragged on for weeks now, made his asthma worse. When she returned with the right spoon, little Perry was sitting on the edge or the bed, feet on the floor, back hunched over. He was trying to breathe and keep from coughing at the same time. When he turned to look at his mother it was such a pitiful look, and there were bags under his eyes, and his eyes were red from crying. "And anyway, if I don't die..."

"You're not going to die." Annie remembered for a moment the horror she had felt once, as a child, when she thought she would die.

"Mommy's little angel is not going to die."

"You interrupted," Perry said.

She waited while he worked out another coughing fit, and patted his back.

"And anyway — if — I don't die — I'm going to flunk — because I'm missing — too much school!"

Annie moved the spoonful of raspberry-flavored antibiotic toward his mouth, not too fast and not too slowly — fearing his reaction. To her surprise, he swallowed the stuff without further fussing. She tried to sit closer to him so she could hug him but he jerked himself away, refusing to look at her, tears again streaming down his cheeks.

"Your teacher told me that you are the smartest first-grader she ever had," Annie said.

"What good is it if I'm sick all the time!"

"Daddy said he'd take you to a different doctor if you don't get better by next week."

"Sure, sure..."

"Now Perry..."

"Sure! He never has any money! Last week he had to borrow — from my money — to get my medicine! Besides, he doesn't really care what happens to me."

"That's not true, Perry. You're his only son. You're his boy! He's very proud of you. And he's always telling everybody how smart you are and how you can read and write already."

"Does he tell everybody how sick I am?"

"Well, he knows you're not going to be sick much longer."

"I know. I know! I'll be dead!"

"Now Perry, I told you..."

"Will it be morning soon?" Perry said, finally looking her in the eye.

"Pretty soon."

"Pretty soon, pretty soon. What **time** is it?" Perry was aware that his breathing usually improved after the sun came up.

"It's three-thirty," Annie said. "In a couple hours it'll be light."

"I know. I know how long it takes." Perry crawled away to the corner of his bed where he had three pillows stacked so he could sleep sitting up. He would not look at his mother again, and he knew it might be daylight before he would be able to fall asleep.

After leaving Perry's room, Annie peeked in on Janey. Janey was nine years old and took after her much more than Perry did. She was fast asleep, hugging her pillow. Sleeping like a little princess, Annie thought. She loved Janey very much. And she loved to look at Janey's long, curly blond hair, just like her own hair had been before it turned mousey and gray. Annie's hair was red now, dyed red (menopause red, Harry called it). She had picked the color partly because Harry often talked about the red-haired girl he had dated back in high school. Now, no matter what Annie did with her hair, Harry would say that it looked like shit.

On the way back to her bedroom, Annie stopped again in the kitchen. Harry sometimes left a love-note in the cupboard where the breakfast dishes were. Each of the four members of the family had their own cereal bowl, and in hers she found the note. It was handwritten with a fat, felt-tip pen:

Dear Annie
I LOVE YOU.
Harry

She smiled. It had been a long time since Harry had told her to her face that he loved her, but he would often tell her with a note. To her face he could say things like "Your hair looks like shit" or "Your belly hangs out like a blob of shit." For him to say "I love you" he had to write a note that she could read while he was away.

Instead of having Thanksgiving turkey leftovers tonight, we'll have beef roast.

Maybe it will be a nice weekend.

They still had Saturday and Sunday.

What if he stays overnight on the island and I make the roast...

She wondered briefly whether Harry could be taking a girl with him in the boat. He had done that once that she knew of.... Annie sighed and flopped into her bed. Tomorrow, no, maybe Monday, she would go back to her diet and start exercising.

CHAPTER 2
The Island

The sliver of angry, red sun lifted off from the horizon and transformed the sky and sea into ripples of brilliant gold. Harry was heading the boat south now, running parallel with the waves, riding up and slipping down off the crests, grinning as he licked the salty spray from his lips. Dropping down off plane through a gentle trough, he snatched up his binoculars and quickly scanned the shore of the barrier island, now less than a mile to the west. Deserted and patient, brilliant green in the early sun, he saw it waiting for him.

No boats. Perfect!

He glanced back, toward Black Caesar Creek, the sun gleaming reflections into his eyes, mirroring diamond-like flashes of light from a speck of a boat off in the distance, heading away into the horizon toward Bimini or the outer reefs.

The guys at work ask what fish I catch.

They have no idea what I do with this boat.

Harry scanned the depth sounder and the island again and abruptly headed the boat straight for it, coming in on a deep-water tongue of the ocean that he knew where he would miss all the reefs at low tide. He throttled the engines down a little, then up at just the right moment, and surfed in with the following sea.

"Perfect!" he yelled, his knees flexed as the boat fell gently off the cresting waves, his knuckles white as he gripped the wheel. And then he saw them. He had to squint to see what they were — people — two people on the shore. No boats, but two people.

"Fuck!"

Harry was coming in too fast and he throttled down again, the boat shuddering as a wave crested and gave the stern a powerful push.

"Nudists! Christ!"

He could see them better now, and he was closing fast. A guy with a beard, and a chick. The chick was wearing a hippie dress or something, and the guy was naked.

Dumb fucker is running for the bushes.

The boat would be close enough to anchor in a minute, and Harry had to take his eyes off the strangers to watch the bottom.

You come all the way out here to be alone...away from everybody...and...

"Fuckers!"

Harry cut the engines way down this time and switched his gaze from the ocean bottom to the shore — and from the shore to the bottom. The engines were purring, and beautiful to hear, but the coral outcroppings were dangerous.

"Assholes!"

Dumb ass hiding in the bushes! Pathetic!

Dumb bitch standing there like she's the queen of driftwood....

Just dumb enough to find my hide-outs. My supplies.

Harry spit over the side in their direction.

Just then, the female lifted her gown and pulled it off over her head. She stood there for a moment, facing the sea, legs spread like a triumphant comic-book savage, head held high and framed in a halo of kinky, red hair, the new sun flashing from her rings and bracelets and the golden ring in her nose. Just at the time when Harry had drop the anchor with not a second to lose.

"Oh, God." Harry's balls were trying to take charge and in a moment the props would be chewing coral. He swung the boat around hard, heading back out into the wind for a second. "Oh God." He scampered up to the bow.

How can she do that?

What a fox!

He flung out the anchor and cleated down the line, tripping on the rope as he paid it out. Wham! Harry landed on his ass, but the bow-rail kept him from falling overboard. He scrambled to his feet as the anchor took hold with the stern just far enough from the island to be safe when the tide ran out. Nice job considering, he told himself, but when he looked up from the ocean bottom, visible now, the chick was gone, melted back into the woods with the freak he'd seen with her.

"Shit." Harry was talking to the breeze. "Shit!" He tried to picture the woman's body, but the image was already fading. It had only been a moment, and just when he had to watch the shallows. He picked up the binoculars and scanned the ride of seaweed and driftwood which marked high-water on the jagged, coral beach. "Damn!" The woman's gown, white and trimmed with what looked like ribbons, was fluttering in the wind, caught on a point of coral near the tree line, where she had left it.

"Well God damn!" More relaxed now with his boat secured, Harry forgot what had to be done next. He needed a beer, that he could feel. There was plenty of beer in the cooler, but the wind and the sea were picking up and the boat was bobbing and twisting up-and-down. He began to pull his gear out from under the bow deck, looking back to shore as often as he could while keeping his balance.

"Bitch!"

It was making him angry now, thinking about how weirds and freaks were always trying to shock people, or getting people to try to be like them and then putting them down when they tried. They were probably laughing at him right now, watching him from the tree line.

She did that just to get me horny.

She waited until I was close enough to see.

And that naked creep in the bushes.... What the fuck!

You get friendly with them and then they tell you how fucked up you are.

"It's my island," he said aloud. "My island!" He knew it would be impossible for them to hear with the wind and the surf. "Harry Schaffner will show you just who is fucked up!" He grinned, to show anybody watching that he did not feel the least bit threatened. "And my brain is all in one piece, too! Not all burned out with chemicals!"

Grinning all the time now, Harry moved his equipment to the stern, propping his M-1 carbine on top of everything so they could see what it was.

They'll split when they see my guns.

After shutting off the fuel cocks, raising the outdrives, and checking the battery switches, Harry looked over the side again at the now murky bottom.

Calm down! Calm down! Don't forget anything!

Bilge pumps on auto — check.

He tested the depth with a paddle, and was happy he had powered up the outdrives higher than usual. Then he picked up his pistol belt, checking the snap on the holster, and hung the belt around his neck. After one, last, quick look at everything, he was in the water with a splash. The water was warm and comfortable, but with the waves licking his ass, Harry had to adjust the heavy belt around his neck so that his canteen hung low and the gun rode high and dry. He decided to haul the gear in with two trips, leaving the carbine on shore after the first while he waded back to the boat for the second load. Testing the freak's intentions in his mind, he pictured them going for his rifle while he was on his way back for the second trip. He fantasized waiting for them to actually get their hands on the M-1 before dropping them with the .45 automatic. With their crummy prints all over the weapon, he would get off free.

Thinking all the time.

Harry grinned.

That's the difference between them and us!

Clear thinking and planning ahead!

Slogging through the waves, he waded with his back to the shore as long as he dared before wheeling around to look.

Nothing.

Come on! I know you're there!

Suddenly, he almost lost his balance when his foot struck a high crown of coral under the sand. He glanced back toward shore to check if they had seen.

Not cool, Harry. Calm down!

That chick was really beautiful....

How do scumbags get all the best girls?

The biggest part of the second load was Harry's large, heavy, red-and-white plastic cooler, which he carried on his head. The pistol belt still hung from his neck, and as he splashed his way in, Harry kept his eyes on the shore where he had left the carbine. He day-dreamed the freaks making a dash for it while he carefully floated the cooler in the water to free his hand for the .45. The gun battle raged in his mind: the dead nudist lying there with the M-1 still clutched in his outstretched hand; the chick running out to Harry naked, throwing her arms around his neck and kissing him and begging him not to kill her, too. No, better yet: the chick was being held captive on the island after the weirdo sank her boat. Harry could almost feel her young, pointy nipples pressing against his chest, and a hot flash rushed through his balls and cock.

God! Why not?

She's really out here! I saw her!

Likes to show off, too!

This could be the real thing!

He placed the second load beside the first, and climbed up onto the coral ledge, crouching and listening while the water ran off his clinging jeans. He had the feeling they were still there, and they were watching.

Well — fuck them!

He pulled some dry things out of his bag and stopped again to listen. The surf was diminishing to gentle laps and gurgles, licking clean the narrow ring of jagged, coral beach which ringed the windward side of island. Smiling now, he sucked in a lungful of the fragrant air he loved so much.

Locating a piece of good, clean drift-lumber to stand on, Harry struggled to get off his wet boots and jeans. He was not wearing underwear, and his pasty-white ass warmed in the sun and dried in the changing, hesitant gusts of wind from offshore. When he was nearly dry, and thanking himself for always keeping his bush neatly trimmed, he pulled on a fresh pair of socks and Levis. After lacing up his boots, he got out one of his favorite T-shirts, which had the word **HARRY** stenciled in big letters across the chest. He pulled the shirt down and smoothed it out, stretching the cotton over his visibly powerful shoulders and flat stomach. His job with the clothing change felt good, and Harry checked the tree line again. He felt comfortable with his guns handy and the boat all squared away. Stretching his arms high and bending over to touch his toes, he felt proud.

I work off every beer I drink, he said to himself, looking at the dress the girl had left behind, still caught on the edge of coral and fluttering. Hooking the pistol belt about his waist, he picked his way over to the gown and snatched it up. It was a nightgown with little, pink ribbons sewed on the sleeves and the hem. Hoping they were watching now for sure, he reverently held the gown out in front of him like a priest holding a sacrificial lamb in a Bible picture. Then, after kissing it, he folded it neatly, laid it on a piece of clean lumber, and placed a small rock on it to hold it down. Nodding once with pleasure at what he had done, he felt that everything was under control.

Ten minutes later, Harry had completely circled behind the point where he was sure the freaks had cut into the woods. He had hidden his gear and was carrying only the handgun and his canteen so he could move quietly and quickly. In a few more minutes he was far enough in where the sounds of the sea could barely be heard, and there was only the buzzing of flies and the occasional flitting of birds through the trees. Harry squatted down for a moment and listened.

They must have a boat somewhere. Maybe in the creek on the south end.

He was crouching near the edge of a small, open spot, bright with the warming sun. The warmth and the solitude suddenly made him horny, and Harry remembered the time when he had stripped and stood in the middle of just such a natural clearing, at noontime when the sun was high and hot. He had stood there and pumped his meat off, naked and sweating, his legs spread and his balls dangling, his head thrown back and facing the sun...

Harry felt the bulge of his balls through the jeans and thought about it. Too early for that now, he decided, and with the possibility of people nearby....

If I can hold it until I get home, fucking Annie will be so good

Then the sinking feeling came, like knowledge: he would never see the chick who had stripped on the shore again. Chicks like that never happened to people like him. She would be at least a mile away by now, hiking over to the south end where surely they had a boat tied up. After all his wild expectations, what kind of a day could he have now? Harry tried to picture Annie, her tits in his hands while he unloaded into her hungry mouth — but the image in his head did not satisfy. He got up slowly, his knees stiff from crouching, and that was when he heard them. Deeper in the woods to the northwest of him came the unmistakable clanking of pots and pans.

They're camping!

Harry dropped down low, the whole, horny sex urge coming back. He could sneak up and watch them. Maybe there were other chicks! And a good place to camp in that direction, he knew, was under the old Poinciana tree. He would be able to crawl under the thorn bushes which completely closed off that clearing on the south side, and watch them as long as he wanted to without them suspecting a thing. It was going to be a warm day, a sunny day — they would be doing their nudist-thing with their clothes off — Harry was sure of that! He began to move on all fours, and in a few minutes he was up to the thorn thicket. It was a beautiful place, and it was impossible to look into the clearing until you were right up on it. Harry had often thought of building a camp there himself, but it was too close to the shore for comfort. He inched his way forward to get a look. The only noise now was the crunching of dead leaves under him as he crawled. A thorn barb caught the flesh of his right arm and he had to back up a little to remove it. When he did, another caught his left arm and another hooked into his jeans. Harry froze for a minute to think, and to stop the sounds he was making.

Why are they so quiet?

He tried to move forward again but there was no way he could do it properly from this side. As carefully as he could, he backed out of the thicket and got up to stretch. If they had heard him coming, it would explain their silence. He decided to go in walking from the only opening, on the other side, as casually and with as much noise as possible.

When he got there, the clearing under the big tree was empty. He slumped down, leaning his back against the Poinciana. This whole business was fatiguing. He should have gone to work on his new trail instead of chasing creeps. Or he could be fucking Annie right now, right under this tree. He remembered the last time he had brought her out to the island and she was too chicken to take her clothes off. Harry had even gone to the trouble of bringing a mattress the week before and setting it up off the ground in a secluded place. But Annie worried about airplanes, or someone sneaking up on them and watching them. He was angry with her for a long time after that because the island was difficult to get to and visitors were rare.

Something moved up in the Poinciana, and for the second time that morning Harry was completely unprepared for what he saw. The platform, built high up in the tree over his head, was new, and the two girls peering over the edge, long hair hanging down, were looking right at him.

"Hi!" they both said together.

"Hi. Uh...." Harry scrambled to keep his balance and his heart slammed up in his chest.

"You were sneaking up on us before!"

"No, uh, I was trying to, um...." Harry's face flushed red.

"Come on, man, we saw you." One of the girls laughed, and the other joined in. "We saw the whole thing. Those thorns get hungry!" They laughed again.

"Well, I didn't know who you were and I thought you might be some rednecks or something."

"Come on, man. You're a redneck yourself."

"Me? Naw, I..."

"Look at you! The guns, the army boots, the cooler full of beer...."

Harry backed up a little to get a better look. "How do you know what's in my cooler?"

"Is there beer in your cooler?"

From what Harry could see of them, they were both naked. He got a flash of tit for a second. "Yeah, but there's other stuff, too, like..."

"Like ham and cheese sandwiches?"

"I didn't check." Harry was smiling, trying hard to be friendly, desperately hoping for acceptance.

"Oh, your old lady's job is making the sandwiches, huh!" The other chick chimed in: "I can see your boat from up here."

"Yeah, well."

"What'd you do with your rifle and your cooler full of beer?"

"I hid them."

Laughing pretty faces framed in wild, kinky hair. "He hid them." They were lowering a rope ladder down from their tree-house. "Come on up!" "Get some sun!"

"Ah, no, ahhhhh.... I get enough sun in my boat for ten people." The offer brought the blood pounding again in Harry's chest.

Do it!

Climb up there and do it! This is your chance!

One of them said: "You have any shit on you?"

The other interrupted. "Do you turn on?"

Harry backed up a little from the rope they were dangling in front of him. If he could only see them better. "You mean marijuana?"

The girls laughed. They were both sitting up now, near the edge of their tree-house, legs crossed, naked. Harry pretended to be completely unconcerned. "Grass doesn't do anything for me." He said.

"It doesn't **do** anything for him — awww."

"Did you ever try it?"

"Sure. Lots of times, but..."

The chicks whispered to each other for a second.

Hey! Harry! Your name is Harry, isn't it? Or is that the name of your T-shirt?"

"My name is Harry, I..."

"Hey Harry! Watch closely now! Does **this** turn you on?" The girls drew together and began a long, passionate kiss. One held the other's head with both hands, as if she couldn't get enough, while the other fondled her own nipples with her fingers and made them grow. Suddenly they both pulled apart and looked down at Harry, an expression of satisfaction and passion-shock on their faces. Then they laughed. "It turns him on! We've got him! His mouth is hanging open! Harry! Did that turn you on?"

Harry swallowed hard and shouted up: "Yes!"

"Our camp is right behind there." They pointed.

"Huh?"

"See that pine tree? There's only one."

"Uh, yeah!"

"Walk straight up to it, go around it, and you'll see the path, same direction."

"Oh. Yeah. Okay." Harry started toward the pine tree, moving under the platform so they couldn't see him for a second. His penis was swollen, and was caught in his pantleg. With a quick motion, he forked his cock over to a better position. The chicks above burst out laughing.

They didn't see that. They're making fun of me.

They got me horny for the fun of it. Same as the creep on the shore with the nightie.

I should waste every one of them. I could. I have the guns. I have control of the situation.

The path behind the tree was clean, and it was new. Harry's hard-on went down nice and easy. Confidence was coming back. He would saunter right into their camp. He would be cool. It wouldn't matter what they were doing in there. Harry Schaffner would be cool. Harry was tough. Harry had guns.

"Anybody home?" The new clearing he found had a familiar look. It was similar to a deserted camp Harry had found a year earlier on the north end of the island. A platform had been built just a foot off the ground with a canvass shelter rigged over it, hanging from scraps of drift rope of all sizes and colors, and strung from surrounding trees. Mosquito netting hung down to form the walls. To the side of the platform was a workbench, a cooking table, and a swing seat — all made from drift items. A stove had been hacked out of a rusty oil drum and the ashes in it were still hot and smoking. On the far side of the clearing was a solitary, Mexican string-mesh hammock tied between two cabbage palms. The hammock was moving. Harry walked through the center of the camp toward the hammock as nonchalantly as he knew how. A bearded man was in it. His head was surrounded with a halo of kinky, blond hair. He was picking his nose with his little finger and pressing the boogers through the mesh. It was the nudist Harry had seen with the chick on the beach. He was smiling and looking Harry right in the eye while he cleaned his nose.

"Good morning," Harry said, shifting his weight to one foot, looking for a good way to stand.

The hippie pulled the pinky out of his nose and swung out of the hammock, smiling broadly, showing all of his teeth. He was wearing a white loin-cloth with piss stains on the crotch, and there were gold rings on his toes. When Harry looked back at the man's face, the big grin was still there, and his eyes were bright blue and unflinching. "Welcome to our camp" he said finally. "And to the island."

"Let me welcome you!" Harry said. "I've been coming to this island for years!" With the big .45 on his belt, there was no way Harry could find to hang his right arm without looking like a gunfighter in a movie, so he tried hooking his thumbs into the front pockets of his jeans. The weight of his body kept on shifting from one leg to the other.

"Are you hungry? Would you like something to eat?"

Harry did not answer immediately, but took a quick swing around to see where the others were. "Where is everybody? I saw two girls back there in a tree-house" Harry pointed in the direction he had come from, but the tree-house could not be seen from the camp. The bearded man did not answer, but at the mention of the girls his grin became even more broad. Almost friendly.

"What do you do here?" Harry said.

The weird moved over to the platform and sat on the edge, pulling his legs up and crossing them, resting his hands on his knees. He was still grinning.

"How did you get here?" Harry asked, speaking louder. It was getting harder to hack that grin, and all those teeth, and the man's nuts hanging out the side of the loose loincloth.

Another hairy man walked into the clearing and began to build up the fire in the oil drum.

"You didn't answer me," Harry said.

"How do any of us get here? To this earth. To this planet, I mean?"

"Shit. That's just dumb shit. Nobody knows the answer to that."

"Then what good are questions?"

"What's your name?"

"Gilli."

"Well, Gilli, I gave up religion when I found out religion doesn't have any answers. None of them do."

"Is Harry the name of your T-shirt, or is your..."

"The answer is blowing in the wind," Harry said, but he smiled as he spoke, to take the edge off.

Gilli's face relaxed. It was a completely open, friendly smile now. "An atheist? An agnostic? Hmmmm... I am a blue-eyed infidel Jew."

Harry turned at the sound of girl voices. The two chicks from the tree-house came wandering into the clearing, still naked. Gilli and the other man paid no attention to them, and Harry tried as hard as he could to appear relaxed, to be cool.

"The tall one, that's Mazie," Gilli said, "and the short one with the big tits is Milky. Those are their dope-head names. Uhh, sit down, Harry. Relax. Take it easy." The big, toothy grin again. "That gun and canteen must be heavy. Sit down. Pull up that stool over there. Sitting like I am takes practice and it hurts at first. An atheist! Harry, we've been waiting for you for a long time."

"Waiting for me?"

"The lady you saw with me before, on the beach, did you get a rush when you saw her, like a hot flash?"

Harry was pulling the stool over, about to sit, but the hippie was trying to embarrass him again. "That's dumb," Harry said. "Anybody would go for that chick." He pictured her pulling off the nightie.

"Sit, man. I have some interesting news for you."

Harry relented and plunked the stool down near Gilli and sat. The man building the fire turned toward them and smiled.

"That's Dale," Gilli said. "Mazie's old man. He's a beautiful person and he hardly ever talks." Dale stopped smiling. "You don't really need your gun," Gilli added. "We are non-violent, for the most part." The grin again. "Are you afraid of us?"

"I'm not afraid of **you!**" That sounded stupid and Harry knew it. Fuck it, what was there to be afraid of? He looked at Gilli and he looked up at the sky. He looked at the sunlight piercing the branches of the trees surrounding the clearing and shot a quick glance at the naked chicks.

Babes. Chicks. Birds....

"The news is that the little goddess you saw when you were setting your anchor this morning thinks you're beautiful. She thinks you're a lot like she is, coming out here alone."

When Harry had stolen the look at the girls, the tall one, Mazie, was sitting by the fire, facing them, tying up her hair, pins in her mouth, tanned little breasts, sitting cross-legged. Harry looked at Gilli.

Did he really say that?

Burned into his eyes, the picture of Mazie's wide-open muff danced across Gilli's face as Harry looked at him, while the realization of what Gilli had just said slammed in hard. Harry relaxed. He smiled a real smile, then unhooked his pistol belt and tossed it up on the platform next to the hippie with a **clunk.** It was a strange feeling that was coming over Harry. A good feeling. It could be nice being here with them in this little clearing. Why not? And then the feeling passed.

"Her name is Faylie."

"Fayley...."

"That's her hogfarm name — f-a-y-l-i-e — her hippie name. Her parents named her Bertha. Bertha! She's a wild girl. Not part of our family but we all love her just the same."

Dale sat down next to Gilli. He was wearing patched jeans and army boots.

"Gotta be tough to get a boat in here on the windward side," Harry said. "The reefs, the shoals.... My guns are insurance for other tough-asses who..." Mazie stood up for a second and repositioned herself, and Harry lost his train of thought.

But we all love her!

Harry's mind raced through the possibilities.

They mean they all FUCK her?

They're all swingers. They're nudists. Hippies.

They can do whatever they want. They don't work. The chicks probably have to ball anybody in the group that wants to.

If a brother wants to fuck your chick you have to be cool about it. Not get pissed off.

Faylie....

God! I want to cum in her right now so bad.

"Did you ever run away from home when you were a boy?" Gilli looked right through Harry when he asked.

Harry nodded and looked away. "A couple times."

"When was the last time?"

"When I split for Florida. Joined the army down here. Got married in Colorado."

"Long time ago?"

"Yeah.... Seems like it. Got two kids."

"You never went back home?"

"No."

"You never went back even to see your mother?"

"No. But she came down here, you know, to see her grandchildren. Our kids."

The grin was gone and Gilli looked serious. "Each day is a new trip. The trip you started this morning, Harry. There won't be any going back from this one, either."

"That's bullshit. What are you talking about?" Harry stood up. The whole band seemed to be trouping into the clearing. One cocky-looking longhair was carrying Harry's carbine over his shoulder, holding it by the barrel. Another freak had his knapsack. Two girls he had not seen before were hauling in his cooler. The man with the carbine walked right up to Harry and extended his hand, still hanging onto the weapon.

"I'm Pete," he said.

"What are you doing with my rifle?"

"We watched you hide it, actually."

The others nodded their heads.

"We don't keep anything from each other."

"Everything is shared."

Pete held out the M-1. "Here!"

Harry refused to take it. The clips were missing.

"Why didn't you leave it where it was?" It was a question and too late for demands. Before Harry could say more, the girl on his right, who had moved in so close she was brushing against him, put her arm as lightly as she could around Harry's shoulder. Harry swallowed. A strand of her long hair blew across his face and tickled his nose. He turned to look at her and her eyes were only inches away. *Christ!* He turned away. The girl on the left pushed in between Harry and Pete. She was older than the others. Harry's age, but thin and smooth like a model.

"I'm Neeta," she said. "Don't mind Pete — he's on an ego trip." She smiled. They were all smiling, friendly and warm. Neeta's bush was poking out from under the T-shirt she was wearing and Harry looked back at her face. His heart was pounding again. They were pressing him in from all sides and Harry hated it. They were trying to make fun of him again, or trying to make him say something stupid as they repeated their names. And the men were letting the women get close. Milky, the short one with the big tits, was right up against his back, mashing her nipples against his skin. He would have to break away. Twist around and dive for the .45 next to Gilli if they resisted. Harry tensed, glancing at Gilli where his handgun was. He felt the girl who had her arm around him begin to stroke the muscle in his left arm.

"It's going to be cool," she purred.

Milky moved off and Mazie, still naked, put her arms around Harry from behind and hugged him. They all laughed.

"We're not making fun of you," Neeta said.

"We're soaking the bad vibrations out of you."

The girl with the arm around him kissed Harry on the cheek, and let him loose. "Sit down next to Gilli — next to your gun if that will make you feel good. Come on." She took Harry's hand. He did not resist, and the others backed off. "My name is Surrendra," she said, "and we are going to sit here together. Can you sit like this? It's good for your head **and** your body." She crossed her legs into the lotus position, like Gilli's were. Gilli's nuts were still hanging out of his loincloth, and he was still grinning.

Harry plunked down on the platform between Surrendra and Gilli, next to the pistol belt. He pulled up his legs, one under the other, and made a face. "I keep myself in good shape, but I can't do this. Not for long, anyway."

"That's good," Surrendra cooed. She was dark, or part colored, and Harry could not look her in the eye.

"How'd you get to be such a grit?" Gilli said.

"Grit?"

"Why are you on this gun trip?"

Pete added, "Were you in Vietnam?"

Harry shook his head.

"How long were you in the army?"

"Three years..."

"How long you been out?"

Harry shrugged. "Ten years...."

"You're an **old** dude," Pete said.

Harry thought about it. He thought about what to do now — how to handle all this. And all these girls! He remembered what Gilli had said about Faylie. "Is this the whole group?"

A few of them nodded. "The whole family."

"Except for Faylie," Harry said, fishing.

"She's around. She doesn't live with us."

Dale looked up in the trees. Harry noticed that Surrendra had looked up then, too.

"Maybe I got on the gun trip the way Faylie got to be Faylie. Maybe I have them because it's easy to get ripped off out here. You can't call a cop out here. Not a payphone in sight."

"Far out."

"Far out."

"Well? How did Faylie get to be Faylie?" Harry said, suddenly finding himself off the defensive.

Gilli stood, grinning a mouth full of teeth. "Where Faylie came from is a million light-years from here. Someday, we will all be a million light-years from here."

They all nodded, as if they had suddenly hit upon a great truth.

"Shit," Pete chuckled.

Harry nodded.

"You are a million light-years from home yourself, Harry," Gilli said. "You just don't know it yet."

Harry did not give up. "Where is Faylie from?"

"Faylie is a PK. A preacher's kid."

"A southern Baptist minister's daughter!"

"Now she's of a new age."

Harry said: "My father called me a redneck atheist. I escaped home soon as I learned how to hitchhike."

"Faylie used to be an atheist...." Mazie stood up and stretched and Harry had to look away from her beautiful body.

"So I just don't know it yet, huh? Where I'm really from?"

Some of the others nodded and smiled.

"You won't want to go back."

Harry pulled his legs apart and stood up awkwardly. "Where are the clips for my carbine?"

Gilli looked at Pete. "Where's the rest of his stuff?"

"Faylie took the clips. I told her not to, but she took them anyway."

"Where is she?" Harry said.

They all laughed. Gilli stooped under the canopy and came out with a large pipe with feathers and beads hanging from the stem of it.

"Smoking time!" Milky shouted.

They all laughed again, except Harry.

CHAPTER 3
Harry's Cherry

Harry knew he was hanging in with them because he was horny. It was stupid. There were five men and only four chicks. Even if Faylie would walk in now, would she look as good as she did when he saw her from the boat? They said she was wild. Could he handle her? Could she be up in some tree now watching him?

Look cool.

What if she comes in right now?

The thought frightened Harry. He was alone on the platform now, and when the freaks lit up the pipe and began to pass it around, he wanted to move away. It was a good moment to split, but he could not bring himself to do it. Standing there alone, he had to decide quickly.

They're sitting there in the dirt naked.

Their cunts are probably riddled with ringworms.

They don't work. They probably steal.

Now they're getting doped on pot.

What are Janey and little Perry doing right now?

Harry suddenly began to worry about his boat at anchor and where he could not see it. The sea had been picking up when he was bringing his supplies in.

I don't need these people. I could be home fucking Annie.

He stepped down from the platform and moved toward his equipment stacked on the ground.

Make a decision! Make a decision!

He pulled a can of Busch out of the cooler. "Anyone want a beer?"

The hippies smiled and shook their heads.

pschttt! Harry popped open the can and chug-a-lugged the whole thing and burped. He pinched the aluminum container and tossed it into the smoking oil drum. Somebody shouted "Hey!" but Neeta clapped her hands.

"Y-a-a-a-a-y h-o-o-o-o-o, Harry!"

Gilli smiled and handed Harry the pipe. "Columbian. It's dynamite."

There was silence as Harry took it. He decided to do it, and do it right. Twice, years before, when Harry had been trying to make it with a girl on Miami Beach, he tried to "smoke shit" with her friends and had been put down for doing it wrong and not getting high.

"Take in a lot of air with it and then hold it in," Gilli advised.

Harry placed the juicy-wet stem in his mouth and sucked, keeping his lips parted slightly around the pipe-stem to allow air in with the smoke to help cool it. He had to suck the smoke directly down into his lungs without holding it in his mouth first, and Harry knew it would burn. He made sure the effort produced the typical hissing sound, and holding his breath with his chest filled, he passed the pipe.

"Right on, Harry!" It was Neeta again.

Harry wiped his mouth with the back of his hand.

Germs! Germs! Do they have to get their spit all over it?

They passed the pipe to him again, stem nice and juicy. This time it was burning better, and Harry coughed.

"Coughing makes you get higher," Pete said. "The better the dope, the more you cough."

Harry reached for another beer from his cooler, but before he had a chance to rip off the tab, Neeta came up and placed her hand over his. It was a gentle gesture. "Give the grass a chance," she said. "Have you done it before?"

"Yeah, but..."

"Did you ever get high?"

"Well, I guess I did. The people I was with all said they were high..."

"What did it feel like?" Neeta's voice was so gentle.

"It didn't feel like anything. It seemed like everyone was pretending to be high."

"Go on."

"Well, I think smoking grass is a cop out. It's against the law so people who do it think they're really brave, but actually it's weak people who do it as an excuse to keep from drinking, like people who can't handle booze."

"Ohhh, Harry. I'm sorry you think that. You are a beautiful person, really, you really are, and you could be so much more beautiful if you would let the sunshine in, Harry, really." Neeta smiled.

Harry noticed the little wrinkles around her eyes. He smiled with her. "You are beautiful," he said. His feet shuffled involuntarily.

All eyes were turned on them.

"Ohhh, Harry.... Listen. Come on with me. I'm gonna get you your first high." She took his hand. "Come on, Harry, I have a joint rolled. A friend gave it to me. I've been saving it. It's two-toke grass. We'll get high together."

Harry followed Neeta up under the canopy and watched her dig around in her things, her bare ass sticking out from under her T-shirt.

"Found it!" A beaming Madonna.

Harry ducked back out with Neeta following. Gilli pushed the pipe in their direction but Neeta declined. She took Harry's hand again. "We're gonna get him his first real high! Come on, Harry!"

"You have matches?"

"Oh! Matches!" Neeta scampered back under the canopy while Harry waited. The hippies were still passing the pipe. There was no talking. Some were still sitting on the ground, some on the edge of the platform. Surrendra got up and stretched.

"The sun! The sun! Warm, beautiful sun!" She pulled off her robe and spread it on the ground to lie on. Harry's eyes hunted for a place to look away. Under the canopy, Neeta was pulling on a pair of denim cut-offs. She came out with the matches and the joint in her hand.

"Ready?"

"Put something on your feet." Harry was glad to have the opportunity to tell her to do something.

"Oh, Harry, sure, my feet!" She ran back in and came back wearing a pair of leather boots. "Let's go!"

Neeta was hard to follow through the bush, but Harry was used to the island. He quickly caught up with her.

"Harry, I put these shorts on so you wouldn't have to think about anything, I mean, so your head will be clear. Your head shouldn't have any hassles for the first high. See, the older you are, the less chance there is that you're gonna get high the first time. You didn't get high on the pipe just now, did you?"

"No."

"I didn't either. Huh! Oh well, I only had one hit. Listen, Harry, see, when you're older, your head doesn't want anything to take it over, so your subconscious like won't let the grass do anything, but as soon as you've tried it a number of times and you become convinced that grass is just a big bunch of shit, then your head relaxes, you just know nothing's gonna happen, right? Then **blam!** You get high for the first time! Oh, Harry! That first high is so wonderful!"

"I don't believe it," Harry said.

"Oh good. Good. Now you're gonna get high. Come on. Right up there is my favorite little spot." She led him to a tiny clearing. Spanish moss hung from the trees which surrounded it, and an aloe plant was growing in the middle, brightened by the sunshine. Coral rock stuck up through the carpet of dead leaves, and Neeta brushed a pile of leaves together to make a comfortable place to sit. "Here. Sit, Harry. And I'll sit next to you. How old are you?"

"Thirty-two." Harry sat on the leaves and wiggled his ass around until he fit in. Neeta plunked down beside him. "How old are you?"

Neeta smiled. "Thirty-five." She put the joint in her mouth and dug around in her pocket for the matches. She had to stand to get them out. Her legs were tan and long. "Gilli used to be my husband," she sighed. "We're divorced. That's funny, I know. I used to get pissed off at him for getting stoned all the time, being a doctor and all. Now I get stoned all the time and it's beautiful! Gilli is an MD. Did you know that?"

"Ummm, no."

A doctor!

"He's pretty far out, but not far out. You'll know what I mean." Neeta sat back down beside him, their arms touching, her long, dark hair brushing his shoulder. She lit the joint and handed it to him. Harry sucked the smoke straight down, letting in a little air by parting his lips. He held his breath and handed the joint back. Neeta nodded and took a hit herself. The forest was perfect stillness. Harry took another hit and held his breath again, letting the smoke burn in. Neeta brushed something off his forehead. "A little bug," she explained. She smiled at him. Harry handed the reefer back but she shook her head. "No, you. I want you to get really high!" The new pull on Harry's guts grew stronger. It was love, real love, he was sure. And it didn't have anything to do with being horny. He knew the feeling. It was love. He took another hit.

"Here, Harry, let me fix it for you so you won't burn your fingers when it gets short." Neeta took the joint and attached it on the end of a twig which she had split with her thumbnail.

Is she nice to me because she wants to get laid?

She's so gentle and beautiful. She's older than Annie and look how beautiful and quiet she is.

It's the dope. All the hippies. They're so gentle-talking because they're all burned out.

Harry held the joint by the twig and sucked in a really good hit and held his breath.

"That's it, Harry. You're really trying."

"It's a bunch of shit." Harry smiled.

"Ohhh, Harry! You just wait and see!" Neeta got to her feet. "Listen, Harry, I'm going back for just a minute to tell Mazie something and then I'll bring back some water because you're gonna get thirsty."

"I hope I can remember all their names. Before, I kept on forgetting who everybody was and I was afraid I'd get the names mixed up."

"Harry! Ohhh, I remember how that used to be. I remember. It seems like such a long time ago now. Harry, it doesn't make any difference how you act. Socially, I mean. Oh, you'll know what I mean when you get back there stoned out of your mind, ha ha, poor Harry, you're gonna be so happy! Everything will be completely different, especially with people."

"Permanently?"

"Oh, no Harry. Just for as long as you're high. Like all afternoon maybe. But if you do grass and things often enough it can become permanent and you can have a good head all the time. Come on, you're letting it burn away without smoking it. You smoke it all the way down and I'll be right back with the water. Okay?"

"Okay."

"I'll be right back." Neeta ducked under the branches and took off toward the camp. "Be right back," she called from the distance.

Then it was quiet.

Harry sucked in another hit and held his breath. He looked at the joint. It was ready to fall off the handle Neeta had made for it. He stuck it on good. It was only about a half-inch long now.

Hell, I'm not going to get high.

Marijuana.

They call it smoking shit. That's what it is, too.

Harry held the burning remnant as close as he could to his mouth without burning himself and smoked it down to nothing.

The red-hot coal dropped to the ground on the leaves and he crushed it out with his thumb.

If, well, okay, if I get high I'm not going to do it again for awhile so I don't get all burned out like they are.

I'm not going to get high — I already smoked the thing.

I'm not going back there pretending I'm high.

When she comes back I'm going to tell her.

He quietly said her name out loud. "Neeta."

Neeta.... The sound of her name repeated itself in his head and it sounded real. Harry straightened up and tried it again. "Neeta."

Neeta.

Harry's eyes widened. He felt good all over his body, and his mind felt good, too! Only his mind itself had never felt good before and he didn't know what to do with it.

What? Is? Am I? Is this? Oh! Oh, wow! Oh! Oh shit! Oh God! Yeah.

Yeah yeah yeah! Oh MAN!

Harry quickly settled back down into the leaves again and pulled up his knees and locked his arms around them.

Oh God!

So this is what they mean....

He looked all around the tiny clearing. The nerves of his body shivered with pleasure and Harry began to grin uncontrollably. He grinned until spit ran down the corner of his mouth. He wiped it away, but not because it was uncomfortable. He felt warm and beautiful, and the clearing was glowing in warmth and splendor in the sunlight.

"Oh God. Oh God. Oh God." Harry listened to the sound of his own voice in his head and laughed.

Of course! What is a sound? Only airwaves out here! Vibrations in my ears! The meat in my brain makes up the sounds!

"Sound!"

No such thing as sound itself.... Harry became amused at the thought of what sound really was, but when he would get near the end of a thought he found he had forgotten the beginning.

Rest for a minute. Look around. Stop trying to think.

Can't stop grinning.

Why should I stop grinning?

Stop thinking. Just look around. Look around.

Harry relaxed and pulled his knees up tighter against his chest. He looked around the clearing.

This is beautiful. Beautiful. Beautiful!

What is beautiful!? What is that? What is...

Harry's mouth was hanging open. For a moment he was able to see and hear for the first time without any thoughts to go with it. Too far into the forest to carry the sound of the sea, the still fragrant air bore only the occasional cry of a bird, and every now and then the click-clacking of a land crab. Each sound broke into Harry's head as clear and pure as crystal. The buzz of a flying insect....

The moment passed.

A new thought floated in.

Neeta....

The image of her settled down into Harry's supremely comfortable brain.

Neeta should be coming back....

Her image took over. He pictured Neeta coming into the clearing, ducking under the bushes, coming in much too fast. It was a powerful visualization. Harry could barely move. All his circuits seemed to be switching on to other things each time he tried to pursue a thought. He stared at the place where Neeta had left the clearing, getting his radar ready to detect her return.

It will be okay.

A little paranoia crept in.

I'll just tell her I'm wiped out. Maybe she'll stay here with me until I snap out of it.

I'll just ask her to. Ask her to take care of me and to go back with me to the camp when we're ready and tell everybody how stoned I got so they'll understand why I can't do anything right now.

He looked up and was amazed to find the sun in the same place it had been when he and Neeta were sitting there smoking together. Streaming in through a tiny break in the trees.

Does marijuana slow down time that much?

Neeta will take care of me.

She is so beautiful for an old chick. For ANY chick.

Is thirty-five old?

Most hippies would say "Don't trust anybody over thirty."

Neeta did not return. Harry looked up at the sun again. It seemed to have moved a little, but he wasn't sure. He thought of calling out to her as loud as he could but was afraid of what the sound would do to his head. He tested his voice by saying her name quietly. "Neeta." The sound of his voice was alien to the sounds of the forest, and he gave up the idea of shouting for her. He would wait. It was nice here, and there were no rain clouds. He would wait until she realized that she would have to come and get him. Harry curled up on the ground, lying on his side, and closed his eyes. Beautiful colors swirled under his eyelids. He adjusted his body on the leaves to avoid the sharp, protruding hunks or coral, piling more leaves under his head. He pictured Faylie pulling off her nightie on the seashore in the early morning light. Hmmmmmmmmm.... He felt so good. He pictured Faylie and Neeta together. The chicks from the camp were not like Faylie. Not flashy. No jewelry. No rings in the nose. Hmmmmmm.... Harry pictured his house back in Miami. It did not seem like home to him when he thought about it. He tried to picture Annie but he couldn't. He pictured little Janey, and he pictured little Perry, and Beercan, the family dog. He pictured Perry coughing, standing in the dark hallway of the house in his flannel pajama bottoms, his skinny little chest heaving for air. "Daddy — can I die — from — this?" A tear rolled down Harry's cheek, and another. He did not wipe them away. *God damn you God!*

Someone was coming through the bush toward the clearing.

What if it's not Neeta?

He kept his eyes closed, tears wet on his nose and cheeks.

"Awww, Harry! You did it! You got your high!"

Harry pulled himself up to a sitting position, wiping the tears from his face with his fingers. He was grinning out of control, so happy that Neeta had returned.

"Harry, awww Harry!" Neeta knelt down beside him and wiped his face with the bottom of her T-shirt. "It was pretty heavy for you, wasn't it? Yeahhhhh, well, I know. I was pretty old when I turned on for the first time and the older you are the bigger a change you go through." She sat there beside him and put her arm around him. He looked in her eyes. He had intended a brief smile, a game-plan smile, but his happy grin rolled right on without him.

"Awww, Harry, you really got high!" Neeta gave him a hug and jumped up. "Come on, old man, get up and see the world!"

"Neeta, no, look, I..."

"You got so high!" She laughed. "Oh, Harry, I'm so happy for you!"

"Neeta, come on, sit down here with me a little longer. I don't want to go out there now."

"Awww sure, I'll sit here with you." Neeta settled back down next to him. "Look me in the eye again, Harry."

The irises or Neeta's eyes were brown flecked with gold, green, and spots of yellow. "Neeta. I don't know what to say, I... Neeta, I'm afraid to go back and talk to anybody right now." Harry shook his head. "But I can't explain it."

"Paranoia. You got paranoid. It happens at first. And as soon as you get afraid of something you come down and your brain takes over again and you can handle things, and when you relax you go right back up being high again. But when you get drunk you can't do that. If something bad happens, you can't come back down and handle it, you just stay drunk." Neeta laughed again. She squeezed his arm. "Isn't that nice?"

"Yeah, but...."

"Don't talk for a minute. Just sit and listen."

"I feel so..."

"Good. Just sit and listen."

"Okay." Harry adjusted himself to a more comfortable position. He closed his eyes, the warm, red light glowing through his eyelids.

How nice it would be to lie here all day! This sunny clearing.

"Neeta..." He felt Neeta stir beside him. "Neeta, don't, ahhh...." Harry felt his hand give Neeta a love-pat on the thigh. "You're beautiful," he mumbled.

Neeta bent over and kissed Harry's head. "You don't look so mean anymore," she laughed. "You look like an angel!"

"I'm a changed person."

"Awwww...."

"A completely changed person...." He felt her stretch out beside him, adjusting her body on top of the leaves and stones.

"I got high, too, Harry."

Harry felt for her hand and held it and their minds drifted off and came back again and drifted off again in peace and harmony on their strange and beautiful, sunlit planet.

Once Neeta spoke. "Harry. Wait until you hear music!"

Several times Harry thought to himself: *Am I passing up another chance to get laid?* But he was feeling so good, so content. Why do anything to interrupt that? He dozed off, then woke again. Neeta was up and brushing the dried leaves off her tan legs. "Come on, Harry!" She held out her hands. Harry grabbed them and struggled to get up, and as soon as he was on his feet Neeta hugged him. Through their T-shirts he felt her small, pointy tits and Harry was surprised at the gentleness of the rush he got from that. "Neeta, do we have to go back already?"

"Yeah, yeah, come on, Harry. It's cool."

Neeta led the way. Harry was afraid, but he didn't know why. He didn't feel that he was in control — control of his head and control of the other people.

Neeta knew what to say. "When bad shit comes and you're high, you come down and handle it and then you can get high again. I told you that already."

"Prove it." Harry had stopped walking behind her and was sitting down in the middle of the path.

Neeta turned toward him, a strange smile on her face. "Little Harry." She came back to where he was sitting and straddled him with her legs: "What would you like to do right now if you had your choice?"

Harry's heart slammed with a rush of adrenalin. He took a deep breath. "ANY choice?"

"You have your choice."

"I — uhhh..."

Neeta laughed.

I wish I could slide my hand under your T-shirt and feel your tits. I wish I could pull your pants down and rub my face in your tummy and lick your cunt and come in your pussy while I'm sucking on your tits....

"I want to tell you I love you."

Neeta smiled. She was still straddling him. "If I back away a little, you can get high again." And she did, and in a minute Harry was back on the trip, but not completely.

And that girl I saw on the shore this morning when I was coming in with the boat. The one with the red hair and the ring in her nose.

"Maybe Faylie's back at the camp."

Harry had really wanted to tell Neeta that he wished he could fuck her, right now, right in the middle of the path. Hold her tight and never let her go. Now it was too late. How could he change what he said about Faylie?

"Come on, Harry baby, let's go!" Neeta was holding her hands out to him again, to get him up. "Did you come down from the high when I said you could have your wish?"

"Yeah..."

"Could you handle my question?"

"No." Harry shook his head and he had to grin. "Uh, no," he said. "I lied."

"That's because you came down," Neeta answered.

"I wanted to say I want to fuck you and hold you tight forever."

It was lunch time. Surrendra was ladling out a mixture of vegetables and fruit in a cheesy-looking sauce that resembled puke. The hippies were eating it with slices of homemade bread. Harry tried one bite of the bread smeared with the mixture and handed it back to Surrendra, who promptly handed the bread with Harry's bite out of it to another person. Harry went to his trusty cooler.

"Anybody want a ham and cheese sandwich?" They all looked at him with funny smiles, and shook their heads. "Neeta — you want one?"

Neeta shook her head again. Pete came up. "I'll take one!"

Harry handed Pete a sandwich and a beer, and took out a sandwich and a Busch for himself. Neeta was over in a flash. "Pete, we want Harry to turn on! Leave him alone!"

Harry put the beer back in the cooler, but when he heard Pete's can pop open, he pulled the beer back out again. He sat down beside Neeta and the other women. The other women were still undressed, and Harry tried not to stare at them. He had completely abandoned his earlier position that the hippies were the intruders on the island. "If you let me visit you guys again," he said to Neeta, "I'll lay off the booze and see what it's like without alcohol" His mouth clamped down on the sandwich, and Harry's face immediately reflected his surprise at how good it tasted. He chewed carefully and swallowed. "Man!" He took another bite, and a sip of beer. "Far out!"

"What..."

"This sandwich!"

"Why?"

"Man is it good!"

"Oh!" Mazie looked at Neeta. "He got high."

"Awww, Harry, we forgot to tell you about food! About eating!"

"Yeah?"

"It's much better."

"Yes."

"Much better high." "Much much better!" They were all nodding and agreeing.

Harry chewed and grinned. Dale sat down with them.

"Hey, man, it's cool to drink and smoke. I do it all the time. You get higher. But not now. I'm going fishing this afternoon."

Neeta jumped right on him for that. "If you drink too much you just get stupid, Dale. You don't get high at ALL! If you talk too much you don't get really high, either."

Dale took his middle finger and shoved it into the crotch of Neeta's shorts with a playful twist. Harry could feel rage his ears turning red.

Neeta jumped away. "I'll be right back with the pipe," she said. "Be right back."

Pete crushed his empty beer can and tossed it toward the trash drum. He missed, and it bounced off the side with a loud **clang!** Surrendra gave Harry a dirty look. Neeta came back and lit the pipe and handed it to Harry first. It pleased him that she was taking care of him in this way. He sucked in two big hits that hurt his chest and handed the pipe to Dale. Each time the pipe made a full round and was back to Harry, Neeta lit a match and made sure it was burning properly. On the last time around, she sprinkled some grains of hashish on top of the marijuana. "Hashish is just concentrated pot," Harry," she explained. "It's scraped from the leaves. It's cool. It's still a psychedelic."

The hash made Harry cough.

"Now don't talk too much, Harry, just sit back and dig it."

Dale shook his head. "You his mother?"

"Dale, I just want him to know we do only psychedelics, no hard drugs."

"So what's alcohol?"

"Alcohol is a hard drug, Dale."

"Yeah, old man!" Mazie said.

"Aw fuck!" Dale said.

Harry uncrossed his legs, which were in real pain now, and moved his back up against a tree. As soon as he was settled, he found himself in full flight again. It was like the first time, only heavier and yet more intelligent. The hippies had tightened up the circle when the pipe was passing around, but now no one was talking. The pipe and the matches lay on the ground in the middle. Harry was sure that he had never felt so good in his life. He was also convinced that there was nothing wrong with grass and he would be doing it again and again for the rest of his life. It was that simple. It was that good. This was knowledge! Today was the first day of the new Harry Schaffner. Today was his rebirth. He wondered for a moment if it could be possible in his lifetime to experience even another rebirth as profound as this. It was a fleeting thought and was quickly forgotten. He felt himself getting even higher. The drug was still building. He wondered if he would be able to explain the feeling to his friends, and to Annie. No. Not possible. He wiggled his toes in his boots. He framed the picture of the pipe and matches lying on the ground in the "V" his boots made as his legs stretched out into the circle.

Neeta bent closer for a second and whispered: "No talking and no thinking too hard."

My legs!

He was grinning. He looked across at Gilli. Gilli still wore that same, toothy, now beautiful smile. Their eyes met. Their eyes communicated a pact of friendship and brotherhood which Harry thought could not be possible. Harry looked at the others. They were all smiling. They were all looking at him except Surrendra, who had her eyes closed. When his eyes met Neeta's, her smile broadened. Neeta had moved to the far side of the circle now, next to Kit, whose long, outrageous beard and hair streamed down from his head like an Indian holy man's.

Harry spoke up. "I love you, Neeta." He paused. "I love you, Gilli. I love all of you."

Harry listened to himself speak. A few hours before, it would have been impossible for him to say what he had just said, to feel what he was feeling now. His voice was coming from a deeper part of his brain that Harry had not known existed, or did not want to know existed.

Surrendra opened her eyes. The hippies did not answer at first, but their faces told him how they felt. The silence was long and beautiful. The voices of the wind and the warmth and light of the sun, all filtered in to them through the forest. A large owl broke free from his hiding place and flapped through the trees overhead. Harry listened to himself say: "Earth is such a beautiful planet..."

Gilli nodded. "We have been waiting for you for a long time."

Harry wondered at the meaning of that. He remembered Faylie. He was glad that she was not there right now. He did not know what to do with loving so many different people at one time. He did not know what love was or where it came from. He did not know anymore where anything came from, or what anything was. But he did know for sure that his love did not come from smoking grass. The grass had simply opened his eyes to what had been in him all the time. That was real, and the love in him was now free.

"Everything is so beautiful and so happy. And so sad."

"Why sad?" Gilli said.

"Because we all can't be this way."

"That day is coming," Gilli answered. Some of the others nodded.

"No, no, the people who don't see and experience this will destroy the world before that can happen."

"They are unhappy," Surrendra said.

"Straight people," Mazie added.

"They like their way of life," Harry said.

Neeta made a face. "Come on, Harry, were you happy with your life before today?"

There was a long silence. "No, well, yeah, maybe, sometimes. No." Harry smiled. "But I didn't know it. If you don't know it, you don't miss it." He settled back again against the tree. Some of the hippies closed their eyes. None of them spoke for a long time.

Dale got up and wandered off with Mazie. Neeta went and got a blanket and took her clothes off and stretched out in the clearing but away from the group. Gilli got up and lay down beside her, still wearing the white loin cloth. Harry closed his eyes and pretended to doze. He thought of the possibilities of coming to visit these people instead of working on his trails, to show them his hide-outs and shelters, his metal detectors and treasure-hunting equipment, his fresh-water system. He thought of getting laid like them, and laying more than one at a time the way he read hippies do.

After a time, Harry opened his eyes, just a slit at first. Off on the other side of the clearing, Gilli was working his head as far as he could get it between Neeta's legs.

"Hey man! Hey man!" Harry awoke from the dream with a start. Kit, the oldest and hairiest, was shaking his arm. He was smiling. "Tide's going out," he said. "Are you staying? If you're leaving, you'd better haul it out a little. Your boat. She's right over a coral head and in a few minutes you won't be able to get her off."

Harry rubbed his eyes. "Oh, yeah, shit, thanks!" He sat up. "I better look." Someone had stacked his guns beside him, along with the missing clips for the carbine. Harry picked up the clips. Did they do this to put him down? "Who found them?" He looked around. The others were gone, and the sun was low behind the taller trees.

"Faylie brought them." Kit spoke softly, squatting beside Harry.

"Did she leave?"

"I don't know.... She's pretty far out. She doesn't live with us."

"Does she have a camp? She lives on the island?"

"If it's a camp, nobody's seen it. She's the one who told Gilli about the island, oh, long time ago. She said Surrendra pissed on

42

your ammo."

"My ammo? Huh? Oh. Oh! She doesn't dig Surrendra?" Harry felt silly using the word "dig".

"No, she meant that Surrendra pissed on your ammo."

Harry frowned and picked up one of the clips and sniffed it. "Christ! She pissed on my ammo!"

Kit was looking him in the eye, smiling. It was a toothy, Gilli-smile.

"Does Faylie always have that ring in her nose?"

"Man, remember? Your boat?"

"Right. Right." Harry stood, and tested his legs. He still felt good, but he didn't feel stoned. "Ha!" he said joyfully. "No hangover!"

"Dig it," Kit said.

When they got to the shore, Gilli and Neeta were in the water, naked. Neeta was pulling on the anchor line of Harry's boat while Gilli pried up under the stern with a piece of lumber. An empty, hollow desire sucked at Harry's gut. *Neeta — tan, slick, sweet animal buddy hug kiss come in you I love you I love you Thirty-five — you are so beautiful! I keep myself in good shape — did you notice that?* Harry was pulling his clothes off to give them a hand and to get in the water with Neeta. But the boat was already moving.

"We've got it!" Neeta shouted.

Harry finished stripping down anyway and pulled his boots back on. He was surprised to find how comfortable he felt being naked with boots on and with all to see. "I have to load up the boat," he called to them as he waded in, realizing too late that he had just committed himself to leaving. Not staying over. He sloshed up to Neeta and took over pulling the boat, but it was already free.

"Far enough?" Gilli hollered.

Harry lifted the anchor farther out and set it.

"Perfect!" Neeta said.

Gilli waded up and laughed and laid a hand on Harry's shoulder. The water was licking their balls. "Where's your gear?"

Harry shot a glance at the sky. "Back at the camp," he confessed, grinning like Gilli.

"Ha, Harry, pot makes you absent-minded," Neeta said. "That's the way it is."

Harry successfully kept his eyes off Neeta's bobbing little tits and watched her happy face. For a moment, the three of them stood there smiling at each other beside Harry's power boat clunking up and down in the waves. Harry reached out and touched his boat, resting his hand on it, then his arm. He looked the machine all over. He had done a good job of putting it together. It was a good thing — a beautiful thing — a powerful thing. "This was just a hull when I bought it — put it together."

"It's a together power boat," Gilli said.

"I take her out in any weather..."

"That's beautiful, Harry!"

"When I get back home after a good day, I feel new all over."

Gilli nodded. "Sounds like that 'I love life — why ruin it with drugs' commercial on TV."

Neeta put a leg up on Gilli's ass and gave him a nudge.

"And what has reality done for YOU lately?" Gilli mocked.

Harry took the inevitable, close-up look at Neeta's tits. Her nipples were long and upturned, the kind he wished Annie had.

"Twin Mercruisers," Gilli said, looking the boat over. "My father gave me a boat during my last year of med school and I didn't get time to really get into it until after I interned. Twin engines. Holman-Moody...."

"Where is it anchored?"

"I got off the power-boat trip and gave it away."

Harry was impressed. It made a big difference that Gilli was a doctor. He shot a look at Gilli's penis. It was smaller than his own, but the balls were like little pears. "It's, um, reassuring — to know that you're a doctor and still do grass."

Neeta laughed.

"Blessed are they that have not seen and yet believe," Gilli said, toothiest grin of all.

"That's from the *Be Here Now* book," Neeta said.

"From the Bible," Harry said.

"From both," Gilli grinned. We're Jews. He let out a loud bubble-fart through the crest of the wave. "The sea is picking up again."

Neeta is a Jew....

A Jewess.

Maybe they all are.

Neeta looks Mediterranean....

Harry was happy, and still had one hand on the boat as it splashed up and down in the waves. "That grass was good. I feel good."

"Oh, Harry, I'm so happy for you!" Just the sound of Neeta's voice could knot up Harry's feelings now. He wondered if there were any more women in the world like her.

"Not many like her," Gilli grinned.

Harry twitched. He wondered about their divorce. "I'd better go get my stuff," he said, breaking away. When he looked toward shore, Kit was dropping down the first load of his equipment.

"I'll bring your shit up to the ledge and you guys can load it in the boat," Kit shouted.

Neeta grabbed Harry's hand. "Come on — let's go!" The two of them waded in as fast as they could, laughing and splashing, the sand pockets of the coral bottom sucking at their shoes. "Kit is a beautiful person," Neeta said. "He's one of the original hippies. He's been grow-ing that hair so long, it's down to his ass!"

"He looks like Jesus."

"He used to be in the Special Forces, and now he's so peaceful and beautiful."

Harry tried to picture Kit as a young man, shaved clean, in his combat uniform and green beret.

"Harry!" Kit was leaning the guns against the cooler and knap-sack. "You going back to Homestead or Miami?"

"Gould's Canal. Right between. Where the trailer is."

"Good! Take me along?"

"Okay!"

Now it was final. He was leaving. Harry was sure he had had enough for one day, anyway, or so he told himself. Neeta helped him

45

carry his things back to the boat, holding the pistol belt and the carbine high and dry while Harry followed with the cooler and his clothes. The waves licked at her tan thighs, and he wished he could watch her wade in from the front and the back at the same time... He made one more trip while Neeta stayed with Gilli.

"Forgot something," Neeta said. "I'll be right back."

Harry dried himself with a towel, in the boat. "Where's she going?"

Gilli shrugged. They watched her pass Kit coming the other way in the water. Kit and Neeta embraced briefly.

"Neeta's special," Harry said, hoping that Gilli would tell her what he had said.

Kit climbed aboard, water running off his long hair and beard like from a wet dog. Harry threw him his towel. "Not taking anything along?"

"Just my pants," Kit smiled, water streaming from his untrimmed bush.

Harry pulled on his clothes and laced up his boots, and stashed the gear under the bow deck.

"No shirt?"

Kit smiled again and pulled on the sweatshirt Harry tossed him. Gilli was still standing in the water, smiling his toothy grin. "What are your trails for?"

"Ahhh — I'll show you when I come back!"

One engine roared to life and then the other. Kit hopped up on the bow deck and grabbed the anchor line. He pointed his arm toward shore. Neeta was wading out to them, holding something high over her head, her breasts bobbing gently up and down. Harry got his chance to see her coming from the front and he laughed. Neeta held out two clenched fists. She shouted above the noise of the engines. "This is for Kit from Faylie!" She pressed a five-dollar bill into Harry's hand. "And this is from Faylie and me for you!" In her other hand was a small, plastic baggie of marijuana. Harry took it and bent over to kiss her but the boat was rocking up and down so hard he bumped her head with his. "I love you," he shouted. "Tell Faylie I love her, too!" *What an easy way to tell them!* Harry looked at Gilli. Gilli and Neeta grinned hand-in-hand in the water as Kit pulled on the anchor rope, drawing the boat away from them.

Harry motioned to Kit. "The anchor drops right into those two hooks!"

Soon as Kit was back in, Harry shifted both engines into forward and gave them just enough throttle to raise the bow a little to cut the waves. His eyes quickly scanned the instrument panel for oil pressure and water temperature while his hands matched both engines at 2100 R.P.M., a good, slow, pulling speed. Kit took up his position behind the port windshield. When everything checked out, Harry looked back. Neeta and Gilli were almost all the way back to shore, Neeta riding piggy-back on Gilli's shoulders. Harry looked at Kit.

"Ready?"

"Ready!"

Harry shoved both throttles forward. The boat shuddered and plunged ahead, quickly getting up on plane. Harry eased the throttles back a little as soon as they were up, and stifled the urge to let out a rebel yell. He had never felt the boat to be so perfect before. So magnificent. They were shooting over the waves like a flying saucer skimming over the ocean. But there was a pain in Harry's soul, too. A stabbing in the heart which would be living with him for a long, long time.

CHAPTER 4
Pot-roast and Dumplings

After helping Harry load the boat onto the trailer, Kit refused a ride into Miami. Harry was puzzled, and Kit had to tell him twice: "I'll be okay. I know my way around here." Barefoot, wearing Harry's sweatshirt.

It was long dark by the time Harry's exit came up on the expressway, and when he drove up to the house, which was only four blocks away, the grassy strip between the sidewalk and the street was parked full of big cars.

"Goddamn niggers!" But through the remnants of his marijuana experience he could hear himself.

He switched on the emergency flashers and hopped down from the truck. The flashers were working properly on the boat trailer as well but the gate on his chain-link fence was padlocked.

"Annie!"

No response.

"ANNIE!"

Harry rattled the gate. He was tired, and pissed off. "COME ON, DAMMIT, ANNIE!"

The house was set way back in the yard, which Annie and Harry had landscaped with tropical plants and trees to block the view from the street. Lights from the front porch and the children's bedrooms glimmered through the foliage. Harry's dog, who usually ran up to greet him, was barking at the fence facing old John Neeley's recently-sold house. Harry yelled at the dog as hard as he could.

"BEERCAN SHUT UP!"

Beercan kept right on barking. It was the standard hate-bark, which the German Shepherd always had ready for the garbage-men. Harry climbed over the gate and strode over to the hole in the hedge where Beercan snooped on Neeley's yard. All the lights were on in Neeley's house, and the draperies and window-shades were gone.

Christ! The house is crawling with niggers!

Couldn't wait till tomorrow! Couldn't wait!

Harry spread the branches of the Florida-Cherry hedge to get a better look. A large U-Haul truck was backed up against John Neeley's front door, and two black men were struggling with a large mattress. The floral design of the mattress was covered with stains and blotches of old cum, clearly visible in the porch light. Harry kicked Beercan in the balls with the side of his boot.

"When I say shut up, shut up!"

The dog held his ground and kept barking. Harry was about to give it to him again when he noticed that Beercan was all wet. The hole which the dog had dug near the fence was wet, too.

"Annie!"

Probably glued to the boob-tube.

Beercan stopped barking.

"Go get Annie!" Harry said. "Come on. Go get Annie!"

Beercan lunged around the house to his doggie-door. A moment later, Annie came flying out the front in her nightgown, hair in rollers.

"Harry! Dammit! I asked you a hundred times not to do that!"

"Do what? Do what?"

"You know what! Sending that damn dog after me like that! You know I'm afraid of him! You know he knows I'm afraid of him!"

Harry waited impatiently for her to come to the fence. "Shut up and watch this. Come on, you're going to miss it. This is rich!" Harry spread the branches of the hedge as far as he could so Annie could squeeze in.

The ugliest black woman Harry had ever seen was holding a huge clock while one of the men was trying to untangle the cord which had caught on the bumper of the U-Haul truck. It was a wall clock centered in a sunburst of peacock feathers. Annie started laughing.

"You missed the mattress they were carrying in a minute ago," Harry whispered. "How did Beercan get all wet?"

"Is he all wet?"

"Christ, Annie! If you don't know what's going on around here when I'm gone, who does? Did those niggers throw water on him? It looks like it!"

"I was watching TV."

Harry turned away from the fence in disgust. "Weren't you even curious what they'd look like?"

"Well, I knew they wouldn't be white. No white people are going to move into a changing neighborhood. Except dumb people like us."

"I didn't know it was going all black when we bought this place."

"I knew. The price was too low. I told you. "

"I love this house! Come on, Annie, give me the key to the new padlock. The truck and the boat are blocking half the road."

"I don't have the key."

"Shit!" Harry stomped up to their front door and jerked it open. "So go in and look for it!"

"Harry, I..."

Harry grabbed her arm. "Annie! I'm tired. I'm hungry. The ass end of our boat is sticking out in traffic. Why didn't you at least have the gate ready for me to come in? Huh?"

"Harry, I thought you'd be back tomorrow. All I have is the key for the old lock. You didn't give me the new key."

"I gave it to Janey to give to you."

Annie sighed. "I'll ask Janey."

Harry followed her in. The television set in the living room was blasting away with no one watching it. Harry snapped it off. "Where is Janey? Where's Perry!"

Annie turned on Harry and raised her voice. "Perry is still sick! He's scared half to death! I'm scared half to death for him! I don't have a boat to go out in and take a holiday, and I don't have a wife to take care of everything while I'm goofing off!"

"I don't have a wife who takes care of anything, either, lazy bitch! Where — is — Janey?!" Harry stomped into the kitchen and yanked open the door of the old pantry, which they had converted into Janey's bedroom. Perry was sitting in the middle of the floor completing a puzzle. He coughed, and smiled.

"Hi, Daddy! Look! I'm almost finished with Janey's puzzle!"

"Dammit, Perry! Why aren't you wearing the pajama top? Why is your bathrobe open! Annie come here! Where's the belt to Perry's bathrobe?"

Perry stood up. He was wheezing for breath. "Right here, Daddy. Mommy sewed the loops back on so the belt doesn't fall off anymore — *cough* — it just wasn't — *long spasm of coughing* — it came untied."

"Where's Janey?"

Perry's coughing became so severe that he had to double up. He pointed wildly in the direction of his own room. Before Harry could turn around, Annie was already running toward little Perry's room, where Janey was playing.

"Don't you hit her, Harry!"

Janey looked frightened. She was in her pajamas, too and her long, blond hair had been tied into pigtails for the night. "I'm sorry, Daddy. I have the key. Here."

Harry grabbed Janey by the neck and twisted her around, shoving her as hard as he dared toward the front door. Janey went sprawling.

"Get up and get out there and open the fucking gate!"

Janey picked herself up, screaming, and limped as fast as she could out into the yard. Annie picked up the key and ran after her. Harry followed. He hadn't really intended to push Janey down. "I didn't mean to push her that hard," he called after them.

Janey kept on screaming.

"For Christ sake, Janey! Stop screaming!"

Janey turned toward Harry, her stomach in convulsions, tears streaming down her face. She tried to speak through the crying.

"Stop it!" Harry yelled.

"I — I — I — can't — stop."

Harry slapped her on the side of the head. "Stop it!"

Annie rushed back and pulled Janey away. "There! You can drive in now!"

Janey ran into the house, holding the side of her head.

"Is my dinner ready?"

"Harry!"

"Well, can you fucking get it ready?"

"It's in the oven! I saved some for you, God knows why! But I saved you some, okay?" Annie turned toward the house.

Harry hesitated, then called after her. "Annie! I didn't mean to hurt Janey. Really!"

"Tell Janey that!"

Just as the door slammed shut after her, Harry saw flashing red lights shooting through the bushes near the street. He trotted out to the sidewalk and was relieved to see that the two officers in the squad car were white. The older of the two had his ticket book out.

"May I see your driver's license please?"

"Yeah. Sure. It's in my truck."

The man followed him over while Harry explained. "I keep my license and stuff in this little magnetic key-case. Don't carry a wallet anymore. Not since the neighborhood went to shit."

"You're blocking a whole lane here."

"When I came home with the boat they had this whole strip here parked up, and my gate was locked. I didn't have a choice."

The cop smiled and handed back the license. "I'll watch the traffic while you back her in."

"Good," Harry said, throwing him a military salute. "Thanks." For a moment Harry was afraid that he might not be able to back his rig into the yard with the two officers standing there and watching, but he was lucky and slopped in the boat trailer right where he wanted it with one shot.

Nothing like a couple beers for precision and confidence!

Back in the house, Annie refused to sit with Harry while he ate his heated-over pot-roast and dumplings. And while he showered and brushed his teeth, she made a bed for herself on the front couch. There was no talking to her, and Harry finally resigned himself to sleeping alone in the big, dark bedroom, his hands on his balls, trying to decide whether to jack off or not. He had forgotten to tell Annie that he wanted to get up early, so he set the alarm clock for 5:30 and fell asleep with a hard-on, Neeta and Faylie and his first pot high all over his mind.

"Harry. Harry?"

Harry opened his eyes in time to see Annie leaving the room, her floppy slippers slapping the hardwood floor. It was still dark outside. A steaming cup of coffee sat beside him on the night-stand.

"Annie."

She stopped in the doorway.

"Annie. Come back and have a coffee with me here." Harry watched her hesitate, and he knew now that she would come back. But to be sure, he added: "Something strange happened to me yesterday. It's why I came back early. I'm not even sure I can tell you about it."

"I'll be right back."

Harry sat up and took a sip of the coffee, swishing it around in his mouth to get the stinking, mossy residue off his teeth. He felt the alarm clock to see why it hadn't buzzed.

"I pushed the button in," Annie said, bringing in another cup of coffee and setting it down on her side of the bed. "I had to get up to give little Perry his medicine, and when I checked on you, I saw you wanted to get up early, so...."

"Yeah, yeah, it's a long story. There's a couple things I have to do today. Shit. Well...." Harry watched while she slipped off her bathrobe. She was wearing panties underneath. That almost always meant that she was getting her period.

"What were you going to tell me, Harry?"

Harry watched his wife's heavy breasts bobble and bounce as she climbed into bed. His left hand lay on his cock, testing the strength of his desire. He needed so badly to get laid, and he needed a way to please Annie. If she was getting her period then it would have to be a blow-job, and the only times Annie would give him a blow-job was after they had had a good time together.

Sneeze! "What are you thinking — **sneeze** — what are you thinking about, Harry." Annie sneezed again and blew her nose. "Do you have more Kleenex over there?"

"Yeah." Harry handed her a Kleenex.

Christ! A runny nose on top of it!

"Oh, Harry, let's have a nice weekend and not fight. We still have Saturday and Sunday. Hand me another Kleenex. Let's be nice to the children, too. Maybe take them to the beach or take them out in the boat. The salt air would be good for little Perry, and he loves the boat."

Harry sighed. His hand roamed over Annie's sumptuous tits. "I'll tell you about the boat in a minute," he smiled. His hand worked its way down toward her crotch, running into the waistband of her panties on the way.

"Oh, no," he mumbled, feigning surprise.

"That's the way the cookie crumbles," Annie said brightly. She blew her nose again — a wet, snotty session.

"Do you have a cold?"

"Just my hay-fever, I guess." Her hand slipped under the blanket to get Harry's cock, which was already nice and hard. She pulled gently on his nuts. Harry groaned with pleasure.

"I'll fix you up," Annie said. She pulled the blanket off and began to brush his belly gently with her mouth. Harry was glad that it was still dark enough where he wouldn't have to face Annie's blobby stomach, her mottled thighs, the sun-burned, turkey-like red "V" of her neck.... He raised his pelvis and strained to move nearer her mouth. She began to lick the underside of his penis while her fingers tugged on his balls. Harry groaned again. Suddenly, Annie's mouth slid over the tip. "Ohhh, Annie, Annie, Ohhhh! Hey! Don't stop now, don't stop now!"

Annie pulled away and reached for another Kleenex. Harry's cock, swaying in the air while Annie cleared her nose, listed to one side.

"Come on, Annie!"

Annie straddled Harry's legs and resumed the feast, her head pumping up and down over his meat. Her breasts hung heavy and full, and Harry strained to sit up a little so he could reach her tits with his hands and play with them while she sucked. All too quickly, he felt himself on the verge of coming.

"Wait a minute. Rest a minute."

Annie laid her head on his chest and nibbled on his left nipple. Harry's eyes were closed. He tried to picture Faylie but he couldn't do it. He could not remember her face. He had not been close enough to Faylie the day before to get a good look. He could remember Milky's face, but Milky was too short and stocky. Her tits were big though, bigger and fatter and longer than Annie's, and they had looked firm. His mind jumped over Neeta and began to dwell on Surrendra — Surrendra with the dark skin and the thick, black hair. Harry decided to pretend that Annie was Surrendra. He slid out from under his wife and kneeled beside her on the mattress, legs apart so Annie could get to his dangling balls. He closed his eyes.

Surrendra. Island princess. Jungle goddess....

Surrendra's gentle, skilled, native fingers pulled briskly at Harry's nuts. Her hot, thick lips kissed and sucked his organ. Cups of eager, live cum loaded up at the base of Harry's tool, building up pressure for the final pumping orgasm down the jungle-queen's seductive throat. Harry's hands reached for the raven-haired beauty's head, but instead his fingers scraped the brittle outer layer of Annie's hairsprayed, reddish-blond, beauty-parlor job. He quickly detoured to his dark mistress' breasts, kneading and squeezing them in his hands.

Annie pulled away. "That hurts!"

"Don't stop now!"

"I have to blow my nose."

"Not now!" Harry yelled.

The exotic, swamp-queen's mouth slid over Harry's moist, distended organ. He tried to hold out for a few seconds more. A drop of thick semen got away from him, but the jungle goddess, wise in the ways of love, whipped the nectar away with a quick, tantalizing lick. Harry felt another drool of cum slide up his shaft. Another quick, expert lick. And a long suck.

"Ohhhh..." Harry cried.

Annie sneezed.

Harry's cock, suddenly swaying free in thin air, burst forth a week's accumulation of sex dreams and semen. He thrust his cock forward in a desperate attempt to penetrate the hungry princess' mouth before all was lost. The beet-red head of Harry's squirting penis slid up into her eye.

"Dammit Harry!" Strands of hot come hung from Annie's nose.

"Goddamn you dumb bitch!"

"Ohhh!" Annie lurched over him and grabbed at the Kleenex box. "You pig!"

"You sloppy old bitch!"

Annie ran to the bathroom.

"Do you know what that does to me?" he screamed after her. The bathroom door slammed shut. While he was wiping off his pecker, he could hear her sneezing and blowing her nose, and then crying.

Harry lay back. He pictured Annie as she was when he met her. She had been happy then, when he was stationed in Colorado— picking her up when she got off at the bar. The weekend camping trips, the long hikes, their dreams of finding gold or uranium. Harry smiled. He remembered how she had hated to leave her mountains, her independence.

He waited for Annie to come out of the bathroom. When she came out, he would hug her, tell her how much he loved her, and they would have a nice weekend. He flipped on the light switch in the bedroom and dabbed at another dribble oozing from the end of his limp cock.

Annie whimpered back into the room, refusing to look at him. Her heavy but lifeless tits hung down over her pasty-white belly.

"Harry, I'm sorry."

"I'm sorry, too!" Harry got up from the edge of the bed and stomped out.

"Make your own breakfast!" she shouted after him.

After showering, Harry put on some coffee, and went to little Perry's room to take a peek. He opened the door gently and tiptoed over to the window to open the draperies. The room brightened with the dawn light. Little Perry's eyelids fluttered, and his bony chest heaved rapidly up and down with each hard-won breath. His eyes opened.

"It's morning," Harry whispered.

Perry nodded.

"You can cough it out now. You'll be able to breathe better as soon as the sun is up over the bushes."

Little Perry smiled faintly. Harry bent over and kissed him. "I have to go away and get a part for the boat, and then I'll be back. It's Saturday. I'll be home all day working on the boat. Okay?"

Perry nodded again.

"See you later."

The tea-kettle was whistling. Harry walked out reluctantly and closed the door.

While he got his cereal and milk and instant coffee together at the dining room table, he tried to figure out the events of the day before. For some reason, it was difficult to get any of it into perspective. Then he remembered he had been smoking grass all that day. And so many new things had happened all at once.

Harry's place was at the head of the dining room table, and he liked to sit there whether he was with the family or not. When they were all together, he was able to see all of them (the children at one side and Annie on the other) and he had a view of the dining room window as well. The other end of the table was right up against the window, which gave Harry a clear view into old John Neeley's back yard. Only it wasn't Neeley's back yard anymore, as Harry was soon to be reminded. While he was munching his Cheerios, Neeley's back door swung open and a little colored kid, a boy about Perry's age, waddled out onto the porch stoop without any pants on. His distended belly and protruding belly-button were poking out under a little yellow-white T-shirt. His big, chunky ass was poking out in back and his black cock and balls were flopping out in front. Harry stopped eating and watched him. The boy wobbled as he walked, as if he were stiff from sleeping. When he got to the edge of the concrete porch slab, he turned toward Harry's direction, put his hands behind his head, and pissed over the side, grinning with two missing front teeth and gums flashing pink like watermelon.

"Annie!"

"Make your own breakfast!" Her voice came muffled from down the hall.

"You've got to see this!"

"I'm in bed!"

"Hurry!"

Annie did not answer. The little boy shook off the last few drops by jerking his body with happy, pelvic bumps, hands still clasped behind his head. Then, instead of opening the screen door to get back inside, the boy simply stepped right through it.

Screen must be ripped!

Harry got up and went to the window. The rip in the screen was almost the length of the whole door.

One night in Neeley's perfectly maintained house and the screen door is completely ruined!

"You missed it!" Harry shouted. He went down the hall to their bedroom and opened the door. He spoke to Annie's back. "I have to get a part for the boat. I'll be right back."

"Again?"

"Yeah."

"Why?"

"The port outdrive was making noise on the way back last night. I know what it is. I had to shut the engine down right before we came in. And the other engine started..."

"We?"

"I had to bring somebody back from the island. I'll tell you about that later. The thermostat housing leaks on the starboard engine — the casting's corroded — I'll need a new one." Harry turned to walk out.

"Harry!" How much will everything cost?"

"Um.... Fifty bucks maybe." Harry shrugged.

"Can't you get it where you work?"

"The boatyard doesn't have a parts store, jeez."

"Harry...."

"Can't help it. I need the parts to get the boat running."

"What about my teeth?"

Harry stiffened. "Look, Annie, I've got the boat paid off, right? The truck will be paid off in only two more months and..."

"I thought you were behind on the truck."

"Three more months, and then we'll have all the money you need for your teeth."

"In three months that tooth will be broken off!"

"Oh, come on, Annie!"

"Tell me something, Harry. Do any of the women working at the boatyard have to clean up their beauty parlor on Sunday nights in order to get their hair done free? Do any of them..."

"You don't need to have your hair done. It looks like shit when you come back. Let it grow long and natural."

"Do any of them have to put pots and pans all over the house every time it rains because the roof leaks? Do they have a septic tank that's overflowing and a toilet you have to squirt soap into every time you flush it or the water won't go down? What about Janey's room? The wood is so full of termites the window frame is falling out and it rains in there and the room is full of roaches!"

"Dammit, Annie! There's no end for Christ sake!"

"What about..."

"What about what I need? I told you it would take a couple more paydays to tie up loose ends before we could get into the heavy shit! As soon as the truck is paid off we can..."

"How about waiting with the boat parts until the truck is paid off, huh? How about that?"

"I have to get the boat fixed!"

"Why? Tell me why!"

Harry pictured Neeta. He heard her happy, school-girl voice.

Awwww, Harry.... You got your first high!

"I have to," Harry said quietly. "I have to."

It's the only way back there.

Janey came up and stood beside Harry in the doorway. "Perry's sick."

"What about little Perry?" Annie screamed. "You promised to take him to a new doctor today!"

"Today? I said next week. This is a holiday weekend. Thanksgiving."

Annie jerked upright in her bed, tits flying. "Get out of here! GET OUT!"

Harry slammed the door and stomped down the hall, Janey following in her pajamas and bare feet.

"Daddy! Perry's sick. He's in his room."

"I'm not going to Perry's room!" Harry turned and faced her at the front door. "Look, Janey, if Perry really needed me right now he would ask me himself, right? You're not trying to bug me just because you heard Mommy trying to bug me, are you? Because I have a lot of things to do today and..."

"He's got asthma again, Daddy. He can't ask you himself."

"He's just trying to get attention."

"But Daddy. You told Mommy that sometimes he can't help it and he's not just trying to get attention and..."

"Janey!" Harry stormed out the door toward his truck, Janey following.

"Are you going away?"

"Be right back."

"But Daddy. Perry's not faking. He can hardly breathe. I heard him."

"Damn you, Janey!"

"Well, can't you maybe take him to the doctor?"

Harry whirled around and grabbed Janey by the back of the neck. "Now listen, kid! You get your ass back in the house and tell Perry I'll look at him when I get home. Now leave me alone!" Harry jumped into the truck and fired up the engine. Janey was crying. Harry rolled down the window. "I said get back in the house!" He watched her turn around. "I looked in on Perry before breakfast and he was okay!"

Janey shook her head and ran into the house. Harry slammed the truck into low and hit the gas. The pickup pulled away with an ominous ripping sound in the back. "Oh fuck!" Harry jumped down and looked. He had unhitched the boat trailer but had left the trailer lights hooked up, and now the cable was torn in two.

More to fix!

If they would only leave me alone! If they would stop bugging me!

Harry stood there for a moment, nearly paralyzed with indecision. Where to hunt for what he needed on a Thanksgiving weekend?

Fucking thanksgiving....

The hippies didn't even act like they knew it was Thanksgiving.

Way to go!

Harry tried to picture Surrendra baking a turkey.

The boatyard where Harry worked did not have the parts he needed to repair his rig, and he ended up taking all morning to find every item he thought would be necessary. It was past noon by the time he returned home and Harry was six dollars into Annie's grocery money, which he had taken along just in case. They all had lunch together, and Harry carried little Perry into the dining room and plunked him into his chair to make him feel a little better about it. "I'll put you out in the sun this afternoon," Harry said. "You can get the sun on your chest and watch me work on the boat."

Little Perry coughed, and nodded. Harry leaned over and buttoned up Perry's pajama top. "Annie, there's no bacon in the scrambled eggs. Again."

"We're out. I didn't have enough money last time." Annie was trying hard to be pleasant. "I'll be able to get all the little things we're always out of today."

"Ahhh, Annie, don't get mad, but..."

"I'm going to get the regular amount of food money, aren't I?"

"Ahhh, no."

"Well, that does it. That does it. That's it. It's hopeless. There's no way out. There's no hope. It's final. It's..."

"Annie!" Harry got up and stood behind Annie's chair and put his hands on her shoulders.

I've got to get the boat ready.

If we split up now, where will I live? Where could I work on the boat? I've got to be able to go back to the island.

"Annie, don't be mad at me. I didn't do it on purpose. I love you. Here, the grocery money. I took six dollars out. Next weekend I'll give you your grocery money and ten dollars to make up for it. All I need to do next weekend is gas up the truck and the boat. I won't short you again."

Annie dabbed at the tears running down her cheeks. "No, Harry. Next week the mortgage is due."

"I'll pay it late. No big deal."

"What about my doctor, Daddy?"

Harry sat back down and pressed his temples with his fingers.

Why didn't I fuck Neeta when I had the chance? Why didn't I stay there?

"Please. I'm getting a headache."

"What happened to you yesterday?" Annie asked. She loaded her voice with hurt and tears.

Harry pushed away from the table. "There's no way you could understand." He thought about it. "You just wouldn't understand."

Janey's eyes lit up. "Did you find the treasure?"

"Treasure!" Annie grumped. "That'll be the day!"

"Daddy." Little Perry cleared his throat. "Daddy, are we going to the movies tonight?"

"Your father spent all the money on boat parts."

Harry finished his coffee and slammed the cup down. "I have work to do. Let me know when Perry's finished so I can take him out in the sun."

Perry coughed. "I don't want to watch you work on the boat, Daddy."

"You need the sun. It will be fun."

"It will be boring, Daddy. Boring! Leave me alone!"

"Mommy! Remember?" Janey pointed to the little empty bowls which had been set at each place.

"There's Jell-O for dessert," Annie said. "Janey made it herself."

"Fuck the Jell-O!" Harry went to the bathroom, pissed, and headed for the front door.

"You didn't wash your hands!" Perry hollered. The effort started him coughing again.

Harry slammed the door. Through the window, he could hear Perry's coughing. It became a long, uncontrollable fit, and Harry hesitated, wondering if he should go back in. Then there was silence. It wasn't until he had gotten all of his tools out and had the bad outdrive removed from the boat that Harry thought of Gilli for Perry's new doctor. As soon as Annie came out he called her over to tell her about it. "Come on over here, where I'm working. I don't want Janey or Perry to hear."

Annie came over to the boat, arms folded across her chest, looking grim.

"Let's admit it," he started off. "Perry's got asthma. It's not just bronchitis. It's hereditary. I had allergies when I was a kid. You've got all kinds of allergies now. The poor kid got it from both sides."

"So? Take him to the doctor like a normal person would?"

"Christ, Annie! Let me finish! I want to tell you about yesterday, and why I need the boat. Perry's lungs cleared out really good that weekend when we took him out. The salt air and the sun... Remember?"

"Oh, Harry."

"Wait! There's more! Yesterday, I found out there's a hermit living on the island. He's been there all this time and I didn't know it. Not only that, he's my age, and he's a doctor." Harry looked at his wife, waiting.

"Shit, Harry!"

"Aw fuck you! Go back to the house and feel sorry for yourself!"

Annie turned to go. She did not stop when Harry continued.

"I'm going to get this machine running and tomorrow I'm taking Perry to the island, just him and me! He needs to get away from you and Janey and your Mickey-Mouse little world!"

"The boat needs fuel!" Annie yelled from the doorway.

The boat needs gas....

Harry had forgotten. Pain throbbed at his temples, and he held his hands tightly against the sides of his head. He thought for a moment. He could sell something. His camera stuff. The Nikon and the extra lenses, maybe. Harry went back to work. He would get one engine running, then knock off to go to the camera shop before it closed and get the other engine ready in the evening. Two minutes later, he discovered that the port outdrive bell housing was cracked all the way through, and it was a part which he had not bought that morning, an expensive part, a part which probably was not available for his old unit except on special order, which meant a week or two wait in addition to getting up the extra money. "Oh god damn you! Damn you God! You dirty motherfucker!" Harry whirled around in circles, yelling, resisting the urge to throw tools or smash something. "Oh Jesus Christ! What did I do? What do you want from me? Why are you doing this to me?"

Annie opened the front door a crack. "Harry?"

Harry walked over to the porch stoop and slumped down on the step, burying his face in his hands. "It's all over," he said, almost inaudibly. "I did my best. I went more than half way. I would have worked in the rain. I would have worked all night with the lights. I would have worked on it sick. But I can't fight God!"

"Harry? What happened?"

"Bell housing is cracked. Can't be fixed. It'll be weeks. Weeks!"

"Harry, I'm going to walk to the store. I'll call you when it's time to pick me up."

"Christ. Didn't you hear what I just said?"

"I can't help you, Harry. Answer the phone, Harry, when I call. I'll have all the groceries. Harry?"

"Yeah, yeah."

"I'm taking Janey along. You take care of Perry. He's going to take a nap now. He says his medicine made him dizzy. Maybe you can carry him out to lie in the sun."

"Yeah...."

"Check on him, will you?"

"Good bye for Chrissake!"

Harry watched Janey follow her mother out the front gate. They were both wearing yellow dresses and white shoes. Janey turned and waved but Harry did not wave back. He closed his eyes.

Awww, Harry, you got your first high!

He could imagine her voice, but could not visualize her face. He pictured her body, long and tan, her loose, up-turned little tits. Beercan snuck up and moved in on Harry with a quick lick on the face.

"Blaaaghh!" Harry came down hard on Beercan's head with his fist. Beercan staggered, and Harry wiped his mouth clean with his forearm. "Beercan, you would like her. Yes you would. Neeta is beautiful, she's wild, she's my age but she's young, Beercan. She would be perfect for us."

Beercan tentatively wagged his tail, and moved in for another lick.

"Sorry, licker dog," Harry said. He got up. "You stay out here. On his way to little Perry's room, he remembered the small baggie of pot Neeta had given him when he left the island. He turned and went to the dresser drawer where he kept his favorite pipe, the only one Harry hadn't thrown out when he quit smoking tobacco. When he went out to the boat to get the grass, Harry noticed the huge thunderheads building up in the west. There would be a thunderstorm soon. Good. Be alone. Perry was not making any noise so he was probably asleep. Janey and Annie would take at least an hour to do the grocery shopping before they would call him to be picked up. It was perfect. Harry took the bag and the pipe out to the little back porch behind the kitchen and sat down on the steps.

Awww, Harry, you got your first high!

He examined the marijuana. It was all chopped up fine, flecks of green and gold and straw color. It excited him just to have it in his hands. He sniffed it. It had the smell of freshly-cut field grass with a sharp, aromatic undertone. There were seeds in it, too, and Harry packed some of the pot, seeds and all, into his pipe. Through the bushes along the fence, he caught glimpses of the colored women who lived behind him, hurrying to get their clean laundry off the line before the rain came. He lit the pipe and sucked in a big, hot toke and held it. When he finally had to exhale, he took a few short breaths and sucked in another burning lung-full, and tried to hold his breath without coughing.

"Pearlie? Yo pussy on fire?"

"Hee hee. Lula Mae, shush up!"

Harry clamped his thumb over the pipe bowl and crept toward the fence. He had never had much to say to the two women who lived in the house behind his — they had been in the neighborhood longer than his own family. In fact, the only social action Harry and Annie had taken toward their neighbors behind them consisted of frequent care of the bushes along the fence to speed their growth, and wiring the back gate shut.

Harry got to the one little hole in the bushes just as Pearlie did. The sight of Pearlie's old, wrinkled brown face inches away from his gave him a start.

"Hi, Mister Harry! How you all doin' today?"

"Ummm...."

"Gimme a hit o' that reefer you smokin' — hee hee — come on, Mister Harry."

Harry grudgingly handed the pipe through the hole in the hedge. Over Pearlie's shoulder, he could see Lula Mae's big ass humping along the wash line — Bermuda shorts with underwear hanging out over the waistband. Lula Mae's blobby-fat legs quivered as she side-stepped along the line. Pearlie got a hit and handed the pipe back, stem juicy with spit. Harry looked at the spit, but before he could think of what to do, Pearlie's brown arm shot through the hole in the bushes and grabbed the pipe back. "Lemme wipe the clabber off for you, Mister Harry. Hee hee — I don' wan' you to get pregnant!"

Harry laughed. He watched Pearlie wipe off the pipe with her shirt tail, and wondered if he would get high. He felt a shot of fear at the thought that he might get too stoned.

"Lula Mae — fetch me my lighter."

"I got matches," Harry hollered. He watched Lula Mae come blobbing over. *Two-hundred pounds of white-man hating nigger,* Harry thought to himself.

"Mister Harry, I didn' know you was a smoker!"

Harry lit a match and held it while Pearlie puffed.

"Mama. Things is gettin' better all the time!"

"You Pearlie's daughter?"

"I think so."

The three of them laughed. Lula Mae handed the pipe over after taking a long pull on it herself. Harry wiped the spit off. "Don't want to get pregnant."

"What your old lady say about you smokin' shit?"

Harry sucked in a long hit. "She doesn't know."

They all laughed again. "Oooooooeee!" Pearlie exclaimed, gold teeth flashing. "I'se gettin' laid awready!"

Harry felt a numbness coming over him, but he did not feel high. He remembered suddenly, watching Lula Mae nigger-lip his pipe stem, that Bo, the foreman at the marine yard where he worked, was always saying: "Never turn down an ugly broad. They are the highway to the choice meat." The sound of Bo's voice was almost real, and Harry could hear him talking in his head. Harry looked hard at Lula Mae and Pearlie, and started to grin. They were OK. They were good people.

Shit — am I getting stoned!

"Laid to the bone!" Pearlie said.

Lula Mae and her mother each took another hit and handed the pipe back to Harry. "Quick before it goes out!" Soon, the three of them were standing there at the fence, grinning and not saying anything. Harry tried to remember why he had hated the two women, why he had thought they were just dumb niggers, stupid, and ugly. He remembered that he hated all the men that hung around their back yard sometimes, jiving and laughing and yelling nigger-talk. Harry laughed. Lula Mae and Pearlie laughed with him.

"Where'd you get this weed, boy?" Lula Mae handed the pipe back through the hole in the bushes. "It mus' be rod."

"Golden-rod. Columbian," Pearlie laughed. "Can you get us some of this?"

Harry remembered Neeta and what had happened to him just the day before. He shook his head in wonderment, smiling. There was no easy way to explain, at least not right now.

"Come on over and sit down," Pearlie said. "Come on! We got

chairs outside!"

"It's going to rain any second," Harry said. "Oh, fuck it!" He went to the gate he had wired shut and climbed over. Pearlie's yard was full of weeds and over-grown bushes. It looked nice and secluded, Harry thought, and the old rattan chairs were comfortable. A bolt of lightning flashed and thunder rolled from, not far off. The sky was darkening fast. It was beautiful.

"Felt a drop," Lula Mae said, wiping a raindrop from her brow.

"We can go inside," Pearlie said.

"I gotta go back," Harry said. "My little boy is home alone and the thunder will scare the shit out of him." He looked at Lula Mae again, thinking of his white foreman at work, Bo, and his theory of sure-fire free pussy. The idea was, you get an ugly chick to ball you — they are easy to lay — and then over a period of time the woman's girlfriends, progressively better looking as you work your way up the ladder, take you away from the uglier ones. Bo was always claiming that his system was a long but infinitely rewarding process. Harry wondered if the system would work with an ugly fat butterball like Lula Mae. He tried to picture what it would be like to lick Lula Mae all over and then fuck her. In order for the system to work, he would have to eat her and then fuck her so that she would have to tell her best friends how good he was.

Lula Mae grinned back at him as he watched her. He pictured his tongue moving around the clumps of wiry body hair which Lula Mae had growing out of her arms and legs in tufts. Harry had never seen body hair like that before and he figured that most colored women didn't have body hair like that. But when he pictured his tongue working into sweaty grooves between her rolls of fat, Harry felt no desire.

"Zat your boy now?"

Harry had heard the cry, too, and jumped to his feet. "Yeah, I gotta split." He grabbed the pipe and vaulted over the gate. Halfway to Perry's room, he remembered that he was stoned. Harry slowed down and tip-toed up to Perry's open door. Little Perry was not there. Harry rushed from room to room, then headed out the front door.

Perry was standing behind the boat in his pajama bottoms, crying. He looked so skinny and helpless. Harry ran to him and picked him up and kissed him. "Awww little Perry," he said, hugging him and carrying him back to the house. "I'm going to take good care of you from now on." Harry kissed him again and set him down on the couch in the front room. He sat down beside him, then picked Perry up and plunked him in his lap. He ruffled Perry's hair and hugged him again. "Everything's going to be all right from now on, little man," Harry said.

Perry coughed. "Daddy — I woke up and there was this loud thunder and nobody was home. I thought you left me all by myself."

"From now on, you can go with me wherever I go."

"Is that a promise?"

"That's a promise."

"What about when you go to work?"

"Awww..." Harry gave Perry another big hug."That's not fair! That's different!"

There was another flash of lightning and a thunder-clap. Rain began to fall. Harry put little Perry down and turned on a few lights. "Listen to that rain, Perry. Doesn't it sound beautiful? Oh shit! I left my tools outside. Be right back!" He ran out to gather up the tools. When he got back in, little Perry was coughing and pointing toward the kitchen.

"Quick, Daddy!" He stood up and doubled over with a heavy coughing fit. "The — pots — and pans! It's leaking!"

Water was already running along the ceilings in the front room and the kitchen, dropping and spattering on the floors. Harry grabbed a stack of pots from the cupboard and placed them under the biggest leaks. A huge cockroach jumped out of the last pot and headed straight for Harry's leg. He stomped on it and shuddered. The hard, outer shell of the roach had made an ugly, crackling sound when its guts split out.

"There's — another one — Daddy!"

Harry wheeled around and stomped, missing it. The roach turned and headed under the couch where Perry was sitting. Perry jumped up and doubled over with another coughing fit. A new leak, directly over the couch, began to spatter down on the boy. Just then, the phone rang. Harry grabbed hold of the couch and pushed it to a dry spot, taking half the rug with it and knocking over two of the pots. Little Perry, still bent over with his coughing, held his stomach with one hand and righted the pots with the other while Harry got the phone. It was Janey.

"Mommy's ready to be picked up."

"I have problems here. Be there as soon as I can!" Harry hung up and ran to the kitchen, where the floor was splotched with puddles of water and the rain drumming the roof with enormous force. He set out as many pots and empty buckets as they had, and went to Perry's room to get the boy's bathrobe. The windows in Perry's room were open, and although the wind was blowing from the other side of the house, the room was filled with sweet, clean, lightning-charged air. Harry stopped in wonderment and looked out over Annie's little vegetable garden, and the roses she was growing under Perry's windows. The full force of the rain abated momentarily, and Harry listened to the water running off from the roof overhang and hitting the standing water on the ground. He watched the plants jerk and bend under the raindrops. A patch of diffused sunlight broke through the clouds, disappeared, and came back again, making the garden glisten and glow.

She planted this stuff here for Perry.

I never noticed this before.

She never said anything about it to me. She put his bed near the window and the roses near the window so he could see them when he's sick.

Perry came in behind him. "It's stopping, Daddy." He coughed again. "I need my medicine."

Harry turned and patted Perry on the head. "Good thing it doesn't leak in here, huh? Which medicine do you need? Is it time?"

Little Perry cleared his throat. "It's in my medicine drawer. Here." The boy pulled out the drawer of his nightstand. It was littered with old spoons and little brown bottles and a white, plastic inhaler. "The spray," Perry said. He bent over for a moment, coughing and holding his stomach. Harry picked up the atomizer and pulled the cap off. "Is there something wrong with your stomach?"

"It hurts when I cough a lot. No, Daddy, you have it upside down." Perry took the atomizer and pulled it apart, putting it back together another way. "This way, see?" He put the inhaler in his mouth, squeezed it, took a deep breath and held it. "Nothing," Perry said, finally.

"Nothing? You mean it's empty?"

Perry tried it again. "It's empty."

"Do you have another one?"

Perry shook his head.

"Can you take a pill instead?"

"I just had — *cough* — a pill before you came in — when I woke up." Perry held his breath again, trying to ward off another violent coughing spell.

Harry slumped down into Perry's little wooden chair.

I'm stoned!

Can I go to the drugstore stoned? With no money?

Can I talk to them stoned? Money! Money! Where can I get a couple bucks fast?

"Come here, Perry, let's put this bathrobe on." Harry had not realized how frail his boy had become, and how dependent he was on his medicine. He adjusted the robe around him as gently as he could and belted it. "We'll pick Mommy and Janey up at the grocery store and then we'll stop at the drugstore for your spray at the same time. Okay?"

Perry nodded, and Harry got the feeling that Perry wanted to ask him about the money for the medicine but was afraid.

"I'll get my feet all wet."

"I'll carry you. Come on. Up we go!" Harry hoisted the boy up and carried him outside. The sun still shone through the clouds, charging everything with an eerie, orange glow. Water steamed up from the puddles in the grass. "Oh, Perry! It's beautiful when it rains!"

Perry tried to cough while Harry was carrying him.

"You know what you and I are going to do when you get better?

We're going to go fishing!"

"You said that — *cough* — before."

"Something else, little man! There is a doctor I know who lives on the island sometimes, and as soon as the boat is running you and I are going there together. Just you and me. He's going to look you over and tell you how you can get better. The salt air will be good for you, too!"

When Harry started up the truck, he remembered again that he was stoned. "Wow! Listen to that!"

Perry looked at his father and frowned.

VVVVVrrrrrooooooom pop pop pop pop... Harry blipped the throttle and listened to the engine he had rebuilt and hopped up himself. "I put this baby together good, Perry! This is a good truck!"

"Too bad — the boat — always — breaks — down."

"I'll get it, Perry. I'll beat it. I'll find a way."

Perry slid down the seat as far away from his dad as he could get. Harry drove carefully, not feeling the normal urge to roar out of the yard and spin wheels around the corner. When they got to the super-market, Annie and Janey were waiting for them with a cart full of what they would need for the week. The sky had darkened again and it was drizzling.

"Why did you bring Perry?" Annie asked angrily. "Now we have to put the bags in back where they'll get wet."

Harry explained about the medicine for Perry, quietly so the children would not hear. "I figured that if you could take Perry into the drugstore and tell them you'll pay them in a couple days, they won't be able to turn you down when they see him."

"You son of a bitch! You go in!"

"No, Annie, look. What excuse could I give them for being broke. You can tell them that your husband..."

Annie wheeled around and turned her back to him. Harry grabbed her by the arm and shook her. "Not now, Annie! Have your tantrum after Perry gets his inhaler! We need you now!"

Annie stared at him without answering. Then she screamed: "You're a coward! Tell them the truth!"

"Get in the truck. We're getting wet," Harry said.

"What about my spray, Daddy? I'm going to die!"

"Stick your head back in there, Perry! Now listen carefully, Annie! I'm stoned. I can't go in there now and talk to them. I'll fuck up my story. You have to do it for me."

"Stoned? What do you mean stoned! You don't look drunk to me. You're just chicken, that's all. You can't face..."

Harry grabbed her arm again. "I mean I've been smoking pot."

Annie stared at Harry for a long time, then turned and climbed into the truck. Harry climbed in on his side, with the children sandwiched together in the middle. Little Perry tried to crawl up on his mother's lap to be near the window. "Roll it down — Mommy — I can't — breathe!"

"I want a divorce," Annie said.

"Oh goodie!" Janey replied.

CHAPTER 5
Hamburger

Peace had been tentatively restored. Harry had discovered where Gilli practiced medicine — the new branch of the public health clinic where battered children were cared for — and Perry got a free checkup.

"Right next to the VD clinic," Harry said. "Remember that place?"

"Don't look at me," Annie said.

"You know, where we had to take Perry and Janey for their vaccinations? Remember the VD clinic next door, and we had to sit on this bench and wait our turn and all these whores were coming and going?"

"That was years ago."

"Well, it's next to that."

"Wait, I have to turn the stove down." Annie headed for the kitchen.

"Daddy said they look neat!" Perry shouted after her.

"What?"

"Daddy said..."

Harry interrupted. "I told him to say that. To tick you off."

"What are you talking about?"

"It's not important. Anyway, Gilli started the place, and now he puts one week a month in there, and other doctors take turns on the other weeks."

"Daddy said I should ask you how they get the sores on their mouths."

"What?"

"The whores!"

"Shut up, Perry."

"Why should he ask me, Harry?" Annie was grinning.

"Daddy said you were an expert!"

"Harry, what did your friend say about Perry's lungs?"

Harry lifted Perry up on his lap. "It's asthma like we hoped. He'll grow out of it. That's the best news. And he's in good shape otherwise. His heart is strong. He needs to eat more but he shouldn't get fat while he has the asthma. We have to clean out his room, and keep the dust out. I'll explain later. And if that doesn't help, we can have him checked to find out what allergies he has."

"He gave me a new spray thing and new pills," Perry added.

"You sound pretty good," Annie said.

"The spray worked right away, Mommy. But it made me dizzy at first. And I thought I was going to get car sick but I didn't."

"That's wonderful!" Annie bent down and gave Perry a kiss on the head.

"I saw a dead boy."

"Oh, yeah, that was rough," Harry said. "They had an emergency."

"A dead boy?"

"They had an emergency while we were there. Actually the kid was brought in before we got there but we didn't know it, and when they wheeled out the body, Perry saw it."

"He was all beat up, Mommy. His mother and father did it. They killed him."

"Harry. How could you let little Perry see such a thing."

"I didn't know they were going to do that! Besides, it's life!"

"No, Harry, **this** is life. Our family. Happiness. Caring for each other."

"Bullshit, Annie! What happiness! Life is waking up in the night and seeing your little boy scared as hell fighting for every breath! That's life!"

Janey came into the dining room. She was trying on the new dress Annie was sewing for her.

"There, Harry! Look at her! Isn't she adorable?"

"The pins are sticking me, Mommy," Janey said, squirming in the dress Annie had pinned together.

"Life is Janey getting her first period," Harry said.

"Harry!"

"See?"

"See what?" Perry said.

"What's a period, Mommy?"

"Ohhh!" Annie dashed back into the kitchen.

Harry raised his voice so Annie could hear. "You should see this guy on the island and then see him dressed like a doctor. Unbelievable!"

"He has a ponytail," Perry said.

Annie came back, drying her hands on the dish towel.

"He said severe asthma like this is often genetic, usually boys, but the kids grow out of it."

"Mommy, he has a beard, too. Yeeeech! But he's nice and he likes me!"

"Not in my family, Harry said, so it must be yours."

"Oh sure, my fault, right. Well, it's not in my family, either, Harry. Did he charge you?"

"No. No. One week a month and he doesn't even charge. He said he doesn't spend any money so he doesn't need any money. How about that!"

"Are you sure he knows what he's doing, Harry? Is he good? I mean..."

"He charges rich people," Perry said.

"He said he charges people he knows are ripping off other people," Harry explained.

Annie was picking and pulling on Janey's dress, changing the location of a pin here and there. "Now slip out of it very carefully, Janey, and put your old dress back on, unless you want to take your shower early."

"Do boys get periods?" Perry said.

Janey stamped her foot. "What's a period?"

"Boys get something else instead," Harry said.

"What do boys get," Annie said.

"Oh, Annie."

Annie ruffled little Perry's hair. "Oh, Perry, you look better already!"

"I can breathe better already!"

"He does look good, Annie!" Harry gave the boy a hug.

"Oh, Mommy, you should see how awful that dead boy looked!" Perry coughed and took a deep breath. "I coughed. I'm still wheezing. But I'm going to grow out of it."

"That's right, Perry. That's wonderful."

"The doctor said if I would've got it when I was older then I wouldn't be able to grow out of it."

"Ohhhh, Perry, that's good news!" Annie looked at Harry.

"He gave me two prescriptions to get filled. I'll go after dinner, but I don't know how much it'll be. Did you ever pay them back for that spray we picked up that day?"

"I don't want to be reminded."

"Yeah, but did you pay them back?"

"Yes, yes."

"You should've seen that dead boy, Mommy. His eyes were still open. I was standing on this thing and when I saw him I almost fell down!"

"They were examining Perry and he had to stand on a chair for a minute," Harry explained.

"His eyes were looking right at me! Yuk!"

"Oh, Harry!" Annie said.

"His mother and father took turns killing him. I heard the nurses talking! They put him in boiling water," Perry said, covering his eyes, "and they hit him and they killed him!"

CHAPTER 6
Family

Christmas came and went. Annie and Harry stayed home New Year's Eve, having exhausted all their money on Christmas presents for the children. Harry also had to save up for the boat engine bell-housing which he had ordered and was due any day. But business at the boat yard was good and there was plenty of overtime.

All through the holidays and the weeks following, one thought lay heavily on Harry's mind: getting back to the island. The memory of that day there with the hippies followed him everywhere and surfaced whenever he had a moment to reflect. Who would believe him? It was tempting, especially during lunchtime at work, to talk about the hippie girls on the island, but he never did. How could he explain Neeta to them, or Faylie! They would tell him to jerk off. They would tell him he was full of shit. There was no way he could convince the other guys that on one of the islands east of Miami there was a white girl running naked and free in the jungle with a ring in her nose. Who could have a sex-dream of a girl like that and expect such a creature to show up in "real life"?

The yearning in Harry's heart grew heavier with each passing day. And making love with Annie became more and more painful and perfunctory. He could do that now only in the dark and with his eyes closed, and rarely communicated good feelings. Annie felt rejected and Harry felt cheated because he could not take pride in her the way she was now. It never occurred to him that Annie had dreams and goals, too; all he could see was what he didn't like: the short, dyed, lacquered hair, the droopy tits, the thick waist, the flea-bites she would scratch bloody on her pasty-white legs.... And yet when he would get high (until the pot supply disappeared) he would see himself for what he was. An oversexed asshole. Why couldn't he leave

Annie alone? Why was he so horny all the time? Why weren't the other guys at work like him? And what was it with all the men who say: "My wife is the only woman I'll ever need." How could that be?!

Slowly, Harry came to remember parts of what he was learning about himself when he was high, on the job with co-workers sharing a joint, and he had also learned to smoke the dwindling supply of marijuana when he was alone and could think without being interrupted. But then the island memories would return. The women, with their hippie names.

Neeta! Exotic Jewess! Golden in the sun!

Surrendra! Dark, Indian princess and a head crammed with silly rules.

Milky! Free blond hair and playful, fully-packed tits!

Faylie! Lean and wild and fearless creature of the forest!

Mazie. Dale's babe. So precious.

Once in a great while, Harry would consider the reality of the hippies on the island. Or at least he would try. He would try to imagine how they got that way. He would even consider the possibility that he was dreaming them all up. He would consider the possibility that his image of the chicks was unrealistic, that they must be real people with real feelings and down-to-earth plans for their future just as everyone else had. But thinking about stuff like that was a dead-end road. He had seen Faylie the way she was. He had heard with his own ears Neeta's cheer and love. *"Awww Harry...."*

The memories held but the reality of the hippies was fading.

Not so with Ruby, a teenage girl next door. Harry would watch for Ruby whenever he was home. And he was getting into watching other colored girls walk by his gate when he was in the yard. When Harry was at work, Bo would call them "jungle bunnies" or "chocolate pussy". The neighborhood at home was turning black with a vengeance, and Harry's prejudices dissolved under the force of flashy black thighs and insolent chunky asses and lilting Dixie voices and sleek dark throats and pretty eyes flashing smiles like Bambi.

Obesity was rare in those Sixties days, and hope sprang in the hearts of many a colored girl with a mirror and a dream.

Once, when Harry had brought up the subject of pretty black

women — how he liked the lean, tall ones — Bo said: "I'll fuck one but I won't kiss one!" From that day on, catching and kissing one of the lithe black deer became Harry's favorite day-dream.

The lunchroom was on the cusp of being desegregated but there was some resentment on both sides, and Harry never forgot a colored boy telling him one day that kissing blondes, their lips are so cold.

"They don't seem cold to me, Harry said, pissed at this unsolicited bit of information.

"That 'cause you don' know no differnt."

For sometime longer, the blacks took their lunchboxes out to the loading dock for breaks, or under the huge, live oak near the fence.

One day, when the men were all sitting around the lunch table, one of the Cuban finishers pulled a girlie magazine out of his lunchbox and carefully ripped a picture out of the middle of it and handed it to Harry. It was a photo of a colored chick, her eyes closed in ecstasy, white cum running down the corner of her mouth and a snotty-looking strand of it hanging from one of her blue-black nipples. The photograph took Harry's breath away.

"My 'mano he get the magazine from Dane-mark!"

Bo kicked Harry under the table and laughed."You look like you're in love!"

The Cuban and another man were flipping through the rest of the book. Harry looked up, hoping not to miss anything. "Any more of this one in there?"

"The rest, they white!" the Cuban grinned.

"Gimme that!" Bo reached over and jerked the picture out of Harry's hand. "Juan Pablo!" he yelled, waving the picture. "Can I keep it?"

The Cuban grinned and nodded.

"It's mine!" Harry said.

"Fuck you, Harry. I asked first. You know the rules."

"Juan Pablo brought it for me. Juan?"

Juan held his hands out palms up and shrugged his shoulders. "The boss-man ask me first."

"Come on, Bo."

"If I give it to you, you'll be in the can all afternoon, jerking off. This is going in my locker."

"Asshole."

"Harry. You got three skiffs out there with new engines waiting for your loving touch and you ain't even halfway through the first one. You been fucking off. Plus you're the horniest dude I ever saw. If you could get your mind off pussy you'd be a good marine mechanic. Your old lady must be a lousy piece of ass for you to be so horny!"

"You want to compare old ladies?"

"You want to compare girlfriends? I'll bet your old lady's the only piece of ass you ever had. I can tell!"

The table was an uproar of laughter. Bo handed back the picture to Harry. "Here! Go jack off before lunch is over. On your own time!"

"Kiss my ass, Bo!" Harry handed the picture around so the others could see it, so they could see how little importance he attached to his ownership of it, hoping they would not wrinkle it up or get food on it.

Fucker.

I'm the best boat mechanic you've got.

That night, while Annie and the children were in the living room watching TV, Harry snuck the photo into the bathroom and masturbated. Before he came, he promised himself to try to find a way to get in with the family next door, to find a way to approach Ruby.

She could baby sit?

Would Annie go for leaving the kids with a black girl?

Do they do stuff like that where she's from?

Colorado? I think so.

Yes!

After seeing a movie Saturday night — a rare event — Annie and Harry went window-shopping along the classy Lincoln Road Mall, Lincoln Road closed off to vehicular traffic but not to pedestrians with money to spend. It was the first time in months that the two of them had an evening out without having to worry about Perry and his asthma. Annie took Harry's hand as they walked along.

"He's really getting better."

"Yeah. For the most part."

"Your doctor friend didn't even have to change his new medicine?"

"No."

"Perry is growing out of it. He..."

"He might not grow out of it for a couple years yet. We just have to pay more attention to him. Love him more."

"You have to pay him more attention! I always took..."

"I know. I know."

"You're the one who..."

"I know!" Harry steered them into the entrance of an art gallery, using the maneuver to get rid of Annie's hand. It was dumb to be seen walking hand-in-hand with your wife when you've been married so long. It made the husband look stupid, like a loser.

"Look at the house in that painting!" Annie said.

"Yeah...."

"Someday we could live in a place like that if..."

"Annie, for chrissake!"

Another, better-dressed couple stopped beside them to look at the paintings. The man was older than Harry and wore slick shoes and a diamond ring. The woman was young with long, loose hair, long legs and platform shoes. She hung on the arm of the man and nibbled at him as they whispered to each other and laughed. Harry moved away from them and Annie followed. The next shop was a boutique.

"Oh! I'd like to have a dress like that one!" Annie said.

Harry looked at the dress, which was a commercial version of a hippie dress. "It would look dumb with that phony, short hairdo you insist on spraying hard like a brick — and you'd have to go barefoot in it which means giving up that ridiculous pantyhose you wear that always bags up at the knees, and you'd have to go without a bra with that dress or you'd look like a gunboat walking down the street."

Annie dabbed a tear away with her finger. The other couple caught up with them and Harry moved on. The next shop was a candy store.

"If I ever find a man who loves me — really loves me...."

"If you loved me you wouldn't have flushed that bag of pot I had down the toilet. There was only a little left and I was saving it!"

"After all this time, Harry! That was after Christmas!"

"So?"

"You were acting terrible then — screaming and yelling at the children — hitting Janey for no reason at all — making all kinds of wild promises to Perry and then ignoring him!"

"Oh, no, stop right there. That was before I started smoking grass. I never did anything like that when I was high!"

Annie did not answer. They moved down the street, not paying much attention to the window displays. It was a cool evening, and Harry shivered. "It would be impossible for me to be shitty when I'm high," Harry said. "I think."

They stopped at a men's shop. Annie reached for Harry's hand again. "Is that the truth, Harry?"

Harry nodded, instinctively pretending to be hurt.

"I have good news for you then," Annie sad, squeezing his hand.

"I have good news for you, too."

"Tell me your good news first."

"I wasn't going to tell you. Sometimes you get me so pissed off...."

"Tell me."

"Two things. First, I got a big raise. Two weeks ago. It showed up on last Friday's paycheck. Yesterday's check leaves me with enough money to gas up the boat after I pay the babysitter! Huh? Ta da! Then, the part I ordered came in and by next Saturday the boat'll be finished and Perry and I are going out to the island together camping and you won't have me around to mess up your weekend! How about that!"

Annie looked thoughtful. "Harry? Let's all go!"

"Naaaa — Annie, I knew you would say that!" I promised little Perry it would be just him and me."

"How much was the raise?"

"Besides, you wouldn't dig the people Gilli has out there. They wear clothes only when they feel like it, and they use drugs!"

"Don't you want to hear my good news?"

"Okay."

"I didn't flush the marijuana down the toilet."

"Yeah?"

"Are you happy?"

"Hey. Come on, Annie. I'm not a little boy. It's not up to you when to give me my toys back!"

"It is when it affects the family!"

"Oh fuck you!"

They walked on.

"Where is it?"

"In my jewelry box."

"I looked in your jewelry box."

"I've been moving it around. If you looked in my jewelry box, then you didn't really believe I actually threw it away, did you?"

"You wouldn't dare."

"Oh come on, Harry. Give me some credit!"

"Hmmmmm."

"What's it like, Harry?"

"Grass? Um, it's hard to put into words."

"Come on, Harry."

"It is, it is. It's hard to describe."

"Harry. You can tell me. We've been married over ten years..."

"Ten years! Ten years of bullshit!"

"Bullshit? You should be married to..."

"No! No, I didn't mean that! Being married itself is dumb!"

"You get away with more shit, Harry!"

"Uh-huh."

"We both love the same two kids is why we need to get along."

"Yeah, yeah. But we don't like the same things anymore. Stop! Don't cry! Don't start that shit! I didn't mean it the way it sounds!"

They turned and watched the other couple pass by.

Annie lowered her voice. "Tell me about pot, Harry."

"You want to try it?"

"No! I'm not going to get hooked on anything! Not me!"

"Hooked?! Annie, you're hopeless."

They walked on.

Annie said: "You told me you used to do it on the Beach. Remember? You used to go to Miami Beach all the time?"

"Yeah, but I never got high then. That seems like such a long time ago.... I tried it. Smoked it often enough but I never got high."

"I was stuck home with the children then. Perry was a baby."

Harry sighed. "When I got high on the island, well, I can't remember exactly how the first time felt anymore." Harry had to stop to think. "That seems strange."

"With the nudists?"

"Nudists. Hippies. Those people — the whole day was so unreal!"

"See? Unreal! That's what they say about it. It twists things in your mind so you think you're dreaming or something like that."

Harry smiled for the first time. "Annie! One thing I know. It doesn't twist your mind. It doesn't twist!"

When they got home the lights in the house were all on. Annie tapped on the front door while Harry rolled up the windows of the pickup.

"She doesn't answer, Harry. Where's your key?"

"I left my house keys on the dresser. Keep your voice down."

"You left your keys on the dresser with her running all over the house?"

Annie dug around in her purse and unlocked the door. They moved quietly through the front porch into the living room. Ruby and little Perry were asleep in the armchair — Perry in Ruby's lap, breathing through his open mouth, his head on her breast, his pajama shirt missing as usual. Ruby's eyes were closed with beautiful, long lashes — face of peace — her arms around their son.

"How beautiful," Harry whispered.

Annie nodded. They moved closer. He's not wheezing."

Ruby's eyes fluttered, then opened wide. "Oh! Miss Annie!" She struggled to get up without disturbing Perry.

"It's alright," Harry said. "Easy. Here, let me take him." Their arms touched briefly in the transfer of the skinny, six-year-old boy, and Harry's heart went out to her. "Thank you," he said. You are good for him. He's been so sick." Harry kissed Perry on the forehead.

Ruby straightened herself up and brushed out her skirt. Harry stood there silently, rocking Perry, who had not awakened. Harry could not keep his eyes off the babysitter.

"How much do we owe you?" Annie said.

She is priceless, Harry said to himself.

Ruby shrugged and smiled. Annie was looking at her watch and counting the hours they had been away.

"Will six dollars be enough?"

Ruby nodded.

"Wait. Let me dump him in his bed first," Harry said. When he came back from Perry's room, he fished out a ten dollar bill and handed the money to Ruby. "I'll walk you over."

Ruby did not acknowledge the extra four dollars, and Harry hoped that Annie did not notice.

"It's only next door, Mister Harry." Ruby smiled.

"Yeah, but you have to go out to the street first and it's dark and late."

"Let him go with you — he's right," Annie added.

The two of them walked slowly through Harry's front yard, keeping some distance between them. Harry waited while Ruby tapped on her front door for somebody to let her in. When the door opened a crack, she turned, gave Harry a little wave, and slipped into the dark house. Harry wondered which one of the large, extended family had been up to let her in. Back home he padlocked his gate and checked the windows of the truck again.

It's only next door, Mister Harry.

That sweet voice....

For a moment, he looked at Ruby's silent house in the gloom.

She usually wears those short shorts....

Fifteen?

That chunky little ass.... Those smooth, long legs.... Oh God....

Annie was in her nightgown already. She handed Harry his pipe and the small baggie of marijuana she had hidden, and sat on the edge of their bed, fussing with the hair Harry hated. There was a brightness in her eyes. "Perry's not wheezing a bit," she said. She waited there while Harry showered and changed.

"Might be just enough for only one pipe full," Harry said, turning the baggie around in his hands. He reflected on how he got it, and how the boat would be ready soon, and what seemed apparent that Annie wanted to get laid, and that he was about to get high.

"It's just like Christmas," Harry said.

"See how nice I am to you?"

"We'll see about that after I get high. Want to try it now?" Harry was glad when she said no. Marijuana had a reputation for revealing the truth about things.

Annie watched him quietly as Harry sat there in his pajama pants, puffing on the pipe, inhaling, holding his breath, exhaling, puffing and inhaling, holding his breath with the smoke deep in his lungs, avoiding Annie's stare. He resisted the urge to ask her not to look at him while he smoked, and instead tamped the pipe out so there would be some left for another time.

Probably thinks I'll morph into a raving maniac any second!

He turned to one side and gazed at the wall, away from her, and waited.

Funny.... Can't remember what it feels like!

At the just getting off stage....

What if I don't get high?

I don't think I'm going to get high.

Harry coughed.

Both times before when I did get high I thought I wouldn't get high.

Harry waited for the first sign of getting high, whatever that would be. He laid down the pipe, which was now out.

Am I getting high now?

The question repeated itself in his head, and turned into a voice, which said: *Am I getting high now? High now? Now? What is NOW? NOW is over, and THIS now is over, over, over....*

"I'm getting high," Harry said aloud. He listened to himself say it, and turned slowly to look at Annie. She was sitting smiling at him.

Does she really love me? She must to put up with the way I am.

All these years....

How could she do that?

Yes, she loves me.

Or maybe it's for the kids.

"I wish you could come with me to this place," Harry said to her, smiling uncontrollably. He tried to stop grinning so much.

"I might like it too much."

"Turn the lights out. But leave the night-light on — it's so bright — in here." Harry relaxed in the darkness. Annie sat down beside him on the bed and touched him.

"Wait — give me a minute — I'm still, ahhh, going up."

"Okay. I'll wait. Don't worry about me."

Harry did not remember Annie's voice ever being so gentle, her manner so soothing. He got the impression that she was in awe of what pot would do, or she was just plain scared.

"Do you want me to leave?" she said finally.

"No, no — just wait. Don't talk. I'm not used to this. Doing it with you here." Harry's eyes adjusted to the dim glow from the night-light. Things in the room began to take shape. A new, heavier but gentle rush flowed through his brain and took him higher. A shiver of pleasure rushed up his spine to his head and back down to his legs and disappeared. *Wow!* Harry closed his eyes. Swirls of the most intense colors played before him. The chromium, toothy grille of his father's old four-holer Buick Roadmaster grinned at him and disappeared from his memory. He opened his eyes. "I just saw the car we used to have when I was a little kid."

"Yes?"

Annie's answer sounded dumb.

Why don't you ask to try it?

You used to be wild.

That barmaid job in Denver.

That billyclub you used on smart-asses....

Harry remembered that he had wanted to fuck her. He wondered about that. It didn't make any sense. It was so good just sitting there that nothing made any difference anymore.

"Oh!" Harry exclaimed, for no reason.

"Yes?" Annie was doing her best to go along with anything that was happening to him. "Is there something I can do for you?"

Harry crawled up on the bed, behind her back, and stretched out, pulling the pillow under his head. "Oh!" he said again. "I feel so good!" He watched Annie sitting there on the edge. "Annie. I wanted to make love to you, but...."

"Yes?"

"Can you do something for me?"

Annie turned and bent over him, looking at his face, like a mother.

"Hey. Don't stare."

"Okay...." Annie sat up again, at the edge of the bed.

"I didn't mean go away. I meant...."

"What do you mean?" Her voice was a whisper. A seductive whisper.

"I want you to — make love to me — to do everything to me while I just lie here. That's my wish. I can't explain it, but that's my wish."

"Okay!" Annie looked cheerful in the dim light. "Where do you want me to start?"

Oh beautiful! She's going to do it!

"Surprise me. And don't talk. Okay? Don't talk."

Harry let his voice trail off, as if the grass were overwhelming him to the point of exhaustion, to give him an excuse to close his eyes and keep them closed while she did whatever it was she was going to do. He listened to the rustle of her nightie as she pulled it off, and his body trembled with anticipation. He knew he was about to be taken away to Paradise. To be sure, though, in a bare whisper as if he were about to lose consciousness, he said to her: "I love you, Annie. I really — do — love you."

As Harry shivered with the most pleasurable and fantastic sensations he had ever felt during a sexual encounter with his wife, the rest of his world of worries and frustrations fell away.

And then it was over, after what had seemed to be a very long and wonderful time.

Annie was struggling to get away from him. She would run to the bathroom and spit it all out, then gargle with mouthwash, which always flushed away what a moment before was such a pleasure for Harry.

When Annie broke from the hands holding her head and yanked open the bedroom door, Janey and little Perry were standing there together in their pajamas, lit up in the shaft of hallway light like angels. Harry scrambled for his blanket and pulled it over him as Annie barreled past the children naked, mouth clamped shut, heading for the bathroom sink.

"Perry's scared," Janey said.

Harry heard the disgusting splatter hit the bowl, followed by gagging and coughing.

Harry yelled. "Close the door, Annie! What are you kids doing here?"

"Perry's scared," Janey repeated.

"Scared of what?"

"I heard noises, Daddy."

"Go back to bed," The harshness of his tone clear and cruel as he listened to himself with expanded awareness

"Can Perry sleep in my bed?"

Harry looked at them. They were so cute standing there in their old, worn-out pajamas. And they looked so small and pathetic. "Wait," he said. He was so high. He looked at them standing there for a long time.

"Wait for what, Daddy?" Perry said. He had his teddy bear in one hand.

Harry realized how much he loved them. "Will you be good and not horse around?"

"Oh good!" Perry said.

"We won't horse around," Janey said.

"Just for tonight."

"Just for tonight."

Annie brushed by the children, still naked, and flopped down in the bed beside Harry, pulling the cover over her. She nestled her head against his chest. The children closed the door behind them. Harry sighed, his senses swamped with the smell of Annie's medicine breath covering up the smell of semen and old pussy. His penis was already asleep.

My first sex with marijuana....

God, I thought I would never stop cuming.

It was a Friday evening and dinnertime, and Harry had just finished his shower. Although he was tired from a hard day at work, his energy came back as he pulled out his camping equipment and checked over all his clothes and guns and gear.

"Daddy. Mommy says dinner is getting cold and we're all waiting for you."

"Yeah, yeah, okay, I'm coming."

Perry kept on standing there. "Daddy, Mommy says you should see what the niggers are doing in Neeley's back yard. She says you'll miss it if you don't hurry."

"That's what she always says. It's their back yard now. They can do what they want."

"Mommy says you shouldn't miss this," Perry repeated.

"Yeah, okay."

Harry ruffled the boy's hair and went with him to the dining room and sat down. It was still light enough to watch the back yard next door. "I remember when there was grass growing in that yard," Harry said. "What's for dinner?"

"Pot roast!" Annie came in and set down a pot full of steaming mashed potatoes. "New Idahoes!" she said.

"What's the big deal in Neeley's yard? Just a bunch of little niggers running around as usual."

Annie leaned over the table and pointed out the window for Harry. "You wanted to know which of the kids were Ruby's, remember? Well, they're both out there now. Look. See the two with diapers by the utility-room door? Those are Ruby's!"

Harry half rose up in his seat and leaned forward to get a better look. "Oh bullshit! Ruby's still cherry. I think. Come on, I'm hungry." Harry slumped back down in his chair, unable to imagine Ruby fucking somebody.

She's mine.

Yeah, right.

Shit!

Annie went back to the kitchen to get the roast. When she returned, Harry was out of his seat now, right up against the window. "Those two?" he said.

"I saw her out there with them this afternoon and I went out and talked over the fence, you know, and she told me the others belong to her mother. Her mother has four little ones there, Harry, you wouldn't believe it, and Ruby's aunt, Birdella, has four more.

"Okay, but did she say she has kids of her own? Those two in diapers are Ruby's? I don't believe it. Christ they're ugly!" Harry returned to his chair. Annie was carving the meat and dishing out the food while Harry continued to look toward the window, his elbows on the table and his head in his hands. "That's hard to believe," he said. "Who's the father?"

"Search me."

Janey spoke up in her little voice. "I think I saw him, Daddy. He doesn't live there but he comes sometimes when you're at work. He looks like a big gorilla, Daddy. Really!"

Little Perry laughed and made a growly, jungle-type noise.

"No, Janey," Annie said. "That's Birdella's boyfriend. She's divorced and Ruby's not married. Ruby's mother had her after Birdella was born, but they seem like sisters even though they have different fathers. And Birdella's husband comes to visit — I don't know what that's all about — and Ruby's mother is on her third boyfriend and that's the man you talked to, Harry, the old one, and he's the father of all those little ones Ruby's mother has. He's not Ruby's father.

Harry shook his head. "Let's eat."

"Daddy, they pee outside," little Perry said.

Janey nodded her head. "The girls, too."

"The old man does, too. In the morning," Perry added.

Janey giggled. "I saw that, too. Ruby's father is real old and has all kinds of teeth missing."

"He's not Ruby's father," Annie corrected. "He's her stepfather."

"He stands there by the lemon tree and only a little dribble comes out," Janey said. Perry clamped his hand over his mouth and looked at Harry. Harry told Janey to shut up.

"They shouldn't do that where the children can see it," Annie said, her mouth full of roast beef.

"Do you have to talk with your mouth full of food?" Harry was talking with food in his mouth himself. "Next time the old fuck does that when our kids are out, you ought to turn the garden hose on him."

"Beercan hates all of them," Perry threw in. "Daddy, please cut my meat smaller. Ohhh look!"

Harry looked up again. One of the children next door, wearing a shirt but no pants, was spraying roach poison all over one of the smaller kids wearing diapers — one of the fatherless children. Harry watched, horrified, as the child laughed, opened his mouth, and let the other boy spray the poison right in. It was a can of Truly Nolen TNT "Truly Nolen Treatment", same brand, same color as the poison Annie used around the kitchen. Harry jumped up, his mouth full of food, and ran out, stumbling over Beercan, who had been resting on the front stoop. Beercan sprang to attention and chased after Harry to the fence, barking.

"Stop that!" Harry shouted. The little black boy with no pants on screamed with laughter and ran after one of the other children, spraying her as soon as he got close. Harry climbed over the fence and jerked the can out of his hands.

"This is poison! You know what poison is?"

The children all quieted down and came over to him, mumbling, some of them sucking their thumbs, eyes wide open in awe at this new thing standing in their yard, giving orders. Not a one of them looked over ten years old. Harry waved the can in front of them. "This is poison. It can kill you. It will kill you!"

He turned around and looked toward their back door, the screen door completely ripped off now. "Where's your mother?"

"My mother's sick," one of the children mumbled.

"My mother's not sick," another said.

Harry bent over the little one with the diapers who got sprayed in the mouth. "Do you feel anything?"

The kid shook his head.

"Where's your mother?"

"I dunno."

"She — she — she gone to work," another volunteered.

"No, she in bed."

Harry stomped over to the back door and knocked. The catch was broken and the door swung open. The kitchen was empty. "Anybody home?" he hollered.

"Come on in," a faint voice called from the front.

Harry walked in carefully, the can of poison still in hand. There were a few squashed roaches on the floor, some of them still wiggling. The sink was full of dirty water, and soiled dishes were stacked everywhere. Harry watched his feet as he walked, following the sound of the television set. Ruby was flopped in an easy chair in the living room, one bare, smooth-as-silk chocolate leg slung over an arm-rest.

"Oh, hi, Mister Harry!" She looked at him, moved her eyes back to the TV, then back to him. She smiled her pretty, dark, Madonna smile, and got up, pulling the hem of her tight shorts down with her fingers. The herd of thumb-sucking, mumbling children gathered around them. Harry held out the can of roach poison.

"The kids were spraying each other. I saw it while I was eating dinner. The window is right at the end of the table. One of them..."

Before he could finish, Ruby took a swat at one of the children in diapers, knocking him to the floor.

"No, no!" Harry said, picking the child up. "This is the one that got poisoned!" He looked around for the boy he had taken the can away from. "That one," Harry said.

Ruby lunged for the boy and twisted him around and whacked him on the ass as hard as she could. **Slap!** "Sammy's a bad 'un — a bad 'un, damn you Sammy!" **Slap! Slap!** "Didn' I tell you to leave the poison alone!" **Slap! Slap!** Ruby's blows were falling all over him now as he lay sprawled on the floor, screaming.

Harry grabbed her other arm. "Don't **kill** him!".

Ruby gave Sammy a couple more swats and straightened up. Her mouth was trembling, and Harry switched to Ruby's smooth, velvety legs and chunky little ass.

"Here," he said, handing her the can.

Ruby went right for the kitchen, blasting a few roaches on the way to the cupboard. "Sink's stopped up again," she said matter-of-factly. She turned toward Harry and smiled again. Her teeth were so perfect and white. Her lips full and succulent.

Annie's teeth are always yellow...

"Let me take a look," Harry said.

Ruby did not move out of the way and Harry had to stand right next to her. His stomach was in knots with the desire for her.

Do other people get as horny as I do all the time?

Harry looked at the scummy water in the sink and plunged his arm in, hoping there would be no slimy surprises. There was no strainer at the bottom and his fingers could feel chunks of slippery garbage in the neck of the drain.

"Do you have a plunger?"

"Mama has one somewhere." Ruby peered down into the dirty water with him, brushing her velvety arm against his. "I'll go look."

Harry followed her out the back door to the utility room, his eyes glued to her white shorts. Her narrow hips, so choice. He watched her poke around in the dark room.

"Here it is!" Ruby handed him the plunger. It had a red, rubber cup with a scrap of dried toilet-paper stuck to it.

Harry had the sink drain working with the third, good stroke, all the water and debris whooshing down with a long, sucking sound. He turned around, smiling. Ruby was gone, and only a few of the little thumb-suckers were left in the kitchen. He went toward the living room and the sound of the TV. Ruby was sprawled out on the couch this time, smacking gum, one hand behind her head. Only one button held her shirt closed, exposing most of her perfect little tits. Harry was sure that her blouse had been buttoned up before. Ruby smiled.

Harry swallowed. "I fixed it."

Ruby nodded her head, still smiling at him. Harry set the plunger down on the soiled carpet and swallowed again. "Well, I guess I'd better go back and finish my dinner."

Ruby gave him a little wave and turned back to the TV. Harry waved back and headed for the kitchen. The hurt inside him was bad. Really bad. He was hopeless. He was a coward and was never going to score with this babe.

I could have fucked her right there with the kids watching and all.

While he stumbled through Ruby's back yard he pictured himself spreading her velvety, brown legs. His lips brushed along the insides of her silky thighs, and his tongue licked her pussy slick as she arched her back and twitched with joy.

Beercan was waiting for him at the fence, wagging his tail.

"Good-old, faithful Beercan," Harry said as he climbed over. He patted the dog on the head and scratched behind his ears, deliberately cleaning the sticky goo from Ruby's sink out of his fingernails with the dog's fur.

"I'm going to the island tomorrow, Beercan," he said. "I'm going back at last."

CHAPTER 7
Hippie Scum

At three in the morning, Annie woke Harry up by pulling back his blanket and kissing around his navel. Harry's first instinct was to pretend extreme exhaustion and let his wife make love to him again, but as soon as he awoke sufficiently to think about his plans for going to the island, he ignored the sexual advances and jerked upright, grabbing the clock and peering at it in the darkness.

"It's three o'clock," Annie said. "There's plenty of time."

Harry dropped his feet over the edge of the bed. "I have to wake little Perry up. He wakes up slow. And I have to check the tide tables and the weather and load the boat."

Annie crawled up behind him and kissed the back of his neck. "Harry. Why can't we all go this time?"

He clamped his hand over his neck. "Why do you do that when you know I have to pee? Why can't you turn me on when I'm home and I'm bored and I'm horny? And I also told you why just Perry and me are going."

"You're horny now. I can tell."

"Annie!"

Annie moved away from him and sat on the other side of the bed. It was dark and chilly, and the only sounds were from a few cars and trucks rumbling down the expressway in the distance. Harry waited for his penis to go down before getting up. He wanted to drop a load into Annie that very minute, but was hoping to see Neeta on the island. Maybe, if he were lucky, he would run into Faylie. If he would ball the old lady now there would be little jizz left to unload.

But if I drop a load now, I won't come too quick if I get a chance to fuck Neeta.

But if I do fuck Annie now, I probably won't get horny enough on the island to get up the balls to do anything about Neeta or Faylie.

If I do run into them....

Fear. Rejection. That's the reason I don't score.

The reason fear is called "no balls".

With a burst of resolve, Harry got to his feet and stumbled toward the bathroom. After he finished washing and shaving, he inspected his face closely in the mirror, and spotted a new gray hair near his temple. The gray hair he pulled with tweezers. It seemed they were popping up all the time now! The hairs coming out of his nostrils he clipped with manicuring scissors. Then he went for the latest problem, which he had first noticed only a few months before: tufts of fine, blond hair growing out of his ears. He pulled these hairs out with the tweezers also, feeling about carefully with his fingertips to be sure he did not miss any. No chick could go for a guy with tufts of hair growing in his ears — he was sure of that. Then there was the pimple check which meant an inspection of his entire body. The only one he could find, a ripe whitehead on his kneecap, met instant death with a thumbnail.

Annie was busy in the kitchen when he came out. She was packing the big cooler. "The baggies with the rubber bands around them are Perry's sandwiches," she said. "You were in there half an hour. It's nearly four."

"Yeah, yeah... "I'll wake up Perry."

Perry was not at all happy to be awakened so early, and he was wheezing and had to take his medicine right away. But by the time the boy was through with breakfast and was dressed for the trip, he was breathing better and was happy to be going alone with his dad on a boat and camping trip. He even helped carry their equipment out to the boat in the cold and darkness without complaining.

"Can I take both my flashlights?"

"Yeah, you can take both flashlights."

"Can I take my BB gun?"

"Yeah. You can take it if you wrap it in plastic so it doesn't get wet."

"Oh good! Do you have any plastic?"

It was nearly five before Harry was ready to drive the rig out of the yard. Annie came outside in her nightie to see them off. "Harry. Be careful."

"Yeah, yeah."

"If it doesn't warm up, come back home. Okay? Perry still isn't very strong."

"He has his sleeping bag and we have plenty of extra blankets. A night in the cold on the island will do him good."

Annie went around to the other side of the truck and gave little Perry a kiss through the open window.

Vrrrrooooom Vrrrroooooom Vvvrrrrooooom pop pop...

Harry waved to his wife and they were off. A little clutch of fear was gnawing away at his gut, but he didn't let Perry see it. There were the extensive repairs he had made on both engines — would they hold up?

Will Gilli even be there? He said he would.

Old Rhodes Key.

Will Neeta be there?

Will Neeta look happy when she sees me?

Will she have a boyfriend? She must have one by this time...

What'll I say to Faylie if I see her?

What if they already left the island? All of them.

The weather forecast looked bad.

Mild cold front coming through sometime today.

The sea will be rough.

The traffic on the expressway was still light. Harry looked at his boy, who was falling asleep with his head leaning against the window.

It was nearly six-thirty by the time they rolled up to the unimproved boat ramp at Gould's Canal. It was still cold, and gray dark and the stars gone. Perry had awakened and was fidgety and anxious to get going. A new surge of confidence and purpose filled Harry's soul when he was able to back his rig down into the water between two other boats and trailers — right where he wanted it with one shot. Harry liked the unpaved and remote launching area at Gould's; there were no signs posting the rules, there were no police or customs agents, no fancy people with clean and pressed yachting clothes and children with braces. There was no bullshit. Plus there was a boat hoist available a few feet inland on the canal for boaters too fucked up after a long day to get their boats back onto their trailers. A good deal for five bucks and a semi sober operator to help. Plus the Pirates Bar across from the crane. Perfect.

Two men walked up out of the darkness, smiled at Perry, and helped Harry shove his boat off the trailer without a word. In a few minutes, he and Perry were in the boat, engines idling, the truck and trailer parked up on the hill in the bushes. Perry pointed to a yellow-legged sandpiper poking along the shore and Harry nodded. A fish flopped ahead of them, breaking the stillness of the lagoon as the boat slid smoothly and quietly out along the coral-rock breakwater. There were no clouds visible on the horizon and a beautiful sunrise was possible. It looked as though the bay would be calm for a while, too. Harry took in a deep breath of fishy-smelling, salt-wet air.

"Perry, get me a beer," Harry said. "I want one before I hit the power."

Perry grinned, and struggled with the cooler lid. It was hard for him to bend with the life-vest he was wearing, but he was happy to be of help. Proudly, he pulled the pop-top tab off the can and handed the beer to his dad. The tab he tossed into the plastic trash can Harry had built into the boat only a week before. Harry chug-a-lugged the beer and nailed the crushed empty into the trash despite a brief gust of wind.

Perry took his place up front behind the windshield. "Ready!" he shouted.

Harry shoved the throttles forward. With a twisting, droning roar, the engines pushed the craft ahead, raising the bow momentarily until the boat lifted over the surface. Harry eased the engines back to 3300 RPM as soon as they were on plane, and tapped the levers gently with the palm of his hand until both engines were running at the same speed. The roar settled down to a melodious, smooth drone. The fear, however, was coming back in snatches, and Harry's eyes searched back and forth over the instrument panel, checking the water temperature and oil pressure of each unit. Then he relaxed and looked at Perry. Perry looked at him and they smiled. At the last marker out past the breakwater, Harry headed the boat 152 degrees toward the Adams Key Channel. The bay was smooth, and in twenty minutes they would pass Adams Key and would be heading east out Black Caesar Creek — the tricky, poorly marked, narrow, deep-water channel out to the sunrise and the blue-water sea.

"One more beer!" Harry hollered.

The sea was picking up and Perry had to move cautiously to the cooler to keep from falling over. Harry grabbed the beer from him and chug-a-lugged it like the first, expertly tossing the can all the way to the back into the trash bucket.

"Yaaaaay-hooooo!" he yelled, bending his knees and flexing his legs as they crossed over the rough wake of a large yacht which had crossed their bow a few minutes before. Perry hung onto the windshield brace as the boat flew out of the water and came smacking down again. Salt spray came over the bow and hit Harry in the face. Perry grimaced, but Harry laughed. "Power boats rule!" he yelled. He was a man. He was alive.

Old Rhodes Key, barely visited because it was surrounded by shoals on the bay side, shimmered in golden, dawn light. Harry searched the shoreline, heading south south-west on the windward side looking for the one, deep spot, the "ocean tongue", where he could nose the bow up near the rocky coast — where it was still deep enough for the props to clear the bottom three hours after high tide. Little Perry, barely able to manage, was dragging the equipment out from under the bow deck and placing it around Harry's feet.

"As soon as the bow is about a foot from the ledge, you jump off!" Harry shouted. "Then I'm going to back her off just a little and start throwing you the stuff. Try not to let any of it land on tar!"

"It's all tar, Daddy!"

"Bullshit! Do the best you can! You've been here before!"

With the sea and wind picking up astern, it was difficult for Harry to bring the bow close to the coral ledge without hitting it, and to keep the boat at right-angles to the shore. They had to keep their balance, too, as each rolling wave would smack and lift the stern of the boat and shove it forward. Working the shift levers and throttles, Harry slowly brought the bow up to the ledge, Perry squatting and hanging off the bow rail, scared but ready to jump. This was a lot to ask and for a moment Harry felt the pain of love for his boy.

"Jump!"

Little Perry hesitated for a second and Harry had to back away and try again. This time Perry was ready and as soon as his feet left the bow, Harry shoved the engines in reverse and the next wave broke over the stern and washed through the scuppers. Now, hands off the controls, he began to heave the equipment toward the shore, with Perry scrambling for each piece and trying to set it up on a place where there was no tar.

"Stay right there!" Harry tossed the last item and backed the boat out. Watching for the next crest, he turned the bow windward atop a wave and plowed past the shoals, setting the anchor with the props still churning. There was little silence when he cut the engines, and the sea was a roaring chorus of nature. Pulling off his pants and jacket and tying his boots around his neck, Harry scanned the shoreline for signs of hippies. He had the sinking feeling that none of them were there.

Should I bring in the M-1?

Fuck it! The 45 is enough...

With a splash, Harry was naked in the water, wading in. He moved slowly, trying to find sandy spots around the jagged coral, having decided to keep his boots dry this time and to take a chance with his bare feet. One large wave almost knocked him down as he struggled forward, hands over his head, holding the bundle of his clothes and his pistol. Little Perry was sitting dejectedly amongst the equipment, trying to get the knot untied on his life preserver. Harry hauled himself up on the ledge beside him, up into the chilling wind. Dripping into his knapsack, he dug for a towel.

"The water's warmer than the air, that's for sure."

"I'm hot. I can't get this thing off."

"Help you in a minute."

"Daddy. Are we going to pitch the tent in? Or on the beach?"

"Don't know yet. It's winter.... First let's look around."

"Daddy, you said we should always pitch the tent first in case it rains. You said..."

"I don't think it'll rain for awhile. It's going to be cold tonight, though. Cold front moving in. We'll pitch the tent in."

Perry smiled for the first time. "Good. Daddy?"

"First I have to see if my friends are here."

"Daddy? I..."

 "Have you heard or seen anything?"

"There's nobody here."

"The ocean is making a lot of noise."

""Daddy..."

"Shit! There's so much tar here I can't even sit down to lace up my boots!"

"I can't get my preserver off."

Harry bent over and helped Perry. Then he hunted for a clean place to sit. He flipped over a piece of drift-lumber and found a wide enough place free of the black goo.

"Daddy, where does that shit come from?"

Harry smiled. The only time that Perry would use four-letter words freely was when the two of them were alone together. "Oil tankers and big boats, I think. And the navy."

"Tar? What do they use it for?"

"No — see — this tar used to be oil. The ships are full of oil and when they leak or when they clean out their tanks by pumping sea-water through them, then oil runs out into the ocean and it evaporates and leaves this black, sticky stuff. It floats in to shore and gets all over every fucking thing, fuck them, fuckers should be shot. Motherfuckers!" Harry had gotten tar on his pants despite his precautions, and had just discovered it.

"Can't they do something to stop them?"

"Who is they?"

"The police?"

"No police out here, Perry. Maybe the Coast Guard, or the navy but the navy does it, too. They claim they stopped. It's a bummer!" Harry was rubbing the tar off his pants with dead sea grass. He noted the fact that he had just used a word he must have picked up from the hippies.

Bummer....

Perry was walking around in circles, picking his path by stepping from one high hunk of coral to another. "Pretty soon the rocks will be **covered!**"he said.

"Yeah, maybe...." Harry noticed the boy was no longer wheezing, but thought it best not to mention it.

"Did this used to be all pure rock? No tar?"

"I remember when there was hardly any tar here."

"Then by the time I'm big it will be covered! Completely covered!"

"Don't worry about it. Come on. Pick up something you can carry."

"Sure, sure — you'll be **dead** then! Why should **you** care?"

Harry ruffled little Perry's hair. "You're a smart little fucker, you know that? A smart little fucker! Come on. You take the canteens. I'll take this knapsack and we'll come back for the tent and stuff." Harry was trying to maintain a cheerful tone, but the lack of signs of the hippies was getting him down a little. He headed toward his new trail, intending to stash their equipment out of sight before looking for Gilli's camp. Little Perry trudged behind with the canteens. In ten minutes, they had all of their gear, covered with a sheet of plastic, hidden under dead leaves and brush at the head of Harry's new trail. The only thing Harry took out was his .45 caliber automatic and the pistol belt, which he snapped around his waist. Little Perry watched him, shivering.

"It'll warm up as soon as we start in," Harry told him. "Plus the sun is coming up."

"I have to go potty."

"Right here. Anywhere. You know that. I'll wait."

Perry pulled out his little pecker and dribbled against a little bush, turning his head from side to side to make sure that nobody was coming. Harry was looking around also, waiting and hoping.

"Daddy! Look!" Perry was behind the bush he had just pissed on, pointing to a perfectly rectangular hole in the ground, about four feet long and six feet deep. "Daddy, a grave!"

Harry picked up the machete which Perry was supposed to be carrying, and crept up to the pit chiseled into the coral. "Oh, that. That's not a grave, Perry. That's a hole they used to hide booze in. Rum bottles. Whiskey. Stuff like that."

"What for? Wow! Is there treasure in there?"

"No, but I wish! That one's already been emptied out. There used to be a law against drinking stuff with alcohol in it, and..."

"Like beer?"

"Yeah, like beer. The people who didn't drink alcohol didn't like what the drinkers were doing, getting drunk, shooting people, smashing their cars into stuff, puking all over everything...." Harry smiled at his own words.

"Well, if it's so bad why did they stop the law?"

"I don't know. There were more people drinking than those that didn't. Or they said that most of them knew how much booze they could handle, anyway..."

"Daddy, but..."

"Anyway, when there was a law against it, this was the only country that had the law, so they used to sneak liquor in from the other countries, and this island was a good place to hide the cases of liquor until smaller boats could bring it in."

"Oh."

"Land of the free. Yeah. Right. Now it's drugs we're not supposed to do. Let's go, boy."

Harry could hear himself making speeches.

Does pot do that?

Make you aware of stuff like this?

"Ready!" Perry took the machete and carried it proudly, following his dad who was ducking under low branches and pushing his way through the thorn bushes by spreading them apart with his hands. Perry took a swipe at one of the thorny branches.

"No, not yet, Perry. I don't want anybody to know this is a trail. We'll start cleaning it up a little farther down." Harry stopped to listen. "Be quiet a minute."

There was only the click-clacking of land crabs.

"We're going to turn off here in a minute, Perry, to see if my friends are here."

"Why didn't you call them up to find out?"

"Ahhh — you know Doctor Gilli — well, this is his time off, I mean, he only works at the clinic one week a month. So he should be here. No phones here, either!"

Perry stuck the machete in the ground and pulled off his extra shirt. "It's hot!"

Harry picked up the machete and headed off the trail toward the hippie camp. His heart clutched with the fear that the camp would be deserted. He had waited so long! When they got to the big tree with the platform up in it, Harry stopped. "Anybody here?"

Little Perry looked up, too. "Wow! Is that a tree house? Can we climb up?"

Harry looked at the rope dangling down. Someone had put knots in the rope to make the climb easier. "Later on we'll try it — you think you can make it? Come on. The camp's right over there."

"I told Ruby about the island," Perry said, out of the blue.

"Yeah?" Harry looked at his boy, remembering him sleeping in the colored babysitter's arms.

"Everybody I tell at school laughs at me and says I'm lying. They say their fathers take them fishing and there's only one island out here with a park on it and you can buy cokes and shit there, and hamburgers there, and..."

"Elliott Key?"

"Elliott Key, and..."

"There's one little spot on Elliott Key where all the Sunday families go. It's right across the bay from Homestead. Easy to get to. There's a pier and stuff. I remember when it was wild, like here, before the government fucked it up.

"Well, they all say I'm lying about this place."

"Don't tell them. I never tell anybody about it."

"Where is Elliott Key from here?"

Harry pointed north. "That way. Come on, let's go." Harry followed the path from the tree-house to the camp. Little Perry followed, chattering non-stop, his breathing apparently much improved.

"Ruby says she believes me, though, and that I am very lucky."

Harry smiled. "Why lucky?"

"Because you take me along."

"Yeah. Once."

"Twice. This is the third time!"

They entered the clearing. The camp did not look deserted, but there was no one in evidence. "Lucky. Yeah.... You were lucky to have Ruby, too. She's nice!"

"I like it when she holds me in her lap. Wow! Look at this place!" Little Perry stood in the middle of the camp, hands on his hips, looking around. "Is this where we're going to pitch the tent?"

"Ahhh, don't know yet." Harry hollered: **"Anybody here?"** No answer. He walked over to the oil drum and the fire hole. There was no evidence of a recent fire. "Looks like nobody's here."

"Look at all the stuff they left lying around, Daddy!"

"Yeah, well.... They're not too attached to possessions. I don't think. Anyway, that's the way they seem to live. Hippies."

"Do they have kids?"

"I didn't see any. But they'll take good care of you, though, you'll see!" Harry walked over to the canopy and peered in. No one. Then Harry remembered the boats. "They might be where they keep their boats!"

"Where's that?"

"There's only one place on this island where they could keep a boat hidden, and that's the creek that runs into the inlet between here and Swan Key. The next island. Let's go down the trail and look."

"Our secret trail, right."

"Heh! Used-to-be secret trail. I think they found it a long time ago. The hippies, I mean. Not the government." Harry moved to the perimeter of the camp and pissed near a cactus. "Let's go!"

It was easy going, once they picked up the trail. Not much had grown in since Harry had improved it the last time. He was surprised, though, to find the trail free of spider webs. "No webs. They're definitely using this trail. Or somebody is." Harry suddenly stopped. A long, fresh, curled turd lay directly in the center of the path. Little Perry smacked into him from behind.

"Wow!" Perry squatted down and looked at the thing while Harry picked it apart with the tip of the machete. "Panther shit, Daddy!"

"No, no.... There's no hair sticking out of it. See? Bobcats and Florida panthers eat stuff with hair on it, you know, and it comes out with the shit. This looks human. Wait! Look!" Harry had a piece of the stool separated from the rest and was spreading it out on a piece of coco-plum leaf. "Pull the canteen out from the back of my belt."

Perry struggled with the snaps, and handed the canteen over. Harry carefully poured a little water over the glittering lump he had found. To conserve the water, he picked the thing up with his fingers and rolled it around as the water dribbled over it

"Yeeeech!" Little Perry said. "You let that stinky stuff on your fingers? Phooey!"

The stone came clean, and glittered as Harry rinsed the crap off of it. "It's a diamond! A big one!"

"Really?" Perry hunkered down next to his dad, eyes opened wide. Harry continued to roll the thing around in his fingers. "It's a partially cut diamond. See the flat sides on it?" Harry stood and held the stone up into a shaft of light filtering down through the trees. "I think it's a diamond. It could be a rhinestone. If it's a diamond, it could be worth some money. It's a large one!" Harry looked back down the narrow, dark trail in the direction they had come. "I wonder how it got in there." He shook his head. "What could we put it in, Perry?"

"My pocket!"

"Naw, uhhh...." Harry looked at the little boy he had ignored for so any years. "Okay. In your pocket. But we should wrap it in something so it doesn't get lost. Do your pockets have holes?"

"Yeah, but Mommy fixed them. Wrap it in a leaf!"

Harry was looking around for something. "Leaf's too brittle."

"A gum wrapper!" Perry beamed. "There's an old one in my jacket pocket." He unraveled the jacket he was carrying and fished in the pockets. "Here! I didn't have a place to throw it the other day. The other kids throw their wrappers on the ground. They..."

Harry gave his boy a kiss on the head. "You're going to be a real man someday. For sure!" He wrapped the stone up and handed it back to Perry to put in his pocket. "Come on! Let's go look for those hippie boats!"

The trail became narrower, then widened again. "It changes because I made it on different days," Harry explained. "Some days I had more energy than others, I guess, and I cleared it better."

Little Perry began to whistle as he walked. Harry stopped him, and bent over to whisper. "The shelter is just ahead, Perry. We should be very quiet from here on. If anybody did find this trail, they could be in the shelter, and we want to surprise them if they are there."

"Aren't they your friends?"

"How do I know it's my friends who found the trail? It could be Cuban smugglers, or something like that. Try not to make any noise. Better yet, you sit down here and wait for me while I sneak up ahead."

"Can I keep the machete?"

"Sure. You keep the machete. Stay right here and wait for me. If you really need me, holler." Harry patted his son on the head and moved off, happy that the boy would heed his dramatization and keep still.

In a few minutes, Harry was close to the only hideout he had near the creek.

That turd was laid on the only clean, flat rock in the trail.

No animal would do that.

No redneck would do that. Well....

No Cuban.

Harry paused at the fork in the trail. The leg heading for the creek was obvious, but the path to the shelter was well concealed.

Down on all fours now, he crawled through the hole he had cut through a thorn-bush thicket the year before. Coming out on the other side, the igloo-like hut Harry had built from hunks of coral rock loomed up from the ground like a wart on the landscape.

"Daddy!"

Harry froze, heart pounding. He began backing up through the thicket, and as soon as he could he turned around and clawed his way back out. Straightening up on the other side, he hesitated, listening. Then he sprinted down the trail, back toward his boy.

"Daddy! Daddy!"

Perry was standing in the middle of the place where Harry had left him. The machete was lying at his feet.

"Daddy..."

"You all right?" Harry picked up little Perry and hugged him. Perry struggled to get down.

"Daddy, a lady, um, oh, I don't know! A..."

Harry put the boy down and crouched beside him, holding his waist. "Okay. Now take it easy. What happened."

"A lady came. She ran up to me. A naked lady! She was a hippie! She was running fast! She scared me! She came running down here and I was going to jump out of the way but I couldn't in time and she almost crashed right into me and she stops and picks me up, Daddy, and she's real strong! She picked me up and kissed me right here. Perry pointed to his forehead. " Yeech! Then she says are you Harry's son? And before I could say anything she squashes my head..." Perry paused and looked his father in the eye. "You won't get mad?"

"No, go ahead."

"She squashes my head, my face, my face right in her titties. And hugs me! Phooey! And she smelled funny!"

"Jeez, Perry! What did she look like? Tall? Big?"

"No. No."

"You said she was strong."

"Well, she was much smaller than Mommy. But Mommy can hardly pick me up anymore. But this lady, she just whooshed me right up!"

110

"Well, what did she look like?"

"Well...." Perry giggled. "She was naked, and, um..."

"What color hair?" Harry wanted Perry to describe Faylie.

"Blond. Blondish red! And she had this ring in her nose! And the air was snorting out of her nose. Like a horse or something!"

"Shhhh. Maybe she's still around," Harry whispered.

"Oh, Daddy, as soon as she put me down she started running again. She can run fast! I could hear her running way down before you came! She was barefoot, too!"

"Toward the camp? Toward the ocean?" Harry pointed. "That way?"

"Yes! Yeech! She was sweaty, too! And I got her sweat on my mouth! She pushed my face right into her titties." Perry looked at Harry, rubbing his mouth disgustedly.

Harry kissed him on the cheek. "Perry, listen. What is all this yeeech business, huh? Didn't you always want to know what a big girl's chest would feel like?"

Perry looked at his father quizzically, and frowned.

"Well, when I was your age I used to wonder how soft they would be, or how firm."

"A sweaty one?"

"Well...."

"Yeeech! This is the second time this week! When you and Mommy were at the movies, Ruby, Ruby mushed my face in her titties and she had a bra on. It poked in my eye!"

"She just wanted to hug you. You're so huggable!"

"Since when, Daddy? You never used to hug me, even when..."

But Harry now had a new picture to erase from his mind.

"I do now, though." Harry straightened up, and listened for the tell-tale signs of an asthma attack which usually arrived when Perry got excited. "Come on! Let's go look for the hippie boats!"

Ruby? Wearing a bra?

He had seen points when he saw her the first time across the fence.

Oh, god, so fine and pokey.

No bra then!

Perry raised his little voice. "You go first! If she comes running back you can smack into her!" He giggled.

"You don't know the creek place. Let me take the machete."

"You have a gun. Will the hippies be sweaty? Will they be naked?"

Harry stopped. "Shit, I forgot to check the shelter!"

"Can I come along this time?"

"For sure!"

Perry followed his father back to the fork, stooping where Harry had to crawl. "The flashlights are back with the tent stuff, Daddy."

"Our eyes can adjust." Harry crept into the narrow opening of the coral shelter and waited for his eyes to get used to the darkness. Perry crawled in behind him.

"My favorite place!"

"You should've been here when I had to back-pack the cement in." Harry bushed his hands along the dirt floor, feeling for the spot where the food was buried. His supply of canned goods was intact. The sealed water bottles along the sides and the waterproof box he kept the metal detector in were also okay.

"Let's go."

"Daddy, I'm tired. Can we stay here?"

"After we find my friends you can take a nap."

Perry grumbled. In fact, he grumbled and complained all the way down the trail to the creek, which was another mile from the shelter. The bright, clean excitement of the open creek, though, perked up both of them. It was a welcome change from the filtered darkness of the trails. The sky overhead was clear and bright blue. The water was clear and smooth.

"Daddy! Look! Fish!"

"No boats." Harry looked down through the water and mangrove roots to the brown, silty bottom. "Snapper. They're good to eat."

"What's that?" Perry balanced himself, moving out slowly along a mangrove root which grew out over the water like an arm. "I see a boat, Daddy!"

"Shhhh. I see it! Let's listen!"

Harry held his breath. He wanted so much for them to be here.

"Daddy..."

"Quiet!"

Down at the bend of the creek, the tip of what seemed to be a canoe was just barely visible. There was a snatch of a man's voice, then laughter. A man and a woman.

"Daddy, you hear that?"

"Could be just some people fishing..."

"Can we go there?"

"There's no trail from here to there... It would take us all day."

"You could swim, Daddy," Perry said with a gleam in his eye.

Harry decided to take a chance. He cupped his hands around his mouth and shouted. "Gilli!"

There was a pause. A faint, male voice called back: "...at the camp..."

Harry waited a moment, then turned and unzipped his fly.

"Again, Daddy?"

"Beer is coming through."

"Here they come!"

Harry shook off the last drops and climbed out on the mangrove roots to where Perry was watching. A canoe with one person in it was heading out from the bend in the creek. It turned and moved toward them. Harry squinted to see who it was.

"It's Mazie!"

"Mazie?"

"Yeah."

Mazie paddled slowly down the middle of the creek, stopping to shade her eyes, trying to spot them.

"Over here, Mazie!"

At the sound of her name, Mazie put a little effort into it, and in a minute she was across from them. She stared long and hard at Harry, paddle in hand just in case. Her hair was in pigtails, and she was wearing a green army shirt with the sleeves ripped off at the shoulders.

"Harry?"

"Yeah! Harry! Just me and my boy!"

Mazie dipped the paddle into the water and the canoe glided toward them, nosing up in between the mangrove roots. The canoe was made of varnished wood inside and canvas on the outside, painted green. It was a type Harry had not seen for many years. And Mazie was kneeling, not sitting. Harry nodded and smiled. Mazie looked them over, then crawled forward and hopped out. She was wearing faded denim bell-bottoms and leather moccasins. "I have to piss," she said. "Get in and I'll paddle you over." She brushed past the two of them and in a flash she had her pants down over her ass, squatting not ten feet away. Little Perry gave his dad a big, wide-eyed look of surprise and headed for the canoe. His little mouth was shaped in a big, round "O".

Harry followed him. "You plunk down in the middle and stay low. Canoes tip easy." Harry crawled past the boy and took Mazie's place, kneeling on the pad. He picked up the paddle.

Damn hippies! She had all morning to piss!

Big deal! We piss in the woods all the time!

I'm not impressed. I'm just as liberated as she is!

"Daddy, you know how to work a canoe?"

"I used to. Was pretty good, too!"

Mazie dropped into the front, facing them. She stretched out her legs and leaned back against the forward thwart. She was smiling, now. "Ready!" she said.

The canoe slid easily off the mangrove roots and into the creek. The current ran slowly toward the direction Mazie had come from. "Tide's still running," Harry said. He was happy to find that he could still paddle a good J-stroke and keep a canoe moving swiftly and in the right direction. Nearing the bend, Harry could see their boats.

"Around the catboat and in between," Mazie directed. Dale, shirtless and his blond hair tied in a ponytail, was bending over the inboard engine of a 24-foot open motorboat. His green army-pants looked like the bottom half of the faded-green shirt Mazie was wearing. He gave Harry a perfunctory little wave of recognition and continued working.

"My old man loves that boat more than me," Mazie said.

"I want to look at it."

"You're probably just like him." Mazie hitched up her pants an inch and gave little Perry a hand out of the canoe.

"Daddy."

"Wait a minute. I want to see Dale's boat." Harry tried to act cool, like he was part of the family, as he stood next to the bow, which was half out of the water. "Is that a Volvo diesel?".

Dale did not answer. Harry tried again. "An MD-2?"

Dale grunted and stood up. Sweat ran down his chest. "Froze my ass off last night and now it's hot. Tempers the body, though. You got a ten-eleven millimeter open-end wrench? A thin one?"

Harry nodded. "In the boat..."

Dale jumped over the side immediately and slogged up onto the coral through the muck. "Where's your boat?"

"East side. Anchored near your camp. The tool box is hard to find, it's..."

"I'll find it." Dale was already moving off.

"Wait!" Harry did not like the idea of the hippies going all over his boat and using his tools. Freaks were fucked up. They lost things. They broke things. They might not return things. "I'll go with you."

"Daddy, what about me?" Perry looked up at them. He was still carrying the machete.

"Come on along," Harry said.

"What about me?" Mazie said. "And what are we going to eat today, Dale, old man. Male. Hunter. Provider."

Dale stopped. He was grinning and shrugging his shoulders. "Eat?"

"Eat. Food. My tits are shriveling up."

Dale was still grinning. "Surrendra said she'd make some island sandwiches for everybody this noon. And we are supposed to catch the fish for the fry tonight." Dale started walking. The rest of them followed. Harry marveled at the width and openness of their trail.

I didn't know this trail was here.

"Island sandwiches!" Mazie said. "They suck! And they stink! We eat meat and they don't, right? So why don't you bring home some meat!" Mazie turned to Harry and smiled. "Puke sandwiches," she said. "They look and they taste like puke, and Gilli grins while he eats them!"

"The sandwiches sound familiar," Harry said.

Dale laughed. "He grins while he eats Surrendra, too!"

Harry took little Perry's hand. Perry squeezed back and looked up, trying to smile.

"I'll take good care of you, don't worry," Harry said.

Dale and Mazie came closer together and reached for each other's hand as they stumbled along. Harry took deep, audible breaths of the fresh, fragrant, clean air. "It's been a long time since I've been here," he said. "My boat needed an expensive part."

"Can you catch fish?" Mazie asked, looking back at Harry.

"Yeah, but — I have some sandwiches in the cooler. Enough for the four of us if you eat meat, ham and cheese sandwiches. There's beer, some apples, some chocolate chip cookies. I didn't bring any fishing tackle this trip, I..."

"Daddy! The cookies were for us! There aren't enough! There aren't enough sandwiches, either! If we eat them all today, what will we eat tomorrow!"

Perry's selfishness embarrassed Harry with the hippies right there. "We share what we have, boy."

Now Harry felt guilty for saying something he did not really believe in.

Hippies are always making you feel guilty!

Everything they have is fucked up so they want the rest of us to share!

Little Perry pulled his hand out of his father's grip with a disgusted look on his face, and walked along by himself.

"Real chocolate chip cookies!" Mazie said. "Far out! Homemade? With the big chips?"

"Yeah."

"Far out!"

Dale quickened his pace, pulling Mazie along. "I could dig a ham-and-cheese and a beer," he said.

In ten minutes, they were at the edge of the camp. The trail had been wide and clear, but still Harry was surprised at how easily they had made the passage from the creek. Only the last fifty feet or so of their trail were rough and uncut, to conceal the path from the camp — just as Harry would have done himself. As the four of them came ducking into the clearing through the thicket, Gilli was standing there in the middle, in the sun, naked except for the white loincloth. He was grinning his toothy, friendly grin, as usual. "I saw your boat. Happy to see you finally came back." He looked at Perry and walked up to him. "How's your asthma?"

"It's going away," Perry said proudly. Perry liked Gilli, but he could not look at the loincloth. "Daddy wanted to come sooner but the boat was, uh..."

"Fucked up," Harry said.

"Fucked up," Perry confirmed.

Harry suddenly became uncomfortable. The gun again.

"Ohhh — fucked up!" Gilli laughed, and gave Perry a pat on the back. "You've grown a little since I saw you last. When you grow a little more — just a little — your asthma will go away even more!"

Harry was very conscious of the .45 automatic hanging from his belt. It had not bothered him with Dale and Mazie. He shifted his weight from one foot to the other, shrugging his shoulders and grinning back at Gilli. "I feel good here," Harry said. It was an honest statement. "I've been working long hours — overtime — and I had the boat to repair." Harry looked away from Gilli. He wondered where the others were and hoped to see Neeta. Even Dale and Mazie had disappeared, and Harry wondered if they were rummaging around in his boat for tools. "I could stay here forever. It's so beautiful and peaceful. No time schedule. No things that have to be done right this minute..."

"Stay! It's easy!" Gilli put his arm on Harry's shoulder. "What would you like to do now — at this moment — more than anything else?" Gilli, still grinning, withdrew his arm and looked Harry straight in the eye.

"Neeta asked me that last time."

"Well?"

Harry looked around him, frantic for something to tell Gilli.

"We believe in doing what we want now. I mean, in the present," Gilli said.

Harry's thoughts were no help.

Fuck Neeta! Fuck Faylie!

"I don't know...." he said.

Just hugging them — ohhhh....

"What is happening now is the only thing that's happening. If you want to do something, do it." Gilli paused. Toothy grin. "Do it now!"

Harry's mind scrambled for an answer. "I want to get stoned and just lie out in the sun in the clearing here. And do nothing. Right now. But I have my boy here instead and that is fine with me!"

Gilli's face fell for a moment.

"When are we going to put up the tent, Daddy?"

"As soon as we decide where to put it, son." Harry rubbed Perry's head.

"Right here?" Gilli said, pointing to a clear space on the other side of their camp.

Harry was delighted. "That's good — good! Come on, Perry! Let's get our stuff!"

"When do we get a taste of those chocolate chip cookies?" Mazie and Dale were back. Dale was naked, and dripping. He had Harry's open-end wrench in his hand. "When do we get a taste of that ham and cheese?" Dale had the smallest penis Harry had ever seen. He looked at Mazie and wondered.

"Help me carry our gear in and we'll eat," Harry said, tough like. He unbuckled his belt and flopped the whole mess, with the canteen and gun, onto their wooden platform. Little Perry sat down next to it, chin in his hands, pissed off. Mazie went over to him and kissed him on the cheek.

"You stay here," she said, "and we'll be right back."

"I have to help carry."

"I'll carry your share."

Harry looked at Mazie and felt his heart begin to tug for her

When they returned with everything, Surrendra was there, with Clyde and Neeta. The three of them were naked, not counting necklaces and ornaments. Clyde, a stranger to Harry, had the biggest cock Harry had ever seen, well, bigger than his own anyway.

Neeta smiled. "Awww, Harry, you came back!" She grabbed Clyde by the neck and turned him toward Harry. "Harry came back!"

Clyde gave Harry a perfunctory nod. Surrendra also did not smile. She had just put down a large bowl and was spreading some goo from the bowl onto slices of what looked like bread. Harry glanced again at Clyde's giant, limp cock.

Little Perry was no longer at the platform but was sitting in the clear space on the other side of the camp where Gilli said they could pitch their tent. He had taken the canteen and pistol belt with him. Dale, Mazie, and Gilli were setting down Harry's equipment wherever it was convenient, and Perry immediately complained. Harry did not hear him at first.

"I said, Daddy, we should put everything over here, where the tent is going to be."

"In a minute, Perry."

"So all our stuff is together in one place!"

"Sounds like a chip off the same block, Harry!" Neeta said.

Harry looked at her, ears burning red, as Clyde embraced Neeta from behind. Harry turned away and studied his equipment lying on the ground, with the picture boring through his thoughts of Clyde's hanging meat dangling in the warm, fallow crack of Neeta's ass.

"Well, Daddy?"

"Yeah, we'll move it." Harry picked up the heaviest item, the tent roll, and carried it on his shoulder over to their spot in the clearing. Then he moved the cooler, and their clothes. The hippies were all standing together around Surrendra's pile of "island sandwiches". Harry dug down into the cooler through the peanut-butter sandwiches until he hit the ham and cheese.

"You and I'll eat in a minute, Perry."

"The chocolate chip cookies were for us, Daddy!" Perry watched his father grab a handful of the cookies that he and his sister, Janey, with Annie's help, had baked for the trip. He turned his back on Harry in disgust and sat down again, cupping his hands over his ears.

Harry walked over to the group. He taped Dale on the shoulder. "Ham and cheese!" He pulled a beer out of his back pocket. "A beer."

Dale nodded. "Aw right!"

Harry walked over to Mazie, who was just about to pick up one of the hippie sandwiches. "Open your mouth," he said. Mazie turned and smiled and opened her mouth, and Harry popped a cookie into it. Then he handed her the whole bunch, and turned back. He glanced at Neeta and Clyde. It was obvious that the two were intimate with each other. Clyde, with his long, dirty-yellow hair in rows of braids like colored people do, with his big cock and muscular legs.

Surrendra was squatting next to little Perry, now, offering him one of her vegetable creations, her hairy muff hovering inches above the ground. Harry squatted beside her, smiling, and watched his son take a tentative bite.

"Phooey!" Perry jumped up and ran to the edge or the clearing and spit. Surrendra shrugged, looked at Harry, and took a bite herself. Her eyes were dark brown and gold, and Harry looked into them to avoid her dark, jungle-gold tits. She chewed slowly and stared at him without blinking.

She's trying to put me down!

She's daring me to look at her tits. Look at her pussy!

"You want a beer?" Harry said, smiling.

Surrendra slowly held the sandwich out toward Harry in both hands, her dark eyes riveted to his, her flowing, kinky-black hair shifting down over her shoulders Indian-princess-of-the-jungle style. Harry reached for the bread and took a bite. Having tasted her food once before, he was steeled for the worst, and chewed the chunky, mucky-tasting stuff without expression.

I can handle any puke this chick can dish out.

Perry was back. "Daddy! You're eating that?"

"Yup."

"Everybody loves my island sandwiches," Surrendra said, taking the thing away from Harry, taking a bite, and handing it back.

"Daddy. Can I take a peanut-butter out of the cooler?"

"Yeah, sure. May I."

"May I have cookies for dessert?"

"Sure, Perry. Just make sure you close the lid each time."

"I go out in the morning," Surrendra said, "and I gather all the wild, good things here on the island and bring them back to make the spread on this bread. I bake the bread in my little stone oven. I can make twenty-three different kinds of bread, all with natural ingredients, all with..."

"Daddy! Do you like them? The sandwiches she makes? That's what I want to know!"

Harry said: "When everything was natural there weren't any antibiotics. People were dying like flies. Ever wander through an old graveyard? Look at the dates on the tombstones?"

"Typical dodge."

"I don't like the taste, Perry." Harry said, turning away and shifting the weight of his body, not used to squatting the way Surrendra was. She got up, however, and walked away, taking the half-eaten sandwich with her.

"Daddy! Can't we camp somewhere else? Away from them?"

Harry unraveled his body and plunked down next to his boy. "Perry. We'll camp here, where it's safe, and I promise you we'll have fun. You'll have fun."

"They're dirty and they're naked!"

"Perry, they're not dirty, they're, well — natural."

"Did you see her bottom? Did you see it? She doesn't even wipe, Daddy!"

Harry glanced around, hoping nobody heard. "Jeez, kid! Not so loud!"

Perry turned away, ending the conversation again. Harry reached into the cooler for another beer. There were only a few left, and he decided to save them.

"Ants!" Perry said disgustedly, slapping his legs. Harry sighed and untied the bedding roll. Spraying the ground with repellant, he laid out his plaid, woolen blanket and sat in the middle of it. Perry climbed onto it with him, a fist full of chocolate-chip cookies crumbling in his hand. Gilli, who had been eating with Surrendra, came over and sat with them, crossing his legs yoga style with his nuts hanging out.

Harry took a swig out of his canteen. He was about to reach into the cooler when Gilli handed him the joint.

"Before you eat," Gilli said. "It's what you wanted to do most, right?"

Harry looked Gilli in the eye and shrugged his shoulders and smiled. He lit the hand-rolled cigarette and hauled in a deep, burning lungful and held his breath. He handed the joint back to Gilli, but Gilli shook his head. "You do it."

Harry sucked in another hit.

The high I got the last time....

What was that one like? I don't remember the feeling.

Will I get high this time?

Same old story.

Harry took another hit, and another.

Dale came over to the blanket, beer can in hand. "Aw right!" he said, bending over and picking up the roach from Harry. He took two long hits before handing it back. The roach was almost gone. Harry held it carefully to keep from burning his fingers.

I'm burning my fingers!

He pursed his lips and sucked in air with it.

They'll put me down if I throw the butt away....

butt — jeez — the roach.

Harry tried to hold it without getting burned, and felt the pain in his index finger. Getting in one more hit, he was relieved to see Neeta coming over. He handed the smoldering remnant to her, copping a look at her little turned-up tits. Neeta finished off the roach with no trouble at all.

"Glad you came back, Harry," Neeta said, after holding her breath.

"Neeta. You're beautiful!"

"Awww, Harry — you're beautiful yourself!"

She turned away and plunked back down next to Clyde on the edge of the platform. Clyde was busy tying his cock and balls up into a red slingshot G-string.

"A hippie princess," Gilli sighed, watching Neeta.

"Milky's gone," Harry said, ears turning red again.

"She's on a mission to the mainland," Gilli grinned. We're out of medicine, which I was supposed to bring along and forgot, and salt, and fresh water — and dope..."

Dope!

"I could've brought what you needed. What do you mean, dope?"

"Grass. Mescaline. Acid..."

Acid.... LSD....

Do they do LSD?

"How do you..." Harry felt the top of his head gently floating off. "How, uhhh... Do you do LSD? Do you..." Harry's face broke into an uncontrollable smile. "Oh shit! Am I getting stoned! Oh shit! My boy. This trip was for me and Perry. I promised him. Him and me. Oh shit."

"Don't talk. Just dig it for awhile," Gilli admonished.

Harry leaned back and propped himself on his elbows. Little Perry tapped on his arm. "Daddy?"

Harry was watching Neeta pull on a pair of jeans. He wondered if his telling her she was beautiful made her do it. She glanced his way as she buttoned up and Harry quickly averted his eyes. Feeling dumb about looking away, he looked back at her but she was talking to Clyde.

"Dad!"

"Yeah!"

"Can I go with Mazie and Dale? In their boat?"

"May I" Harry looked at Gilli. Gilli nodded.

"Okay. Be a good boy. Don't fall in the water!"

"Oh good! They're going to fish. Dale said I could hold one of the poles."

"Okay. I'll come and see you down there later."

Perry ran over to Dale and Mazie and told them it was OK. Dale was wearing clothes again. Harry was relieved. He was stoned. It was hard to tell what was happening. He needed a rest.

"Bye, Daddy!" Little Perry waved. Harry saw it but it looked like Perry was on a movie screen and the little boy in the picture was waving at him. Harry waved back. He closed his eyes for a few minutes, then twitched suddenly and sat up. Gilli was still sitting there. He looked serene.

"Gilli! I saw things!"

"What things?"

"I saw a hat that my mother used to wear — in perfect detail! In color! I saw my Uncle's vicuña coat! It was a heavy coat — beige — I can even feel the texture of it in my hand! Right now! That was years and years ago! I was twelve maybe! Eleven..." Harry could hear himself raving on and on.

Gilli grinned. "We should call you Zonker because you get off so good. It was a long time before I could see objects. Colors, yes, but objects? Not at first."

Harry closed his eyes again, but he opened them immediately, wanting to tell Gilli more. He felt proud and happy, and he felt so good all over. "Gilli — how long were my eyes closed the first time?"

"A minute. Maybe two..."

"Jeez, it seemed like ten minutes! My uncle's coat.... The thickness of it, the color, the feel of it! How can I remember that? My brain — it's just a bundle of nerves and stuff — a hunk of meat! A hunk of pink meat and I can go in there and pick out pictures from years ago! And facts? And the feel of things?" Harry closed his eyes again for a minute. "Gilli! Where in my brain — in the meat — are the pictures shown? Who is watching them? Can my brain watch itself? That's impossible!"

Gilli waited for Harry to calm down. "We call them movies. We call it our movie screen. Research has not found the point in the brain where humans and animals see and watch them."

Harry clasped his knees and pulled up closer to Gilli on the blanket. He looked into the hippie's eyes. "You are a true bro, Gilli."

"And you are my brother."

Harry suddenly cupped his ears in his hands. "Where — are the movies — showing? Where is the screen? It's impossible!" He continued to look at Gilli, into Gilli's blue eyes. "It's wonderful!"

Gilli nodded, grinning his big-tooth benevolent grin. "It's called the Cartesian Theater."

"And where do we hear? Who listens to the sounds that go in our ears?" Harry thought about it. The wind brushed the leaves of the trees above them. From the shore, Harry heard a snatch of Neeta's voice, calling Clyde. A crab click-clacked somewhere in the ground nearby. Surrendra — dark, sweaty, fully-formed, and naked — floated down beside them on the blanket.

"Doctor Gilliveh," she said.

Harry closed his eyes to the intrusion. Strange, sucking noises came from Surrendra's direction and Harry had to open his eyes again. Surrendra was sitting directly in front of them in the lotus position, her hands touching at the fingertips, her eyes closed and her pussy hanging out. She was doing breathing exercises: taking a deep breath, holding it, then parting her lips slightly and letting the air out slowly with a weird noise. *"heeeeeeeee..."*

"You should ask Faylie about where you hear sounds and where in your head you see the movies," Gilli said, ignoring Surrendra. She's always getting into that when we're all stoned and nobody wants to talk."

"heeeeeeeeeeeeeeeeeeeeeeeeee...suck suck..."

Harry tied to avoid looking at Surrendra. "Gilli! I'm thinking about stuff I never thought about before! This marijuana is really beautiful! Sounds! There is no such thing, is there? Just waves and ripples of air hitting our eardrums and making them vibrate. And the vibrations sending signals — electric signals — to... Wow! To where? And electric signals are not sounds!"

"It's easy to talk when high," Surrendra said. "Hard to listen."

Gilli nodded. Big toothy grin.

"heeeeeeeeeeeeeeeeeeeeee...suck suck"

Harry looked at Surrendra disgustedly but felt his balls tighten up unexpectedly.

Who does this Indian think she is?

Does she have to meditate right in my face?

She's a Jewess. Not Indian.

"Gilli, I.... Uhhh... Now I forgot what I was thinking. Shit." Harry laughed. "Far out!" Harry was immediately aware that he had just used a hippie expression again.

Far out! Far out!

"heeeeeeeeeeeeeeeeeeeeeeeeeeeeeeeee..."

"Faylie! She's really a philosopher, huh? I would..."

"Harry." Surrendra called him by name for the first time. "It is not cool to engage in conversation with people who are high. Easy to talk, hard to listen. Can you remember that please?"

"Big dreamer and hermit," Gilli said. "You would dig Faylie. She's wild. And tough."

"suck suck"

"Did Faylie have to go to religious schools? I had to. Study Latin and the Bible. All that shit. The other kids I knew didn't have to. Their parents let them chew tobacco and stuff like that."

"Most of us here were born Jews. Not Faylie, I don't think. Now listen, Harry, Surrendra was right. Hard to listen, easy to talk when you're high. So quit talking. For now. Just for now."

Jews....

A Jewess....

A Jewess at the well in the Bible.

Harry closed his eyes again, trying to picture Faylie on the shore pulling her nightie off. Instead, he pictured little Perry standing alone on the trail, crying. "Wow! How long've we been sitting here?" He looked at Surrendra, and shot a look at her crotch. Her wrinkly, dark-skinned pussy was opening, all by itself, and her red clit was hanging out. Surrendra opened her eyes and looked straight at Harry, making him jump. Her eyes suddenly softened and Harry realized that her face was really beautiful and young.

She spoke to him, as if describing something she could see from far off: "Faylie is in her swing, suckling her puppies. One puppy is sick, is dying. The sick one lies in a basket at her feet."

Gilli looked at Harry and raised his eyebrows. "Surrendra is clair-voyant," he said.

Harry smiled at the two of them.

Clairvoyant....

Yeah, right.

"Where is her swing?"

Surrendra spoke to him, eyes half closed. "Faylie lives in the Val-ley of the Morning Glories. Elliott Key, Gilli? Her swing hangs from a mahogany tree at the south end of the valley. The morning glories are not blooming now, but..." Surrendra opened her eyes and laughed. It was the first time Harry had seen her look happy. Suddenly, the meat in Harry's pants began to grow as he pictured Surrendra lower-ing her wet snatch onto it. He remembered he was stoned. Leaning back, away from her, Harry tried to relax. He grinned, and let himself be, simply, a stoned person. He tried to remember to shut up.

Surrendra, friendly and alive now, slapped Harry's boots lightly with her brown fingers. "You're stoned!" she said kindly. "Want your boots off?"

"Yeah..." Harry reached to the side and pulled his clothing bag under his head so he could lie back. Surrendra began tugging at the laces of his boots, kneeling at his feet.

"Faylie told me she loves to suckle the puppies because their sharp little teeth make her nipples tough." *Oooooof-plop.* One boot off, one to go. Harry looked over to Gilli who was still sitting like the yo-ga god and grinning. Gilli nodded and tilted his head in Surrendra's direction and nodded again.

"I can't believe this," Harry said in Gilli's direction. He closed his eyes. The other boot slid off. Not knowing what to do next, or what was expected of him, Harry remained silent. Surrendra's firm hands clasped his right foot and began to knead it. Harry felt her change position on the blanket and the sole of his left foot slide up against her muff. Eyes still closed, he stretched his left leg tentatively and pressed the heel of his foot gently against her pussy. She was wet. His heart began to pound. Surrendra quickly picked up both feet, and laying them up on her thigh, began to pull and jerk Harry's toes, alternately beating the soles of his feet with her fists. A ripple of pure nerve-pleasure shot up his spine.

"It's the grass and Surrendra," he heard Gilli say.

Another wave of pleasure rolled up his body and rolled back down again. "Ohhhhh!" Harry groaned involuntarily. Suddenly Surrendra stopped. Harry's feet, tingling, tried to convey the texture of Surrendra's thighs to Harry's brain. Something had happened. He opened his eyes carefully. Gilli and Surrendra were both looking at something over their shoulders, behind them. Harry struggled to sit up. On the far side of the clearing between the trail to the tree house and the trail to the creek, was Faylie, her legs spread in an arrogant pose, her jeweled hands on her hips, her head back, the halo of her red hair in the sunlight, blinding little jewels of light flashing from the be-jeweled choker around her throat, the bracelets on her arms and around her ankles, the rings on her fingers, the bright gold ring in her nose... Harry's mouth hung open. His eyes fixed on Faylie's nipples, earthworm red, extended, evil and enticing things protruding from tiny, firm, pale tits. Harry squinted to see better. Faylie's eyes were riveted on him, across all that space, and when Harry's eyes met hers he recoiled with the green fire of them.

"She's curious about you," Surrendra whispered, bending toward Harry. "She told me to tell you about the puppies' teeth."

Harry could not move.

"She steals all that stuff she wears from wealthy boaters." Surrendra paused. "You can get her if you chase her, but you have to run her down. Hunt her."

Harry made an effort to stand, but remained sitting.

"You'll have to put your boots back on or you'll never do it. You'll cut your feet to ribbons out there. You can do it."

Faylie remained standing on the other side of the clearing, defiant and radiantly beautiful and sinful. Harry swallowed hard. Their eyes remained locked across the distance.

"Keep looking at her and very slowly pull one boot on and then the other and don't look away from her."

"I don't know if I can," Harry whispered, not moving.

Do it! Do it!

The forces inside Harry's head beseeched him.

Hurry! Now! Do it!

Still sitting there, Gilli was bending over and tying up the thongs on his clear-gum sandals.

"Gilli, you bastard," Surrendra snapped.

Harry looked away from Faylie just long enough to see Gilli whip his loincloth out from between his legs. Harry looked back at Faylie. Faylie had turned a little, and was facing the hippie, now. Gilli slowly rose to his feet, and with a yell he leapt naked and wild and white across the clearing. Faylie's ass disappeared into the woods like a fleeing cotton-tailed rabbit.

For a moment, Harry and Surrendra stood together and listened to Gilli crashing through the brush into the distance.

A doctor! Harry thought. *A man! More of a man than me!*

Surrendra was walking away from him.

I could fuck Surrendra now!

No! She knows I really wanted Faylie. She'd put me down.

If I were drunk instead of stoned...

Harry slumped back down to the blanket.

What if little Perry needs me?

Harry pictured his boy.

I'm always ignoring him.

He's just a little boy who didn't ask to be born and I don't love him and hug him and listen to what he's saying. Nobody listens to what he's saying. He must think his ideas aren't worth anything by now....

Jeez! When you're stoned you can really see how it is for other people. For Perry. A little person.

Surrendra came out from under the canopy wearing a long, yellow caftan. It was getting chilly. Harry had forgotten it was still winter. He wondered about the time. How long had he been dreaming? It was afternoon on the island, and beautiful. He watched Surrendra glide toward the trail to the boats.

"I have to lie down. I feel stupid. And weak." Harry called after her. "Will you check on my boy for me? He's with Dale and Mazie. I'm all hung up. I have to — think."

Surrendra turned, smiled, and nodded.

Harry rearranged himself on the blanket as comfortably as possible, pulling all his gear and his pistol belt around him so he could reach everything without moving. It felt good to lie in the sun on the blanket surrounded by the soft clumps of his possessions. The tent roll — well, he would pitch the tent later. The canteens.... He reached for his canteen and took a swig.

God, this is a beautiful life!

Harry watched the ice-cream clouds move slowly across the sky.

Thank-you, God! Thank-you!

He chuckled at his thoughts. He had not believed in God for a long time. Fifteen years? Not since the last argument he had had in a high-school religion class and discovered that God as he was described by the church couldn't possibly exist. Lying on his back here on the island, Harry remembered the weeks of shock he had gone through at that time without the comfort and security of the help of Jesus and the promise of Heaven to carry him through, and the years of rebellion and bitterness which followed while all his redneck neighborhood friends still believed and would get pissed about any contrary suggestions.

The church teaches you to believe in crap then leaves you with nothing!

Three pelicans, gliding in formation, slicked across the sky over the clearing. Harry closed his eyes. Colors flashed and whirled in his head, and began to take shape. The mouth and throat of a toad filled his whole field of vision for a moment, then changed into the toad's eye. The eye became larger and more colorful, the pupil an infinitely deep black, and the flesh around the eye was a mosaic of jade and rubies. Harry opened his eyes. He remembered the big turd he had picked apart on the trail and he reached for the gum wrapper, half expecting it to be empty. But the diamond, or whatever it was, was there. He had not imagined it. It was real. Harry was rolling the gem around between his thumb and index finger, holding it up to the sunlight, when Dale ambled into the clearing with his open-end wrench.

"Your wrench," Dale said, tossing it onto the blanket.

"Where did you get it?"

"From your boat."

"So put it back in the boat."

"What is that?"

"I don't know. It was sticking in a big turd in the middle of my trail this morning." Harry held his arm up to Dale, who was standing over him.

"Oh! Far out!" Dale said, taking the diamond and examining it. "I've been trying to find one of these for a long, long time." Dale handed it back. "That's a real diamond. That burned-out chick that Gilli likes so much — she rips jewelry off of yachts and stuff and swallows the jewels and shits them all over the place. Mazie found a big ruby in one of Faylie's turds last summer and got a hundred and fifty dollars for it at a pawn shop in Miami. That money lasted a long time..."

"Yeah?"

"Don't let Surrendra see it — she throws them away. She says they're bad karma. She's fucked up, too."

"Here," Harry said. "Keep it."

Dale picked the gem out of Harry's hand. "Far out!" He held it up to the light. "Soon's my boat's ready I'm going to cash this mother in!"

Harry pictured Gilli pinning Faylie back against a tree and pumping his meat into her. He remembered how horny he had felt before coming to the island and how relaxed and comfortable he felt now. Dale was walking away. The wrench still lay beside him on the blanket. Soon he would have to get up and check the boat — make sure the toolbox was closed — then pitch the tent — and play with Perry. The thought of Perry brought a pang or apprehension in his chest. Harry rolled over on his side and closed his eyes. He would get up in a few minutes and take care of everything. Just a few minutes...

A gentle breeze blew over Harry as he slept, and the peaceful hippies, one by one, returned to the camp.

The sun was already below the treetops when Harry finished pitching the tent and stowing their gear inside. Leaving Perry, who was helping Dale and Mazie clean fish, he went out to the ocean to check his boat and to swim. The coast was beautiful, calm, and deserted. Neeta and big-dick Clyde came into the water with him for a few minutes and the three of them played catch with a baby coconut. Harry felt empty inside, though, needing Neeta to love him — she was so beautiful in mind and body — and needing Surrendra to love him, enfold him with her dark, exotic flesh, her meat — and needing to conquer Faylie, to drop a load into this female from outer space.

The three came back dripping and laughing to the smell of roasting fish. A measure of wholeness returned to Harry's lost spirit as he toweled himself off naked and unashamed in the presence of the others and in the coolness of late afternoon, so alive.

"Daddy! They don't fillet them!"

"It's okay."

"They're going to eat them with the bones still inside!"

"Well, uh...." Harry pulled on his pants and laced up his boots.

"Daddy! Did you see the fish I caught? Dale says it's a snapper! Will you fillet it for me?"

"Sure, sure. You find a board or something, and get out my filleting knife and the frying pan."

"Oh good! Do you want to eat some of mine?"

"Sure! I'll eat some of yours!"

Neeta came over and handed Harry the pipe. "Awww, Harry — isn't he a beautiful little person!"

Harry took a long hit. "Yeah. Thank you. You are fantastic. Beautiful. And you take good care of me."

"Awww, Harry!"

Harry watched Neeta run over and hand the pipe to Clyde, and then to Gilli, Dale, and Mazie.

Girl with a pipe....

Harry was picturing a painting.

A painting of real life.

He watched Neeta sit down on the platform next to Surrendra

and start talking. One by one, the men would come over to them to get a hit off the pipe. In a short time, they were all stoned once more, Harry with just one hit. For fifteen minutes which seemed like a wonderful hour, no one talked. Harry watched contentedly as Perry carefully approached Mazie's cook-fire with his little frying pan with the two fillets in it. A discussion followed, with a lot of head nodding. Then Mazie took the fillets, dipped them into something, and laid them back into the frying pan.

What does Faylie eat?

If the guys at work could see me now!

Annie would flip!

Everything is so different here.

It's so easy to get used to. It's like I've been here all my life!

The hippies were all standing around, eating fish with their fingers. Perry ran up to Harry. "Ours will be done in a minute, Daddy!"

Mazie came over with the frying pan and set it down beside Harry. There were four, golden fillets in it.

"She cut them in half to make them fit, Daddy! Here's your fork, and here's mine. Ohhh, we forgot to bring the salt — oh — here it is!"

Harry sprinkled salt over the fish and broke off a mouthful with his fork. He aimed the fork load toward Mazie. "Wanna try it?"

Maze shook her head and smiled. "I'll bring the pipe back," she said. She was still wearing the big sleeveless army shirt and the jeans they had seen her with in the canoe. Harry watched her amble back to the group while he tasted the fish.

"Oh WOW!" Harry exclaimed.

Perry looked at his Dad and tried the fish himself. "I caught it all by myself!"

"Man, this is good!" Harry said. "Wish we had potatoes now, and biscuits, and..."

"I used a crab feeler for bait. Yeeeech! Dale put it on the hook for me."

"Christ this is good!" Harry said loudly, through his second mouthful. "This has got to be the very best fucking, far-out fish — I don't even like fish much, I..."

"Daddy. You don't have to say that just because I caught it!"

"Can't you taste it?"

"Well.... It tastes okay."

Mazie came back and plunked down beside Harry on the blanket. "I filled the pipe first. Neeta said you have trouble getting high."

"Not anymore!"

"You should've seen how my pole bent when I hooked him!" Perry said, his eyes big with the excitement of it. "Then, he swam right under a mangrove root and Dale thought we might have to break the line, and just when Dale got his knife out to cut the line, my fish — this fish that you have in your mouth, Daddy — he swam right back out again and got himself caught! By me!"

"Man! It's the best fish I ever tasted!"

Mazie laughed. "It's the grass, Mister Harry."

"Grass?" Perry said.

"It makes food taste good."

Harry looked at her, chewing slowly.

"You should know," Mazie said. "Well, now you know!"

"You mean you weren't exaggerating" Perry looked at his Dad. "It is the best fish you ever tasted?"

Harry nodded, and ruffled little Perry's hair. "You're a smart little fuck," he said.

"He is," Mazie said. "He's a beautiful boy!" She lit the pipe with a farmer match.

Little Perry grinned. "Can I have some of that?"

Harry's heart skipped a beat. *Hippies don't like to say no to their kids — I read that — they hate all rules — they...*

"It might burn your throat," Mazie said.

Harry puffed to get the pipe going, and handed it to Perry. Perry got a whiff of the smoke and gagged.

"Phooey!" I could get asthma from this stuff!"

Harry smiled but turned down another hit, and handed the pipe to Mazie. The pipe was going out and he held match for her while she drew down on it. While she was inhaling, Harry remembered Dale's small penis.

"I like to get super-high right before evening comes," Mazie said after holding her breath.

Perry was talking, too. But little Perry's words piled up in Harry's head like so many pebbles. He had gotten off deep, and now Mazie was talking again.

"I like to walk around the shore in the evening, stoned, watch the birds come out, watch the sun go down on the other side of the island.... That's something to see. As soon as the last of the sun disappears the birds cry, and you can see them flying low and fast over the tops of the waves, just barely missing the water. It's far out."

Harry turned down another hit. He nodded his head toward Perry so Mazie would understand.

"Right before the sun goes down, there's complete silence," Mazie continued. "There's — oh! Far out! What was I saying? Wow!"

They both laughed.

"Fuck it," Harry said.

Mazie laughed. "Fuck it."

Gilli sat down with them and picked up the pipe. Surrendra came next, and Neeta. Neeta introduced a joint she had just rolled and gave it a start around the circle. Clyde came, too — his huge cock bulging under his jeans — and Dale. All of them were dressed now, for the cool evening air and the bugs. Clyde dropped a small chunk of hashish into the pipe, lit it, and handed it to Harry. Harry gave in and drew down hard.

"Carefully, Harry!" Neeta said.

The burning toke went down fairly easily, but by the time Harry had the pipe passed to Mazie, he knew he would have to cough. The coughing fit that came was a horror, and for a moment Harry thought he had permanently damaged his lungs. As quickly as it came, however, the severe burning passed. And he surprised himself at being able to handle a second hit of the hash, at Clyde's insistence, without any more trouble. Little Perry looked over at his dad disgustedly and began to wander off. There was a long silence.

"Harry. What do you do here on the island?"

Harry looked at Surrendra and smiled. It was his new, stoned smile. "I hunt for Black Caesar's treasure," he said quietly. "The colored pirate. And now I get high."

Gilli grinned back and nodded.

"Awww, Harry — that's beautiful," Neeta said.

Long, happy silence.

Surrendra spoke again. "Do you get high at home?"

Harry thought about it. For a second, he forgot the question, he was so zonked out. "I got high a couple times at home, with the grass Neeta gave me when I was here last, uhhh — Neeta, that was beautiful of you — to give me that grass to take home."

"Awww, Harry, thank you. That was from Faylie, you know."

Everyone nodded approval. There was another long silence.

Neeta's eyes brightened. "Did you turn your old lady on, Harry?"

Harry shook his head. "She's afraid of it."

"Were you ever afraid of it?" Clyde said. "Before I tried it the first time, I thought I might go crazy or something."

Harry looked at Clyde and saw him in a new light. There was no more trace of hostility, which Harry thought he had sensed before. "I — was worried about it the first time I tried it, but I didn't get high, so the times I tried it after that — uh — forgot what I was going to say. Man! It sure makes food taste good!"

Laughter and nodding.

"Sex, too."

"Yeah?"

"Yes."

"Yeah, oh definitely."

"Hey, Harry," Neeta said. "Did you ball your old lady when you were high? At home? Oh, you don't have to answer that."

Harry smiled, closed his eyes, and opened them again. He had never been able to be open up with personal stuff before — people in a group — before, but now.... "Yes!" he said suddenly, sitting up straight and clasping his knees. "Yes!"

"Oh, Harry, that's wonderful!" Neeta said.

"It's a long story," Harry said.

"Tell it," Mazie said.

Harry hesitated. "Well.... Years ago — before Perry was born — I was really crazy about this showgirl on Miami Beach, you know, she.... Aw shit! Ahhh...."

"Take your time, Harry."

"Yeah, man."

"She was tall and lean and.... Oh, God! I really loved her! There wasn't a bone in her body! She could move like a snake and for a time there was nothing else in the whole world."

"Awww, Harry, that's beautiful!"

"Were you married then?" Mazie said.

"Yeah. We already had Janey, my little girl. "Now I remember what I was going to say! Reba and her friends used to smoke pot all the time, and I didn't want to be put down, so.... Shit! Forgot again!"

"Good grass," Clyde said. "Good hash."

"Oh, yeah! Rebecca's skin used to feel so, uhhh, like velvet! Even her feet were smooth and velvety. I used to kiss her feet, lick her toes — I loved her so much! One time, when we were swimming at the Twenty-First Street beach — it was about three in the morning — full moon — one of those special times..."

"Oh, Harry!" Neeta said.

"Well, Reba came up out of the water and there was this long, thick glob of snot coming out of her nose, you know? She came up right in front of me, blowing water, and I held her face in my hands and sucked the snot out of her nose and swallowed it — I loved her so much it was heaven to do that — and at that moment she knew how much I loved her."

"Oh, Harry!"

"Anyway, I used to hold it against Annie, my old lady, because her skin felt crummy compared to Reba's, and, oh — it just wasn't as good, the whole number with the old lady. In fact, even though I haven't seen Reba for years now, I was still holding her against Annie all this time, well, the last of that grass you gave me, I got high and laid the old lady and it was really far out. I should say she laid me! And then I got to thinking, maybe I was getting high back then with Reba and just didn't know it. I don't think so, though. And I haven't had a girlfriend since Perry. Reba was so pissed when she found out Annie conceived Perry when I was going out with her." Harry suddenly became embarrassed. He was telling too much. "Anyway, that's the story."

Dale, the last one to join in, came over and flopped down on the blanket. He looked pissed. "It's easy to talk your ass off but hard to listen when you get high. Plus I swallowed a fish bone for Chrissake," he said. "Well, I didn't swallow it — it got caught in the back of my throat."

"See? That's what happens!" little Perry said. Perry had come wandering back and nobody had noticed him.

"Dale, you okay?" Mazie said.

"Yeah...."

"Daddy?"

"Pass the pipe," Dale said.

"Think it's out. Empty."

"Shit!"

"Daddy?" Little Perry tapped his dad on the shoulder from behind.

"You know, we're gonna have to score pretty soon," Neeta said.

"Milky is going to score."

Mazie, who was still sitting next to Harry, patted his hand. "You coming back next weekend?"

"If the boat doesn't fuck up."

"Hey. Our boat'll be ready by then," Dale said.

Neeta handed Dale a roach and lit it for him. Mazie now had her hand resting on Harry's arm and it made him nervous. He looked at her and smiled. Suddenly, he realized how much he liked her and wished he could hug her. Looking back at Dale, he realized how much he liked all of them. He loved them. What a wonderful family! Mazie squeezed his arm and withdrew her hand, and Harry remembered Dale's tiny pecker.

They say it doesn't make any difference, but...

"Maybe Harry could bring back a bag next time."

"Grass?"

"Yeah. We'll take a collection and you make the score for us and bring it back next trip."

"Dumb-dumbs! Milky's already got all our bread for the score!"

"You going to count on her? Let Harry!"

"Awww, Harry, can you do it?"

Harry's heart pounded up. They lived in a different world. What could he do for them? "I was hoping I could get some grass from you," he said. "The guy I know — he deals everything — he's not in town right now and..."

"Aw fuck, Harry," Clyde said. "Not you! Don't give us that bullshit! What guy? What dealer?"

"Come on, Clyde," Neeta pleaded.

Harry, caught in the lie, hoped that the darkness of sunset was enough to cover the burning red of his ears.

"Daddy?"

"What, Perry?" Harry turned to his boy, happy with the intrusion.

"Everybody smokes nowadays," Clyde said. "You can score reefer anywhere."

"Daddy? That lady. She wants some food."

Gilli suddenly uncoiled. "Faylie?"

"Yeah," Perry said.

"Feed your animal, Gilli," Surrendra purred in her dusky voice.

"Awww, Sura," Neeta said. "He can't help it."

"Where is she?" Harry said. His boots were on and Gilli was barefoot.

"I didn't catch her before," Gilli grinned. "Faylie and the jungle out there have an agreement.

"Hey!" Dale said. "Feed her! She pays her way!" Dale dug down into his pocket for the diamond and held it out. "Harry found it. He gave it to me. From a Faylie turd."

They all looked at the gem except Harry and Gilli, who were looking at each other. Gilli was grinning.

"She's over there!" Little Perry pointed to a figure in the shadows near the edge of the clearing. The braceleted arms crossed over her chest. Harry jumped up.

"Any fish left?" He got a few negative murmurs.

"Daddy. Can we give her some chocolate chip cookies?"

Chocolate chip cookies....

God am I hungry for chocolate chip cookies!

"Yeah," Harry said, stepping over the others and heading for his cooler. "And a ham and cheese sandwich!"

"She probably won't eat the cookies," one of them said.

"She won't come over here," Neeta said. "Hungry or not."

"And definitely not the ham. No meat."

"Chocolate's not good for you, and cane sugar...."

Perry held open the cover of the cooler. "Peanut butter, Daddy? Will she eat one of my peanut butter sandwiches?"

"Peanut butter. She'll eat that," Surrendra said.

"But not the white bread."

"Your daddy dude is horny," somebody said.

"Like Faylie fucks rednecks now? I don't think so!"

Harry hovered helplessly over the stuff in his cooler while the comments he was hearing repeated themselves in his mind.

"A hard-boiled egg!" Perry said.

Harry dug out an egg, which Annie had peeled for him and put in a baggie next to another with a peanut-butter sandwich on white bread.

"If she doesn't dig it, she's not hungry," Dale said.

"Snap the cover back on the cooler, Perry," Harry said, heading for the other side of the clearing.

"Hold it! Hold it, Dad! She said for me to bring it!"

Harry stopped cold, helpless again, his resolve to confront Faylie slipping fast. He handed the food to the boy. "So that's why you're so willing to share all of a sudden!"

"Daddy...." Little Perry took a look at Faylie, who had moved back into the trees. Perry took a look at her and waved for her to come over. The shadowy figure did not move.

"Coming along, Dad?"

"She might be tripped out," Neeta said softly.

"Burned out," Dale said.

"If she's tripping, she's not hungry," Surrendra said.

Harry looked at Gilli, who nodded, grinning.

"Coming?" Perry asked again.

Harry patted his son on the head. "Come on — let's go!" Harry was afraid, but he was so high and feeling so good inside that it didn't matter anymore what good or evil was coming up.

Little Perry picked his way slowly through the dark camp, holding the egg and the peanut butter sandwich out in front of him. Harry took a deep breath of the fragrant, cool, evening air.

Jeez, she is beautiful standing there!

God, did you make her for me? Did You make her for me like you made Rebecca for me when I needed her? Did you bring me here for her?

Am I for her? Oh God she is beautiful! Wild and so beautiful!

Faylie kept a cape clutched together at the throat. Her hair radiated electric fire about her head, and her eyes bored clean into Harry's soul. He stopped directly in front of her.

"Here!" Perry said, smiling, handing up the food.

Harry could feel that it was hard for Faylie to take her eyes off him, and his heart leapt with joy.

"Here!" Perry said, thrusting the hard-boiled egg under Faylie's nose. Faylie dropped to her knees, letting her cape open just enough to let little Perry in. She hugged him — arms of a goddess, arms encircled with bracelets in the twilight — Perry holding both arms up in the air to keep the food from getting crushed — looking up at his dad with the most contented smile on his face, eyes bright and happy.

Harry could not say anything. But she knew. He could feel it and she could feel it and there was no doubt. It didn't matter that they were different — they had been designed by the same god. Faylie stood and looked back at Harry, one slender hand holding the cape together and the other clutching the baggies with the sandwich and the egg. Their eyes locked into each other's.

The wondrous terror of an encounter like this had happened to Harry before.

REBA: What's your name?

HARRY: Schaffner. What's yours?

REBA: Rebecca.

Harry's heart had slammed at hearing the name. He had heard it first in Sunday school, and as a horny little boy had pictured an exotic female.

HARRY: You are a Jewess.

REBA: You are a German. I can tell.

HARRY: Your olive skin. Your nose. It comes straight down from your forehead like a Greek goddess.

REBA: Kiss it.

HARRY: (Kissing her nose) I want to suck your mouth.

REBA: Your kiss makes me wet.

HARRY: (heart pounding)...

"It is a long trip from where you are to where I am," Faylie said slowly. Calm, untroubled, confident female voice. "A million light-year trip. I made it. You can make it."

"Wow!" Perry exclaimed. "She can run!"

"Shhhhh." Harry swallowed hard. The sounds of Faylie's flight into the forest fell on Harry's brain like bright autumn leaves.

"I love you, Perry," he said finally. He put his hand on the boy's shoulder. "Come on. There's a whole world out here we haven't even seen yet."

Perry grinned. "How do you know there's more if you haven't seen it?"

"God tells us things in some way," Harry said. "Or something does.... You're barefoot!"

"You're stoned," Perry said. He laughed. "You're stoned!"

"Yeah."

"Daddy?"

"Yah?"

"I liked it when the lady hugged me this time!"

"Yeah, Perry, lucky you, yeah. I could dig hugging her, myself. "

"I won't tell Mommy."

The hippies were all looking up at them when they returned to the circle.

"Wow!" Harry looked at the others. "Can't relax after that!" Harry plunked his ass down but could not get comfortable.

"Far out chick," someone said.

"I'm shook up," Harry said.

"You're receiving her vibrations," Surrendra said, in her low, witchy voice. "You pick up vibrations easily for an oil head."

Oil head.... beer drinker?

Redneck....

Harry clasped his knees, trying to get settled.

"Awww, Harry! Don't worry about it. I found some more Jane. The pipe is still going. Here."

Harry took the pipe and pulled on it while Neeta lit a match.

"We're all going to dump our bodies someday anyway, no matter which road you truck on down," Clyde said. Clyde, with his blond hair braided in long corn-rows, was getting to be more understandable all the time. Harry looked at Gilli and Surrendra. Surrendra laid her dark head in Gilli's lap.

"Stars are coming out," she said.

Harry tried to pass the pipe to Mazie. "No more, man. You do it."

"I'll help you guys get more grass," Harry said. He took a long, burning hit and held the smoke in as long as he could. "Or I could take one of you in and bring you back next weekend — or— uhhh..." Harry laughed. "What — oh, fuck it! I can't talk, I... Man am I getting fucked up! Oh, beautiful! Beautiful!"

"Oil gets you fucked up," Surrendra purred. "Psychedelics get you high."

Dale laid his head in Mazie's lap and looked up at the stars. Or planets. There were just a few of them because the sky was still light. Harry looked at Dale and Mazie. It was nice to see such tough-looking people so peaceful.

"Harry," Neeta said. "Don't worry about the grass. We can do without. We do that often. And Milky's coming back soon. And Pete should be back any day now, too, with a whole boatload of tea. Don't worry about it, Harry. And — be quiet now. Shhhhhh!"

Harry looked at her. He was so in love with her.

I can love her and Faylie and Mazie and even love Surrendra all at the same time!

It's all real. I love all these people.

I wish I could dissolve into them.

Neeta... I wish I could hug her and hold her.

She's so beautiful! So wonderful!

"That's not for a month at least, Neeta. Pete has to stop twice to pick up travel papers, plus changing boats at Andros."

Harry watched Mazie's mouth talk. Her voice seemed to be coming from a dream.

They're talking about running dope.

Here I am with a bunch of dope smugglers. And they're beautiful people!

"I know. I made a trip with him. It's a long, heavy trip. A long, heavy voyage."

Harry pictured Pete, who had been with the hippies the first time he ran into them. He remembered Pete to be arrogant, cocky, smooth-shaven with long, black, curly hair.

There was a long silence as the pipe went around. Harry looked around for Perry. He spotted the boy pulling their equipment into the tent. Perry looked their way and Harry waved to him.

"I'm getting the beds ready, Daddy!"

"Okay!"

"Awww, Harry. You really love him!"

"Yeah."

"I'm glad you can stay this time, Harry."

"I love you, Neeta." Harry grinned with the revelation of it. The others looked at him. Harry shrugged.

"Awww, Harry...."

"It's true. I love all of you. Actually, I... Oh, I don't know."

"Awww, Harry, you get stoned so good now, you get so high. You're making up for all the years you should've been turning on. The same thing happened to me, didn't it, Gilli?"

Gilli nodded. "Harry, how long are you here?"

"I have to go to work Monday."

"Come and live with us," Gilli grinned.

Harry looked Gilli in the eye to see if he was putting him on. It was getting too dark to see. "I can't," Harry said. "I wish I could."

"Then do it," Gilli said. "Bring your family."

Harry shook his head. Gilli did not understand.

"None of this seems real," he said finally.

"What is real?"

"Pontius Pilate," Harry said. "I think."

Gilli laughed. "You're stoned."

"Is Faylie real?"

Dale mumbled from the depths of Mazie's lap. "That diamond is real."

"She doesn't hang around here much," Gilli said. "But she's been watching you. She sees something in you."

"She sees clear," Surrendra intoned. "When you live alone with Nature you get a special vision."

"It's the acid," Mazie said. "Acid makes you see things the way they really are. And Faylie's tripped more than all of us put together."

"She's burned out," Dale said. "Too many trips."

"Depends on the trip," Gilli said. "Look at Pete."

"Pete's only tripped at parties and with groups of people," Mazie said. "He hasn't had a chance to get into his head."

Surrendra sat up for a moment and looked around. "Maybe Faylie's a gun freak. Good thing her camp's on Elliott. I think."

"LSD?" Harry was still thinking about Gilli's offer to stay with them. The offer troubled him.

"Don't knock tripping at parties, man," Neeta said. I tripped at a party once and I got off so heavy I had to split to an empty room. Man, it was heavy!"

"That's why we don't do acid at parties."

"What's it like?" Harry said. He looked at Neeta. She would tell him. He had asked people about acid before, about what it feels like, and none of them could tell him, or would take the trouble to tell him.

"Awww, Harry, don't ask me that."

"I'm high," Dale said. "Too much talking going on."

Harry sat up straight and looked at all of them. "Every time I ask that question. I get that shit," he said. He would force them to tell him. Fuck it. He looked at Gilli. "Come on, Gilli."

"First of all," Gilli said, "Nobody can get the pure stuff anymore. The Sandoz." He looked at Harry. "Pure LSD-25."

"We can," Dale said.

"Yeah, but what's it like?"

Long silence.

"And mescaline," Neeta said.

"Be careful," Mazie said. "A lot of the street shit that's supposed to be mescaline or acid is really PCP mixed with speed and shit like that."

"There's Owsley acid," Dale said. "That stuff is pure."

"If you can prove its Owsley. You should still be careful, Harry."

"I'm not ready for it anyway. Well, maybe I am but — I don't know — now I forgot what... Oh! When we gave Faylie that food she said it's a long trip from me to her or something like that. Did she mean, uh..."

"She means you haven't tripped, Harry," Neeta said.

"Did she really say that?"

"Yeah."

"Awww, Harry...."

"Yeah."

"Tripping," Gilli continued, "tripping takes over your whole brain, no, I shouldn't say *takes over* but — no, because if you are near other people, part of your brain tries to stay alert in order to keep defense mechanisms working, and if you are in a social situation after you've dropped acid, you won't really get into it because your head is too busy with all the things it has to handle.

"Fuck, Gilli!" Dale sat up. "Too much talking. We were listening to the birds and the ocean! Now he knows less than before! He wants to know what it **feels** like!"

Surrendra laid her sexy, dark voice on Harry. "Did anyone describe pot to you before you ever got high on it?"

"Yeah. I thought I knew what it would feel like. But when I finally did get high, it was like nothing I ever experienced before. It still is."

"Oh, Harry, it gets better all the time, too," Neeta added. "If you don't do it every day."

"Bullshit." Dale said, lying back down.

"Acid's like that, only a hundred times more," Gilli said.

"A hundred times?"

Gilli hesitated. "If you do it alone, out in nature — no social situations. Yes."

"Like out here?"

"Awww, Harry!"

"Would you?" Mazie said.

Harry hesitated. "I don't know."

"If you drop out here, for the first time," Gilli said, "and if you go off into the woods to be alone before you get off, or find a spot on the shoreline alone, you will be walking into a whole new world."

"You are living on a planet which you have not ever seen," Surrendra purred.

"Will I come back all fucked up?"

"You're fucked up now," Surrendra said.

Harry's heart reeled.

"Harry, she means that, well...."

"Timothy Leary said that most people have..." Dale stopped in mid-sentence. "Shit. I'm not talking any more when I'm high. All this talk sucks!"

Gilli finished for him. "Leary says that the very worst that can happen to you from the acid experience is that you come back to the life you were living before the trip."

"Right on!" Mazie said.

"Would it change me?"

"Harry, if you want to trip then the best thing for you to do is not think about it but just do it. Not evaluate what is happening from a lot of preconceptions which a lot of people laid on you before the trip."

Dale groaned from Mazie's lap. Harry stopped asking questions.

"I'm going for a walk on the beach," Surrendra said, getting up.

Should I get up and go with her?

No. She's been lying in Gilli's lap. She and Gilli are tight...

"I'll walk with you," Mazie said.

"Aw fuck!" Dale said, with his head in Mazie's lap.

A hundred times more than pot!

A hundred times! Could I handle that?

How can anyone handle that!

Harry and Neeta pulled in closer to Gilli when the girls left for the beach. Dale lay there on his back, in the middle. "If only they had space travel now," he mumbled.

"You're traveling in space now," Gilli said.

Dale laughed. "Fucking hippie!"

Long silence.

Looking up at stars.

"A hundred times more powerful than pot, huh?"

"Oh, Harry, it's not just more powerful. It's a hundred times more different, too. More than you can imagine it to be. Different from anything you can imagine."

"Hmmmm...."

"It's not like getting high, Harry. But you get high, too."

Gilli raised one finger. "The path to inner space is long, treacherous, and pleasant. But..."

"Jewish hippie!" Dale said.

"But many surprises await those who travel upon it. It is hard to find the path, also. One must first be able to hear the laughter of the travelers who are already on it — to listen to them — and pick up the tread."

"Awww, Gilli — that's beautiful!"

"Sounded like owl shit to me," Dale said.

"Awwww, Dale!"

Harry looked at Neeta and marveled.

"Where does Faylie live?" Harry said.

Dale got up. "I'm getting some firewood," he said.

Harry made a motion to get up with him but Neeta touched his arm and shook her head.

"She lives in an old chicken coop, Harry," Neeta explained. It was a chicken coop. It's all clean inside and covered with rugs and tapestries and things she ripped off here and there. I saw it once. It's near a valley that's covered with purple morning glories. It's far out, Harry. Really far out."

"On this island?"

Gilli shrugged his shoulders.

"Awww, Gilli."

"Where'd Clyde go?"

Gilli grinned, and pointed toward the beach.

"Mazie says it's Elliott Key," Neeta said. "But I think it's this one. Maybe she moved."

"Here? Harry said, looking at Neeta's face in the moonlight, wondering, stoned, floating. "Old Rhodes Key? You said you saw her camp."

"Oh, Harry, I was so tripped out that day. It felt like a three day trip. I don't even remember what island we were on. I thought it was this one but Mazie says it was Elliott Key. We hardly go to Elliott Key anymore. It's right across the bay from Homestead. All the beer-heads with good boats go there, Harry. The gov made it a park or something. It's easier to get to and it's got boats around it on weekends."

"I know. I don't go there much either. Not anymore. But it's big."

"It's long. Eight or nine miles long..."

"It's big all right. You can go for miles without seeing a man." Harry's eyes gleamed. "Clyde has explored Elliott Key," Gilli said. "He's found abandoned houses from the old settlers, old bottles, artifacts — all stuff he can sell. He's very intelligent. You should talk to him."

Harry recoiled at the thought of getting tight with Clyde. "Did he ever find Faylie's hideout?"

"No. I think she rips off people when they leave their boats for a time."

"Daddy?"

"Yeah..."

"When are we going to sleep?"

"I don't know." Harry stretched his arms. "I'm tired. Maybe in a few minutes."

"Okay."

Harry looked at Gilli and Neeta. "Dale didn't come with the firewood."

"He's with Mazie and Surrendra — and Clyde," Gilli grinned. "Clyde likes to organize sex orgies on the beach when the moon is full."

"Ohhh, Gilli! Don't give Harry the wrong impression. Clyde's not a devil cultist or anything like that. He just likes to get things together."

Gilli leaned over and kissed Neeta on the ear.

"Awww, Gilli."

Harry's ears burned red in the darkness.

"Daddy?"

"Yeah?"

"Can I light my lantern?"

"May I. Okay."

"There's no kerosene in it."

Harry got up and pretended to stretch and yawn but he didn't manage the fake very well. Too high. "See you later," he said to Neeta and Gilli. His voice was trembling.

"Can we go out to the boat and get the kerosene, Daddy?"

Harry picked up his boy, hugged him, and carried him toward their tent. "Not now, Perry."

"Awww...."

"It's too dark. It's too..."

"With the moon?"

"Too many big fish out there," Harry said, hugging him again, and putting him down. "Let's check out the bedrolls. There's supposed to be a cold wave moving through here. Should be here by now. Forgot about it."

Sex orgy! In the moonlight!

Mazie!

Would Dale let Clyde fuck his chick?

Mazie was the one necking with Milky in the tree-house — I forgot that!

If Surrendra would fuck Clyde, would she fuck me? I'd eat out her pussy!

Clyde has such a big cock. And those balls!

It must make a difference. It must!

"Daddy! Look!"

Harry peered into the tent. Perry had both flashlights on so he could see. He was zipped up in his sleeping bag.

"Mommy fixed the zipper. Now, if it gets cold, I'll be warm enough!"

Harry crawled into the tent.

"Aren't you going to close the door? Close the door!" Perry laughed at himself. "I mean, zip the door?"

"Well, if we were alone I would, but..."

There still might be a chance. I'll sleep with my head next to the opening in case they want me.

Harry began to turn his bedroll around but decided against it. Fuck them.

"Good!" little Perry said. "It's safer to sleep with our head away from the door. Wild animals come."

"Yeah."

"Daddy? Will we be together tomorrow? Just you and me, I mean."

Harry lay on his side and looked at his boy. So frail, but he had never seen him so happy and asthma free. "Just you and me tomorrow, Perry. Tell you what. If a big ship goes by way out there, or a barge — if the weather is okay — we'll take the boat out and chase it. We'll go right up to it. Remember we talked about that once?"

"Yeah, but I don't believe it. You said the ships are so big that when you get close you get a scary feeling. I don't think they're that big."

"You just want to be sure that I'll do it. To prove it to you."

Perry grinned.

"Turn the flashlights off. Batteries."

They lay in darkness for a moment. Perry breathed a loud sigh of contentment. Harry wanted to ask him if it would be okay to take one of the hippies along to chase a big ship — if one of them wanted to — but he changed his mind. If he should be so lucky, he'd work it in with Perry when the time came. It felt so good to lie there in the darkness in the tent with the flap open — alone with his boy on the island. Was it the grass? He closed his eyes and pictured himself flying over the waves in his boat.

The sky was dotted with ice-cream clouds, the sea was choppy and blue and green and the engines were droning with effortless power as the boat skipped alongside the giant barge, the island a dot of green on the horizon. Perry, so special, his orange life vest covering his chest and neck and his hair blowing back away from his forehead, the boy grinning and looking at his dad and looking back at the awesome size of the barge.... Beautiful, special Neeta, her tanned breasts bare to the sun and wind, black hair whipping about her head, one hand free for balance and one hand gripping a hand-hold, legs spread and knees slightly bent, absorbing every bounce and slam with ease.

Harry opened his eyes again and looked out through the tent flap into the moonlit clearing of the hippie camp.

CHAPTER 8
Family

Janey was the doorman. Each time Harry or Perry made a trip from the boat back to the house with an item of equipment, it was her job to open the door and to close it after them. When Harry came up with the big tent roll she opened the door wide, but when little Perry came up, loaded down with canteens, flashlights, and his knapsack, she let the door close on him before he was all the way through.

"Dammit, you fuckin' creep!"

"Perry, watch your mouth!" It was Annie, yelling from the depths of the kitchen, where she was making a late but big, Sunday-night dinner.

"I brought you a present, too! Boy, was that a mistake!"

"A present?" Janey opened the door wider and watched Perry set his load down.

"Yes! A present!"

Janey eased outside. "Can I see it?"

"May I see it. Are you worth it?"

"Doorman!" Harry was standing there with the big cooler.

Janey popped back and held open the door. "Did you like the chocolate chip cookies, Daddy?"

"Yeah, they were good. Thank you!" Harry set the cooler down and gave Janey a hug. "Were you a good girl while I was gone?"

"Yes. Were you a good boy?"

"Yes," Harry answered.

"No," Perry said.

"Come on, Perry. We still have a lot to unload."

"I have to go potty first!" Perry hung back until his father was out of hearing distance. "Janey. You should've seen the island! It was..."

153

"Well, if anybody will ever take me!

"You interrupted, Janey!"

"Only babies call the bathroom *potty.*"

Perry looked at his older sister impatiently.

"I'm sorry I interrupted," Janey said.

"Okay. Uh, it's still in the boat. I have to go potty first." Perry started for the bathroom and then remembered. "Janey," he said in a low voice. "The whole island was full of naked — hippies!"

"In this cold weather?"

"Oh, Janey! You missed the whole point. As usual!"

"Well, I got cold today."

"Today! Sure! Janey. They do whatever they want. They sleep on the ground if they want to. They wear rings on their toes! And there's this lady there, she has a ring in her nose!"

"Doorman!"

Janey went to open the door again and Perry headed for the bathroom. "And I caught a fish!" he yelled over his shoulder. The bathroom door slammed shut. Muffled now, Perry's voice kept on. "And we cooked it and ate it and Daddy said it was the best fish he ever tasted!" Harry stopped inside the front porch and listened. "Yeeeeeech!" The bathroom door opened and little Perry came running back out. "Janey! Daddy! There's red Kool-Aid in the potty!"

"Flush it," Harry said. "I thought you were helping me."

"I am, Daddy! But I have to go potty first!"

"Go like we do on the island!" Harry went back to the boat, with Janey following.

"Daddy, can I come along next time?"

"Uh, sure!"

"Really? Really, Daddy?"

Little Perry screamed from inside the house. Harry wheeled around and headed for the front door just as Perry came tearing out. "Daddy! Daddy! The potty-seat's overflowing!" The three of them stormed into the house, meeting Annie in the hallway. Water was already running out from the bathroom onto the hallway carpet. Harry pushed them all aside and looked.

"It's going down a little," he said. "Don't flush it again until I find out what happened."

"But Daddy, I can't wait."

"Piss outside!"

"People will see!"

"They saw you on the island!"

"Ohhhh! Daddy, those were hippies!"

Harry gave the boy a swat on the ass. "Get going!"

"What hippies, Harry?"

"Annie, did you flush a rag down the toilet?"

"I don't think so."

Harry stepped over the puddle and grabbed the wastebasket. "There's no Kotex in here," he said, rummaging through the basket.

"Okay, so I flushed it down."

"Only it didn't flush down. Like I told you it wouldn't! Goddam you, Annie! And the kid comes in here and the toilet's full of blood for chrissake!"

Annie turned to leave.

"You get the plunger and fix it, Annie! You get the snake and clean your bloody Kotex out of the pipe!"

"And you cook dinner!"

Harry grabbed Annie's arm. "Are you going to flush one more rag down our toilet?"

"No."

"You'd better not!" Harry headed for the front door.

"You have to fix it now, Harry. I have to go, too!"

"Go in the bushes!"

"Harry?"

"All right! All right!" Harry stomped down the hall for the closet where the plunger was. Perry and Janey were standing next to the bathroom door, waiting.

"You two go outside and finish unloading the boat. Perry, you know what to do. Do it right."

Harry stared at the toilet bowl, flooded to within an inch of the top with bloody water and shreds of toilet paper.

Who needs a bathroom? Who needs all this shit?

This whole house. Who needs it? The roof leaks. Roaches live in the walls. The shutters are rotten and falling off and the zoning inspector gives me ten days to get them squared away. Thirty days ago.

Who needs a zoning inspector? Miami didn't have a zoning inspector before!

Janey and Perry were talking in the little hideout they had constructed under the bathroom window in the bushes. Harry climbed up to the edge of the bathtub and tried to see them. They were supposed to be unloading the boat. Janey was unwrapping something. He couldn't see Perry.

"Oh! What is it?" Janey said.

"Coral. I found it just for you. Mazie said it's a good piece!"

Harry watched Janey turn the rock around in her hand. "Who's Mazie?"

"A hippie. She's nice. She helped me cook the fish I caught. She wears clothes, well, most of the time." Perry lowered his voice. "There's these ladies there walk around naked all day. There's this weird one, she can really run, too! And climb trees!"

"What did Daddy say?"

"Nothing. He likes her. She hugged me!"

"So?"

"I could feel her titties!"

"Perry, I'm going to tell Mommy."

"See!" That's the thanks I get! You're welcome, Janey, for the present!"

"You kids get your asses over to the boat and get busy!"

Annie came in with a plastic squeeze bottle. "Dishwashing liquid. It'll make the water go down." She squirted two, long shots into the bowl. "What are you doing in the bathtub, Harry?"

"Oh for chrissake!"

The mess in the bowl began to move, then went down with a long suck and a gurgle.

CHAPTER 9
The Party

"Don't worry about your crummy coat," Harry insisted. "It's a wonderful, Spring evening. Spring! It's going to be warm and balmy all night! Did you smell the air this morning when we got up? It's here! It's not going to cool down now."

"Another long, hot summer coming up," Annie sniffed, poking through her clothes in the closet.

"It's almost dark outside and you can still feel it. Go outside and smell the air! First evening in Spring! It's going to be warm and balmy all night!" Harry repeated.

"I can smell it through the window."

"Month after month of beautiful tropical nights coming up! Swimming in the moonlight! Coming back from the island without freezing my ass...."

"Why don't we go swimming tonight, Harry? Instead of going to that crummy party?"

"Crummy party." Harry turned away from her. "I'm going outside for a minute to smell this good air. It's changing. South wind. You can smell the Caribbean!"

"Oh, Harry."

"Annie, look, you're always complaining about my friends, what bums they are. You complain that all we ever do is go to movies, right? I mean, I'm in a good mood and I'm trying my best to stay in a good mood, okay? This party is for you, too!"

"Okay."

"Gilli's a doctor. The party's at his brother's place. His brother's a psychiatrist or a psychologist. A PhD, anyway. That's two doctors, right? No bums."

"I said okay!"

Harry headed for the front porch and yanked open the door. A flash of white fur, which was Annie's big, half-Persian cat, shot between Harry's legs and into the house. Harry wheeled around and with a surprise bit of agility and luck, he caught the animal with the side of his foot and kicked it halfway across the porch. The cat, knowing from experience that Harry would pursue it without giving up, regained its balance and dashed back toward the door. Harry jerked the door open again and boosted the animal on its way with his bare foot, sending it flying over the concrete stoop.

"Oh God!" Harry looked down at his big toe and wiggled it. It felt sticky but it looked OK. "Damn!" He went back to the bedroom where Annie was dressing and sat on the edge of the bed, pulling up his foot to inspect it."

"What happened?"

"I kicked Fluffo out the front door."

"I hope you broke your toe!"

"I think my big toe went right up her ass. But I guess it didn't. It looks okay." Harry pulled his foot up as high as he could so he could sniff the toe. Eeeewww!"

Annie laughed. "You deserve it!"

Harry ran to the bathroom and turned the bathtub water on over his gooey toe. The bathroom reeked of cologne, deodorant, and FDS. "Annie!"

No answer. Harry dried off his foot with toilet paper and stormed back into the bedroom. "Do you have to spray your pussy with that shit?"

"Harry...."

"Some greedy jerk-off in New York City decides he can make a killing by telling all the women in the country that their cunt might start fuming in the middle of the day and so who's the first genius on the block to run down to the store and buy a can of — Feminine — Deodorant — Spray? Annie Schaffner! Christ!"

"So? You wash your asshole with Listerine!"

"There's a big difference between cleaning something and spraying over the crud!"

Little Perry was standing in the open doorway, knocking. "Daddy. I have to go mess, and the bathroom is full of perfume!"

"So go mess," Annie said.

"Mommy. The perfume. I'm allergic to it. I might get asthma. I might get an asthma attack!"

"Okay," Annie sighed. "I won't use it in the bathroom anymore."

"Why use perfume at all?" Harry said. "Who needs perfume?"

"What do I do," Perry demanded, "about right now! I have to go mess now!"

Annie jumped up. "Open the window!" she screamed. "And get out of here! Both of you! Leave me alone!"

Harry walked back to the bathroom with little Perry. "Just try to handle it this time, and I'll see to it that your mother stops this bullshit with the perfume from now on."

Perry went in and slammed the door on his father. "Handle it!" he mumbled through the door. "Handle it! Does he think I'm stupid? Did he listen to the words — that I was saying? No! No! Handle it, he says! Handle..."

BLAM! Harry struck the bathroom door with his fist. He pictured Perry jerk with fright. Before Perry could recover, Harry made it to the kitchen where he had the first bag of grass he had ever scored in his life, twenty-five dollars worth, and some cigarette papers. Janey was sitting there at the counter, picking the seeds out of the stuff.

"How's it coming?"

"Daddy, there are so many! How about these little ones? Should I pick out the little ones?"

"Uhhh, not the real little ones. Where's the pile that's left?"

"Just this little bit over here." Janey brushed the hair out of her face. Her bangs were growing out. Harry was now insisting that Annie let Janey grow out her bangs.

It took Harry three papers and five minutes to roll the first joint, and it still looked lumpy and crooked. Carefully, he tore the thing open, saving the precious buds inside, and started over. The second result was not much better than the first, and there were bits of the bitter marijuana in his mouth from licking the paper, and some on the floor which had spilled when his hand trembled. "Shit!" Harry was on all fours, scraping up what he could from the tiles.

Annie came breezing in just as Harry was getting up. "Well? How do I look?"

At first, Harry did not know what to say. He knew that he had already criticized Annie to the limit of her patience, but... "I don't know," he said, shaking his head. "That pushup bra will have your tits in everybody's face all night. And those jeans with your old cowboy boots? Yeah, yeah, that's okay, but do you have to spray your hair? You sprayed it like a brick again. I told you..."

"Yes, Harry, but you've been wanting me to wear this bra and this open blouse for a long time now, so now I have the guts to do it and phhht! You have to bitch!"

"Yeah, but..."

"You told me before that these damn dope freaks wear costumes because they know that all clothes are costumes, right? So I come out in a costume, my costume, and you bitch."

"Yeah, but..."

"Harry. The first time you saw me waiting tables in Central City I was dressed almost exactly like I am now and you were so far gone over my tits you forgot what you were going to order. So this is my costume now! Okay? Annie Schaffner! Cowgirl barmaid from the Rocky Mountains!"

"Cowgirl!" Harry snorted. "Barmaid!"

"I could tell everyone I was a truckstop waitress when you were in the Army."

"Annie, for chrissake, look, these people are heads! That means they use psychedelic chemicals to adjust their brains. They see through a chick wearing a push-up bra. You're saying: Look at these tits! But don't touch, they belong to Harry! Just get horny."

"You want me to go to the party with this blouse but without the bra?"

"Yeah! Yeah! That would be groovy. Yeah! And brush that hair-spray out and let your hair go wild." Harry went back to rolling joints. Janey was still picking out seeds, pretending she had not been interested in the conversation. Annie came back just as Harry finished another lopsided joint.

"Ohhh, Harry, I can't do it. I can't do it. No. I can't make myself look like a young woman anymore!"

Harry was busy turning the joint he had just rolled around and around in his hand, refusing to look at his wife.

"My — you know — they're hanging down too much. I can't go like this. Look. No, don't look!"

Harry looked at her. Annie's breasts were a little droopy, but they were also heavy and full, and the sight of them through the sheer, décolleté blouse turned him on. "Hell. That's all right!" He pulled her in and gave her a hug. "Mmmmm — I can feel you on my chest, yeah."

"No, Harry. I can't go like this. I can't. It's just not me." She lowered her voice. "Harry. Let's stay home tonight. Go to bed early. Have a little party right here."

"No, Annie. Come on. Don't do this to me."

"I can feel you, too."

Harry broke away from her. "We're going. I told them I would be there. And you look beautiful that way. Period."

"I'm putting the bra back on."

"Annie, you know, you're about ten years behind the times. You.... Oh, fuck it, do what you want!"

"I will."

When Annie came back into the kitchen she was still wearing the jeans and cowboy boots, but this time with her old, blue bikini top. Harry still had not rolled a good joint. "Hey! That's all right!" he beamed.

"If I go like this, will you stay with me? Not desert me at the party like you usually do?"

"Yeah, yeah...."

"Promise?"

"Yeah."

"Daddy can't roll them," Janey said.

"I'm having trouble with this, Annie. And I'm not even dressed yet. Fuck!"

"Don't look at me. I don't know how. Why don't you take one of your old pipes and bring the pot along in a baggie?"

"One of my old pipes...." Harry mumbled. "Annie, they use special pipes with this shit. They..."

"Take one or your pipes, Harry. I'm sure it will be okay."

You're sure. You're sure. What do you know about it! No, I have to roll these jays, and that's it. At a party, when you arrive, you pass out a joint that you brought along, you know, like..."

"Oh, Harry!"

"The other people, their chicks roll the joints!"

"Guess I'm not a chick!"

"Can I try, Daddy?"

"No." Harry looked at Janey. "Okay, try it. But don't spill any."

"Harry, she's just turned ten years old and now you've got her rolling marijuana cigarettes. I'm worried, Harry, I mean, these people have much too much influence on you. Having your ten-year-old daughter roll joints for you just doesn't make any sense. They have too much influence over you and you should know it!"

Harry held his hands to his temples, feeling a headache coming on. "Damn it! Damn it! Damn it, Annie!" He stormed into the bathroom and slammed the door.

Harry cruised around the block again while Annie held the address in her hand. "That must've been it, Harry. The third house from Coral Way."

"There would be cars parked in front, like I said..."

"That's it! That's it!"

Harry slammed on the brakes. The car behind them waited patiently. It wasn't safe to honk at big pickup trucks.

"The cars are parked behind the house. I saw them," Annie said.

Harry pulled over and allowed the cars behind him to pass so he could back up.

"Harry. It's a mansion! I can't go in there dressed like this. I can't!"

Harry moved over and checked out his face in the rear-view mirror to make sure his hair was right. His hair was growing out a little, over the ears, but he still touched it up now and then with scissors, and still looked like a redneck. They were now halfway down the drive.

"No, Harry. No, no, either you got the address wrong or it's the wrong night or something."

"Look. There's a van back here, and a panel truck. That panel truck has got to belong to a freak, and..."

"And a Cadillac."

"Lincoln. It's a Lincoln."

Harry nosed the pickup between the panel truck and the garage.

"The garage is bigger than our house, Harry, and it has rooms upstairs for servants. Stop. Stop, Harry! I'm not going in!"

Harry looked around and opened the door, lowering one booted foot to the ground.

"Harry!"

"Yeah, yeah..."

"You at least look civilized with that turtleneck shirt and those pants but all I'm wearing is this bikini top with cowboy boots? Oh, Harry, come on, let's get out of here before somebody sees us. Harry!"

Suddenly, the yard lights went out, blanketing them in darkness. Then the lights went on again. Harry looked up at the lighted windows on the third floor. "I think I saw Neeta," he said.

"What?"

A shriek of laughter slipped out from inside the big house. The back door opened a crack and a large man with a shaved head and a big, black beard looked out.

"I'm looking for Gilli's brother," Harry called.

"Yes! Yes! Come in! Come in!" The man's voice was as impressive as his size. He came out toward them as Harry motioned for Annie to get out. Gilli's brother walked in quick, giant strides, and was up to Annie's side in no time. He was dressed in a natty, dark blazer with white trousers and white deck shoes. "Come on, come on, don't be afraid," he boomed to Annie. Annie took his hand as she climbed down from the high truck.

"I'm Annie," she smiled.

"I'm Harry."

"I'm Joel, Gilli's brother. Welcome to my madhouse!"

"Thank you." "Thank you."

Joel looked at them both, eyes glinting with power and good humor. "Well, well! You two look almost normal! You look sane!"

"Yeah, well, I uh...." Harry said.

"My house here is full of crazies and hippies! Hippieeeeee!" Joel took Annie's hand and led her to the house with Harry following. "You're not a hippie, are you?" he asked, looking down at Annie.

"No, no..." Annie smiled sheepishly. "Just a housewife, I guess."

Joel's giant, beautiful body stopped hauling. "A housewife! You've been liberated and don't even know it! Wonderful! Glad you came! St. Paul tells us: 'Don't neglect to show hospitality to strangers, for hereby some have entertained angels unawares!'" Joel looked at Harry. "But I don't suppose that applies in **your** case!"

"I thought you were Jews," Harry answered firmly.

"St. Paul's letter to the Hebrews, boy!" Joel resumed pulling Annie toward the big house. "Stay with me, you two! I don't understand these hippies! And I don't have a soul to keep me company. Plus I'm presently between wives!" He laughed and hauled them through the huge kitchen, where here were a few hippie chicks in long dresses milling around. On into the living room, flickering with dark candlelight in the bizarre fragrance of incense and marijuana smoke. Harry recognized Gilli's toothy grin glowing through the gloom, but no others. Everyone was ether sitting or lying about on the parquet floor on mats or pillows. There were no chairs.

"Awww, Harry, you came anyway!" Neeta appeared and gave Harry a hug and a kiss, then turned to Annie. Annie froze, and pulled her hand away from Joel. Neeta was wearing only jewelry and a leather loincloth, and her loose, upturned breasts poked clean through her beads and black hair.

"Annie, this is Neeta," Harry said. "Neeta, Annie."

Joel roared with laughter at the awkward introduction. "Come on, Annie! Everything's going to be all right!" He got Annie's hand back again. "Come on back to the kitchen. We need a drink!"

Annie smiled and let Joel drag her back toward the kitchen. She waved goodbye to Harry. Harry swallowed.

"Harry, she's beautiful!"

Harry assumed Neeta was lying. "She has the joints we brought in her purse," Harry said. "Maybe I should..."

"Harry, that's okay, we have some super hash and a water pipe — it's been around a couple times already — now what happened to that thing...." Neeta looked around. "Harry, listen, Gilli and me are back together again. Isn't that wonderful?" Neeta embraced Harry again and he hugged her back, the old yearning for her cutting away at his guts.

"I'm happy to see you're happy," he said.

"Awwww."

A strange-looking dude floated by with the biggest, blackest beard Harry had ever seen. He handed Harry a burning, corn-cob pipe. "Good shit," he mumbled as he faded down the hall.

Harry and Neeta stood there looking at each other while they took turns on the pipe. As soon as he felt himself getting off, Harry handed the pipe down to one of the freaks sitting on the floor with Gilli.

"Ahhh," Harry said to Neeta, grinning and shrugging his shoulders.

"Oh, Harry, you don't know where you belong now, do you?"

"Where do any of us belong? Wow!" Surprised by the force of the grass he had just smoked, Harry suddenly became aware of Neeta's spirit, gleaming pure and bright from somewhere behind her eyes, coming through into him and mingling with his spirit through the pathway the two of them had just cut with their eyes. "Neeta!" he exclaimed quietly, his eyes widening, drinking her in.

"I — feel it, too!" They stood there, neither of them smiling now, locked in with the scary wonder of each other. Neeta broke the transmission for a moment, standing back a little and looking Harry over carefully up and down before locking in with his eyes again.

Harry's mouth opened and he took a deep breath, forcing himself to break away from Neeta's eyes to look at her body. For the first time in his life, he could do it — look a woman over thoroughly without shame. He saw the creases in her skin near her armpits.

Thirty-five years old....

The veins in her thin arms.

The bony hands, thumbs hooked into the thong of her loincloth....

A loincloth!

Neeta raised her arms and pulled her hair back, flipping it behind her shoulders, baring her breasts, the strands of beads lying now between her breasts on her tanned, bony chest, her breasts pointy but fragile with her age, swinging out over the sides of her ribcage in a delicate balance.

Harry's hands yearned to reach out and feel Neeta's tits.

He looked back into Neeta's eyes and caught the path back to the spirit in her head just as Neeta cut the path off. He was visibly shaken by what had just happened to him.

"For the second time in my life," Harry said slowly and carefully, "I have felt the spirit — the spirit — of another person — and it was more powerful — and more beautiful — than her beautiful body — your beautiful body — and — nothing else — is — important."

"There the two devils are!" Joel's voice boomed. He came up from behind and pressed a shot glass into Harry's hand. Annie was trailing behind Joel, a coquettish look on her face, looking at Harry, playing games. Harry downed the shot of whiskey and pulled off his turtleneck shirt, tossing it toward an unoccupied space near the wall.

"Harry, put your shirt back on," Annie said. She was holding a cocktail, smiling, acting, not about to show any unhappiness in her face. Annie in her brown cowboy boots, jeans, blue bikini top with the heaviness of great white tits bulging out the sides, her lacquered hair.... Harry — naked to the waist, tan and muscular from all the days outside at his job, his head floating in new discoveries — took a deep breath and smiled and shook his head at Annie and shrugged his shoulders.

"I feel free right now. I feel naked and free, even in this big house, these people strange to me, the darkness, the light, the smells, the bodies."

Annie turned away quickly. "Boy is he bombed!"

They were interrupted by sounds of a commotion in the kitchen.

"Your favorite dope smuggler is back with more free bags," Joel sad, to no one in particular. Neeta split for the kitchen.

Annie turned back to Harry. "There's a man back there, Harry, with long, beautiful black hair like a girl. He came back from Jamaica or somewhere with his own boat about a week ago. He looks like a god, Harry. He says he met you on the island. He has such good manners and has such a beautiful, low voice." Annie reached out and touched Harry's shoulder. "Put your shirt back on, Harry."

"Pete? Has good manners?" Harry moved away from his wife, remembering the bit about free bags, and rolled on toward the kitchen. He felt like he was walking through a movie. Not a set, but a real movie. Pete stood in the center of the kitchen, obviously the center of everyone's attention. He was naked to the waist, also.

"You tell him to put his shirt on?"

"You're not a hippie, Harry. You look ridiculous."

A tall chick with a butch haircut was raving to Pete about the romance of dope smuggling: "It's unreal — I mean — you come back like Prince Valiant after spending month after month in the mountains — on the high seas — the dope_peddlers, the narcs, the United States Coast Guard, all trying to rip you off and now you're here. Right here for God's sake! In Coral Gables! I love you for that!"

"Give me a blowjob."

The chick sucked in her breath and kept right on yapping. "I would love to make love to you, Peter. I could make such beautiful love to you. We could..."

"Just suck me off," Pete said.

The girl shut up and stepped back a little, just enough for Annie and Harry to see Pete grab her wrist and pull her hand away from his open fly.

"No, no," Annie said, shaking her head. "This is too much, Harry, this is too much. We don't need to know these people, Harry. I want to leave. Right now!"

Pete caught Harry's eye and nodded. "Harry! I remember! This your old lady makes the ham and cheese sandwiches? You make good sandwiches!"

"Harry, let's go!"

Harry shrugged and headed for the whiskey bottle he had just spotted on the counter.

"You have sloppy-looking tits," Pete said to Annie.

Annie stamped her foot. "Harry!"

Harry took just one little pull of the burning whiskey in the bottle. He shook his head like a wet dog. "Blaaaagh!"

The tall chick with the butch slid up to Harry and touched his wrist. "Are you an oil head?" she said gently. Her face was close to his ear. "Alcohol is very bad for you. It causes brain damage and a lot of other things that are bad for your body.

"You have a very nice body," Harry said. He tried to stop smiling so much. "I'm high," he explained. "Not used to it. Yes, I will stop drinking. This is as good a time — as any — to declare — yes, I am through drinking." Harry looked at the woman's mouth, Pete's hard and clear demand for a blowjob still ringing in his ears. The girl definitely had an erotic, pouty mouth. For a few seconds Harry forgot himself as his mind floated over the girl's lips and teeth. Pete moved up beside them while Annie stood in the middle of the kitchen, hands on her hips. The other people there, who had been very quiet, all left.

"I want to suck your mouth," Harry said, close to the woman's ear. He said it as evenly and as sincerely as he meant it, and his own words repeated themselves over and over again in his surprised brain as his hands reached for her head and pulled her parted lips to his. Her mouth was willing, hot, and tender, and... **SPLAT!** Annie struck Harry across the side of the head with a wet, cold dishrag.

Harry turned away in disbelief, watching — like in slow motion movies — his frightened wife standing her ground and the chick reaching out for Annie's arm and cooing to her like a mother: "Don't be angry — don't be frightened." with Pete cackling while cracking his knuckles.

"Give me the keys to the truck, Harry!"

"Give me the joints Janey rolled," Harry said, hunting for a towel.

Pete laughed. "Harry, when you going to shit-can this broad?"

Annie yelled at Pete, then at Harry. "Harry, do something about that stuck-up bastard!"

Pete laughed again. "You have a beautiful mouth, too, Annie. But there's too much garbage coming out of it."

Big Joel, who had been standing and drinking in the hallway, left and came back with Gilli. Gilli was wearing a home-made suit, cut from what looked like bed sheets. He was barefoot, with the usual rings on his toes. For once, there was no grin on his face. "Annie," he said soothingly, taking her arm. "You are Harry's wife? Perry's mother? Listen, Annie, listen. Because we love Harry and your little boy, we love you, too."

"Oh, bullshit!" Annie said, pulling her arm away. "I want to go home!"

"Just listen to me for one minute, and then decide if you want to go home," Gilli continued. "Come out in the hall where it's quiet."

"Truck keys, Harry!"

Pete cackled.

"Please listen, Annie, because half of the people here right now are not from our family — our band — and Peter here, well, he would like to be soon as he gets his head together. Harry, well, Harry is our special case. Our new friend from the work-a-day world. Our contact with consensus reality."

Harry watched Gilli lead Annie out of earshot.

"Can you dig a pound of really dynamite weed?" Pete said to Harry.

"Uh, yeah, um, no! I'm broke," Harry mumbled.

Why doesn't he give me a free bag like Joel said he would?

Harry watched Gilli and Annie talking in the hallway. He was surprised and relieved to see Annie smile.

Far out! He's talking her into smoking! Oh, shit, he's lighting it up or himself. No! She's taking it! Suck it in, Annie! Good! Good! Hold your breath! Hold it in! Good! Good! Fuck, it's her first time, she won't get high. She hates the idea of getting high. Thinks she'll get hooked. That's it. Get another hit! That's it! A good one, Annie! Come on! Fuck, Annie, don't cough! Don't cough! Shit! Don't let that stop you! It'll go away!

A hand touched Harry's shoulder.

"Hey, man! Kit!" Harry was happy to see the peaceful hippie again. Kit was the man he had taken back to the mainland on his boat the first time he met the group.

"Aw right!" Kit said. "What's happening?" Kit's hair still hung all the way down to his ass.

"Gilli's turning my old lady on to grass," Harry said. "First time for her." He jerked his thumb toward the hall, only Gilli and Annie were no longer there. Just then, Clyde barged into the kitchen from the back door. His hair was braided, as usual, in corn-rows, and the bits and pieces of his elaborate costume were adorned with pheasant feathers. "Hey, Harry! Kit! Kit! Goddam! Where you been?"

"Gilli's place in Costa Rica."

"Take your bike?"

"All the way! But I brought it back on my boat. It was being re-built down there."

"Far out, bro!" Clyde gave Kit a hug.

"Bathroom's over there if you want to put something on your jock itch," Pete said.

"You got a big mouth, creep!" Joel boomed. He ambled right up to Pete and towered over him. "One more turd from that mouth and I'm going to cripple your body!"

"Love! Peace!" Kit said.

Clyde put his arm around Kit. "Listen to this shit, huh? Remember the new era? The new world that acid and pot was going to bring in? Huh? The Sixties? A couple years go by and it's all over? What happened to the planet turned on to beauty, love, and peace? Fuck! I used to believe all that shit!"

"Didn't we all," Kit said.

Pete said: "And now we need an armed redneck on the island for protection?"

Harry looked at Pete and then back to Kit. Kit must have been one of the originals to have his hair so long now.

All the way to Costa Rica on a motorcycle?!

Through Mississippi? Texas?

Through Mexico?!

Dirt roads and jungle and bandits!

How did he live? Where did he get the bread?

Pete mumbled something to Joel, and in a flash, Joel had him spun around with one arm locked behind his back. "Okay, wise ass! You've got one minute to get your van full of dope out of here! This is my place! This is my party, not Gilli's! Territorial prerogative, boy! Something you'd better learn about if you want to stay alive! Joel walked Pete right out the back door.

"Cars!" Joel said to no one in particular when he came back in. "Cars parked all over the place and on the neighbor's grass! In ten minutes we'll have the Gables police checking us out! That fucking Pete! What does Gilli see in that bum? And that grass he brought back. He was ripped off! Nobody got high! You get high? I didn't get high!"

"I got high," Harry said.

"That's shit Neeta brought over — where'd I put that stuff — keeps her grass in an empty vitamin C jar for God's sake — excuse me, Lord — typical hippie — a vitamin C jar..." Joel rambled his way out of the kitchen.

Gilli appeared. He clapped his hands twice and grinned. Joel came up behind him. Gilli and Kit embraced briefly, without words.

"Announcement!" Gilli grinned. "With this party we will now add to the reunion of our bodies a reunion of our spirits via the new sound system my blood brother Joel has put together in what used to be his recreation room in the garage but what has now become, whether he knows it or not, a temple of..."

"Oh bullshit!" Joel roared. "As soon as all you freaks are gone, the ping-pong table comes back out!"

"A temple of sound!

"Neocorticular masturbation!"

Gilli turned to his brother and blew him a kiss. "And my brother would like to state the rules of the new recreation center," Gilli grinned, "as soon as we can all get together."

"Everyone out of the kitchen and join the party," Joel said.

In the short time Harry had spent in the kitchen, the living room had filled with new people, all of them strangers to him. He tried to find Annie or Neeta in the dim, smoky light.

"All the persons who use psychedelic drugs exclusively please rise. All the oil-heads sit down and grope for the glasses you set down here and there, so they don't fall over and stain my carpet. The oil heads stay here — you make too much noise. And we don't want any poisoned brains around for the concert!"

"Everyone going to the concert form a circle around the room and join hands. No, standing up. That's it. Spread out more. Somebody turn on the lights. Okay, stand facing the middle of the room, okay, now you oil heads sit down all in the middle or the room facing out, that's right, face the flower people who are standing around you."

More lights went on and Harry spotted Annie on the other side of the room, joining hands with the "flower people". He smiled at her and gave her a little wave. Annie smiled back. She looked stoned. She did not wave back. Harry thought that she fitted right in with her boots, jeans, and bikini top. He backed up to get into the circle, and shot a quick look at the chick who was next to him. She smiled and took his hand. Clyde was on Harry's left, and he took Clyde's hand. It was strange, holding hands like this, and Harry could feel the current running through the circle of joined hands and spirits. Just then, Neeta and another woman came in, carrying stacks of what looked like folded bed sheets. Surrendra, the jungle goddess from Gilli's band, followed them carrying a small, embroidered bag. The three women broke into the circle and faced the participants. Surrendra's eyes caught Harry's, and she smiled. She approached Harry first.

"Silence, please!" Joel boomed. Joel broke into the circle on the other side of the room and took Annie's hand. Harry nodded to him and smiled, and Joel nodded and grinned back. The girl holding Harry's other hand squeezed it as Surrendra came up.

"Open your mouth," Surrendra commanded.

Harry opened.

Surrendra took a pebble out of the sack and placed it on Harry's tongue. "When you close your mouth," she said slowly, "you will have made a pact of silence. You will remain silent for a long time, and you may not speak until the concert is over." Harry closed his mouth over the smooth pebble and rolled it around against his teeth. Surrendra moved on to the girl next to him and repeated the act.

Joel left the circle to turn the lights back out. The huge room was illuminated only with candle-light now. Neeta was standing before Harry, holding out a thin, white, pullover smock. "Remove all your clothing, Harry, except for rings or jewelry, and put on this robe." The chick next to Harry squeezed his hand again and released it, and Clyde let go of his other hand. Neeta moved over to the girl. "Remove all your clothing, Liz, except for jewelry, and put on this robe."

Harry was about to place his gown on the floor so he could pull off his boots. Without warning, Harry found out that inability to make decisions was part of getting high on grass.

Think! Quick! I'm not wearing underwear!

I can pull the robe on and then get my boots and pants off, or...

Fuck. That would look dumb!

Am I the only one without any underwear?

Wearing boots?

Whatever I'm going to do, I have to do it now!

Oh, the hell with them!

Clyde nudged him and whispered, breaking the pact of silence. "Wait till you hear the sound-system Joel rigged up!"

The girl next to Harry was stripping.

I'll whip off my pants and when I pick up my robe I'll look at her then!

Harry dropped his robe on the floor and struggled with his boots. He caught the eye of a *Playboy*-type chick sitting in the center with the oil-heads, a cocktail glass in her hand, mesh-stockinged legs pulled up under her ass. He watched her watching him as he pulled off his bell-bottoms. His hairy legs looked wiry in the flickering candle-light.

Annie, on the other side of the circle, was slow to realize what was happening.

"Oh no! Ohhhhh no!"

"Shhhhhh!"

"Quiet!"

"No talking!"

Dumb bitch...

Harry bent down to pick up his robe, copping a look at the chick next to him, who was doing the same. Their eyes met. They smiled. The robe was a light, white flannel, and hung down almost to the floor. Annie found a place among the oil heads in the center, and sat down. She would not look in Harry's direction. The straight people in the center were quiet, but Harry could hear them breathe. He could not hear the dopers breathing, and the difference was remarkable. The oil heads were very intent on watching the "flower children" strip and pull on the robes, but so was Harry. He noticed that half of the men were not wearing briefs. And the few women in the circle who had been wearing bras were discarding such dainty and sexy underthings. Harry marveled at how much he had been missing all the years of marriage with Annie.

After passing out the pebbles to everyone, Surrendra donned one of the robes. Neeta and the woman with her did the same. Neeta said: "We will now go to the Sound Chamber, where we will explore our minds and communicate with our spirits. Follow me single file. When you are out in the yard, you may spit out your pebbles, but you must still remain silent." Neeta held one of the pebbles high. "Now I will begin my own silence, she said, placing the pebble in her mouth. Then she walked up to Harry and took his hand. It was the second time that evening he had been chosen to be first. The group in the circle shuffled out single file behind him. He turned to catch Annie's eye, but she was looking the other way. The night air was perfumed, balmy but refreshing — a tropical spring night. With light from a distant yard lamp, they threaded their way through the silent, dark vehicles in the yard and up to the outside staircase on the side of the garage. Harry cast a fond, quick look at his pickup truck as Neeta mounted the steps.

There was no second floor. Once inside, they had to step down again, on carpeted steps which ran the width of the small building. The steps covered all four sides and were wide enough to be used as seats. The room, dark and ominous, glowed in the light of a single, electric globe placed over a pit in the center of the floor. Harry looked up at the ceiling, from which hung drapes of silk. The windows, which he had seen on the outside, were not evident now but covered with little tapestries. Pillows had been provided on all four sides, and the group dispersed, each person finding a place on one of the sides at various heights. Neeta whispered into Harry's ear that she would need help with the door. Uncertain whether he should sit with one of the women or pick a place to be alone, he was glad to be of service. Swinging and bolting the outer iron door was easy, but Joel had to come up and help him with the inner wooden door, which was obviously warped. Joel whispered into Harry's ear: "Fear not. The angel of The Lord is in your head."

The brief flash from a powerful strobe light startled everyone for a moment, and Surrendra, standing in the center of the room near the globe, pressed her finger to her lips, beseeching everyone to remain silent. To demonstrate, she clapped her hands together just once, almost soundlessly. From up above another, brighter flash of light struck the room with a crackle and the smell of ozone. Surrendra pressed her finger to her lips again and nodded. The drapes of silk hanging above them in the semidarkness appeared to be red, and the walls of the room purple. The carpeting of the steps and the pillow covers seemed to be in varying shades of burgundy and purple, also. Neeta took Harry's hand again and placed him about one-third of the way down on the least populated side of the room, and Joel and Neeta took their places on either side of him. Surrendra was now bending over the glowing, moon-colored globe down in the center. Gracefully, she lifted it from its socket in the floor and held it high. As the globe dimmed and died in her hands, a red glow of fire and coals glowed in the pit which the globe had covered. Again, she touched her finger to her lips to indicate there should be silence. A humming sound came from several places high up on the walls, barely audible but which Harry recognized as small ventilating fans. Harry looked around as Surrendra left the glowing pit and climbed up to Gilli to sit with him. Eyes now adjusted to the fire-like light down in the small pit. Harry shook his head and smiled with the pleasure and comfort of this strange place. All about the tiered room were the robed bodies of the others, all one now, all brothers and sisters in the family clothing which eliminated the need to deal with body messages and social intercourse. Suddenly, some of the others began to move sideways. Smoke was coming from the pit and it was coming in tiny, white, cloudy trails, up the rows, up toward the tiny, almost silent, exhaust fans in the walls. The sweet smell of hashish and marijuana gently flooded Harry's brain. He leaned over sideways and put his nose in line with the trail of thick smoke coming his way, as did Joel and Neeta and the others. He recognized Clyde on the other side, on all fours, his braided hair hanging over his face which was splitting a trail of smoke and sending it over his shoulders. The movement of the people was breaking up all the smoke trails, though, and in a few minutes, the entire place was a haze of psychedelic perfume. The fans shut down. Harry followed Neeta's lead, exhaling as quietly as he could, then taking deep breaths and holding them. The room became a vat of the sound of breathing.

A Fellini movie!
Where have I been all this time?
How long has shit like this been going on?
Joel must be rich to have a place like this.
I'm not getting high... Am I?
Or am I....
Am I?
Am I?

Some or the robed figures already had enough and were reclining back against the pillows now, satisfied, silent, dreaming? Harry took one last super lungful and rested his back against the step above him. He felt a foot move out of the way as his head touched it, but Harry did not look up. He had never been anywhere where he felt such a sense of safety and belonging. His eyes focused on the glowing coals below. The fire was going out. The moon-globe, which Surrendra had hung on a hook above the pit, began to light up faintly as the fire beneath went out. Before the room could clear up, the pure terror and the wild animal cries of a growling, electric organ pierced the space between Harry's ears, and there was music. Oh, such music! The concert had begun.

It was dark and quiet now in Joel's back yard. Annie stared straight ahead as Harry wiped the condensation off the inside of the windshield in front of her. He gave her door handle a pull to make sure it was latched. They drove out as quietly as possible.

"Turn right, Harry — turn right!"

"I know an easy way home from here. It's okay."

"Oh."

Harry was bursting with happiness, but he was bitter at the same time. He needed to share what he had experienced in Joel's Sound Temple, and he was also sure that Annie was pissed off. Maybe if she could stay high....

"You want to smoke one of the joints Janey rolled?" he said. "We never passed them out."

"I did. Half an hour ago."

"You did?"

"Yup."

Harry smiled. "You high?"

"Oh, Harry, I am soooo high!"

Coral Way stretched out in front of the truck forever. "It slows time down," Harry said.

"I know. Harry, we've been driving toward that traffic light down there for five minutes!"

Harry shot a look at his wife. She was smiling. Her plastic hairdo and the swell of her tits as they passed under a street light burned a strange but vivid picture into Harry's movie screen. Harry cleared his throat. "I'm happy you got high."

Annie did not answer.

"I was hoping and hoping there would be a way to get you to try it."

Annie moved closer to him. "I know why now." She laughed. "They told me that all you people did in that place with those robes was listen to records."

"Oh, Annie. You should've heard it. It was hi-fi heaven!"

The traffic light at Le Jeune Road came closer, closer. It had been on green for a long time, so Harry slowed down, expecting it to change before they hit the intersection. The car behind them honked. Harry glanced in the mirror. It was a milk truck. He looked at the speedometer. Fifteen miles per hour. He stepped on the gas. Miami was asleep. The light was still green as they rolled on through the intersection.

"Did you see that other light?" Harry said.

"I just saw something.... Oh, Harry, go around the block. Turn, okay?"

Harry smiled and made the first right.

"Look at the houses, Harry."

"I can't. I'm driving."

"When we get back on Coral Way, slow down, and I'll show you which window to look into."

Eventually they got back onto Coral Way. "Slow down, now."

"What about the pigs, Annie? I can't go too slow!"

"Oh, Harry, don't call cops pigs. That's dumb."

"Yeah."

"Here! Here! Stop!"

Harry stopped the pickup and checked his mirrors to make sure there were no other vehicles behind them. Annie was pointing to a lighted picture window on her side of the street. The draperies were open. A man, in a bathrobe, wearing bright red slippers, his legs crossed as he sat before the window, was on the telephone. A little girl in a nightie was standing beside him. The man's head was bald. He was holding something up in his free hand, like a medicine bottle, and staring at it while he talked. Their living room was richly furnished and old-fashioned. Behind them was a grand piano. An old woman, or a woman with thick, silvery hair, was lying on the couch, her head propped up with pillows. She was lying on her back, facing the ceiling.

"Oh, Harry."

"Yah, there's a whole story there." Harry started the truck moving again. "You look at people and you see their movie. Gilli was telling me that one time. Psychedelic drugs make you sensitive."

"That I'm never going to do. Psychedelic drugs. Even if it's true they're not habit-forming like other drugs. I don't want to get into it. Maybe I'll do grass again, but not the heavy stuff. Ever!"

"Grass is a psychedelic drug, Annie."

"Oh. Oh, right."

"I have this little book. From one of the young guys at work. It's about grass, peyote, mushrooms, LSD...."

"Don't do LSD, Harry."

"I'm reading up on it. It must be amazing shit."

"Joel told me it burned out Doctor Gilli's brain."

"Joel said that? Naw...."

"Well, not in so many words. But he said he'd never try it himself. He said he had doctor friends who have patients who are all burned out."

"Doesn't sound right."

"Well...."

"Gilli said that when the CIA tested LSD to see what it would do to an enemy, or to see what it'd do to us, that it didn't turn the people into helpless sheep — it made individuals out of them! He said that's why all the governments all over the world are against it. They would lose control of the people. Control! Can you imagine?"

"Harry! I'm sorry, Harry. I can't listen. I'm too high."

"Yeah... Me, too. Listen to the tires..."

"They're singing..."

"It's so beautiful — driving like this..."

Annie sighed, and settled back. "I understand now how you can love this truck."

Harry looked at his wife and smiled. "Instead of sheep they found men the next morning — with some of their indoctrination erased."

They rolled on in the pre-dawn darkness and silence. Coral Way continued to stretch on and on. Then Twelfth Avenue stretched out before them. The deep tread of the truck tires singing.

"Harry?"

"Yeah?" He turned his head toward her just as they passed under another street light, and Annie's tits bulging out of her bikini top made Harry horny again.

"I'm sorry I didn't go with you to the Sound Temple."

"Sound Temple!" Harry snorted. "But that's what it is, for sure!"

"The first thing I thought of was orgy! While you were gone, they explained it to me."

"They?"

"There was this couple — they were real hippies, Harry. I always hated hippies. They were really nice. They were angry with Joel because he used physical force to throw Pete out, that horrible creep. How come you know Pete?"

"He was on the island when I met Gilli."

"He's disgusting."

"Yeah..."

"I told them with people like Pete, force is necessary. They didn't believe me. Don't ever get like them, Harry. Don't ever become a vegetable."

"They have their reasons, I guess," Harry said.

"We'd all be communists by now if we were all like them."

Harry sighed. "I'm sorry, Annie. I can't handle this right now."

Twelfth Avenue rolled on and on. They crossed the Miami River. "So beautiful," Harry said. "So what was the excuse for the gowns?"

"They said Joel has a lot of rules. No talking while everyone is trying to listen to music. No social activity while he's playing his albums. No leering at other people because everybody looks the same in those bed sheet things. Like, no flirting. That kind of stuff."

"Ah so."

"When we smoked joints," Annie said, "they brought out this huge, Chinese gong hanging in a frame, and started beating it. Harry, you should've heard! At first, I just heard the loud chime, you know, bong bong bong while they were beating on it with this leather hammer. And then, real quiet at first, I heard this crying, until the whole room was full of like people wailing! And they were beating the gong faster and faster, with the crying and wailing coming right out of the metal! And then the sound of wind came! First it sounded like the wind in the pine trees like back home in Colorado — it was so beautiful! But the wind came out stronger and stronger until it was like a storm, like a blizzard in the winter in the mountains, with the crying voices underneath, with the sound of that beautiful gong chiming away underneath that! Then whoever it was suddenly stopped beating the gong and it all died out. But it took a real long time to die out, Harry! Like minutes to die out. And then they split, just like that — this hippie couple — and they waved at me and shouted: 'Peace!' Just like that!"

Harry smiled.

"So — I'm glad I didn't make the Sound Temple after all, Harry." Annie patted Harry on the arm. "This is our corner."

"Finally!" Harry shook his head.

"It was sure a nice drive!"

"How much did you promise Ruby?"

"If we stay all night? Ten dollars."

"Ten dollars? Shit, Annie!" Harry pictured the chocolate babysitter with eyes like Bambi and long legs like velvet. His penis stirred. "For ten dollars, I'll eat her pussy."

"Harry!"

"I'll eat Ruby's pussy for nothing!"

"HARRY!"

"Eat **your** pussy?"

"It's a deal!"

"Wait till you ball stoned!" Harry patted Annie's head and nodded.

"And the children will be asleep."

"Yeah."

"When you pull in the drive, turn the lights out so you don't wake up little Perry."

"You have to open the gate. I have a hard-on already!"

"Oh, Harry. Okay."

Harry pulled up to the gate and switched out the lights. Beercan ran up to the fence, wagging his tail and sniffing.

"Harry, you should've seen the colored girl that came in after you people went off in your bed sheets! Your robes or whatever,"

"Yeah?"

"You like niggers so much, Harry. You missed it."

"Get out and open the gate."

"Her name is Comet. She's over six feet tall, Harry, and beautiful. Like a model. She told me she knows the island you go to. She says she has a lover on the island who knows you."

"A lover?"

"She says she balls men and women, Harry."

"I can't picture you in a conversation with somebody like that." Harry was looking at Annie's tits. "Who does she ball on the island?"

"A girl. Her name is Faylie. Faylie! Imagine that name — those hippies!"

"Faylie. Yeah, Faylie... A lesbian? Aw!"

"Do you know her? Do you know Comet?"

All Harry wanted to do now was to pump an endless hot load into Annie. Into any woman. Like immediately. "Uh, I ran into Faylie. Perry told you about her, remember? I never saw anybody colored on the island. You going to open the gate?"

"She said sex is her specialty, Harry. Comet did."

"Annie...." Harry was having trouble putting all this new information together. He watched Annie open the gate. Beercan would not get out of the way, and Annie was afraid to push or kick the dog. While he waited, he thought about the Sound Temple, and he thought about his mother. His mother loved music. She had a collection of classical records and often spent hours listening to them. He remembered how his father had bitched about the money she had spent on loudspeakers when stereophonic hi-fi sound systems first came out. But then, later, he played country music on it.

Mom, if you could only hear music the way I heard music tonight!

Annie finally got the gate open all the way, and Harry eased the truck up the drive.

I wonder what Ruby looks like tonight.

Faylie and Comet! Black and over six feet tall? Faylie is so light...

Snap out of it! Annie's ready to get laid! Keep her on it! Walk around the house naked. Feel each other up in the dark.

Harry wanted everything to go right as he remembered how getting laid high for the first time was for him.

Don't mention other chicks.

Don't spoil it for her.

CHAPTER 10
Family

Harry had told Annie over a week before about the big new raise in pay he would be getting at the boatyard, and she was thinking about it. The raise would be a big one for them. And she was happy about Harry being so valued where he worked.

"I'm going to need more grocery money from now on, Harry," Annie said. They were sitting down to dinner the night of Harry's first, big payday.

"Come on, Annie, for chrissake!"

"Well, soon as the truck's paid off then. That's soon."

"What about your dentist?"

"Well, that too."

Harry picked at one of the noodles on his plate with a fork. "Noodles! Is this part of your grocery money presentation?"

"You told me not to buy potatoes if I can't afford Idahoes. Remember?"

"I said that?!" Harry thought about it. "I work hard every day. I do every job at work like a fucking master. Shit! So what do I get at home? Shit!" Harry could hear himself but could not stop.

"Well, you get to work on all the big boats now. That's some compensation. They're cleaner — you told me yourself — and there might be bigger tips from the owners."

"Tips? Ha ha."

We don't tell the wives about the tips.

Harry got up and yelled out the back door because the kids had disappeared. He had come home later than usual and was still in his work clothes. "I bought us a couple surprises on the way home," he said, as he sat back down.

Little Perry and Janey came running in, all excited. Janey headed

The mother of some of the children, Ruby's aunt Birdella, came flying out with a broom in her hand. Annie backed off and turned the water away as the black woman rushed up to the boy still hanging on the fence with his pants at his feet and his little, black member at half mast. Birdella wailed at him with the broom. With a rip, the boy was down and trying to scramble away on all fours. Birdella was relentless. **Wham!** The broom bounced off the fence. **Whap!** Her torn blouse hung over one naked, brown shoulder down to her right nipple, and the top button of her shorts popped.

Whap! Whap!

Birdella's thighs stretched and quivered firmly with each blow. The boy tried to crawl between her legs.

Whap! Whap! Whap! Whap!

When Birdella finally dropped the broom, the boy was hanging onto her legs, silent. Birdella looked up and saw Harry in the window. She flicked the hair away from her face and smiled. Harry gave her a little wave. Birdella gave Harry a little wave back and then she jerked away from the boy and kicked him barefooted right in the head. Sauntering back to her house, she stopped once to shoot Annie a bird. Annie looked up at Harry through the window and bitched something at him. Harry shrugged. Beercan stopped barking and trotted back in through his doggie door. He lay down at the window where the three of them were still standing, and began eating himself.

"White stuff comes out of him, too," Janey said

"We have to get out of this neighborhood," Annie said firmly, after they had all settled down to eat.

"What's the surprise you brought home?"

"Two surprises," Harry said.

The kids hollered "Oh good!" both at the same time.

"I bought two new speakers for our old stereo," Harry said, "and — I bought two — two — headsets. Earphones! I bought two pair so you and I or the kids can listen with the headphones on at the same time. Together!" Harry beamed. He shoveled in a mouthful of pork roast with applesauce on top, and waited for Annie's reaction.

Annie did not speak.

"Phooey!" little Perry said.

"Phooey, Daddy!" Janey said. "What did you get for **us?**"

"Yeah, Daddy! What did you get that **we** like?"

Harry gave the kids a mean look and turned to Annie. Annie had stopped eating and was staring at him.

"Yes, Harry, what did you get for **us?** I mean it. I worked hard on this dinner because we were celebrating your first payday with your new raise and all — look, you're eating your favorite vegetable — Brussels sprouts — which I had to walk clear through niggertown for — I did that for you — the children hate them — and..."

"Niggertown?" Harry snorted. "We have two black guys at work with more smarts and skills than the white guys. Except for me, of course."

Annie looked up from her plate. "It's black now??"

"Daddy! We **hate** Brussels sprouts!" Perry hollered.

"Shut up and eat your noodles," Harry said.

"He has a right to talk, Harry. I made this dinner for **us**, Harry. The children do like pork roast — I have to even carve it because you're too lazy to learn how. And I made your favorite cake which the kids like, too, and which I don't even eat. Now what did you buy for us?

"These groceries," Harry said triumphantly. "This house. Your clothes..."

"What clothes? When? A house with a leaky roof!"

"A boat I'm not allowed to be in," Janey added.

"You shut up!" Harry said.

"She has a right to talk, too!" Annie said.

"And **you** shut up!" Harry jumped up from the table. "Enjoy your cake!" he yelled as he stomped out of the dining room.

It took Harry over an hour to get their record player ready. The speakers were easy to hook up, but the headphone jacks were the wrong size and he had to hunt for adaptors. When he was through testing everything, he took a shower and changed.

"I'm sorry I yelled at you," he said to Annie when he came out of the bathroom.

Annie would not answer. She was sitting on the living room couch, doing nothing. It looked as though she had been crying.

"Where are the kids?"

"Outside."

"In the dark?"

"They're in the yard."

"Annie — I remember how enthusiastic you were about the sound of that gong the hippies played for you at Joel's house, and I knew you'd never heard music before with a headset, stoned, so I thought that..."

"Ohhh, Harry. Just shut up!"

"Aw fuck you!"

"The boat. Thousands of dollars there! The pickup truck — just for you! Everyone else has a car — for the whole family! You have to have a pickup truck!"

"Annie goddam it!"

Annie got up and walked out toward the kitchen. Harry followed her. "Wonderful Friday evening!" he shouted. "I used to go out on payday night!"

"So you could pick up some colored whore?"

"What?" Harry grabbed Annie's arm. "Where do you get that shit?"

"I can tell how you look at them!"

"Annie...."

"Leave me alone, Harry. Let go of me!" Harry let go. He had really looked forward to this evening. "I'm sorry," he said. He had looked forward to the life he was going to have with Annie now that she found out what it was like to get high. And now this. "I was looking forward to this evening at home together," he said quietly.

"So? The evening is here!"

Harry whipped around and left her standing there. "You're always trying to make me feel guilty!" she heard him say from the other room. "Guilty! Guilty! All my life I'm supposed to feel guilty! Maybe I'm just no good! Okay! I'm no good! So leave me alone if I'm no good! Just leave me alone!"

Harry flopped into the old couch on the front porch. The only light burning there was the dim, yellow, bug-bulb, which neither of them ever bothered to turn off. Harry and Annie had made love there once, in the shadow of that light, while the children were asleep. It had excited them so much to be naked together for the first time on the porch — the porch actually served as their living room — and although they later remarked to each other what a stimulating event that had been, they only made love on the front porch that one time.

There was a brief lull in the Friday night traffic which exited the expressway farther down the street. Harry looked out through the screened windows, into the darkness. The children's tire-swing hung silently from the huge poinciana tree in the center of the yard. Off to the side, Harry's truck and boat loomed up in the shadows. Cool, night air crawled in and touched his face and arms, carrying with it the *schlop-schlop* of colored teenagers strolling by on the sidewalk, in bedroom slippers with crushed-down heel stays, Harry assumed. A snatch of conversation wafted in with the fragrant, night air, filtered by the trees and bushes. A boy's machine-gun laugh. A girl's lilting banter. Not a fat girl — Harry was sure he could tell — and he smiled in the quiet of his front porch. *schlop-schlop-schlop...*

Harry closed his eyes and let his mind wander. *The girl with the appealing voice straddled him, closing her eyes in dreamy ecstasy, while her dark, mysterious cunt slowly enveloped his white cock.*

Eyes open, he turned on his side and pulled a joint out of his shirt pocket. He held the thing out and examined it in the dim light. Jimmy, the black janitor at the boatyard, had given it to him. Jimmy had cashed his check early at the liquor store, during lunch break, and scored a bag of "rod" there in the parking lot.

Harry had expressed surprise that Jimmy smoked pot.

"Ever'body smoke reefer!"

"Bullshit."

"This here's Columbian, too, "Jimmy said. "You gonna get laid!"

Brakes squealed out on the street, followed by horn-blowing and cussing. Harry resisted the urge to fantasize getting up, grabbing his carbine, and blowing the head off every scumbag out there. He shouted to Beercan to stop barking, and reached for the matches to light Jimmy's joint. For a moment, it was still outside again. Harry heard little Perry calling Janey in the distance, from their hideout behind the house...

Jimmy's reefer had a strong, aromatic flavor. Harry pulled in a hit and held his breath. A whiff of the colored girl's voice came in through the filter of the front yard hedge. He lay back against the couch.

Bo says they're all ugly. How can he be so blind?

Another hit and Harry slowly exhaled the smoke out through his teeth. He was high already — or getting there, anyway. It was getting easier all the time. He would have to remind himself to tell Jimmy how potent his grass was. Cars roared by, lights flickering through the shrubbery. Another hit.

Bo would fuck one, but he wouldn't kiss one.

That's what he said!

Kissing with one would be the best part!

How does a dumb-ass oil-head alkie like Bo get to be foreman of the whole fucking yard?

Suddenly, Bo's voice rang out clear and unexpectedly in Harry's head: "Trouble with you rednecks is you come to Miami and to tell us things we already know!"

Calling me a redneck.... Harry smiled. *Like he's not?*

"Good reefer, Jimmy!" he said aloud.

He pictured Ruby. Every time he had seen her, he wanted to kiss those beautiful lips. Or he would imagine them hot and sucking, sliding up and down over his cock. He knew they would be warm lips, hot with blood. His blond high-school girlfriend had thick, warm lips. Kissing her was a thrill every time. Annie's lips were always, well — he could not recall — not exactly cold, but....

Harry caught himself staring at the half-burned joint in his fingers. Struggling to his feet, he headed inside for the shelf where his LP records were stored. He wished he had some good, hard rock to play, but he hadn't collected much music before he learned to turn on, and now there was little at home to choose from. His body actually shivered at the thought of twenty minutes of country or the Boston Pops. He began to flip through the classical stuff his mother had given them. Every birthday, and each Christmas, his mother would pack one record in with the gifts she would send — a classical symphony piece — with a note: "For the whole family." Harry pulled out one LP which still had the note attached.

FOR THE WHOLE FAMILY
With love,
Mom
(This is one of my favorites)

Harry had never really thought much about these notes before. High now, he saw the hope his mother had sent with each gift — hope that one day Harry and her grandchildren would get into classical music. She loved it so much. And Harry knew most of the symphonies by heart. Hour after hour on Sunday afternoons his parents would listen to the phonograph, or the Mormon Tabernacle Choir on radio, or the New York Philharmonic. Or he would hear his mother playing the old up-right piano downstairs when he was much younger and took naps.

Must've been four years old then — maybe five. Oh, hell, who knows!
That two-tone Sunday suit! It was wool! It itched so much!
Sibelius' Symphony No. 2 in D Major, Opus 43
My parents....
Me and Perry. Janey....

A wave of guilt washed over Harry's soul. Little Perry! How often Perry would run up to him with a problem and Harry would brush him off. Or Perry would rush up, all excited about something he wanted to share with his dad, and Harry would be too busy.

Harry clapped on the headset, set the tone-arm down on the record, and rushed to the couch so he could lie down and close his eyes before the music came on. He had already tested the volume control for the maximum sound he would be able to stand. For a few long, slightly scratchy seconds, Harry waited for the music his mother preferred over country to fill the sound temple of his mind. And then it came. It came in from both sides. Harry recognized the melody from the first few notes. How many times as a youth had he rejected this Sunday afternoon noise?

It came in quietly at first. It was a story. A story in sound and it arrived as a surprise even though he had expected something special because he was high on pot. Its beauty unfolded in flowers of light behind his closed eyes. It came to the center of his brain and spoke. It was God speaking and Harry was Sibelius. And He created music. But it was more than that. It was a window into Heaven. It flowered and overwhelmed him and his head *became* The Temple of Sound.

"Harry. **Harry!**"

Harry jumped up to a sitting position and yanked off the headset. "Oh! You scared me! Annie!"

"The record was over about five minutes ago and I thought maybe you fell asleep and you wanted to go to bed, or..."

"Woe! You scared me! I was — uhhh — daydreaming, I think. I was thinking about sound. What it is."

Annie sat down on the couch beside him. "Let's not fight anymore," Annie said.

"Listen, Annie — I was thinking about sound."

"Hmmmm...."

"If you could cut somebody's head open without killing him, while he's listening to music or whatever, you'd never be able to find the place in his brain where he hears the sound. The brain is just a piece of meat!"

"Well, everybody knows that, Harry."

"Yeah, but do they think about it? I mean, do they live with it? Why doesn't anybody wonder where the stage is, where the movie screen is?"

"Harry, you're stoned."

Perry came into the room and sat down quietly by the window.

"Listen, Annie, I've been noticing — when I get high — I think about all kinds of groovy stuff. It's more than thinking. It's like everything becomes clear. It's like they've been teaching us all kinds of dumb bullshit and when I'm high I can see through it all!"

"You're hallucinating, Harry. Harry. Do you think the children should hear this stuff?"

"The children! What the fuck do they have to do with this?"

"Because you've been using drugs, Harry!"

"Big deal! It's just like Prohibition when alcohol was against the law! Listen! Grass has been making me smart!"

"Oh, Harry...."

"For example — and remember, I was thinking of all of this for the first time since that record went off — and look at all the stuff I thought of!"

"Harry...." Annie made a motion to get up.

"Wait! Wait! Let me give you one example. If it's stupid, then tell me back when I'm straight tomorrow what I said that was dumb. Okay? I was thinking about where the sound is in my head. It's not in there, Annie! There's no sound coming in! Just a lot of compressed air waves from the earphones hitting my eardrums, which vibrate, and give off electric signals which follow little paths through my brain! And if you could dissect my brain while it's listening to music, all you will find would be little currents of electricity. No sound! There's no sound! Not in our brains, and not outside our brains, either. That's compressed air out there. Okay? Right?"

"I guess so."

Electric signals are not sound! The sound can only be in the soul. Except there's no soul, either!"

"Ohhhhhh, Daddy! Our teacher in school, Mr. Northrop, he said that one day there will be computers everywhere and they won't need people!"

Harry readjusted himself in the couch and listened to what Perry had just said repeat itself over and over in his mind. "I'm so high, I forgot you were listening," Harry said.

"See?" Annie laughed.

Janey came in and sat down.

Little Perry grinned. "Daddy's stoned."

"So?" Janey gave Perry the finger just as Harry turned to look at her. Perry shot a bird back.

"They are working on computers now that are supposed to end

up pretty good," Annie said.

"Yeah? Listen! I read that all the countries in the world couldn't put together a computer good enough to equal what a little child's brain can do."

"They're learning," Annie said. "The engineers."

"Okay. Let's go into the future. Here's this computer the size of New York City. It equals the human brain. The whole world worked on it. You talk to it and it answers. It has all human knowledge stored up. It has a TV screen so you can see what it sees. You know what's wrong with that? There's no little man inside. It's not aware of itself. It doesn't even know it exists. One of us has to look at the TV screen to see what it came up with. One of us has to be there to listen to what it is saying. Where in the computer does the computer hear sound, or see, or feel? Huh?"

Harry got up from the couch thinking he had made himself clear. Annie shrugged her shoulders.

"Wait till I tell Mister Northrop!" Perry exclaimed.

"Mommy, Perry went potty on a fence post. The one next to the washing machine."

Perry shook his fist at Janey. "Little tattle-tale!"

"You know the ball thing on top of the pipe? Well, it comes off real easy, and Perry takes it off and stands on the washing machine and pees into the pipe. Yesterday, he took my pet lizard and put him in..."

"It's not **your** lizard, you little snitch! Those lizards are in the yard for **everybody!**"

"He took my lizard and put him in the pipe and put the cap back on so he couldn't get back out, and then today he took the cap off and peed right into the pipe!" Janey ran out of the room, crying.

"That lying little **creep!**" Perry screamed. Crunched up with fear, and expecting the worst, he turned to his dad.

Harry looked at him. Perry was so skinny and weak from the months and months of asthma he had endured, and Harry was glad he resisted the urge to smack him.

CHAPTER 11
Saturday Morning

Dear Mom, and Dad,

First of all, I'm sorry for not writing sooner. I have a whole stack of your letters here and I will write as I go through them. Little Perry still did not write his thank-you letter for the Christmas presents you gave him, but I will see to it that he writes it today and will enclose it with mine.

Speaking of Christmas presents, I know I thanked you for them at Christmastime during that phone call, but I forgot to mention that after all these years I am getting into classical music, and I especially like Sibelius' 2nd in D Major, which you wrote was Mom's favorite. Or one of her favorites.

Harry stopped writing and looked out into space. He wished there were a way to get his parents stoned before a concert, and considered writing them about his recent marijuana experiences. He loved his parents but had never expressed that love much. If parents and children loved each other, why couldn't they be honest with each other?

The other night, I was listening to Brahms Piano Concerto No. 2 and I thought of you, Mom, because it was so beautiful. So I want to thank you again for all the records you've sent me over the years and which took me so long to appreciate. Plus I probably wouldn't be able to like classical music now if you hadn't forced me to listen to it over and over again when I was a kid. I remember, too, all our neighbors only liked country, and that's all we heard on the car radio unless we had to go the city. Here in Miami there are a couple stations but you have to know where they are.

Harry decided to spill the beans.

I was smoking marijuana when I was listening to Brahms. Music doesn't just sound better with psychedelic grass, Mom and Dad. It's whole and it speaks without words and you can hear what the composer was dreaming and you can hear what he could hear.

When are you guys going to come and visit us? Don't forget, Perry and Janey are getting bigger and you don't want to miss them at this stage. Anyway, when you come, I want to turn you on to the way I listen to music.

Perry came into the room where Harry was writing. Harry was reading over what he had written and was shaking his head. "So corny," he mumbled.

"What's corny, Dad?"

"Nothing...." Harry took the letter and tore it up into small pieces. "Hey, Perry. How many months has it been since Christmas, huh? Did you ever thank Grandpa and Grandma for the magic set? The Bible stories and the Plastigoop set? Let's see, what else did you get?"

"Bird stickers!"

"Well, did you write a thank-you letter yet?"

Perry stomped his foot, and fumed. "Every time I come in to talk you bug me. Bug me, bug me, bug me. You don't care about me, you don't want me to have any fun, all you want to do is bug me. Leave me alone!"

Harry looked at his boy sadly. He loved him so much, and he had neglected him for so long. Now, Perry didn't trust him anymore. "What did you want to talk about, boy?"

"Mommy told me to tell you the washing machine broke down again. She wants you to come fix it right away because nobody has any clean clothes — and — there are some hippies outside and Mommy doesn't know if she should let them in and you should come right away!"

Harry's heart pounded up. "What hippies? From the island? Do you know them?"

"One is from the island. Yeeeech!"

"Which one?"

Harry heard Annie shout his name from somewhere outside.

"Which one, Perry?"

"I don't remember his name, Daddy. Aren't you even going to look? Mommy's calling you!"

Harry slid his chair back timidly and got up.

Do they have to come now?

Do they have to come when I'm busy?

The washing machine's all fucked up. The kids are fucked up. Annie's all pissed off....

"It's the one with that hair, Daddy. Those nigger braids?"

Harry looked out the front door. There was no one there. "Don't say nigger, Perry."

"You say nigger!"

"I'll explain later. Come on!" The two of them went around the outside of the house to the back where the washing machine was hooked up. Clyde and two hippie girls Harry did not recognize were there with Annie. Annie's hair was in multi-colored plastic rollers, and her mushy, pasty-white belly hung out over the waistband of her wrinkled white shorts. Spidery threads of varicose veins, on legs mottled with fat, completed Annie's picture. Harry tried to smile and look pleased with his visitors. Clyde was grinning that toothy smile like Gilli always did. His hair was not braided this time, as Perry had reported, but was all combed out in a strikingly radiant, blond-afro halo. The white girls with Clyde wore long, colorful dresses. They smiled at Harry. They looked cool and peaceful.

Clyde and Harry did a double-handed handshake number. The handshake went okay without a hitch, and Harry relaxed a little. They all stood there grinning, except Annie.

"Harry, when I came back here the drain was backed up and smoke was coming out of the machine, so I unplugged it. There's a load in there and I haven't even started the rest of the week's wash. I need to get some of this stuff out on the line before noon or it won't dry!"

"Far out," one of the girls said. The girls looked so clean and nice. Harry looked down at the turds and toilet paper floating in the puddle of water around the machine.

"Drain's backed up," he said.

"Gross," one of the girls said. They began to whisper to each other. Suddenly, Janey came tearing around the corner of the house.

"Daddy! Daddy! The potty is overflowing!"

Harry stood there helplessly, embarrassed not only about the appearance of his wife, but at his entire situation. Annie made a face at the hippie girls and glared at Harry, hands on her hips.

"Here's what's happening, man," Clyde ventured. "Dale has his diesel boat totally together and it's over at Gould's Canal, waiting on us. Gilli's there. Mazie, Neeta, Milky — the whole family. They were just thinking of waiting until summer comes before going back when we scored this truly righteous acid and..."

"Harry's busy!"

Harry shot Annie a hateful look. "Waiting for summer?"

"Been some cold waves coming through."

"Not buggy there in summer?" one of the girls said.

Clyde kept on. "We scored this acid and we're going to do it this afternoon or tomorrow morning. Or Monday."

"Yeah?"

"Gilli said I should come get you."

"Janey!" Annie snapped. "Perry! This isn't for you! Go and play somewhere!"

"Far out," the long, cool, hippie girls said.

"I do have some work to do on my boat before I can use it again," Harry mumbled. Perry and Janey held their ground, looking at each other and back up at the hippies.

"No, no man, you can come with us. We'll probably be back tomorrow night for the last load of supplies and shit."

"What about me?" Annie demanded.

"Come on along! There's room, Dale's boat is big, the weather's good."

"Come on along," the hippie girls chimed in.

"LSD?" Harry said.

"The best, man. Owsley."

One of the girls said: "Gilli said pure Sandoz LSD-25."

"Really clean shit." I thought he said it was mescaline, though."

"I've never done acid before."

"Shit!" Annie said. "This is too much. Too much, Harry! Harry? If you get hooked on LSD you're through!"

"Hooked," the girls laughed. "Hooked."

"You can't get hooked on acid, Annie," Harry added.

"How would you know?"

"I've been reading up on it."

"I know! So you've been telling me! What about my wash?"

"The book I have now, which you refuse to read, was written by two doctors."

Annie spun around and plotched her way back to the washing machine, barefooted through the turds and toilet paper. She pushed the plug back into the socket.

ZAP!

Annie's arm jerked away as soon as she touched the timer. "Damn it Harry. I could get killed!"

"Far out," the chicks said.

"Come on in the front yard where we can talk," Harry suggested.

"You stay right here until you figure out what we're going to do!" Annie hollered.

"You figure out what to do. I'm, going with them."

"You bastard!"

"You got wheels?" Clyde asked. "We hitched out here."

"Yeah. Let me go inside and change and get my gear together."

"Did you turn on yet this morning?" one of the girls said. She moved up right in front of Harry's face. "It's not cool to trip if you're stoned."

"Don't eat, either. No food," the other one said.

"Harry! Don't you dare take that truck! I'm going to have to take the clothes to the laundromat, and I haven't done the shopping for the week! And who's going to fix the drain? Who's going to fix the drain, Harry?!"

Janey looked worried but Perry looked up at his dad grinning, waiting for Harry's reply.

"I worked hard all week," he mumbled, "and now I'm going to fuck off."

"Gilli said we're coming back tonight — not tomorrow," one of the girls said. "Right, right," the other one said.

"I'll take care of all your stuff tomorrow," Harry said.

Clyde nodded. "We got to go now. Today. Weather's good."

Harry was surprised that the hippies were trying to help and showed no signs of contempt for Annie. She seemed surprised, also. Harry rumpled little Perry's hair and looked Annie in the eye. There were tears in her eyes. "It'll be alright, Annie. It'll be alright."

"When my man trips," one of the girls said, "he's so peaceful and beautiful the next day."

"Right," the other girl said.

"LSD makes you crazy," little Perry said.

"There was this boy at the park," Janey added. "He was Perry's age? Well, a crazy hippie came with a knife and pulled his pants down? And he cut his thing off."

"Janey!" Annie said.

"Really! My teacher told us! She said the man was taking LSD!"

Harry picked up the garden hose and went over to the spigot to turn it on. One of the hippie girls was leading Janey to the side, assuring her that the story couldn't possibly be true. Harry wondered. He watched silently as Annie grabbed Perry and headed him toward the back door. Perry wrenched himself away, turned toward Harry and pointed to where his little pecker was, shaking his head.

"Disgusting!" Annie said.

"Far out," Clyde said. "Hey, man, we have to get this trip together."

Harry hosed off the concrete slab under the washing machine. "I had a chance to trip on acid years ago but I was chicken and I turned it down," Harry admitted. He turned off the water.

"Yeah, Harry, that little Jew bitch you used to run around with — you should've stayed with her. You should have..."

"Oh!" the girls said. The hippie girls looked Jewish.

"Fuck this!" Clyde said. "Are you coming?"

"I'm coming. Let me run inside and get my gear."

"You won't need anything."

"You got any fresh water left on the island?"

"Far out," the girls said.

"No," Clyde said. "We'll need water."

"See, Harry?" Annie laughed. "They're burned out! You had to think about water! Do you want to get like them?"

"Oh, Annie, shut up!" Harry headed for the back door, where Perry was standing. Perry dashed inside.

"When you get back, we'll be gone!" Annie yelled after him.

Harry zoomed through the kitchen, letting the screen-door slam behind him. Little Perry looked at him from the hallway, fingertips of one hand crammed in his mouth pretending like he was scared.

"Come off it, Perry. Where's my knapsack?"

"You left it in the boat."

"You been playing in the boat again? I told you not to."

"You don't need anything," Clyde repeated. Harry didn't know that Clyde was right behind him, and he jumped. "I keep all my camping gear in the boat now, so I don't forget anything, and now I can't decide."

"Just a water jug," Clyde said.

"You got a first-aid kit in Dale's boat?"

"Uhh..."

"We'll take mine." Harry pulled out his dresser drawers, hoping for inspiration.

"Jeans, a sweatshirt, and boots or sneakers," Clyde said.

"Yeah, yeah..." Harry changed quickly, and showed Clyde where to fill the water can. Annie followed the group out to the truck. "Remember, Harry? You said marijuana doesn't lead to hard drugs? Well?"

"LSD is a psychedelic drug," Clyde corrected. "Hard drugs are addictive. Like oil. Alcohol." While Harry climbed into the truck, the tall hippie girls and Clyde piled in on the other side.

"Four in front is against the law," Annie said.

Clyde slammed the door and poked his head out of the window. One or the chicks was on his lap, trying to squeeze her head down so she could see.

"The girls can sit in the back," Annie said.

"Listen," Clyde said quietly. "Don't get on everybody's trip, okay? Everything's going to be alright." He gave Annie a thumbs-up gesture.

"It's going to be okay."

Harry started up the engine.

Vvvvrrrooooooooooom!

Vvvvrrrrrooooooooooom pop pop pop pop...

"Far out," the hippie girls said.

When they were out on the street, Clyde said: "Your old lady's fucked up."

"Yeah."

"So are you," one of the girls said. Harry's ears turned red.

"After today, you'll be alright," the other girl added.

"Slow down, man. Easy." The closest girl put her arm around Harry's shoulders. The truck joined in with the flow of traffic on the expressway, and for a time no one spoke. Harry relaxed, but the woman's arm was electrifying.

After today, I'll be all right....

What is this stuff going to do to me?

Neeta said that Faylie meant I would be okay after I tripped, too. Wonder if Faylie's still on the island....

LSD.... Remember reading — a reporter dropped acid at a hippie pad — he had a cold or something and he sneezed once. When he sneezed, he sneezed flowers. That's what he said. Sneezed flowers.

"Will I remember my name?" Harry asked.

"Huh?"

"Will I know who I am?"

"Yes. Yes." The girls laughed.

"You don't know who you are now," Clyde added.

"Is everything going to change shape?"

"Everything changes shape all the time," Clyde said.

Harry kept quiet for the next few minutes. He was definitely afraid. He was afraid he might not be able to handle LSD. It was not a long drive to Gould's Canal where Dale's boat was waiting, and he had questions.

"Could I go crazy?"

"No," the girls said. They laughed. "No."

"Nahhhh," Clyde said.

"What about bad trips? Can a bad trip scare you into suicide? Or into something else stupid?"

"That army scientist," Clyde said. "They probably pushed him out that window. LSD is the only drug where they even banned research! They're afraid of the truth."

"You can't have a bad trip if you do it away from people," one of the girls said. "Out in nature."

"I had a bad trip once," the other girl said.

"That was at a party," Clyde said. "In an apartment building. Shit, all that plastic, all the chrome, all the other people...."

"That makes a difference?"

"We evolved in the jungle. You've got to trip at the home where you're familiar. At home in the jungle."

"It's so beautiful," the girls said. "So beautiful."

Harry changed lanes. They were out on the South Dixie Highway now, headed for Allapattah Road.

If it makes a difference where you trip, then it must be a close shave.

Surviving it must be a close one.

"Will I be able to talk to people?"

"Don't worry about it, man. It's going to be cool. You're with good people. That's important."

"Yeah."

"Yeah." The arm around Harry's shoulder gave him a squeeze.

"To reach the fifth level of enlightenment," one or the girls said, "you should try to be alone for awhile, after you get off."

"The fifth level is the level of Pure Light," the other chick said.

"There's no numbers on the levels," Clyde said. "That's shit."

"Your ego will die temporarily," the chicks said. "Ego death."

"What's left if your ego's gone?"

There was silence for a moment. "Your same mind but without judgment."

"Your mind uncorrupted."

"Your mind but only with what you learned from experience, not what you have been taught."

Harry turned briefly to study the girls' faces. They seemed too young to be so intelligent.

"Your ego returns when you come down later," Clyde said.

"Your spirit remembers the trip, though," one of the girls added."

"You missed Allapattah Road," the other said. "Just passed it."

"I'm a little nervous."

"Turn here! Turn here!"

Harry turned the truck around. It was hard to steer with the four of them crammed in the front seat. The slender bodies of the hippie girls did not seem to turn him on now; they were just in the way. It was the idea of dropping acid that was dominating his thoughts. It was a heavy thing to do, to try. Harry realized that he had felt inadequate years before when he had been given the opportunity to trip on LSD and turned it down. Like he wasn't man enough. Like a cannibal youth who has to kill a man to become a man. Tomorrow Harry would wake up a man at last, he thought.

"Here!" the girls said. "Turn here!"

Harry squealed the super pickup truck onto Allapattah Road. Gould's Canal and Dale's boat were only a few minutes away now.

"It's going to be alright," Clyde said. "It's going to be cool."

Harry thought about Neeta, but he didn't want to ask if she would be there. He thought they mentioned she would be. The hippie girls were running their fingers through their long, beautiful hair, shaking their heads like young animals. They were keyed up, too, Harry suddenly realized. They knew what was coming. They knew.

"Never met anyone who tripped and was sorry," Clyde said.

"No," the girls said. "No." They shook their heads and their beautiful hair again. The rich, everglades farmland stretched on and on. Harry's stomach rumbled. He had missed lunch.

Good. You're not supposed to eat. I'm going to have a good trip.

If they can handle it, I can handle it.

"Today I'll know what even research doctors aren't allowed to find out," Harry said.

"You missed Gould's Canal Road," Clyde said.

"It's because he's older," the girls said.

"Acid is heavier for older people, yes."

"More adjustments to make."

"Yes."

"Older people have really far-out trips."

"Make a U-turn."

"Wait for that car to pass."

"The weather's perfect!"

Harry pulled in a deep breath. He wondered what Annie was doing.

"Smell this air," he said.

"Mmmmmm," the hippie girls said. "Mmmmmm."

CHAPTER 12
Electric Meat

Only Surrendra was missing at the small, working-class marina. Dale and Mazie were there, and Gilli, Neeta, Kit, Pete, and Milky. Even Gilli's brother Joel was there, his black Lincoln Continental parked beside Dale's boat at the canal bank. Joel recognized Harry. "You're going to blow your brains out with these freaks?"

"Yeah, I guess so," Harry said, lowering his big water-can into the boat. "My first trip."

"To the island? Or with acid?"

"With acid. You going?"

"Shit, no!"

Right off, one of the hippie girls who were with Clyde attached herself to Joel. Harry went back to the pickup for the first-aid kit, but stopped where Neeta was. He tried to hide the uneasiness he felt. "You coming along?"

"Ohhh, Harry, I don't know.... Joel says he can get us on the Goodyear blimp this afternoon. Isn't that wonderful? I've never been up in a blimp before, so...."

"Where's Surrendra?"

The Goodyear blimp? When there's a trip like this?!

"Surrendra was supposed to be here, Harry, but she and Comet hitched a ride out to Elliot Key this morning on a police boat. You know, Faylie's mother died last month and she just got back from New York after the funeral and all and last night we got a telegram that her father was just killed in an automobile accident. Isn't that awful the way things all happen at once like that? He was probably distraught or whatever, you know, anyway, Surr is going to try to find Faylie's hideout on the island and break the bad news to her, and she took Comet along because, you know Faylie and Comet love each other. Faylie's been alone for such a long time and..."

"Shut up for a minute everybody!" Dale shouted. "Who's going and who isn't?"

"I'm going!" Harry hollered. He noticed that a few of the fishermen who had been working on their boats around them had stopped and were watching the hippies and discussing them, but there were no signs of hostility. The people at Gould's Canal were always good that way, Harry thought.

Wonder if they know we're going to trip on LSD?

"Neeta, is Comet the black dancer at Joel's party?"

"Listen, Harry, I have to see who's going on the blimp ride."

"Yeah. Sure."

"Come on!" Dale shouted again. "Let's get this shit together!"

Two of the fishermen laughed and smiled.

"I'm going with Joel," the hippie chick on Joel's arm said. Harry remembered the feel of her arm around his shoulder when he was driving them all down in his truck.

"I'm going with Joel on the blimp, too!" Mazie said.

"Aw, fuck!" Dale said. "Who's going with us?"

A discussion followed. Gilli stood off to the side, grinning. Harry went up to him. "I'm nervous," he said.

"I feel that fear every time I drop," Gilli said. Right after you swallow it down. "Too late now!" Gilli laughed. Just let yourself go. Go with the flow. Remembering that you will survive. Nobody ever O.D.s on the pure stuff. Just don't try to control where you go on the trip."

"Okay, but, I can't get used to the idea that nobody can tell me what it's going to be like."

Gilli shrugged. "Did you know what grass would feel like?"

"A little."

"Bullshit," Kit said. "You day trippers!" Kit was wearing only a pair of cut-off shorts. His long, brown, frizzy hair dangled down to his ass and radiated all about his skinny, tough body.

"Okay, but I've been doing a lot of reading about acid and mescaline and I think I know what to expect."

"You still don't know what to expect."

"I mean, I know it'll be heavy."

"And beautiful," Gilli grinned.

"You'll see Earth as a planet. See it."

"You going?" Dale said.

"Wouldn't miss it for anything," Kit said. "Except for maybe a good, steady, shit-together woman."

"Sandra's going," Dale said. "And Pete and Milky."

Sandra was one of the two hippie girls Clyde had brought to Harry's house. She walked up to the group with Pete holding her hand. Harry tried to be cool.

Pete! Will I have to handle Pete on my first trip?

Sandra broke away from Pete and got in Harry's face. She was as beautiful as a magazine model, Harry thought. But he still felt no desire. In just a little longer, he would know LSD.

LSD-25....

"Neeta told me to look after you," Sandra smiled. Harry's heart pounded with the love he felt for Neeta. Clyde came up and pulled on Sandra's arm.

"Get in the boat. Both." He turned on Gilli, and shouted. "Get in the boat, man! You got the dope?"

Gilli nodded, and Harry glanced over at the fishermen.

"Let me see it," Dale demanded.

Gilli poked around in the carpet bag he had slung over his shoulder. Everyone stood around. Gilli looked serious now. In his hand was a small, glass vial with a little cork in the end of it. In the vial were twenty or thirty tiny, purple pills not much bigger than a pinhead. Gilli grinned. "Owsley. We'll drop it after we get there," he said, no grinning this time. "In case we get checked out or the boat breaks down."

"The boat's not breaking down," Dale said.

"It's Saturday. Marine Patrol in full force."

"We'll drop when we get there," Gilli repeated.

"Whatever," Clyde said.

"There will be a lot of weekend boaters today, too."

Sandra suddenly grabbed Harry's hand. "I forgot it was Saturday. Too many people. You won't miss me if I don't go." She grabbed Clyde's arm. "I changed my mind," she said.

"Oh, come on, Sandra," Milky said.

"Fuck," Dale added. "The chicks always bug out."

Sandra bolted and ran toward Joel's Lincoln, which was pulling out. There was a long discussion.

"Fuck!" Dale said again.

Neeta got out of the car and Sandra got in. Joel honked the horn and pulled out in a cloud of dust.

"Aw right!" Clyde shouted as Neeta ran up to them.

Everyone clambered into the boat, and Dale started the diesel engine. It ran with a healthy, even sound. **donk donk donk donk...**

A boat full of long hairs — and Harry. He accidentally bumped into Milky's tits. The nipples felt hard through her T-shirt.

"Forgot the lines!" Dale shouted, but two of the fishermen rushed over and motioned for them all to stay in the boat. They unfastened the lines and tossed them in, all the while keeping their eyes on Neeta and Milky.

Pulling away from the dock, Dale stood in the middle at the controls, legs spread, hands on the wheel, hair blowing in the breeze. The others stood alongside the gunwales, hanging onto the hand-grips. Harry stood on the starboard side behind Neeta, letting her long hair flick past his face. The sun was high and the wind had picked up.

donk donk donk donk donk donk donk donk...

Salty spray broke over the bow and spattered their lips. They all smiled. The sun was hot. Harry flexed his knees for the next bump and licked his mouth. He looked at the hippies, each of them in a different costume. Their hair and their adornment were wild and free and outrageous. Harry was happy, and he felt wonderfully alive.

Far out on the horizon, the thin, green line of the islands slowly became visible.

Dale's boat was dependable, but slow. They had been beating the Easterly headwind for almost an hour, and now the seas were six feet or better. Dale and Gilli decided that, with the windy weather, they were relatively safe from weekend boaters or a check from the Florida Marine Patrol.

Clyde passed the binoculars around. "The abandoned pier on Elliott is clear!" he announced. "No boats!"

Milky and Neeta cheered — no having to wade in with their stuff on the windward side. Harry was happy it would be Elliott key instead of Old Rhodes because he was hoping they might find Faylie's camp. But thinking about Faylie, fear began to gnaw at his empty stomach. When Gilli pulled out the vial of tiny pills and began passing them out, Dale cut the engine back, keeping the bow into the wind while they all tried to keep their balance. Right off, Dale lost the tiny pill which Gilli had handed to him, and there was a scramble to find it but without success. Gilli continued by placing each hit of acid in their mouths with his fingers. When he came to Harry, Harry opened his mouth and stuck his tongue out a little, just as he used to do at Communion at church when he was younger, to accept the "body of Christ."

This ye do in remembrance of Me.

For a second, Harry thought he didn't receive anything, but exploring his mouth with his tongue, the little chunk of chemical turned up. He corralled it over to the teeth and crunched it. It felt like a tiny bit of pencil eraser. He swallowed.

Too late now!

He saw Neeta watching him. She was smiling. Harry smiled back and gave her a little wave. "Too late now!"

"Awwww Harry. It's gonna be beautiful!"

"You are beautiful!" Harry shouted back. The hippies were all licking their teeth, making sure it all went down. Dale shoved the throttle forward again and Harry nearly fell. Ahead, the island waited.

"Anybody bring a watch?" Dale shouted.

They all shook their heads. "No."

"Good! Good!"

donk donk donk donk donk donk donk donk...

Harry wanted to shout: "I'm so happy!" but he kept silent.

These strange people — it felt so good to be with them!

donk donk donk donk donk donk donk donk donk donk...

When they finally approached the leeward side of the island, the wind died down quickly as they closed in on the abandoned pier. The sea settled down also, and the rare fragrance of the lush vegetation of the key permeated the air. Harry took a deep breath. How he loved that smell! He wondered how long the acid would take to hit him, and hoped it would not come until they were all on land and the boat was secured.

He was glad it was not his boat this time.

Dale pulled the throttle farther back, lowering the bow a little and raising the stern to give the prop more clearance. The hippies were all looking over the sides as the shallow and sandy bottom glided by in the clear water. It was high tide, Harry guessed, and if it was then they would not be able to get out until the next high tide, which would not come until the middle of the night. But he had not checked the tide tables for that day, and did not say anything.

"A couple of you get up in the bow to raise the stern higher," Dale shouted. Harry and Neeta scrambled forward. Clyde came up behind them. The sea gurgled and bubbled under them as the bow cut slowly through. They passed over grass, sponges, and a school of needle fish.

Neeta was breathing deeply and sniffing out the wonderful scent of the island. "It's so beautiful! I can't believe I'm getting another chance to do this! It's so beautiful!"

The bare coral on the shore was nearly covered by the tide, and the profusion of mangrove roots looked half submerged. The path behind the huge, wooden pier suddenly became visible.

Dale cut the engine. "Ahhhh..." They glided between the two outer pilings. Harry crouched, mooring line in hand. The bow clunked gently alongside the pier, and Harry wound the end of the line around a piling, leaving enough slack to allow for the boat to go down when the tide would run out later. Dale did the same at the stern. In a moment, the eight of them were standing on the pier, looking around, looking down at the boat.

"Not another boat in sight!" Dale said. "Far out!"

"Leave the water can in the boat?"

"Why not?"

"If somebody else ties up here, and we need water...."

"Yeah," Milky said. "I don't want to come back and some redneck is parked here drinking beer and I'm tripped out naked and his face is turning into a mush of wormy colors and I need a drink."

Harry hopped down into the boat and hoisted the heavy can up onto the pier. He thought about the "mush of wormy colors" and tried to imagine what that would look like. He hadn't felt anything yet and it must have been nearly half an hour since they all swallowed the tiny pills. "We could hide the can farther down the trail and have everybody memorize where it is," he said.

"Good idea!"

Harry took a piss against the rusted-out hulk of a pre-war Ford automobile, which had been barged over to the island years ago when Elliott Key was inhabited by several farmers. The car was off the trail near the pier. The trail, in fact, used to be a rut road which ran from the bay side of the island to the ocean side — less than a mile. Near the center of the island, the trail met the crossroads where it joined the road which used to run the length of the island, about eight miles. Both roads were now overgrown with bushes and dead vines to the point where even walking was going to be difficult, but Harry was picturing it, how it must have been back in the old days. Something he did every time during visits here with his own boat.

The hippies decided to hide the water can near the crossroads, where any of them would have access to it, no matter from which direction they were coming. Without a word, Dale and Harry each took a handle of the can and followed the others as they left the pier.

"Hot today," Pete said, taking the lead.

"No wind." Gilli said.

"It's blowing the treetops."

Milky spoke up. "Too much talking!"

The trail was too narrow for Dale and Harry to haul the can walking side-by-side, and Harry worked up a sweat immediately. He still did not feel the acid. The pills were so tiny — how could they possibly have any effect? Gilli stopped and waited for Harry and Dale to catch up. He pointed to the south. Nothing but impenetrable jungle in that direction, Harry thought. "There's a house in there," Gilli said. Last year I got a ride past here in a sport fisherman. I saw the roof of the house from the tuna tower."

"How far?"

"Not too far from the pier."

"Shit, Gilli." Harry grinned. "I know about the two houses on the ocean side, but I've never seen anything in here. Just the little caretaker's shack up ahead."

"You been here before?"

"Oh, yeah. Before I switched to Old Rhodes Key. This hasn't changed much. More beer cans on the trail. Rhodes Key is too hard to land on so it stays pure."

"Pure, ha ha, funny."

"Far out!" Milky said from farther down the trail. She had just reached the caretaker's shack. The hippies stopped there, and when Harry and Dale caught up to them they set the water can down. Neeta stood in the doorway of the shack and waved. It was a one-room, bare-board structure. Part of the roof had fallen in, and to the side of it was an ancient trash pile full of broken bottles and dark, rusted tin cans, with a few, brand-new Busch-Bavarian beer cans thrown in. Harry took in a deep breath of the fragrant air. He loved this place. If it were not for the abandoned pier, he would have established his camps on this island. But the pier on the bay side made it a popular piss stop for weekend boaters.

"Let's hide the water can here," Dale said.

"No, man, let's take it to the crossroads like we decided." Harry bent to grab one of the handles but hesitated. "That way we can get at it from any direction."

Dale shrugged. "I'm getting off, I think. I can feel it."

Harry scrutinized Dale's face. What does it feel like?"

Dale gave Harry a blank look. "Anybody getting off yet?"

"No."

"No...."

"We should be off by now."

Pete and Dale moved the water can off to the side and covered it with dead branches. "Okay, everybody, this is where the water is! Anybody need a drink?"

There were no takers.

"Let's get trucking down to the ocean side," Neeta said, "where it's safe. We could be getting off any minute!"

"Yeah."

"Yeah — let's go!"

Where it's safe....

Harry hesitated

How heavy is this shit?

With a pill that small, it can't be that powerful.

He remembered the first aid kit, still in the boat. The hippies were already starting to continue on. "I'm going to run back for the first-aid kit! I'll put it with the water can!"

"Hold it!"

"Come back!"

Harry turned back. They were all standing there, waiting.

"We're going to do another one just to be sure," Pete said. Gilli was already passing out the tiny pills.

"You people are crazy," Kit said, but he took a pill and swallowed it. Harry followed suit. "I'm running back for the first-aid kit," he said again. "Everything we might need is in there."

"Okay, man."

"We'll walk slow," Neeta said.

Harry took off, chewing the hit of acid. It still felt and tasted like a tiny bit of pencil eraser. He already planned to get a drink of the water on the way back to rejoin the group. It was hard for Harry to respect the hippies when they were too dumb to get a last drink of water before hiking over to the ocean side of the island.

Dale's boat was bobbing and bumping gently near the end of the old, tilting pier. It was beautiful to be alone there for a moment — no sight or sounds of other people — just Harry and this beautiful place and God.

And God....

Harry hesitated, then jumped down into the boat and pulled out the first-aid kit, which was in a waterproof ammunition case. He placed the case on the pier and climbed back up.

And God....

Harry knelt there on the wooden planks for a minute, one hand on the metal case. A spare .45-caliber automatic pistol was in that case, too, with an extra clip — all part of his first-aid gear, and he reflected on the presence of the weapon.

And God....

It had been a long time since Harry believed the Sunday school lessons about God and Jesus and salvation. The fear of Hell and death and the pressure of sin and guilt had remained to a certain extent after Harry lost his faith, but he could no longer believe that Jesus answered prayers and things like that.

The strange feeling he had before jumping down into the boat passed, and Harry turned to debating with himself about leaving the gun in the boat.

What if the acid makes me crazy and I want to shoot myself?

Better hurry and make up my mind.

Some real assholes come here sometimes and they bring their guns with their boats.

The hippies are too dumb to take a drink of water before a hike.

Do they take me along for shit like this? To look out for them?

Wonder how much time I have left.

First they say it's good shit, then they all take an extra hit.

Better hurry and catch up to them.

Harry got to his feet and started down the trail with the kit. He was surprised to find himself a little out of breath, and by the time he got to the abandoned caretaker's shack he felt a strange pressure on him to hurry and get the first-aid case hidden before he would have to rest. As quickly as he could, he cleared away a spot a little away from the water can, and covered it with brush so even the hippies couldn't find it — because of the gun. Then he stood there, panting, memorizing the place, trying to catch his breath. Fear crept up on him. In the book he had been reading about LSD, they warned about illegitimate street acid, how some of it had been analyzed and found to contain the deadly poison strychnine. Harry looked down the trail in the direction the hippies had gone. He had intended to run after them to catch up after hiding the kit. Now, breathing hard and feeling weak and powerless, he would have to walk. If he could walk... He stumbled forward. His breathing was noisy and rapid.

I waited too long! I should've stayed with them! They must be clear to the other side already!

Harry stopped walking and grabbed hold of a tree trunk to steady himself. He tried to control the breathing, to no avail.

Maybe it's not poison.

Maybe it's the acid and I'm fighting it! The book said not to worry about your body.

What if there's something wrong with my body that I didn't know about?

Harry slid down to the ground to rest.

If it's poison, Gilli and Kit would know about it by now and they would be coming back this way.

Stop breathing for a minute and listen.

Listen.

The sun's heat — warm and loving — the wind rustling the treetops. The cry of an unseen bird: "Keeeeaw caw caw caw caw."

"Keeeeaw caw caw caw caw."

Harry's body shivered and trembled. He tried again to control himself.

Faint snatches of sound carried in from the bay alerted him.

An outboard! I'm too close to the pier!

What if the boat docks? What if I'm discovered like this?

Harry struggled to his feet and pulled off the sweatshirt, tying the sleeves around his waist so he would have his hands free. He searched his beleaguered mind for the instructions he had memorized from the book on LSD in the event of a bad trip.

Let yourself go.

If your heart feels like giving out, relax.

If you suddenly get hot or cold, relax.

Don't try to figure out what is happening to you.

Don't try to control!

Harry moved down the trail a few feet, where the sun was breaking through the treetops. He stood here with his feet apart and his arms hanging down, sweating and shaking. He smiled. He nodded his head and looked up. There were so many different kinds of trees and they were all beautiful. He was going through exactly what the book said he might go through. It was going to be alright. He grinned. His breathing settled down. And for a moment, his body shivered in ecstasy.

Go on!

Go on! Get past the crossroads in case that boat docks and they come down this trail!

Get past the crossroads and hide in the woods! And rest!

Harry lurched forward and then, to his surprise, he regained his balance and natural grace. He could move swiftly again. And the trail seemed to widen. The trail became much wider than he remembered it, but it took him a longer time to reach the crossroads. That spot was clear of trees and brush — just grass and coral rock and the beauty of the sun's penetrating heat. Harry hesitated there and looked down the trail to the north, and to the west from where he came. His body felt young now, tanned and beautiful in its gentle trembling and sweating in the sun. He felt the primal urge to strip naked and run wild and free, but his survival instincts kept him in check.

I need to hide.

Thank you, God. It's so beautiful!

He headed east again, toward the ocean side. Back into the jungle. This is where the hippies would be going, to see the ocean rolling in while tripping. A powerful weight pressed upon his thoughts now, slowing him.

Get in there and hide!

Soon! Soon! Hurry!

Harry looked to the right and the left as he continued onward. A bright place to his right appeared.

Can I get in there?

I can crawl in! I can crawl....

Harry got down and crawled. Pushing his way through the vines and bushes, he was able to straighten up after a few seconds, then had to go down again. In a minute, he was clear to walk upright. He moved as far off the trail as he could before dropping to the ground. Flopping over on his stomach and bare chest, he spread his arms and legs and distributed the weight of his body so that the sharp tips of coral protruding through the dry carpet of leaves could not hurt him. The dry leaves and the mossy coral smelled fragrant and good. He laid his forehead down now, burying his face in the jungle floor. A shiver of pleasure ran up his spine and back down through his balls and down his legs. His hands found knobby hunks of coral firmly embedded in the ground. He gripped them and shuddered in spasms of pure joy. Tears ran down his cheeks as he pushed his face farther and farther into the bed of leaves, funky and sweet.

Go with the flow. Relax. Relax.

Trust your body. Trust your mind.

Surrender.

Harry lay there weeping. He knew he was weeping for happiness he did not understand. But he knew he had never been so happy or imagined such happiness could exist. "Ohhhhhhh," he sighed, and he closed his eyes, quickly opening them again and raising his head.

Man!

He carefully closed his eyes again, steeling himself. But there was no steel in him. Pink flesh and blood rolled onto the movie screen in his mind through the closed eyelids, then the picture fell through outer space, through a black void, past pinpoints of colored light like stars, into a new galaxy where giant wheels spitting flame and circled with moons roared slowly past his field of vision. Past a dull, giant sun. Past a serene planet which looked like Earth. Coming down for a landing on a moon. Coming in much too fast. Harry's ears roared with thunder. Eyes still closed, he pulled out of the dive and glided over the surface of the strange moon, down through paths and tunnels of an infinite city of blue and pink beings shaped like teardrops and packed together like sardines, all singing and speaking in strange and beautiful voices, noting his swift passage. Nothing was familiar. Harry could not tell where the non-living structures of the city ended and the living beings began. His space travel slowed, melted, and joined in. There was no more Harry. Just movies. Voices. Falling through the strange moon packed with the pink and blue teardrop creatures. Back into space. Floating by gigantic, slowly revolving wheels. Pinpoints of light up ahead. Past the orbit of tiny, piss-colored Pluto. Speeding up and a roaring in the ears. Down long tunnels of incredibly black nothing. A film of blue ahead, like the tissue of a blue morning glory. Earth. Beautiful Planet Earth.

Silence....

"Keeeeaw caw caw caw caw." The cry of a bird. The click-clack of a land crab. Harry's eyes opened slowly, tentatively. He found himself lying on the ground of a beautiful, warm place. Plants and trees budding with life surrounded him with intricate profusion. The Garden of Eden. The sound of the breath of the body which carried him: the electric atoms of the atmosphere of the beautiful planet hissing past the teeth and lips of his flesh-and-bone vehicle. Harry's body righted itself and sat, so the head could look around. Bees and flies swung through air-highways between trees and plants, some coming, some going.

Highways!

They have regular highways through the branches and they all use the same ones!

The sky above was a thin tissue of electric blue, purple, and white. The head of the man called Harry looked down. The electric-blue sky shown between the roots of the trees and through the spaces between the beautiful, dry, fallen leaves. It was the center of the universe, and the sky appeared above, all around, and below the man. It was not possible but it was there. The man struggled with the thought but there was no thinking. Just seeing, hearing, smelling. He brushed away the leaves and saw clear, blue sky beneath, with nothing holding up him or the ground cover. A thought intruded, and he stared at where the horizon would be, seeking to banish the vision with logic,

to force the sky to stop at the horizon where the ground should begin. But the bright-blue sky continued to shine through the gaps in
the leaf clutter beneath him.

After what seemed to be a long, long time, Harry came back to
himself. He was sitting in a small depression in a kind of clearing.
The sun was still high and it was very warm there, but pleasant. Harry
felt uncomfortable in his clothes. He looked as hard as he could in
the direction of the trail to satisfy himself that he knew where he was.
Then he pulled off his boots, socks, and pants, and spread out the
pants so he could lie on them, making a pillow of the sweatshirt. The
effort fatigued him mentally, and he wondered what more there was
to come. Without having to decide, he distributed his naked body on
its back, facing the mother-warmth of the sun, and surrendered himself once again. The atmosphere of the planet shimmered above him
and flowed and eddied in delicate, electric color. The material of the
air, and then of everything he could see, now became real and showed
itself in its actual nature, nothing solid, all negative and positive
magnetic charges in different configurations, all electric, all energy.
Harry's body trembled in neural orgasm. He was going. He was dissolving into his various parts, into positive and negative electric
charges of which all atoms are made.

Atoms are not made of solid material.

Nothing is.

No need for the origin of matter.

Matter is nothing. Nothing Is.

The most intense and exquisite sensations ran up and down Harry's body, and just as he was about to rise up and collect himself, his
legs stiffened and his body expanded and blew apart in a silent explosion of energy and light. And when he looked down at his feet, his
body was no longer there.

A bee appeared. Its sound was a symphony of integrated mechanical genius. It hung in space and time — or out of space and time —
wings suspended, then flowing slowly into a stroke downward, then
wings bending and flexing ever so slowly, then beginning the return
stroke with the hairy body of the insect slipping sideways through the

swim of electric atmosphere, then slowly pulling away. Harry looked down at himself again. His body had returned.

I disappeared!

Time stopped! Stopped!

Harry disappeared again. The man sat up. There were small bushes next to him, their branches intertwined at one point. A beetle with long legs was walking along one of the thin, smaller branches. The beetle was plain, and brown. He walked along smartly, like he knew what he was doing but was in no rush. He swayed from side to side as he walked, as if he were enjoying it. He came to a fork in the branch and, without hesitating, took one of them. He came to another fork and again made his way without hesitating. Near the end of the narrowing twig, he had to choose another fork. Without a pause, he swung onto the branch which, at its end, was touching the tip of a branch on the next bush. Effortlessly, the beetle crossed over to the other bush and continued on. Another, smaller bug now appeared when the first was out of sight. Using the same path, this smaller bug casually moved to the next bush, picking all the right forks in the road.

The man's body was bathed in delicious sweat. He rolled over on his stomach and dug his feet into the coral carpet and grasped the earth with his fingers and wept again, and shuddered with pleasure; he was so happy and alert. His nakedness was beautiful and right. His body lay free and open, and the planet's sun caressed and nourished it. The man stared at the chunk of coral protruding through the leaves, inches from his eyes. The fungus on the rock shimmered with color. The plasma of the rock flowed in slow motion, turning in upon itself, boiling, viscous, and electric, changing without changing. There were no more thoughts again, only the movies. The movies in the man's head grew larger and spread wider at the sides of his vision until the picture came near to joining itself behind his head to form a complete sphere. The man's body shuddered, and he pulled himself up to a sitting position again, and looked all about himself. A thought penetrated: it seemed a work of gods, this planet he found himself upon.

Delicate ferns, painted and fashioned in fragile iridescence, sprang from the porous coral. Wild flowers bathed in sunlight appeared on all sides. A butterfly, then another, fluttered about in the clearing, landing and taking off again, the undersides of their wings brown, the inside surfaces an electric purple which was visible only when they flew — delicate, deep purple flashes of color as they flew ever so exquisitely about the garden, wings moving too slowly to possibly support flight. Wings moving so slowly the man could study them. A single, blue morning glory appeared near him, nestled alone in the grass. The vine was not visible, only the flower. The man leaned toward it. The delicate tissue of the flower trembled before his gaze, inviting him to explore its depths. Furry wands swayed within its center. A black bug , an intricate and mobile machine itself, poked about deep within the flower. The man looked closer, slipped down inside, and dissolved into the morning glory.

A short time later, Harry found himself beside the flower again. He appeared to be dying. He looked at himself, surprised that his body was still there.

I left my body!

I almost didn't come back!

Time! A little longer, and I wouldn't have come back! Another second... *Second!*

A voice said to him wordlessly:

THIS IS THE BEGINNING

Harry carefully rose to his feet, naked, legs spread wide for balance.

He surveyed the planet. He was a warrior.

The sun dried the sweat off him as he turned and his eyes swept the edge of the clearing, hunting for other sights, hunting for other creatures, other wonders, other signs of this god. Or gods. He spoke quietly, almost in a whisper, as he turned his eyes hunting.

"God — I will live here for you. I will hunt for you. You can ride me while I hunt."

THIS IS THE BEGINNING

"My body is beautiful. I will train it and use it. When I run, you will be able to feel me leaping."

"I am free, now! Free! Free!"

"They won't capture me again! I'll never let them capture me again, now that I've seen..."

A new feeling gently washed through Harry. And there would be more. The second pill they had taken was dissolving into his machine, and he could feel something coming.

THE BEGINNING

NOW

The man remained standing there, in pure silence and light, for what seemed a long, long time.

Harry was bending over and picking up his things. With the moving about, it felt as though he was tiny and in a control room behind his eyes, thinking to the muscles in his body, commanding them but without the act of making commands. Each move he made seemed to be in slow motion, and his clothes looked funny.

Shake out pants legs.

Slide right foot in. Slide left foot in.

Before pulling the jeans over his ass, he pissed, fondling his balls and watching the golden stream fired in sunlight strike the rocks and explode into globes of iridescence.

Pull sock on. Pull other sock on.

Pull boot on. Pull other boot on.

Lace boot. Lace other boot.

Time had slowed down to near nothing but it seemed perfectly normal, and Harry's boots were flowing in his hands as he threaded the laces through the upper grommets. He laughed at his clumsy boots but sobered when he saw the cow in them.

The leather....

When he stood back up, his belt was uncomfortable and he pulled it out of his jeans.

Let the jeans hang low if they want to.

Tie shirt around waist. Let the sun soak into the chest and back.

As soon as Harry had finished girding his body, he found himself floating away again. It was an already familiar sensation and he allowed himself to drift off. Standing there in the clearing, leather belt dangling from his right and with the buckle flicking the ground, he felt his personality, his mind, his ego, sitting beside himself in his head, in his Awareness. He was not what he had thought he was. He was deeper, peaceful, and the warrior part was stored safely in a secret place. His returning ego quickly fell away again along with all his thoughts. He was there, seeing everything without thoughts, without words. Knowledge and experience were there without words. The planet shimmered clear and beautiful with him, but he was not separate from it. Everything simply and exquisitely was. It did not need the old Harry Schaffner to tell it what to do or to interpret it or to judge it. Everything simply was, and it was good. He no longer knew or cared who Harry Schaffner was. A long time went by. A long time went by like this and the man slowly sat down and when the vehicle was parked and comfortable, it switched off and disappeared as he was melded with Planet Earth and the fragrance of it and the diversity of it and the wonder of it for a long time. And for a long time he was nothing and he was everything.

Voices.

Faint snatches of an approaching conversation. Distant, earth-creature voices.

Harry Schaffner returned and his brain was now conscious of itself. His machine resumed operations. His ego was taking over the body's controls and the brain surveyed the situation. The sun was still high and the sky was still clear.

The sun is still high!

Time stopped!

Time! Time! Time! Time is an Illusion!

All of this is an illusion! The Earth! The Universe! My personality! Me!

THIS IS THE BEGINNING

"Yeah, yeah," Harry said aloud, smiling.

NOW IS ALL THERE IS

"Yeah, yeah, yeah.... Yeah" Harry wanted to cry out with joy but

the voices he had heard were the voices of strangers on the trail. He
crept slowly through the clearing and into the surrounding bushes,
trying to get a glimpse of the trail to see who was coming. He found
that he had developed the stealth and grace of a cat — or an aborigine
scout. The ability had been there all his life but Harry had never
known it.

Paths and tunnels through the dense forest growth opened up
like magic before him as Harry bored ahead — swiftly now and with
renewed confidence in his machine. Suddenly, he was only a few feet
from the trail. Off in the distance, a girl's voice, then a man's — coming from the direction of the pier. Harry sprang out onto the trail
silently, leapt into the air once, for the fun of it, then disappeared
into the bushes on the other side to wait for the strangers to come
into view. It took them a long time.

"...and when Dad got home, he took my dresser drawers and
dumped them all out. He ripped my bedding off my bed and threw it
all out in the hall, and..."

The girl was past her teens. She was wearing short boy-shorts,
sneakers with white socks rolled down to the ankles, and a white hal-
ter. Her blond ponytail bobbed along as she walked. The man was a
little older, also clean looking, with a trimmed but large moustache.
The two of them were straight out of an ad for Salem cigarettes. They
passed by Harry's hiding place without a care. "...and Mom was furious, really furious, and when the police came — finally — they
threatened to lock her up, too, if she wouldn't shut up." The girl had
big, firm tits and a nice, chunky ass. The couple passed out of sight,
and their movie ended.

Harry loped back out onto the trail and stretched. Again he
looked up at the sun, which still had not moved.

A mosquito was filling up on the psychedelic blood from Harry's
forearm. He watched the mosquito's movie.

Feeling his subconscious coming out once more, Harry sat down
in the middle of the path and felt his ego slide away again, along with
his personality. No thoughts. Pure observation. A South Florida deer
fly, the type which can bite without stopping to land first) swung into

the clearing and hovered near Harry's ear, then descended and hummed over to the top of a weed which was residing in the ground just beyond Harry's right boot. It was a large fly with large, compound eyes, and the humming of the fly's machinery was wonderful, balanced, and integrated — a precision machine-noise. When the fly alighted on the tip of the weed but did not shut down, the weed swayed with the fly's weight and wings in slow motion. Ready to take off at an instant, it was facing Harry and observing him, humming, humming, humming... Harry leaned forward to get a better look at it. The hum of it, and the perfect balance of all the fly's machinery spoke to Harry of the fly's design. The eyes of the fly grew large, and as Harry looked at them he suddenly found himself in the fly's control room. The room was charged with green light and hummed with high, delicate energy. There was no vibration. Through the wonderful windows Harry could see his own machine sitting out there on the trail. The view was bright and dazzling, and covered much more of a wider range of vision than Harry was used to. Suddenly, the fly's engines revved up to a higher pitch. Harry saw his own body tense. The fly was considering attack.

flash!

The world outside the control room blurred with the speed of the insect's inhuman acceleration as it launched.

Harry Schaffner had regained the controls or his own machine just in time to observe his right arm already half-way through the arc of a violent swing as his hand opened and came down on his left forearm.

Whack!

Smear of blood!

Harry looked at the thin trace of blood on his forearm and the specks of gray fly-material which trailed along with it, while the memory of the shattered and dying humming sound repeated itself over in his mind.

End of fly movie. The rich and varied fragrance of Earth returned.

My brain can operate without me!

My brain and me are two things.

No. Everything is one thing!

The man sat there, awestruck with the memory of the fly's control room, from inside its brain seeing himself sitting out there, giant-sized through the green, cut-glass windows of the fly's movie-screen. A wonderful flying machine, fueled by red meat. Compound eyes? He had seen a single picture. Just like his own from two eyes. A single picture.

Not like that science book picture of what flies see.

Must be the same for dragonflies....

Harry's thinking ceased again.

An old bottle protruded from the plants growing at the man's feet. It was four sided and made of cloudy-clear glass, and stoppered with a chunk of pale cork. There was a little sand inside. The man turned the bottle around-and-around in his hands. He picked up a small stone and struck the bottle with it. The bottle rang out with all the tension of the magnetic forces which hold glass together. The tension was the glass! The man struck the bottle again and again, marveling at the sound. He held the stone to his ear and rubbed it. The electric tension in the atoms of the stone were not just merely evident — the tension was the stone. The man got up and began to walk, tapping the bottle with the stone in rhythm with his steps. Movies of what may have happened to the bottle during its lifetime played in his head. Early settlers in old-fashioned clothing spoke to him of their dreams and ambitions as they handled the bottle. And in the sound of it as the man struck it with the stone, an internal voice said:

I AM

A Malayan coconut palm hung out crooked and bent, but rich and full over the trail, shading it. The man felt a strange presence as he passed the tree, and he speeded his steps without thinking, until he was clear of the feeling. Looking back, he could almost see the presence, which was dark with soft spikes of energy. Walking backwards as he looked at the apparition, Harry bumped into a huge gumbo-limbo tree. He turned, and encircled the maroon tree trunk with his arms, hugging it. The trunk felt amazingly strong and as tense as steel. Carefully laying the stone and bottle on the ground, Harry stood and embraced the tree again, pressing his naked chest against the coolness of it, wrapping his legs around it, pressing his head against it. He closed his eyes. The presence of the spirit of the tree was real. It was not friendly or unfriendly. Harry closed his eyes and waited for the tree to communicate with him in more detail. He imagined that the tree would tell him how strong it was, how beautiful it was to be so strong and flexible, roots radiating out in the ground the way it was with its roots in the sky as well, both to nourish it. The wood-steel of the tree swayed and creaked and groaned in the wind up above as Harry pressed his ear against it and waited. A vision was coming that he could feel. Harry prepared himself, clenching his eyelids for the alien shock of it, whatever it might be. The gumbo-limbo creaked and groaned and clunked its branches against the trees around it, the contacts ringing down the steel trunk to Harry's ear. The vision came. The inside of the man's head filled with dazzling light as a thousand leaves, happy and green, danced in the sun of the planet.

Harry stepped back from the tree, surprised. The message was not what he had expected: strength, serenity, and peace. It was a message of unrestrained joy. He looked up at the tree's top, swaying and dancing in the sun. And the sun was still high.

Harry remembered Faylie. He wondered where on this long, beautiful island garden Faylie's nest was. There were no thoughts in his head regarding what he would do if he should run into her, or what would be expected of him, or what his capabilities were. Harry was free from that, for now. Faylie was indeed somewhere, and Harry simply moved on down the trail. The ego which had been Harry Schaffner gone.

Once, a thought intruded regarding the straight, strange couple he had observed earlier, their coming back down the trail and meeting him on the way back to the pier. Harry smiled. He did not think about it further or make any decisions. He was so right inside now — so in tune with himself and the planet. The movie of the couple walking down the trail played for a moment in his head. They were like animals in the zoo.

But without a fence to separate it could be complicated.

In a zoo you looked at them and you moved on.

Harry was getting back into familiar survival patterns. He stopped his loping about and listened. He was sweating again, and the sweating of his muscular body was delicious. He wondered where the hippies were. The sky up ahead was a brighter, more alive blue. He was nearing the ocean side. He had been walking such a long time, it seemed. Such a long time.... He continued on, happy, free, and alive. The last time he had walked this same trail it had taken him only a few minutes to cross the island to the sea.

Not more than fifteen minutes, he thought. He laughed.

Minutes!

Harry felt tired, and he began to breathe faster. He realized that he had returned to ego-reality and was going to have to rest. There was a depression in the ground up ahead, beside the path. The hollow was filled with leaves, and no coral protruded. Quickly, he veered off the trail and slumped into the bed of grass on the far side of the hollow.

Flesh and blood vehicle landing. Rest. Rest.

The grass was thick and green and plump with moisture. It had crushed down beneath him as his vehicle first descended upon it, and now the grass around the edges of his body was springing back up, blade by blade. What food his dead body would make for this beautiful, rich, green stuff! Harry lay there, watching, observing, panting in heavenly exhaustion. Slivers of iridescent red flashed through the bushes from the flowers they bore. A breath of wind traveled over the man's body as his cares slipped away, bringing with it a snatch of the sound of the surf, and the smell of the ocean. The man sighed. The grass continued to right itself all about his sweating machine. The man's ego was nearing death again, and his eyes began to flutter and close. All the colors of the Universe swirled in his head. A coral rock sticking up at the edge of the hollow flowed and rolled in a cosmic boil. The flesh and blood machine sank down further, the weary head propped with one arm, the elbow buried in the hungry grass.

The soil is so thin....

The man laid his head down, too weak to hold it any longer. The grass fenced in his eyes now, as he lay in it, and his body shuddered and adjusted itself to die in this lovely bed, to rot and to nourish this creation of living green. The grass began to sing. It began to sing in a wonderful choir of a million voices. A million enchanting voices, all singing the same, haunting note of sadness and joy. The voices bent in on the man, and grew in spine-tingling beauty. The flesh and blood body shivered in ecstasy, and the eyes ceased their fluttering, and closed. For a long time.

The man's body stirred, and Harry returned.

The grass sang!

Harry opened his eyes cautiously, not moving anything else.

I came back. Again!

I came back!

Harry's teeth began to chatter, and the chattering felt good. His arms and legs began to tremble. *Good!* He let himself go. He had already decided to surrender long before. Eyes open. The planet shimmered in all its glory, a fairyland of color and life. He laid his head back on the ground, to die.

It feels good to die....

I used to be so afraid of death.

The children.... Annie.... You'll be all right.

You don't need me.

When you come to this place someday you will be dying and you will know.

It's all right. It's all right....

The man's body trembled one last time, and lay still. Harry Schaffner was gone.

CHAPTER 13
Real Meat

"Harry!"

Harry had just emerged from the forest and was standing on the shore facing the ocean. Spray from the restless sea licked at his boots as the water shot up through the porous coral. His legs were spread wide and his palms were pressed against his legs as he allowed the sun and sea to love him. He stood as if proud. His chest was still bare. His hair was tangled and matted, his face radiant.

"Harry! Oh, beautiful! We were worried about you!" Neeta strode over to him, dressed in her beads, and rubber sandals for her feet. Her hair was wet from the ocean, her lean body alive in the sun. Tears ran down Harry's cheeks. When she came up to him he held his arms out and they embraced. They wept together. Then they stood back, holding hands, and looked into each other.

"Neeta."

"Harry. I'm so happy for you."

"Ohhhh," Harry said, grinning like Gilli.

"Oh, Harry," Neeta said, smiling, happy. "Gilli and Kit are looking for you."

"Yeah?"

Gilli and Kit!

"Oh, Harry! Your first trip!"

"Yeah...."

"We didn't know how good the acid was. We didn't know one tab would be enough. I'm still getting rushes, Harry, and taking off into space, and oh, it's so wonderful!"

They hugged each other again. Harry dissolved right into Neeta through her beads and bare chest against his bare chest. They swayed together like that without individual identity for a long time.

"Wow, Harry!"

"Wow, yeah..."

They were back apart, into their own. Harry touched Neeta's damp hair, her wet, salty cheek.

Off in the distance, down the shore, Dale came shimmering toward them, naked, his long, blond beard blowing in the breeze. He carried a long walking stick, like the staff of Moses in old Bible pictures. Shimmering and glimmering, he approached them, taking long strides, yet never seeming to get there. And then, after a long, long time, he was there.

"Heavy shit," he grinned.

"Harry's first trip," Neeta reminded.

Dale nodded. "Pretty heavy trip."

"I saw the world," Harry said. "The planet turning." He looked up at the sun. The Earth had rolled away from it but the sun was still fairly high.

"Time stopped."

"We went so far."

"It's called tripping!"

They laughed together. Harry watched the horizon as the ocean curved around the planet. The horizon line was clearly drawn with a thin, bright line of the most wonderful electric green. The atmosphere just above the horizon was flashing puffs of white energy, off and on. The hippies saw it, too. "It must be real if we all see it," Harry said. "That green line."

"Nothing is real," Dale answered.

Harry's body shivered with exquisite, electric energy. He was looking at the flower in Neeta's hair. The flower was delicately structured, but the color was a brilliant yellow. He saw Neeta bending over to pick it and he saw her standing somewhere pushing the stem of it into her wonderful, thick hair and while he was seeing this she felt him and smiled an angel smile and Harry saw that none of this had any place in the evolution of things as it had been explained to him up to this point, and God said to him right there:

I AM

"Let's get the water," Dale said.

The water!

"Water," Harry said aloud, thinking about water, its texture, its fluidity, its color, what it does, what it is.

"Water...."

"Runny water," Neeta said.

"Runny. Far out!"

The three of them stood there, immobilized by the exotic qualities of water but laughing at the seriousness of it.

WATER....

Dale stooped down and picked up something out of the seaweed at their feet. He turned it over and over in his hands, than handed it to Neeta. Neeta looked at it and handed it to Harry. It was tiny and made of white plastic. It was part of all the junk and litter that floats in to the island from boats passing by. Small as the end of a finger, it was divided into two halves, each half a tiny little triangular cup. There were holes in it to simulate cloth. There was a tiny little strap at each end, a quarter of an inch long.

Dale suddenly shouted: "It's a Barbie-doll bra!"

A Barbie-doll bra!

Harry handed it back to Neeta after they realized what it was.

"You're a girl," Dale said. "You keep it."

They were standing close. Dale and Harry were sweaty. Neeta was clean and fresh because she had been in the ocean. Her loose, golden, up-turned breasts poked through her beads. The plastic doll-bra fell to the ground and Harry looked up into Dale's eyes. Dale was looking back at him. They could see each other's spirits. Harry began to see Dale's life story. It seemed a strange, beautiful story.

Our spirits....

Spirits?

"We can see into our brains through our eyes," Dale said.

Neeta was walking back toward the trail. Harry remembered the strangers he had seen — the couple — and he remembered that Neeta and Dale were naked. And their nakedness was right.

"Did you see the people?"

"Yeah..."

"Weren't they funny?"

"Yeah."

"Plastic."

"Hey, we can cut in here," Harry said. "We can pick up the trail from here." He turned into the jungle, and Neeta and Dale followed.

"Wow, Harry!" Neeta said. The path Harry had taken opened up dramatically into a large clearing. The ground in the clearing was bare of vegetation. Huge and jagged bursts of coral rose up out of Earth, thrusting at the sun. Here and there, ironwood trees, long dead, cleaned-bare and bleached by the sun, twisted and turned and pierced the sky with their strange and angular shapes.

"Moonscape."

"Earth!"

"Yeah!"

"Earth!"

The clearing was ringed by the jungle, brilliant green, and dancing with sea-grape leaves. The three of them picked their way over the coral and stopped to rest. The sun had never seemed so bright and so clean; and Harry had never felt so beautiful, clean, whole, alive, and justified. "I found this place years ago," Harry said. "When I was straight. And I liked it then. But I didn't see this! This way! Not this!"

Dale was already up into one of the bleached, tree sculptures, and he looked like a vulture up there. Harry picked up a piece of fallen wood and was amazed at its weight, and the tension and strength in it. The Feeling was coming on again.

Neeta was sitting on one of the lower limbs of the dead tree. "Wow, I'm getting off again."

"I'm getting off again, too," Harry said. He looked down for a place to lie. All sharp, protruding coral. He eased himself down, anyway, and arranged is body to distribute the weight of it so he could be comfortable. He was surprised at how easy and how quick he was able to do this.

No one talked.

The dead coral was as warm as stone would be in the sun, but alive with moss and fungus. The stone began to flow before Harry's eyes. And the little holes in it, the pores, rolled and shimmered and looked back at him. He reached for the sharp edges with his hands to get a grip on the surface of the planet. A sweet, roaring rush came to his ears. He closed his eyes.

A long time passed.

Dale was climbing down from his perch in the tree. The tension in the ironwood rang out as his body clattered down it. Harry opened his eyes, and again found himself in Paradise. He raised himself and looked at Neeta, who was climbing down, also. "I came back!" he said to her.

"Here we are!" Dale said.

"Where is that?"

"I keep on traveling to this strange planet," Harry said. "I don't know where it comes from — I couldn't have imagined it because nothing there is familiar. Nothing! It would be impossible for me to imagine this place. I've never seen anything like it. The buildings there are the people, and the people are little red and blue wedges and they have instant communication with each other and..."

"It's a big universe," Dale said.

"Do you believe there might be such a place? In the Universe?

"I believe it."

"I believe it ," Neeta said, helping Harry up.

"Neeta. You are so beautiful."

"That's why I don't let straight people hassle me," Dale said. "They haven't even seen their own planet. And they want to tell me what to do — what's right — what to believe. They're ridiculous. I feel sorry for them."

"Some of them feel sorry for us," Neeta said.

They laughed.

"I didn't know," Harry said. "I didn't know there was more. I lived half my life..."

"Look at me!" Neeta said. "I'm an old lady already!"

"What a wonderful old lady you are!" Harry said.

"Awwww, Harry!"

"Imagine us all real old!" Harry said.

Dale laughed. "I see it! I see it!"

"We forgot we went to get the water."

"Water!"

They began to move on. Harry remembered again that Dale and Neeta were still naked. He remembered the couple. But it wasn't the couple that would give them any trouble.

"There might be others at the pier."

"Next time let's do this on Old Rhodes. No pier."

"Yeah..."

"You gotta know what you're doing to land there."

"Yeah."

"Know what we're doing?" Dale laughed.

"What did you guys do with your clothes?"

"We stashed them on the trail, near the crossroads."

"Oh. Well...."

"Awww, Harry — don't worry about it."

"I'm not worried about clothes — just you and Dale."

"Awww, Harry."

They all turned off of Harry's short-cut and onto the trail. The fragrance of the tropical vegetation there caused them all to stop again, as they sniffed the air and looked all around. Harry kept on shaking his head in wonder — and sadness. "It's sad," he said finally.

"I know," Neeta said.

"Fuck." Dale said.

"No, it's true," Neeta said, touching Dale's arm. "You're just a boy. We wasted half our lives not knowing."

"You got a long way to go yet."

"Let's cross the log again," Neeta said.

"What log?"

"Before, when we came down here, there was this log, right over a sinkhole, and we could walk right over it without falling. I could never walk a log without falling off before."

"Our clothes are on the other side of it," Dale said. They pointed to a place in the forest and headed toward it. When Harry saw the log, and how deep the sinkhole was beneath it, he recognized the place. "I could never walk across a log before, either."

Dale was ready to go." Try it!"

"Awww, Harry, you can do it when you're tripping!"

Harry shook his head, then remembered the instruction that had shocked him when he was a boy, remembering even the fierce tone and voice of the instructor, and the smell of sweat in the school gym.

"Never say I can't!"

Harry stepped up onto the log and crossed over the sinkhole as if he had been doing it for years.

"See?"

Harry crossed back for the fun of it. "Too much!"

"Far out!"

Dale and Neeta dug out their clothes. Neeta pissed in the flowers before pulling on her jeans. The drops of golden urine hung like jewels from the hair on her muff when she got up. Harry pulled on his sweatshirt, now that they were in the shade. Neeta was still topless, and Dale helped her tie on her bikini top.

"Now we can go anywhere and do anything," Harry said.

"When people hassle us, we should kill them," Dale said.

We should kill them....

A warning flashed in Harry's mind. Did LSD make Dale say that? He thought about it. Killing people who force others to conform to their ignorance. The thought was entertaining.

Second warning signal!

Could I kill on LSD?

Could I kill straight?

Yes, but for a good reason.

"Fuck 'em" Harry said.

"What?"

"I was thinking about, um, oh, fuck it."

They all laughed.

"I'm reprogramming," Harry said. "My computer."

"You know about computers?"

"I read, uh, John Lilly's book. The Human Bio-computer."

"I'm too spaced to follow all this."

"Yeah."

"I'm way down from where we were before," Neeta said.

"I'm not."

"Forgot where we were going."

"Water?"

"Water!"

They continued on, the paradise trail stretching out endlessly before them. Birds, butterflies, flowers, vines, exotic scents, Busch-Bavarian beer cans. Saturday?"

"Saturday."

Saturday!

"Wow!" Harry said. "Saturday! Is it still Saturday? Far out!" Harry laughed, and shook his head. "Just the idea of Saturday. What a thought!"

"Tomorrow's Sunday," Neeta said.

They all laughed again.

Sunday!

Sunday!

Annie. Little Perry....

Janey. Poor Janey! I never pay any attention to little Janey. She's such a beautiful kid. Where are they now? How far away from them am I now?

"Huh," Harry said.

"What?"

"I was thinking about Annie. My old lady. I never thought about her before."

"Yeah."

"Awww, Harry...."

"I never considered her as a real person before. You know, with her own plans. Her own dreams."

Neeta gave Harry a friendly poke, and laughed. "Your family will never know what hit them when you get home!"

They walked under the Malayan coconut palm, where Harry had encountered the strange Presence. This time he felt nothing.

"Man!" Dale said. "When I walked past here before, there was a weird, powerful thing there!" Dale looked around for it.

"Shit!" Harry said. "Oh! That's too much!"

"What? Why?"

"Shit," Harry said. "I saw it, too. I mean, I felt it!"

The trail darkened as heavy clouds covered the sun. They passed the hollowed-out place where Harry had died in the grass. "I died in there," Harry said. "The grass — the grass was singing!"

Dale grinned. When they passed the gumbo-limbo tree, Harry told them about the vision of the leaves dancing in the sun.

"Harry?" Neeta said.

"Yeah?"

"You were lucky. Really lucky. My first acid was at a party, and it was a long time before I found out what it can do for you."

"I was lucky with my first trip." Dale said

A small, white butterfly landed on Neeta's wrist. They stopped to look at it. "The only white one here!"

"Its brain is so tiny!"

"Smaller than its eyes!"

"Imagine what the movie screen in there looks like!"

"Total!"

"Far out!"

The butterfly took off. The trail opened up into the crossroads.

"Which way is Faylie's hide-out?" Harry said.

They stopped and looked about.

"Harry — the only time I saw it I was so tripped out."

"But it's this island? Not the other one?"

"Yes." Neeta paused. "I think so."

"Yeah."

"It's in a little valley like. All purple morning glories! Glorious! You can't miss it! She lives off the land! She..."

"She lives off the rich boaters she rips off," Dale interrupted.

They laughed.

"She's got this abandoned chicken house, Neeta said. From the old days. The old settlers. And a tree house. And a swing! She lives in the trees!"

"Must be near the north end," Dale said. This island's pretty long.

"Comet stays with her sometimes."

"Lately...."

"Lately!" They all laughed at the word.

"We could fly a plane," Dale said. "We could fly over. Hunt for the morning glory field."

"Far out!"

"Far up!"

They moved on. Toward the bay. Toward the old pier and the boat. The thought of the pier gave Harry a start, a shot of adrenalin. They would likely be contacting other people at the pier, straight people, strangers. But maybe some of the other hippies would be there already, and it would be wonderful to be all together again.

If they all survived.

"Wonder what Milky and Kit and Gilli are doing?" Harry said. "And Pete, and Clyde..."

"Awww, wow! All our friends! All together! All tripping!" Neeta plunked down, right in the middle of the trail. "I'm pooped!"

"Aw fuck!" Dale said.

Harry sat down also, and Dale gave in. The Feeling came down upon all of them as soon as they were silent for a moment. The coral stone began to flow beneath their bodies. The island garden shimmered in all its color and glory. Peace descended. Harry's body trembled once, and relaxed. He closed his eyes and lay down on his side, not caring about the pebbles and the dirt as his head touched the ground. His body became lighter, lighter, and then he broke free. Ribbed, purple tunnels to infinity. Gentle, rushing music. Past giant wheels of time and space, into pinpoints of black to new lands. A river the color of slate, soundless, fluid, but not moving. A strange city up ahead. A piercing beam of light from the city hunts for him, finds him standing in the river, blinding him. He settles back into his body. He opens his eyes.

Neeta and Dale were gone. How could they leave him? Harry remembered the bottle and the stone he had found earlier. Where did he leave them? He got to his feet, his heart pumping him into action again. He jumped up-and-down a few times to warm up. He felt so good, so good. And so powerful and graceful! He realized that he needed to be alone for a while.

The bottle and the stone!

Why do I feel such a pull toward them?

Did I leave them at the gumbo-limbo tree? Where the grass sang? Too far to go back! Too far?

Harry looked up at the sky.

Plenty of time!

Time!

TIME!

He flopped back down to the ground. *Time!* Holding his hands to his temples, Harry forgot the advice to relax and to go with the flow of things. He tried to wrestle down the concept of time. It slipped away.

Leary says if you're trained in religion or philosophy you can see what is right or wrong without thinking.

TIME!

Harry shook his head violently.

Stop! Relax!

"Okay!" Harry relaxed. He pulled his legs up under him and looked around.

Still so beautiful!

Is it permanent? Will I forget this?

It doesn't matter. Nothing matters....

Matter? What is matter?

STOP TRYING TO THINK!

Something was coming toward him, from the direction of the pier. It was a clinking noise — the sound of someone striking a stone against Harry's bottle.

The bottle!

Harry jumped up and peered down the tail. The sound came nearer. Nearer.

The bottle!

Gilli!

Gilli approached him, grinning his toothy grin, tapping Harry's bottle with the stone. He handed the bottle and stone to Harry. His white loincloth was dirty. The rings on his toes had bits of grass and flowers stuffed into them. He looked natural. He looked right. Harry closed his hands around the bottle and the stone, mouth hanging open in wonder. Gilli put an arm around him and hugged him.

"Did you know — these were mine?"

"I knew they were somebody's!"

"Somebody!" They both laughed.

"They had been placed on the ground — reverently," Gilli said.

Harry nodded. "Yah. Yes."

They stood there, grinning at each other.

"Brother," Harry said finally.

"Brother!"

Harry wondered where the others were and what they were doing. But at the same time, it didn't matter what they were doing. It was a beautiful way of thinking about the others, and the detachment was new to Harry.

"They're where we hid the water."

Harry nodded, and grinned even more. "Telepathy."

"From here," Gilli said, pointing to his head, "to here," pointing up at the heavens, "back to here." Pointing to Harry's head. "Cosmic feedback."

Silence....

"Where is the Valley of the Morning Glories?"

"Let's go look for it," Gilli said. "You need water first?"

Harry thought about the water and was surprised. "No!"

They stood there, immobilized by the moment.

"Do you know where the Valley of the Morning Glories is?"

Gilli grinned. "In your head."

"Yeah, but..."

"It's somewhere here," he laughed.

Here! Here! Here!

"Paradise is always only a veil away," Gilli added. "Look. Look at this island now. You've been here before but today it is Paradise."

"Yeah...."

Faylie.

She exists, but where?

"What would you do with them if you found them?"

"Them?"

Comet....

Are they actually real? Nearby? Now?

"Real!" Harry snorted. "Reality! Oh shit!"

"What would you do? With both of them, "Gilli insisted.

Harry grinned. "I would... I would fall in love with them!" It was true.

"There's a better chance we can find the water," Gilli said.

"Okay."

They were walking down the trail toward the pier now.

"I dissolved into a morning glory flower."

Gilli nodded, always grinning.

"Once I lay down and I died. While I was dying, the grass around me — it was springing up all around — the soil was thin — the grass needed my body. I was dying and the grass was singing. It was so beautiful!"

Gilli nodded.

Harry put the stone next to his ear and rubbed it with his thumb. "I can still hear it. The tension in the stone. The magnetism of the atoms. It's all electric, not material. We are all electric. I can hear the tension in the glass, too." Harry struck the bottle with the stone. It was a beautiful sound. He began to beat on the bottle. **kling kling kling kling kling kling kling kling...** The ringing of the glass brought back The Feeling. The Peace. He forgot where he was, where he was going, what day it was, what time it was, and who he was. **kling kling kling kling kling kling kling kling...** "I forgot who I was," Harry said finally.

"Do you remember now?"

"Yeah! Sure! Ah...."

"Who are you?"

"I'm, ah, Harry Schaffner, and, um...."

"Who is Harry Schaffner?"

"He's ahhh...."

"Harry! Gilli!" Neeta ran up to them and gave Gilli a big hug. "I was coming to look for you guys!"

The hippies were all sitting around the abandoned caretaker's shack. They had the water can out. They were all there except Dale. Gilli and Harry drank from an empty Busch-Bavarian beer can they were using for a cup.

"Dale's at the pier, checking out the boat. It's near low tide."

Milky was sprawled out on her back in the dirt, her pearly-white tits nursing the sky, her legs spread open and her clit hanging out. Harry wondered about people walking up the trail from the pier and seeing Milky like that. He grinned like Gilli. All the hippies were like that, all hanging out, not giving a care. It was right, Harry thought. They were right. He wondered about Dale, alone at the pier, naked to the scrutiny of the other boaters or to the Florida Marine Patrol.

"Gilli's a doctor — they won't hassle us," Clyde said. "They know him."

Harry nodded. Clyde had known what was on his mind.

Clyde let out a long, rappy fart.

Why is farting wrong?

It's the way our machines were designed.

Milky stretched and stood up. "Far out! Wow! Here we are again!"

Harry looked at her. Again, he had forgotten where he was or what they were all doing.

"Who wants to go with me" Milky said. "Look for that house in there." She pointed in the direction of the pier. "Gilli? You said it's in there!"

Gilli did not answer. He and Pete and Kit were all sprawled out on the ground around Neeta, holding hands, eyes closed. Pete looked so serene. Clyde had disappeared.

"Harry?"

Harry nodded. "But the only house I know of is on the gulf side. Your feet. Are you going barefoot?"

Milky kissed him. Her fat tits against Harry's arm sent a tactile dream charging through his head. But it wasn't desire — it was just so good. He watched Milky pull on a pair of army boots.

Naked in army boots!

Harry flashed on a scene at the boatyard, his job there, his old life. What would his new life be? Would it be permanent?

"Come on," Milky said. Let's go see Dale. We need a guy with a gun sometimes, but some of us reject that." She started trucking down the trail.

She doesn't sound high.

Did I bring a gun?

We came in Dale's boat....

It's in the first-aid kit.

The pier was not far away, and Harry steeled himself for the rednecks that were certain to be there on a weekend.

Weekend! Weekend!

What a weird custom!

CUSTOM!

Customs suck! We're all robots!

I am, anyway....

Milky stopped. There was a leaf sticking to her big ass. "In here," she said. "Gilli said if we crawl in here we'll find it."

"It!"

"Funny. Yeah.... Pretty heavy shit we dropped, but it comes and goes now. It's wearing off. You down? Be careful. It'll come back when you least expect."

"You be careful then, too."

Harry squatted and peered into the jungle where Milky was pointing. "Crawl is right! I can't believe there's a house in there..." He was about to ask Milky if he should go first, when she dropped to allfours and started in. He followed right behind. "You get all the spiderwebs on your face," he laughed.

A chick you can have fun with, like a guy!

The tunnel through the bushes and thorns was hard going.

"It's good to get scratched and bloody," Milky said, breathing hard. "It's good karma. Sets up defense mechanisms in your bloodstream."

"Oh? Yeah?"

What a pink crack! Rashy looking. Will I get laid?

She's probably been laid five times today already.

Tomorrow's Sunday!

Sunday!

The tunnel opened up above them and Milky and Harry stood and looked around. Milky was brushing webs away from her face and tits. Harry's penis began to unravel at the thought of her heavy tits dangling all over him — and Milky saw it. They were both breathing fast from all the crawling and stooping.

"Take off your jeans," Milky said. "It's groovy, tripping in the woods, free and naked."

"I was doing that before, when I was alone and I was first getting off. But I saw a couple on the trail so I put my pants back on and..."

"Whatever," Milky said, sounding disgusted. "Fuck the rednecks!" She took off, hunting her way through the grown-over path. Harry let her go and unlaced his boots and pulled off his jeans. He folded them carefully, placing them in the middle of the path so he could find them again. They were near the bay — that he was sure of. He could smell it, and see it in the sky. And all around, the crabs were click-clacking in their holes. He took a deep breath of the fragrant atmosphere, and felt the weight of his balls with his left hand, lifting them and dropping them. His penis stirred and Harry pulled on it once to gauge the effect of LSD on it. He was horny again but The Feeling was coming back to him, too.

Alone again! Peace again! Far out!

He stretched on his tiptoes and reached for the sky.

I'm an Indian. A hunter. Stalking game!

Stalking pussy!

Harry felt something different.

A Presence!

What?

YOUR GOD IS HERE

A breath of wind stirred the bushes and blew over his naked skin and caressed his genitals. "Follow me," he said aloud to The Presence, and set out after Milky, and found the house he did not believe was there.

"Milky?"

No answer. The old, falling-down frame building, slowly feeding the jungle with its rot, was straight out of a storybook. At one time it must have been a dream house for someone. Little walkways led off in all directions, deep into the forest. The walkways were bordered with bricks and were hedged with tropical plants and bushes of all descriptions. The flowers of the plants perfumed the air.

"Milky?"

The fairyland quality of this place weakened Harry physically but flooded his brain with wonder.

Am I hallucinating?

Is this possible? In real life?

"Real life!" Harry shouted out loud. "Real life!"

REAL! What is that now?

He climbed up onto the front porch, which had been screened in at one time. He felt the rough-hewn door frame with his fingertips, and saw the builder there working as he must have worked so many years before, when the island was virgin country to a few Florida farmers.

When the man who built this was real.

I'm hallucinating it better than it is.

No. The pathways are real. The blue roof, all the tropical plants....

They were imported by somebody. Somebody with a dream. Somebody who loved the island.

The porch groaned under his feet. Already, many of the rotten planks had tropical storm damage or been kicked in by previous visitors.

In the kitchen, Harry ran his hands over the counter, which had been covered at one time with Linoleum. A small hand-pump was fastened to a pipe in the middle of the right-hand counter, which sloped a little so the water from the pump could spill down into the sink. To the left of the sink was an old-fashioned drain board and dish-rack.

Over the sink, and looking out over the pathways and garden, were two small sets of French windows. Almost all of the glass had been smashed out, and bits of glass littered the sink and the floor around it. The empty window frames were opened out and hung there, crooked, their weight having pulled the hinges out of the rotten framing. Harry turned, and his feet crunched in the broken glass. Looking down, he shocked himself with his naked body culminating in his hiking boots, cock dangling out, legs more hairy looking than he remembered them to be. He was coming down from the acid trip and was more aware of his nakedness, aware of where he was, what day it was, and who he was with. But who **he** was had changed. He wasn't sure how much he had changed, but he had changed.

I'm changed," he said, nodding his head, and standing there all alone in the middle of the wrecked kitchen.

I am never going to forget this day. Impossible.

This day! It is still the same day! The same day!

Tears rolled down his cheeks.

Tomorrow is still Sunday!

Still Sunday!

Tomorrow....

He squatted down in the middle of the kitchen and wept until he could no longer weep. When he got back up, he felt renewed, and he wiped the tears away with the palms of his hands. He wandered carefully into a room off to the side.

A small bed-frame stood in one corner — a full-length narrow cot. A dresser lay down on its side against another wall, all of the drawers pulled out and smashed. A human turd, dried and curled, lay in one of the drawers, framed in shit-stained Kleenex. Mouse-turds carpeted everything. A broken mirror lay under the cot-frame.

Vandals....

Too many idiots can afford boats.

There was no closet, but a row of shelves ran up one narrow wall. The shelves were empty, but the top shelf was out of reach and partly out of sight. Harry pulled a dresser drawer over to make a step. He ran his hand along the top shelf. The dirt, grit, and the mouse shit rolling under his fingers made him shiver. He felt a little piece of something and brought it down for inspection. It was a tiny piece of white rubber — the broken half of a little wheel, a little rubber tire for a child's toy automobile. Harry turned the fragment around in his fingers, an exciting signal of recognition opening in his memory. "A Tootsie-Toy wheel!" He stepped down and rolled the tiny object around with his fingers. Movies of the toys he owned as a little boy played on his screen.

The yellow dairy truck with two trailers!

The hole in the little half-tire was streaked with rust where the axle-pin had held it on.

Aunt Wilma gave me that set! I was so happy when I opened the package. Dad spanked me because I wouldn't say thank you. For a whole week he put it on a shelf and wouldn't even let me look at it. And then he...

What's little Perry doing now? What's little Janey doing? They can't play out of the yard. They can't use their bikes. All the new neighbors....

Some of those negroes hate us so much we can't take a chance.

Perry — I still never have time for him.

He always wants to see animals — go to the zoo — go to Lion Country Safari.

Pretty soon he'll be big. Big like me.

Harry placed the broken Tootsie-Toy wheel back where he found it, then decided to keep it. He wondered how much warning the little boy who lived in this room had before they moved. Or little girl.

Harry had to piss. He looked around and found a back way out. Here the steps down had completely rotted through and he had to jump about four feet. **Plop!** The short distance down from the back door to the ground surprised him because he had seemed to be airborne for a long time. He remembered he was tripping.

"Milky?"

His urine splattered golden afternoon sun drops over the unprotesting weeds behind the house. How good it felt to piss naked in the woods!

Under the weeds he spotted a rusted-out toy dump truck.

"Milky!"

Milky.... Why am I calling Milky!

One of the quaint, gravel-covered bordered paths led right from where Harry was standing to the side of the house and around toward the bay. The Peace began to descend upon him again, and he made his exploration of the path slowly and carefully, so as not to disturb the feeling. He made the curve toward the bay and saw that the path disappeared straight into the jungle. In a moment, he was back to stooping and crawling. As overgrown as it was, it was easy to see that at one time this had been a stately walkway to somewhere. Varieties of cactus were growing all along the borders, and huge Poinciana trees arched their limbs overhead. Harry paused to rest, sitting on one of the coral rocks which formed the border.

I can smell the bay!

He heard voices in the distance, and a child yelling.

The pier! I must be near the pier!

Harry got up and moved forward in a crouch, being careful not to make any sounds. He knew he was near people and he wanted to scout them, observe them without being seen. The prospect was exciting. Better than watching movies. Testing survival techniques. Moving about in the jungle inches from your enemies.

Enemies....

Harry sighed. *Why do I think enemies?* He caught a glimpse of the waters of the bay, glimmering through the leaves up ahead, and a snatch of white flesh.

Milky!

Milky was stretched out on her belly at the end of the path which ran right into the water. She was looking in the direction of the pier but turned for a moment when she sensed Harry's approach. She held a finger to her lips and turned back to watch. The sight of her big white ass reminded Harry of his big toe sticking up Fluffo's hole when he kicked Annie's cat out the front door back home.

Home!

Harry crawled up beside Milky and lay down in the dirt with her. He kissed her shoulder and she kissed him back on the mouth, then pointed toward the pier. It was hard to see the pier because of the mangroves growing out into the water.

He whispered: "They spot you?"

"No. Dale is there alone. I can't tell if they're hassling him or not."

Harry tried to position himself so he could see through the mangroves, but he wanted to see the whole bay, too. The twin red-and-white smoke-stacks of the Turkey Point electric power generating plant were a shock. Miles across the bay on the mainland, Miami was running full blast. The barely-visible smokestacks shimmered on the horizon in the afternoon sunlight, the air swept clean by the easterly breezes blowing toward Miami from the sea. "I forgot where we were," Harry whispered.

"Crawl up a little farther so you can see the pier."

Harry crawled up. His elbows and forearms were in the water now. A tiny fish about an inch long darted out of its home in an old beer can, scouted around Harry's fingers, and scampered back into the can. The fish was colored the most brilliant two-tone yellow and purple Harry had ever seen.

"We're so close!" Harry wiggled around so he could see everything at the pier.

"Shhhhh."

There were three boats. The tide was low, very low, and Dale was in the water, hauling a line from the gunwales of his own boat to an outer piling. Harry remembered that Dale's boat was an inboard, and that the prop could be stuck in the sand and coral bottom. It was harder to see the other two boats because they were closer in, but also alongside the pier. They were large outboards. A baby was on board one of them, and it was crying. Harry heard a slapping sound. Dale looked up from his work. He looked tough with his wild hair and trim body. He was working in his jeans, and his jeans were soaked and clinging. The baby was crying louder. Two men laughed. Harry could see one of them. He was wearing plaid swimming trunks and a Day-Glo red hunting cap. Big pot-belly. The other man was the one Harry had seen earlier on the trail. There was a lot of milling around, clunking and bumping — sounds which the water carried so beautifully — and talking. An older woman with a sailor hat on was casting from the end of the pier. The plug splashed in the water right next to Dale. "Oooops! I almost caught that man there!"

"Aww, shoot! Try again!" The strangers laughed.

The baby stopped crying. A beer can sailed over Dale's boat and into the water, too light for Milky and Harry to hear it land. Then a white rag or a ball of paper went flying after it. A diaper! Harry raised himself up to get a better look.

"Harry, they'll see you."

"They should see us," Harry whispered. "They think Dale's alone."

The half-submerged diaper and the beer can began to float away from Dale's boat, out to sea. Dale was standing there in the water now, hands on his hips, glaring at the people. The two men were both on the pier. The younger one still had a beer in his hand. He stood there like a rooster, hip thrust out to one side, one hand on his hip, the other hand clutching his beer in front of his chest, posturing. There was a little boy, too. He came running out onto the pier holding a live crab by the leg. "Got another one!"

"Land crab! Ohhh, look at the land crab!"

More laughing.

Someone turned on a radio. The sound of the radio blared across the water, advertising Clearasil acne pads and ointment for pimples. The boy must have been dangling the crab in front of the baby, which Harry could not see.

"Leave your sister alone now. Leave her alone."

"She likes it dad. She likes it."

"Leave her alone, boy, with that thing!"

The boy strode disgustedly out to the end of the pier. Winding up like a baseball pitcher, he slung the crab as hard as he could out into the bay. The crab separated into two pieces. "Look! Look! His claw ripped off!"

"Ahhh — look at that!"

"You see that, Alice? Alice? Awww fuck you!"

Someone was fiddling with the dial on the radio.

"No game today — remember?"

"Pa — I'm tryin' to get some music!"

The radio played "Night Train".

"Leave that on," one of the women said.

Harry slumped down. *Night Train!* His memory flooded in. Years ago, when he was in the army, every overseas bar had a band. After getting drunk, Harry would always try to get them to play Night Train.

Another beer can sailed over Dale's boat and landed softly in the water. A rush of adrenalin zapped Harry's bloodstream. He crawled back and got to his feet. "Time to stop the bullshit!"

Milky jumped up after him. "Wait! Harry, no! Wait!" Harry was running and stooping and clawing his way back down the path, with Milky hot behind him.

"Harry — you're tripping! You're tripping!"

"I came down!"

"It comes and goes! You can still trip out! Harry!"

"Not like before!

"It can get heavy! Harry! You don't know it yet! You can't judge! You don't know what's happening. Out there. In your condition!"

"**Really** happening?" Harry whipped around and faced her, forcing Milky to smack into him, shocking him with her opulent flesh. They were both breathing hard. "Milky. Milky, ha, listen! Today — for the first time — for the first time — I can see — what is really — actually happening!"

Milky's eyes looked sad.

"It's true, isn't it? See? And what about Dale?"

"Dale knows how to handle himself."

"So do I, and without my fucking gun."

Milky said, "I hope they heard that!"

Harry tried to concentrate and to get his shit together in the face of Milky's hot tits. "Okay — but — what if Dale needs help and the others don't know he's here. Shit. Ohhh!" Harry was still breathing hard and ready to kick ass. He turned away, but walked this time, toward the house and the trail which had brought them there.

"None of you rednecks can handle shit like Dale can!"

zap!

Harry had forgotten that he wasn't one of the hippies, and that he was considered a redneck. He stopped at the opening in the bushes where they would have to get down again and crawl. He turned to get one last look at the beautiful lost dream house.

Milky touched his arm. "It's true," she said.

"Yeah — yeah — maybe."

"All you oil-heads want to do is own things and defend things and fight over things."

"Yeah..."

Milky smiled. Harry had not seen the real woman in her before. Or her distinctive personality, her intelligence. He grinned, and was surprised to feel a trickle of spit running down the corner of his mouth. Milky's hand got to it before his own did, and she wiped it away. "See? If you were in complete control now, you wouldn't be drooling. It's the acid," she said gently. "The acid." She had to look up to him when she talked because she was so much shorter.

One of her nipples grazed his stomach.

"Huh!" Harry said, looking into her eyes. He had never liked short, heavy girls, and he was now aware of how many personalities he had passed over because of the way their bodies were constructed.

"Huh!" he repeated, shaking his head in bewilderment. He wanted to hold her hand. The Peace was falling over him again. Harry had been alone through it all — all day. A long, long, long day. Plus there was so much more to come. The boat was grounded with the low tide and it would be long dark before they would be able to get off. Still looking into Milky's spirit through her eyes... "Huh!"

"What?" she said gently.

"I never really saw you before."

Milky nodded, also looking through his eyes into his spirit. His brain. One step more and she was holding him and he was holding her, trembling with the richness of the contact. But he did not dissolve into her. He was himself. And his penis was coming to life. "I used to wonder if — ohhhh..."

"What?"

"I forgot what I wanted to say..."

"Oh, bullshit, Harry!" Milky pulled away and laughed. She headed back toward the house. "Come on! Come on!"

He followed her up onto the sagging porch and into a room he hadn't explored earlier. There was a mattress on the floor and Milky sprawled right down on it and pulled off her boots. "Boots off, Harry!" she laughed.

Harry no sooner had the last sock off when Milky pulled his face into her tits and mashed him over onto his back. Sandwiched between Milky's rubbery, warm, motherly body and the gritty mattress, Harry lost all initiative and in a moment, Milky was lowering her wet cunt over him and they were balling. Balling, balling, balling — Harry's head rolling back and forth, eyes wide open in amazement — balling, balling, balling — never had he experienced such abandonment, such feeling in his nerves, such involvement in the pure act of fucking. "Cum in me, Harry! Cum cum cum in me, Harry! Cum cum cum..."

And Harry came. He came forever — pumping cum in endless throbs — thundering gobs of cum visible in his head — the vision of her face on his screen flashing and arcing and dissolving as he came — and suddenly Milky's head detached itself from her body and smiled down upon him from the sky which now was showing clean through the ceiling of the room, her head floating away up into Heaven.

And then Milky's body disappeared, the room disappeared, and Harry disappeared.

They found themselves back on the mattress on the littered floor on the beautiful planet God had made for them, the fragrance of His Work wafting in through the busted-out windows of the house, the Beauty of Nature bending and swaying in the breeze.

I was wrong....

There must be a creator.

Milky lay beside him. They held each other for awhile, Harry with his head on Milky's breast.

"I've been alone all day."

"You have, haven't you."

"I got separated before I got off."

"Wow, Harry."

"I didn't know I needed someone later. It's so good to be with you."

"Oh, yes Harry. You're beautiful."

"I had a beautiful trip by myself."

"It's good that you were alone. You were lucky."

"Before today, I thought my mind was made up about everything. I thought I knew everything I needed to know." Harry repositioned himself against Milky's flesh, the banquet of her body. "Your body feels good."

"You feel good against me."

"When I came, your head came off and floated straight up to Heaven..." Harry rubbed his nose in Milky's wonderful chest. Her nipples were wide and rubbery.

"Clyde said that."

"What."

"My head came off."

"Oh.... Yeah?"

"Not today."

"Oh. Today! Wow..."

"I laid Pete before, though."

"Yeah?" Harry flashed Pete on his movie screen. It didn't matter somehow.

Milky put her hand on Harry's penis, which was soft and now sliding around. Harry propped his head up and looked at the weird, slimy organ.

What a trip God had with that.

"Lay back," Milky said.

Harry leaned back a little.

Milky kissed the head of his penis. She licked it clean as it grew. His penis grew straight up in the air, swelling, throbbing, hunting.

"Lay back."

Harry obeyed and laid back, hands under his head. He closed his eyes.

Again! Oh dear God! Again! Oh God!

"Dream."

"I am dreaming."

Milky's warm lips slid slowly down Harry's cock. She began to suck. She sucked and licked and swallowed and sucked until there was no more man there — no more Harry, no more world, no more past, no more future. There was only Harry's dream, and the dream was real.

CHAPTER 14
Family

Harry dropped Milky off on Dixie Highway near the Cutler Ridge Shopping Center, and watched her run across to the other side during the red light. Tits flying under her T-shirt — lit up and onstage before the rows of headlights — drivers bent over their wheels with poisonous engines rumbling for the green light. It was Saturday night in The Magic City. The light turned green and Harry was slow to react. His pickup moved out but shiny passenger cars began burning rubber to get around him. Harry was accelerating slowly as he looked from side to side in amazement. Looking into the cars at the duded-up young people inside.

What's all the competition? What's the hurry?

Up ahead there had been an accident, and a patrol car was flashing intense, blue pulses of light.

Harry was fully aware that he had changed. He had seen so much.

Will it be permanent? Am I burned out?

He smiled, and passed a few of the cars which had slowed down to rubber-neck the accident scene. He felt good and he felt right. Another red light came up. He caught some plastic people in the car beside him looking up at hm. He smiled and they quickly looked away. He was streaked with dirt and driving barefoot, but they couldn't have seen that. His hair was a tangled mess. Good! He was a human animal and it felt right. He was returning from an incredibly long expedition into inner space, but the city seemed no longer his home. The light turned green.

This place is not right, not right.

More cars zoomed around him.

Old pickup goin' down the road.

Some dumb redneck?

Fuck 'em!

Straight people would have very little to show for their way of life to Harry now. Endless circle of expressway entrance ramp, then the far-out ribbon of smooth-cruising freeway! Harry adjusted his ass and stepped it up to fifty. *hisssss zoooom hiss* Three more shiny cars with the windows rolled up and the door buttons pushed down hurtled around him. Then an old, Porsche sailed by, top down, the driver's hair whipping and snapping in the wind.

Narrow, low windshield.... A Porsche SPEEDSTER!

The one I always wanted!

Harry probed his feelings. The old need was gone — simply not there — gone! He tested himself. A rich man flags him over in his mind. The man says: "Look, I don't need this here Porsche and you've always wanted the Speedster model — they don't make them anymore — but I had this one rebuilt like new. Ready to race." Harry shook his head. A car like that wouldn't help much now.

Hey, man! Harry's got a Speedster!

Hey, man, look at Harry's new wheels!

Big deal. Harry adjusted his ass again to get more comfortable. The traffic on the expressway had thinned out. He could cruise in peace. And in peace was the only way he could be described at this moment.

The truck was humming, beautiful and the tire treads sang.

I'm glad I'm a mechanic. Thank you for letting me learn machines.

I KNEW ABOUT MACHINES BEFORE THE EARTH WAS CREATED

I HIDE IN THE COCKPITS OF THE SPACE MACHINES THAT CRUISE GALAXIES

Our machines are poisoning the planet.

YOU ARE STILL LEARNING

I won't live long enough to...

BUILD A MACHINE THAT WILL HARNESS THE WIND AND THE SUN AND I WILL RIDE WITH YOU

Harry stepped on the gas and the truck shot up to sixty, tires singing.

I'll do it! I'll do it!

Back when they all were returning from the island only an hour before, in the middle of the night, sky bursting with stars, planets and galaxies, Dale's boat plowed toward Gould's Canal and "home". Miami. The faithful diesel doing its job easily. **donk donk donk donk donk donk donk donk ...** All the heads, all the brothers and sisters, standing at the gunwales and leaning into the wind and spray. Naked torsos, bodies straight and alive, faces beaming, hair wild and free. God's children. God's toys on Planet Earth. The human earth-cams of the angels.

Suddenly:

AIRPORT

Left Lane

EXIT ONLY

A chill ran up Harry's spine and goose bumps raised on his arms. He had been listening to a voice somewhere in his own brain, and when he asked it questions, it answered. Was that voice always there? Was it God?

REMEMBER WHEN YOU WERE A LITTLE BOY?

Harry's body shivered.

WE USED TO TALK THEN

Yeah, yeah...

Harry negotiated the ramp onto the Airport Expressway. He was almost home, and he slowed down to enjoy what was left of the trip.

Are you my subconscious?

YES — BUT...

My spirit?

I AM YOU

Then why do we have to talk? Sounds like two of us...

THIS AFTERNOON ON THE ISLAND THERE WERE TIMES WHEN WE WERE TOGETHER AND YOU TWO DISOLVED

This afternoon....

Seems like yesterday. Like two days.

TWELFTH AVE

Right Lane

EXIT ONLY

Almost home...

HOME....

Look at all these houses! One right after another. Rows and rows of them.

Whites, Cubans, Haitians - and then my place. My house. It's so strange, so strange....

Where is my real home?

Where do I come from? How will I ever get back?

Will I ever get back home again?

Harry pulled up to his gate, which was chained up, and left the headlights on and the motor running while he unlocked it. He looked fondly and with fresh eyes at his whole scene, shaking his head with wonder at what trip he was on in "real life": the eight-foot-high barricade he had built in the middle of the yard so he could drive the truck behind it and load up his family in case there was another riot. Or shoot from behind it, or... And the variety of big , tropical palms he and Annie had planted in the yard to make it look like a South Seas paradise. The huge hulk of his power boat looming in the shadows beside the house. The children's swing seat hanging quietly from a limb of the giant poinciana tree. His outdoor workbench, Harry's favorite spot, waiting silently under another limb of the patient poinciana.

Harry swung one half of the gate into the yard, then the other. The gates squeaked. Beercan came dashing around from behind and jumped up on Harry at the sidewalk. Harry wrestled his dog down to the ground. "Took you long enough!" Beercan and Harry rolled around in front of the headlights of the truck. "Ha ha you hairball. What you get outta that, huh? You furry creature! Yuk! You drool!"

"Awww right!" one of the two black men said as they walked around the pickup blocking the sidewalk.

Harry smiled and shoved his dog away. There was the truck to pull in — yes — and he had to take a piss.

Awww right!

Cool black dudes.

New neighbors?

After parking the truck, Harry paused momentarily in the jungle of his front yard. A car hissed by down the street, lights flickering through the trees and bushes. An empty can clattered out onto the road farther down.

Beercan stood beside him, tail wagging.

Beercan, you can think.

You're not just all instinct.

House looks weird just standing there.

My house....

Once inside, he looked in on Annie first. He could barely make her out in the darkness, but he could hear her breathing. Her covers were pulled up and she was hugging her pillow.

Annie, Annie....

You're a real person — like me — you have dreams, too.

What happened to your dreams, Annie?

What have I been doing to you?

He looked in on Janey. Janey was completely hidden under her blankets, and her pillow was on the floor. Harry picked up her pillow, brushed it off, and placed it gently beside her head.

Janey, Janey, who are you? Who are you?

I don't know you at all.

I never took the time to know you.

Harry moved quietly through the kitchen and down the hall to Perry's room. "This is too much," he whispered to himself as he sneaked open Perry's door.

Too much! Everything is so clear in my head!

I've been living like a zombie!

What've I been doing all this time!

He could hear little Perry's wheezy breathing before he could see him, the skinny little boy all sprawled out on his back, his mouth hanging open like a dead man. Perry's pillows were propping up his head but his blankets were lying on the floor in a heap, and Harry carefully covered his boy.

Poor little guy....

Your little spirit — your little spirit computer got a crummy deal, didn't it. All locked up in such a fragile little body, always getting sick, getting sick on your birthday so you couldn't even open your presents, getting sick when you're out playing, lying awake so many nights sitting up just to get enough air to stay alive....

Harry leaned over, touched Perry's hair, and kissed him. He knew now how much he loved that little boy, and how sad a burden that love might be from now on.

He wanted to stay with Perry longer but the urge to piss was overwhelming.

The bathroom light became bright slowly, then lit up upon stark, white, porcelain brilliance. The machinery of the bathroom and Harry's new face in the mirror over the sink was a shock. Flesh and blood for sure. Skin and bone and gristle was what he had been made of all this time but hadn't realized to what extent. His eyes were wild and free as he looked at himself without prejudice for the first time. And as dirty, sunburned, wind-burned, and uncombed as he looked, Harry also saw himself with new potential. It was scary. He had become the brave, adventurous, free spirit he had always imagined himself to be after so many years of bullshit, pretense, and wishful thinking. Or did he? He stepped back from the mirror a little to see if the robot-like flesh-and-blood quality he now felt for the rest of his body — his vehicle through this life — was as pronounced. He shuddered. Getting close again, he looked into his eyes and spoke quietly to his image in the mirror. "You are free now. As free as you can be in this body. See you later. Got to piss."

Harry decided to pee sitting down so he could do it without making a lot of noise. Sitting there naked on the cold seat in the middle of the equipment of the bathroom, he promised himself to piss outside whenever he could from now on. He pissed for a long time. The toilet paper roll was empty. Harry stood up, cranked the flush lever, and wiped his dick off on the corner of Annie's towel while his urine swirled down the drain along with gallons of fresh water, the drain often sluggish, .

He was looking at himself in the mirror again.

So this is you. Or me. Or whatever.

*So this is why hippies say **whatever** all the time!*

SO WHAT ARE YOU GOING TO DO WITH YOUR LIFE NOW?

What am I going to do?

Oh wow, it's still the weekend!

*All this time has passed, all this stuff has happened, and tomorrow is still Sunday? **Sunday!***

We'll all be home together.

We could be so happy together! Little Perry — you want to talk, or show me something, I'll listen to you — I'll listen to you! And Janey....

Little Janey! And Annie!

Annie!

CHAPTER 15
Sunday

"Sunday," Harry mumbled. "Beautiful Sunday." He watched Annie pull the comics out of the newspaper. "When the kids get up, they'll flush the toilet. It only works if there's a long interval in between. I saw the note you put on it."

"They can go in the bushes." Annie stopped reading and looked at Harry, all sprawled out on his side of the bed. "You want another pillow?"

"Naw. I don't think I'll be able to read, anyway."

"Harry? What was it like?"

"Ohhh...." Harry shook his head and shrugged.

"Not much, huh?"

"There aren't any words to describe it!"

"Oh, Harry...."

"Because it's new and people didn't do LSD in the old days, there aren't any words in the language."

Milky's head blasting off her shoulders when I came. Where did it go? What did her neck look like?

"You just don't want to talk about it."

I don't remember seeing her neck.... Then her head was back and her face was in my face....

Harry looked at Annie. "Was grass different for you than what you imagined?"

"Well, yes, but...."

"LSD is indescribable. Period."

"Don't do it again today, Harry, okay? I don't want you to get hooked."

"Today? Oh, Annie, I couldn't do it again today. I'd have to rest up and think about it a long time before I could do it again. It takes so long — so long. One thing, I know today is Sunday, right? But I can't picture today as Sunday because I've been through so much, so much, in the last few days, I mean since yesterday afternoon when we dropped the acid, that I still can't picture today being Sunday. I believe it, but.... Harry stared straight ahead as he talked to her, the realization coming to him that he still might not be back to normal.

What is normal?

Annie slid over next to him and laid her head on his shoulder. "Tell me about it."

"Ha! Oh, Annie — I'm so happy and so confused right now."

"Want me to leave you alone for awhile? Should I get up and wake the kids and make breakfast?"

Harry took her hand and looked at her. "No. Well, no. I.... I need to share what happened to me — and still — I don't think I can. I..."

"It's okay, Harry."

"All this time — the last couple years — I thought that I — my personality — was, uhhh, cast. Like I knew who I was and what I wanted. But now...."

"Like what?"

Harry shook his head again. "I'm so happy! I feel so good! But I can't describe...."

"I was awake when you came home but I pretended I was asleep because, well, I was worried. I didn't know what you would be like after LSD. I read about married people getting divorces after doing LSD because one did LSD and the other didn't, and they saw things differently after that.

"Oh, Annie..."

"Well?"

"I guess it could happen."

"Look me in the eye."

"Annie...."

"See?"

Harry looked Annie in the eye and smiled. "Everything's going to be all right. From now on. Like decisions. I was always hassling myself about how to make the right decisions, you know, and yesterday I saw

— so clearly — that decisions just come, if you let them. You don't have to make them ahead of time and then worry about whether you should change your mind later. It all works out by itself."

"I don't agree with you."

"You haven't seen it yet."

"Seen what, Harry?"

"You haven't tripped."

Annie looked away. "Harry, if you think that you can use psychology on me to get me to trip, you're wasting your time."

"How can you say that when you just said you were wrong about grass. Marijuana."

"Harry! Don't be stupid!"

"Oh, Annie. It's too bad you feel that way. Too bad. Don't let it spoil our Sunday, okay?"

"Daddy?" Little Perry was standing in the doorway in his pajamas.

"Hi, boy! How're you feeling this morning?" Harry looked at him. "Come here. I want a hug!"

"Daddy? The kids next door. They're hanging their dog."

"Chomper?"

"No. Chomper's too big. They're hanging that little puppy they got last week."

Annie jumped out of bed. The hem of her nightie was stuck up her ass, and Perry covered his mouth when he saw it.

"Annie. Don't get into it. Don't get all pissed."

"You! You!" She turned on him. "You just stay there in bed while I run out and handle it!"

Harry sighed and sat up on the edge of the bed.

"Don't exhaust yourself, Harry. I know how tired you must be after those hippie girls you were with Saturday!" Annie and Beercan went tearing out the back door.

"Hippie girls, oh, Annie...."

Harry pictured the tall, cool girls who had come with Clyde the morning before.

Don't remember seeing them on the boat, though....

Harry ambled to the dining room to watch what Annie was

going to do. Janey was already at the window.

"They're trying to get the rope around his neck again," Janey reported. "It keeps coming off."

"Too dumb to tie a good knot!" Perry explained.

Harry hiked up his pajama pants. "Let me in there."

There were half-dozen or so of the brown thumb-suckers milling around in Ruby's back yard. They were trying to get a noose around their new puppy's neck. Harry watched as Annie came running around the side of the house with the garden hose.

Shit, Annie! You can't keep on hosing down the neighbor's kids! They'll call the cops! "Janey! Run out and shut the water off. I'm going to stop Annie!"

Harry got out there just as Annie's hose dribbled off.

"Dammit, Harry!"

"Annie — Annie — look. It's against the law to..."

"Against the law! Since when do you care what the law says? Huh?"

"Alright, alright. But there's a — uhhh..."

Harry was watching Ruby's back door just as Birdella came out in one of her sexy, Daisy Mae, Dogpatch outfits: short-shorts and a bare-midriff peasant blouse dangling loose over her nut-brown shoulders.

"Harry, you bastard!" Annie bitched.

Birdella's black thighs snaked straight toward Harry at the fence, her body trailing the little droolers. "Mister Harry — you better do somethin' 'bout this old lady 'yourn befoe I has to put a clamp on her."

"Yeah, well..." Harry swallowed. He tried to concentrate on the problem, but his eyes were on the possibilities of the black woman's mouth.

"Those brats of yours were torturing that little puppy!" Annie screamed. "People like you shouldn't be allowed to have pets!"

"Lissen, Honey, I..."

"Don't you honey me! You just keep an eye on those little monsters you've been popping every nine months so you can get a higher welfare check!"

"Dumb honky bitch!" Birdella made a point of pulling down the hem of her tight shorts with her long fingers. "Harry — i'fn wouldn' be for you — you know — I could put her big mouth in jail? You know that?"

"Yeah, yea, maybe. But..."

"But what?"

"I turned the water off, Daddy!" Janey said, running up.

"Turn it back on!" Annie said.

"Annie, shut up!"

Birdella smiled. She tugged at the sleeve of her blouse, which was way down one shoulder. "Now see?" she said to Annie. "I can **talk** to your husband."

Beercan and the puppy were nuzzling each other through the fence.

"I'll bet that's not all you'd like to do with him!"

Oh, perfect! Harry thought.

"Hmmmm. Well, Miss Annie, you must know what he ain't gettin' nuff of."

"Oh, he's getting everything he needs! He's getting everything!" Annie stopped because Birdella was already sauntering away, swinging her chunky ass.

"Dumb nigger!"

Harry grabbed Annie and shook her. "That's enough!"

Annie broke away from him and ran inside. Harry turned to the neighbor kids who were still at the fence. "Don't hurt that cute little puppy of yours, okay? He's too good for that. You take good care of him. Okay?"

"Okay Mister Harry." "Okay." "Okay."

Birdella turned at the back door stoop and gave Harry a little smile and wave. He waved back, and when he got in the house, with Birdella's chocolate body dancing in his brain, Annie was crying. Avoiding her eyes, Harry got into some old jeans he didn't mind messing up, and stalked out to the septic tank to check out the plumbing, hoping that his activities would get breakfast started. The cover on the underground tank was made of concrete, and had an iron ring in the center of it. Harry had to get a pipe and a crowbar to lift the slab off, and when he did he was dismayed to find that the tank was full and was not draining properly. A slimy sea of turds, toilet paper, and foamy scum was covering the inlet pipe from the bathroom. Harry looked around for a stick, and poked it into the pipe just as somebody in the house flushed the commode. With a juicy rumble, a wad of brown scarf shot up into the air and caught Harry in the face before he had a chance to dodge it.

"I want you guys to look at me," Harry said, parading his shit-stained face and chest through the house. Perry and Janey followed him into the kitchen where Annie was laying bacon strips into the frying pan. "Phooey!" Perry said.

"Harry!" Annie said.

"Janey did it," little Perry volunteered. "She was just in there."

"I put a note on the potty," Annie said.

"Guess Janey just spazzed out again," Perry concluded.

"Don't you hit her, Harry! I'm warning you!"

"Hit her?" Harry smiled and tasted shit on his mouth. "Blaaaagh! Gimme a paper towel! I could get sick from this crap. Annie — come on out and hose me off."

"Okay... Janey! Come and watch the bacon!"

"Is Daddy still inside?" Janey was hiding around the corner.

"He won't hurt you!"

Harry sighed and ambled out the back door. It was going to be such a nice Sunday....

"So you were pretending to be asleep when I came in last night, huh?" Harry was wolfing down his bacon, eggs, toast, and grits.

"Well — I was afraid."

"It's okay."

"I was really afraid."

Harry nodded. "When I climbed into the bed did you feel me touch you?"

"Mmmm hmmm."

"You're mumbling, Mommy," little Perry said. "No mumbling!"

"Perry." Janey said disgustedly.

"Janey can't read a simple note that says DON'T FLUSH printed — in capital letters!"

"I had my mouth full of food," Annie explained.

"You explain mumbling to them — that's beautiful," Harry said. "When I was a kid, no talking with a mouthful was allowed ever."

"That sucks," Janey said.

"Janey...."

"Well — all Perry ever does is boss people around!"

"When I slid into bed I really needed to be with someone. To have someone. I'd been through such an experience! But my mind is still free and for some reason — I can't explain it — I must have expected you to have fur or something. Fur on your body like an animal would, and..."

"Fur!" Perry snorted.

"You don't know everything yet," Harry said. "Anyway, Annie, I was so shocked when I came in contact with your skin, your hairless body, that I jumped away."

"Hairless body!" Perry said.

"You're the hairless one!" Harry said, turning on Perry. "You look like a little plucked chicken when you're naked."

Little Perry looked down at his plate. His mouth curled down and tears began to flow.

Harry ruffled Perry's hair. "Aww, come on, guy. I didn't mean that."

"Yes you did!" Perry screamed. He jumped up from the table and ran down the hall to his room, slamming the door behind him.

"And he didn't even finish his breakfast," Annie said.

"He didn't even touch his egg," Janey added, giving Harry her mean-look.

"He's very conscious about his body — being skinny," Annie said. "And he really needs to eat as much as he can."

"Oh!" Harry shoved his chair back. "Alright! I'm an asshole! I'll go get him and beg him to come back." He paused. "Don't look at me like that. I know I was an asshole."

Poor Perry....

Poor Little Perry.

"It's true," Harry said aloud. I know I've been an asshole. And I know Perry's had a hard time."

It took a little doing to get Perry back to the table. When they were together again, Annie was bursting with something she had to tell them.

"While you were in Perry's room — you know — our nigger next door? Well, Ruby..."

"Don't say nigger!"

"I learned that from you. We don't have niggers in Colorado. Well anyway, you know how they just boot all the kids out the back door in the morning in their underwear so they don't piss up the bathroom, and then they pass them sandwiches out through the hole in the screen so they don't mess up the kitchen? Well, while you were in Perry's room..."

"You should see their kitchen, Mommy!" Janey interrupted.

"Yeeeech!" Perry added, his mouth full of fried egg.

"Don't talk with your mouth full, Perry," Janey said.

"Fuck you!"

"Perry!"

"Go on, Annie." Harry was finished, and resting his chin in one hand, watching the neighbor's back yard, looking for the puppy. Hoping to see Ruby.

"Well, Ruby came out there — you should see the clothes she's been wearing lately — and her mother came out and..."

Harry perked up. "What kind of clothes?"

"Expensive clothes. Sexy clothes. Well, her mother..."

"Daddy's always watching her, Mommy, and talking to her over the fence. One day I left my ball outside and..."

"**My** ball, Janey!" Perry shouted, spraying grits.

"Janey..." Harry said, giving her a look.

"May I finish?" Annie said, giving Harry a look.

"So here's Ruby," Janey continued, "hanging up laundry like this..." (Janey got up and turned her back to them and wiggled her ass) "...and Daddy's sneaking up to the fence and he throws the ball and lands it right on her butt!"

"She didn't get mad or anything!" Perry added.

Annie was staring at Harry and shaking her head.

"They threw the ball back-and-forth for awhile but Daddy kept on dropping it and missing it."

"Ruby can catch much better than Daddy can," Perry said.

"May I finish my story now?" Annie said. "Nice going, Harry!"

Harry's ears turned red.

"Oh, forget it. I don't want to tell it anymore."

"Awwwww," they all said.

"Well, when Ruby's mother came out, Ruby said to her in her bullshit, sophisticated, put-on voice: 'Mother? Shall we serve the children outside this morning'"? Annie looked at her family, laughing. Harry nodded his head.

"You don't think that's funny?" Annie said.

"No."

"I think it's funny, Mommy," Janey said.

"Then why aren't you laughing?" Perry said triumphantly.

He bowed to them all, cracking his knuckles and grinning.

"So much hostility," Harry mumbled. "There's so much hostility here. I don't understand it. Well — yeah — I do understand it. Maybe."

"Just so long as you understand why the toilet won't drain."

Harry straightened up. "I fixed it," he grinned.

"Oh good!" Perry said, jumping up and running to the bathroom.

"So soon?"

"Yeah. I was afraid the drain field was full of roots and dirt and shit, but the outlet pipe was just clogged, rusted out or whatever. I have the cover back on already."

"I'm flushing it!" Perry yelled from the bathroom.

The three of them sat on the edge of their seats, waiting.

"It's okay!" Perry shouted. He came back to the table with a truly happy expression on his face.

"He was terrified when the plumbing broke down," Annie said.

"That was the end of the world, huh Perry?" Harry said.

Perry pouted. "Not funny, Daddy."

"Miami might be at the end of the USA," Harry said. "The only big city that still uses septic tanks instead of sewers in old neighborhoods?"

"Harry," Annie said. "Your hair is getting kind of long... You should shave, too. You promised me when you started letting your hair grow you would keep it neat and combed."

"You look like a beaver," Perry grinned.

"Like a hippie," Janey laughed.

Harry cut Janey off with a look. "Would you guys appreciate me if I fixed the washing machine? Would you lay off then?"

Annie smiled. "I'm sorry, Harry. But you should get a trim. Anyway..."

Harry sighed and got up from the table. "I'm letting my hair and my beard grow out," he said sadly. "I've been thinking about it."

"Harry. Soon we won't be able to remember your real face anymore."

"With a beard it will be my real face. Beards are natural for males."

"That's right," Perry said. "Your beard just grows!"

"No, Harry," Annie said.

"Annie — should we go out and shave Beercan's head so we can see what his **real** face looks like?"

"Ha ha — ha ha," Janey said.

"That's a good one," Perry said.

"I've been thinking about it a lot," Harry said, "and shaving and all that other crap is bullshit."

"Pretty soon I'll be old enough to shave!" Perry beamed.

Harry nodded, patted Perry on the head, and went outside to the washing machine.

The sun was higher now, and all the moisture had steamed off the grass, even under the huge poinciana where Harry's workbench was. He pulled the plastic cover off of the little sofa he kept out there and plunked down into it. He was back to feeling peaceful inside, and happy, and he wished now that there were some way he could impart this feeling and this knowledge to the rest of the family. To make it up to them.

Annie came around the side of the house but stopped before Harry noticed her. She was unsure of herself, as always, and had learned to hate it. Harry was what some women called a "hunk", and from the beginning Annie knew that keeping him would be a challenge. When they first met, when she was a tough-ass barmaid and he showed a particular interest in her, she assumed other things about him. The other staff would call him "your redneck who can read" because Harry could be crude but seemed half-way educated. In fact, the other girls were jealous and Annie had determined she would always find a way to keep him, a promise to herself she often regretted.

Annie snapped out of her hesitation and walked up to Harry at the sofa under the tree. She was smiling. "Thank you for fixing it. The machine," she said.

"I got lucky again."

Annie stood there.

"Come on," Harry said, patting the cushion beside him.

Annie sat down and Harry put his arm around her. She frowned, then smiled again. "I always hated this old sofa out here in the middle of the yard."

"It's not the middle of the yard."

"Well, practically. You can see it and that's the point."

"I'm not into points today."

"You never are."

"Hey! Relax! We don't have to argue. It's become a habit."

"A habit you started. Years ago."

"Yeah, yeah.... Annie, we are going to have a nice Sunday."

"Okay. Okay. You're right."

Silence....

"Where are the kids?"

"Um, they're out in back trying to save those baby possums. They have milk in an eye dropper I gave them."

"I promised to look at the possums and I forgot."

"They're nice children, Harry."

"Yeah...."

"I wish you wouldn't go crawling and begging after Ruby when they can see it."

"There you go again."

"Well, they're just children."

"That's not it."

"Did you see anything? Did you hallucinate?"

"Huh? Yesterday? Wow!"

"Wow?"

Yesterday....

Only yesterday!

"The LSD, Harry."

"Seems like I was gone two whole days. Everything I saw, though, was real."

"What did you see?"

"God." Harry hesitated. Well, I saw Planet Earth. Don't laugh. And it seemed created. Like it didn't happen by itself. Like there's a creator, or creators."

"Oh, I always knew that."

"Well, maybe you're smarter than I am. Anyway, while I was tripping I saw that billions of years of evolution couldn't have made everything on this planet from nothing. The universe from nothing. It was so clear in my mind that I didn't even have to think about it. It was there. I'll never be able to forget it."

"That's faith, Harry."

"No, no! I'll never get my faith back. It's knowledge." Harry thought about it. "It's perception, I mean."

"Go with me to church." Annie gave Harry a love squeeze. "Only this time you don't just drop me off. You come in with me. It's only an hour, Harry. Next Sunday. And we can take the kids."

"It's not the church god, Annie. It's not the church god. The real god is something else, something else so far out, so fantastic, so, um, unbelievable actually. Not that petty, feudal king of everything in the

Bible who has tantrums."

"Forget it, Harry. Forget it." Annie got up. "I have to check the machine."

"Check the machine." Harry closed his eyes. He was back in the army. They were flying him overseas in a troop transport and there was still over an hour to go to reach the Azores Islands, where they were to re-fuel, and two of the four engines were out, one on each wing, and the airfield was reporting crosswinds at forty miles per hour. The captain had relayed that information to the troops and crew, and told them all to get ready. A huge, smart-ass black airman, who had given Harry a hard time earlier, was now pressing his hands against his temples and praying out loud, his face chalky looking, drained of blood. Harry remembered shouting to him that if there were a god the engines would be turning, there wouldn't be any fleas, or mosquitoes, or germs, or Air Force planes. Harry smiled, thinking about that, remembering how everyone had immediately turned on him — whites and blacks — hollering at Harry to shut up and start praying. He recalled how low they were when they finally spotted the island with the single runway the size of a Band-Aid and the fire-trucks all deployed down there, the captain telling them that they would have to make it on the first shot and that was it. Harry-the-atheist silently said to God: *If you are there, please save us — don't let me burn alive — in Jesus' name — Amen.* Later, as they were making their way down the boarding ladder, the wind blowing their hats off and tearing at their uniforms, Harry paid his dues and said aloud: "At the last minute, I prayed." The big spade who had been so terrified earlier looked Harry in the eye and said: "Oh, it weren't nothin'. These here planes fly just as good on two engines as four. It weren't nothin'." Just then the man's hat blew off while he was still on the ladder, and Harry watched him scramble for it half-way down the field.

"Harry?" Annie patted him gently on the shoulder. "Harry?"

"Huh? Oh! Yeah! Hmmmm — that was nice."

"You had a nice nap, didn't you," she smiled. "Move over a little."

Harry moved over on the sofa, which was now surrounded by

rows of dripping, white bed sheets, hanging from the creaking lines.

"I'm sorry I was crabby before."

Harry put his arm around her. "Were you crabby?"

"Hmmm — yes."

"Kids still feeding the little possums?"

"They're working on the fort in back. And spying on Lula Mae and Pearlie."

"That Pearlie turned out to be a really nice person. I got high with her once. Oh, I told you about that. Didn't I?"

"You told me. Harry. Did you know she's running a whorehouse back there."

"Naw, she's too old and fat."

"Go back there and look, Harry. She has them waiting out on the back stoop right now. Her and that fat daughter of hers, and..."

"Come on, Annie. It's their trip, not ours."

"I have a little headache."

"Yeah?" Harry rubbed the back of Annie's neck. "You know the sure cure we found for headaches."

"Oh, Harry...."

"Remember the time you had a migraine and you were willing to try anything? That was the second time you got high on pot. Migraine gone!"

"Harry — I don't want to be stoned all day."

"Well, whatever. Try a couple hits anyway, or just one hit. You'll still be able to function only your headache will be gone. Feeling good beats feeling bad."

"Do you have a joint rolled?"

"There's a roach in the ashtray next to the bed."

"One hit only!" Annie got up and ambled off toward the house. Harry stretched and went up to the front gate to watch colored people. Three of them going by on the sidewalk just as he got there — teenagers — two boys and a girl. They were all duded up and the girl was wearing a pink Sunday dress. They stopped jiving with each other when they saw Harry. One of the boys spit in Harry's direction.

"Don't be nasty," Harry said. "It's Sunday." Harry was smiling and trying to catch the girl's eye. They stopped.

"See this fist?" one of the boys said. "If you wouldn't have that dog layin' over there I'd jump this gate right now and make you eat this fist."

"Aw fuck you." Harry smiled.

"You prejudiced?" the girl asked impishly.

Harry shook his head, still smiling. He was surprised at how well and how peaceful he felt, even with this new confrontation.

"He just horny."

"Jus' horny."

"See? We're brothers in more ways than one."

The girl laughed, and one of the boys smiled. "Show him your new garters," the girl said to the mean one.

"Come on — show 'im!"

The mean one grinned and pulled up his trousers, revealing a muscular leg enclosed in a long black sock held up with a red elastic garter. "So's when I stomps white folks my socks don't work down."

Harry shrugged. "It's Sunday, man."

"You scared?"

"You bullet proof?"

No answer.

"Well," Harry said, starting to turn away. "I don't want a headache — not on Sunday."

"You know what's good for a headache?" the girl said.

"No, what?" Harry turned back to them. "My old lady has a headache."

"She white like you?"

"On the outside."

"Good. Oh, good. You tell her what my mama told me when I'd be gettin' a headache. She say: 'You fill yo mouf up wif milk and hold it, and then you start buttin' yo head up agin' the wall. When the milk clabber, yo headache be gone.'"

Harry laughed. It was sincere laughter, and now all of them were smiling. Harry wondered if they smoked pot. He realized that he felt good enough and didn't want to turn on more, so he didn't mention it. The colored people moved on. They did not seem to be angry now.

"What was that all about?" Annie said. She had the burning roach in her hand.

"Hey! All right!" Harry said. "You're doing it outside now. Beautiful!"

"Harry, in this neighborhood, what difference does it make?"

"Oh, ha ha!" Harry grabbed Annie and hugged her. "Everything's going to be all right from now on, Annie!"

"Oh, Harry, I love you! I love you!"

"I love you too, Annie! I love you, too!"

"Let's go sneak around the house and look at that fort Perry and Janey are building!" Annie sucked another hit off the smoking fragment she held in her fingertips, and took Harry's hand and pulled him toward the side of the house.

Harry remembered what it had felt like to come in Milky, her heavy jugs in his hands, her beatific smile as her head ascended into Heaven... "It's going to be a nice Sunday, Annie," Harry said. "A nice Sunday!"

CHAPTER 16
Monday

Harry was only a minute or so late in getting to the lunchroom, but he was the last one in. He wearily pulled his brown bag out of the refrigerator and slid onto the bench at the long, wooden table — between Bo, the yard foreman, and Bo's stuck-up, queer-looking son, Timmy. Bo looked at Harry, made a face, burped, and spoke: "Suck on any niggers this weekend?"

"Aw fuck you."

Bo watched Harry unwrap a sandwich. "Where'd you say your old lady was from?"

"Colorado."

"That there sandwich is a nigger-rig if I ever saw one."

A few of the men looked over at Harry to check out what he was eating. Harry held out the sandwich, raised the top piece of bread a little so they all could see, and announced: "Ham and cheese." He shoved it under Timmy's nose. "Ham and cheese. Okay?"

Timmy raised his delicate, blond head and opened his mouth seductively for a bite. Surprised, Harry let him get a mouthful, then wondered why he risked his health with Timmy's germs. There was no telling what Timmy might have had in his beautiful mouth before that.

"It sucks," Timmy said, looking Harry straight in the eye and smiling.

"Beats that pussy yogurt you're eating. Strawberry flavored, huh? Is the strawberry flavor artificial?"

"I don't eat anything artificial."

"Hey, Bo! Where'd your kid learn to eat all that pussy diet food? Huh?"

"Leave him alone."

Harry looked at Timmy. "I'm supposed to leave you alone."

Timmy looked at Harry and slowly opened his mouth as wide as it would go, all the masticated ham, cheese, bread, and butter all gooey, stringy, and plastered over his teeth.

"Hey, Harry!" It was Juan, the Cuban. "We saw you guys Saturday! Nice!"

Saturday.... Saturday!

"Yeah? Where?"

"Nice what?" Bo said.

"Gould's Canal. Before noon — you was all standing there — next to that big car." Juan turned to the others, getting excited as he always did, spreading his arms out to show the size of the car. "Big black Lincoln! Lincoln Continental! And all those beautiful girls!"

Bo looked at Harry and snorted. "Hey, Red! Look at this guy here! If you was a chick, would you go for him?"

Red, the new mechanic, looked up from the magazine he was flipping through and grinned. "Harry or Timmy?"

"Harry! Harry! Fuzz Face!"

"I wouldn't give 'im mouth-to-mouth, if that's what you mean."

"See, Harry?"

"See what!"

"You go out with them?" Juan asked, his brown eyes dancing.

"We went to Elliott Key."

"Elliott Key. Oh! Good! Elliott Key is nice, nice."

"There ain't nothin' you can do on Elliott Key you can't do anywhere else," Bo said. "It's only good to take a piss on if the sand fleas don't turn your peter into a submarine sandwich!"

"Good one, Bo."

"No pigs there," one or the younger men said.

"Yeah, but the Marine Patrol.... Plus the feds are going to put park rangers out there soon."

"The Marine Patrol ain't that much. They never get outta their boats."

"Bullshit. Busted my brother. No registration. Two joints in the tool box. One leaky life-preserver."

Harry looked up to see who mentioned joints. It was Ronnie, a college kid who worked part time. Kept the yard clean and the boats mopped out. "What'd they do about the pot?"

"Dropped the charge. They don't bust you for holding — you know, your personal dope stash — well, they lost the joints, too. But they got 'im into court, anyhow, and..."

"I don't wanna hear about dope," Bo said.

"You drink, don't you?" Harry said.

"Drinkin's legal."

Timmy looked up from spooning his yogurt and sent his father a disgusted look. "Alcohol is a drug, Dad."

"And you been lookin' funny lately, Ronnie," Bo said, pointing his finger down the table at him. "If I ever catch you smokin' that shit on the job your ass is gonna go up in smoke. I don't want any accidents!"

"Accidents? What?"

"Things is tight nowadays, and accidents are expensive."

"It's alkies have all the accidents, Bo," Harry said.

"You smoke that shit, Harry? Wait! Stop! I shoulda known! Look at you — ha — you haven't shaved for a week. Hair's all uncombed — I seen it before. Dope! It's the dope! You people get yourselves hooked on that shit and your whole appearance goes to shit!"

"It's the wind out there — the wind messed up my hair!"

"Windy! So wear a hat!"

"When's the last time you changed the oil in that hat you're wearing, Bo? Huh?"

The whole table laughed.

"He wears that hat because he's bald," Timmy said.

"Timmy?" Bo showed Timmy his fist.

"Never did try that stuff," one of the men on the other end said. "Never did try it. Lot of people doing it, though."

"Beats dealing with an oil head."

"Oil head?"

"A drinker."

"Go to Elliott Key," Juan grinned. "Get high...." He raised his hand above his head. "Take clothes off — run around all over the place naked."

Harry was wondering how much Juan knew about trips there when Bo interrupted.

"You do shit like that, Harry?"

Harry shrugged. Then he decided. It was good and it was right. "Yeah, I do shit like that."

"Run around without clothes on — with women?"

"You should see them!" Juan said.

"You do them, uh, psychedelic things? Pills? All that stuff?"

"Just psychedelic drugs," Harry said. "Yeah. I do that."

Timmy touched Harry's forearm. Harry looked at him and Timmy nodded.

Timmy!

That explains it!

Timmy is a head!

That's why he's so quiet. So gentle.

"You know where you'd be if the boss-man heard that?" Bo said. "Huh?"

"I do good work. When I wire a boat you don't have to check after me. When I drop an engine in, it's perfect. All the time I've been working here. Can **you** say that? You got a customer back last week, bitching about that outdrive you fucked up! You oil-heads are always fucking your jobs up!"

"Don't get pregnant," Bo said. "So I'm an oil head? Anybody want to step outside and call me that?"

"Beer drinker," Ronnie said. "That's all it means."

"What kind of pussy talk is that?"

"Alcohol drinkers are oil-heads. That's almost everybody in here. It's even legal."

"Oil heads! How sweet."

"Fuck you, Bo."

"Fuck you. Fuck you. Ever'time I get you in a corner, that's all you can come up with. You know, when you was in the bottom of that Owens this morning this long-hair hippie comes up — the office sent him out — askin' for part-time work — says he knows you — and I wouldn't give him the time of day. Wouldn't talk to him. Know why? 'Cause..."

"Bo godammit!"

"'Because if a man can't take care of himself, and be neat, how's he gonna do on the job?"

"What was his name?"

"Oh? They have regular names, too?"

Harry got up in disgust, and shoved the rest of his lunch back into the bag.

"Sit down. You'll get over it."

Harry swung a leg over the bench. It was a tight place to get out of. Before he could get the other leg over, Bo grabbed his arm.

"I'm not through," Bo said evenly.

Harry sat back down.

"Tell me one good thing about hippies."

Harry set his jaw and looked Bo in the eye. There was no use explaining anything to Bo, or was there? His mind searched for something about the hippies Harry knew that Bo would understand. Harry looked at Timmy, but Bo's son had retreated from the conversation, his eyes closed, his chin resting on one propped arm.

"Name one good thing," Bo repeated.

"Their whole way of life, Bo. They're happy all the time because they live in tune with the planet, they roll with it instead of fighting it."

"Oh, Harry, that's dumb!" Bo wiped the remnants of a third sandwich from his lips and tried to unscrew the lid off his dessert.

"What you got in there?"

"Pudding."

"Your old lady make it?"

"Yeah. She made it."

"From a recipe or a mix?"

Bo looked up at Harry and grunted as the cover loosened.

Harry could not resist. "She must have the grip of an army sergeant to get the lid on so tight."

"Harry...."

"You ever do LSD, Bo? Bet you'd be afraid."

"Acid," Ronnie said. "Yeah."

"How about you, Bo?"

Timmy revived and touched Harry's arm again. He made a face and shook his head, pointing at his father. Bo was busy spooning in the chocolate pudding.

"After you do acid a few times," Ronne continued, you don't want to do it anymore."

"Hey, Bo," Harry said. "You ever dream about sex?"

Bo looked at Harry and sighed. He looked up at the lunchroom clock.

"I mean daydreaming, Bo. You know. You think up a real fantastic chick in a real fantastic situation and you imagine what fucking her would be like?"

"Oh, yeah man," Juan volunteered. "I do that all the time. Big, beautiful women with big ass, big tits, experienced but look like fifteen years old, all that shit."

"Big ass!" Bo snorted. "Cuban pussy!"

"How about you, Bo?" Harry insisted.

"He chicken to talk," Juan said.

"Picture yourself without your old lady," Harry said. He leaned toward Bo and folded his arms on the table. "It's warm and sunny, and here are three women, all part of your hippie family, and they're naked because it's hot, and you've just taken a pill that'll give you all kinds of energy and makes you see clear and feel good, and you're lying there in the sun on this blanket and the chicks start sucking on everything on you that can be sucked on. Huh? That's what hippies do. On weekdays!"

"Harry...."

"Okay. Pretend that you're one of the hippies."

Bo looked at Harry, opened his mouth, and burped. Then he got up and slammed his lunch-bag into the refrigerator. "Five minutes," he said to the men as he walked out.

The fridge.... It takes longer now for the bulb inside to go on.

Time slowed down again.

"That was acid you were describing?" Ronnie said. "Sheeeeit."

"I was trying to make it sound real for him. When I first got home time slowed down so bad.... You can't describe stuff like that. You gotta be there."

"Oh. Yeah, I can dig that."

"Home, after tripping, it took five seconds for the fridge bulb to come on, seemed like, and it made me jump! My hand suddenly lit up and it looked like an animal claw reaching in there." Harry turned to look at him. "You don't do acid anymore, Ronnie? Yourself?"

"Naw — well, I would do it now, I guess. It's been a couple years."

Harry looked at Timmy. Timmy nodded and closed his eyes again. The air-conditioner on the far end of the room kicked on. Harry closed his eyes for a moment also. He felt so good inside. Ever since the trip. So good!

And Ronnie....

I thought there was something special about him!

His attitude.

Harry, eyes still closed, was aware of the sounds of the other men leaving the room. Then he felt Timmy get up. It would be hot out in the yard, and the boat he was working on was a mess.

Give me one more minute....

An outboard in a test tank outside started up. It sounded like Elliott Key. The air-conditioner was beginning to sound like Elliott Key, too. It began to smell like the island. Water gurgled and sloshed through the coral on the shore. The tide was coming in. *Awww, it's so beautiful, Harry!* he heard Neeta say. He opened his eyes. The chipped paint of the long lunch table stretched out before him. The dirty ashtrays. The discarded sandwich baggies. A matchbook from the Topless Tomboy Club.... Dust-laden sunlight from the high windows streamed into the dirty room. *Awww Harry!* Neeta said. *Whatcha gonna do now?*

CHAPTER 17
Ronnie's Brother

It felt like it was near quitting time, and Harry wearily pulled himself out of the old Owens cruiser he had been working on and dropped his cramped legs down to the asphalt below. Juan and Ronnie were standing around waiting for him. They were talking about pussy.

"Whew — I feel stiff all over," Harry said. "Not much room in there." He unplugged the portable fan and blinked his eyes. Sheets of electric purple were reflecting off all the boats in the yard, and a broad beam of purple had just radiated from Juan's wristwatch crystal. "Wow," Harry mumbled, rubbing his eyes.

"So," Juan continued, "when she turn her back on me, after I go to all the trouble get the rubber on, I think, hey man, this is your wife — she not suppose to shut me off, you know, so I jack off in the rubber!"

"Right in front of her?"

"To her back. But I wiggle the bed. I grunt. You know."

Harry looked at the skinny, happy Cuban, shook his head, and smiled. Another sheet of purple flashed off the chain-link fence on the far side of the yard.

"She no care. She preten' she asleep, you know. So I turn around and sit on the bed and I roll the rubber off and sling it over my shoulder, you know, and whop! Right on the, you know, little — idol — statue — on the wall, her statue of the virgin, and the rubber it hang there. Dripping cum? Ohhhh, you should see her then! She get mad! Oh, she get so mad!"

"I'm seeing purple," Harry said.

"Purple?" Juan put a hand on Harry's shoulder. "Harry, I have a question."

"Yeah," Ronnie said. "Juan is cool."

"You ever get the purple flashes after tripping?" Harry began rubbing his eyes.

Ronnie looked at Harry for a moment. Then he remembered. "My brother did."

"Harry," Juan said. "You can get LSD?"

Harry shook his head. "I was going to ask you guys."

"Nobody doing acid anymore?" Ronnie said.

"I did last weekend."

"Where you get it?"

"From friends — but I don't know if I can score any from them to bring home, you know."

"I scored on some last year. Ten hits for twenty bucks and it wasn't even acid, it turned out. Blotter acid but not the good stuff."

"Shrinks used to get pure Sandoz 25," Ronnie said. "Legal. And there's still some Owsley around."

Harry ignored the supply problem momentarily. "Tell me about your brother and the purple. I got the purple this morning on the way to work, but it went away when I got here so I forgot about it. Now it's back."

"You see it now?" Juan grinned. "The purple you get from the good stuff. The LSD-25."

"I can see purple around your teeth! Wow! Smile again!"

"You make fun!"

"No, Juan, no!"

"My kid brother had that," Ronnie said, "But it went away. We used to drop acid all the time."

"Now I can't see it. It went away." Harry stiffened up. "Now it's back!"

"You get used to it. What's on that island, hey?"

Harry thought about the island. He flashed to the time he was lying back in the hippie camp with the others and naked Surrendra, the dark, jungle queen, was pulling his boots off and massaging his feet. Harry shook his head violently to clear his brain. "I'm having trouble today. Trying to figure out what is real and what isn't. Man!"

"It's all real. You're a lot like my brother."

"I ever see your brother?"

"I don't think so, I..."

"He look like Jesus," Juan grinned. "Long hair. Wear sandals."

"A couple years ago — no, more than that — we were going to fish in that little canal along 117th Avenue, you know, past Bird Road? And I had three-hundred hits of Owsley Berkley White micro I scored — pure LSD-25 — it came out to sixty cents a hit what I paid for it, but I was getting a dollar and a half or two dollars a hit? Worth a fortune to me now. All gone. Well, Stevie — that's my little brother — he was still in school, shit, still in the ninth grade? Tenth grade? Anyway, there was this like a little grove by the canal where nobody went and we gave Stevie a hit and he had one, g-o-o-o-o-o-d trip, I tell you." Ronnie was getting excited telling this, and waving his arms around. "Everything must've been right for him that day because it changed his whole life. For over a week that's all he ever talked about, that trip, how beautiful everything was. He quit school. He quit his newspaper route. All he did was walk around looking at flowers and getting up early to watch the sun come up. Really fucked up good! So after a couple months went by he started begging me for more acid and begging me not to sell it all, you know, but I felt guilty for fucking him up. And shit, my mom and dad were hassling both of us all the time, you know — do this and do that — so one day I got pissed off and we went out in the empty lot next door where we had a little fort, and I let him drop with me. After that, I quit selling the shit, let's see — we had about, um, over a hundred hits left — and I liked it, tripping with my brother. We used to fight over everything before that, but now we were buddies all of a sudden, it was really cool, and he always wanted to trip because he wanted so bad to get back to that place in his head where he went to that first time. Sometimes we'd drop in the morning, right after getting up. This was in the summer now. Or we'd drop in the evening. Usually we'd have big plans about what we were going to do that night, and a lot of times we would drop right before dinner, planning to split right after dinner when we would be just getting off, you know? Well, sometimes dinner would get held up, like my dad would come home late from the job and want his shower first — shit like that — and here Stevie and me'd already dropped and we'd be getting off sooner than we planned, like right in the middle of dinner, and my parents would be hassling us, like when are you going to the barber? Or, why didn't you take the garbage out? You know. And my old man's face'd start flowing like putty while he's talking to me, and my mother's shitty jewelry would be flashing all these weird colors and the meat on my plate would be moving."

"Did they know you guys were on drugs?"

"No man, not for years!"

"What happened after that?"

"Well — wait, Bo's looking this way, no, never mind. Well, one day, about a week after school started, only we didn't go one day, I went to get a hit and it was all gone. Those pills were so tiny! Well, I told Stevie and right away we were figuring out how to get the bread together so we could score some more, but as soon as I hit the street, something happened, I don't know, and I just kept on realizing — Wow! The whole summer — what happened to it? Like one day sort of flowed into the next and we weren't getting anyplace, so Stevie and me just quit doing acid, just like that, and we went back to school. And I haven't done any acid since."

Juan smiled and pointed at Ronnie and nodded his head. "Bo say LSD is habit forming. Habit forming! Ha ha!"

"That's bullshit," Ronnie said.

"What happen to your brother? Tell Harry what happen."

"Well, Stevie, he moved into the vacant lot next door. One day my old man came home drunk and he went out in the field and burned down the fort with all Stevie's hippie books in there, and his blankets and, you know. And then that new north-south expressway went in along 117th Avenue where Stevie liked to trip and they bulldozed the whole grove flat. You don't think you can score the acid, huh?"

"No. I don't know. I'll try."

"Was it good shit?"

Harry nodded and smiled.

"I didn't know you were into psychedelics. Hard to tell. You just didn't show it."

Harry shrugged his shoulders. It would be easy to let them think he'd been doing it for years. "I just got into it recently."

Bo came ambling up. "So this is where the fish are bitin'!"

"Fuck you, Bo."

"Fuck you, Bo."

"You jerks are on the clock!"

"It's near quitting time, Foreman Bo!"

"You guys think you can't be replaced?"

"Nobody like us."

"Nobody good lookin' like us neither."

Harry watched Bo walk away. "What happened to Steve?"

"Oh, Stevie, he's on a heavy trip now. No drugs at all, no booze, no cigarettes. He lives in a chickee out in the everglades. Runs around like a native. I saw his camp once. He's done left the planet!"

A chickee in the everglades! Harry thought to himself.

He didn't leave the planet, he joined it!

Bo stopped and turned around — hands on hips under his beer belly — and Harry swung back up into the Owens. "Got to lock up my tools," he explained.

A chickee in the Everglades!

The boat he was working on was dirty inside but Harry pictured a tanned, bearded white man, looked sort of like Ronnie, naked save for his shorts, lying on his open platform under a thatched roof way out in the open country, all alone, hands behind his head, dreaming.

Ronnie reached over the gunwales so Harry could hand up his tools. Harry said: "Think he ever got back to that place he was looking for?"

"Place?" Ronnie said. "Oh, you mean Stevie?"

CHAPTER 18
Tuesday

Harry plunked down at the breakfast table just as Annie was pouring him a new coffee. "Your coffee got cold, so...."

"I know. Thanks. I'm so late this morning. I think I'll stay home."

"Harry...."

"I'll be okay in a couple days. Call them and tell them I'm sick. Okay? I never call in sick and everybody else there does."

"Okay. Short paycheck, though."

"Yeah, yeah." Harry looked up to watch the morning commotion in Ruby's back yard. "Here they come, Annie!"

Annie rushed up to the window in time to see all the little thumb-suckers next door come flying out the back door. Each one had an article of food in his hands. One of the smaller ones lost his sandwich immediately to their mongrel dog, Chomper.

"Mother," Annie mimicked. "Shall we serve the children outside?" Annie sat down with Harry at her place on the side of the table.

"I had the most realistic dream this morning," Harry said. "I can remember the whole thing right now so clearly."

"Oh, Harry, they're poisoning each other again!"

Harry looked out and watched one of the kids chasing one of the smaller children with a can of roach poison. Suddenly, the smaller child stopped and turned around, opened his mouth, and laughed all the while the poison was sprayed in. Another child ran up, grabbed the can away, and sprayed himself in the mouth. Another was lying on the ground with his arms and legs up in the air, jerking and kicking in imitation of a dying cockroach.

"Another weird thing about the dream was the colors," Harry said. "Annie, I never saw colors like this in a dream before!"

"I think I dream in black and white," Annie said.

"Another thing about the dream is that I remember the beginning of it, too!"

"Tell me about it."

"Aw, Annie. You're so nice to ask," Harry laughed. He watched Ruby come out and saunter over to the children who had the poison. She was in the robin-egg-blue bathrobe and her hair was in a rag, but Harry overlooked all of that and concentrated on Ruby's chocolate legs flashing through the slit in her robe as she walked. Ruby was yelling something, but the window was closed and they couldn't hear.

"Good! Good!" Annie said, when Ruby began kicking the child with the poison. "Way to go!"

"Oh, Annie."

"You were telling me...."

"Well, the dream started with two of me, two of me in my head, not one, and I didn't have a body or anything like that. There were just these two of me in my head. There was the real me, or the spirit me, and the ego me. The ego me was real tiny, like a little dot inside my brain, where it sits and runs the controls, the machinery. I could see it, no, I could see where it was, but it was too tiny."

"Harry, I wish you hadn't taken that LSD. I'm worried."

"Come on, Annie. Well, from this tiny place in my brain where **me** was — is — I could see everything in there. Listen, Annie! My brain was all pink and red and flashing light, and all these brain-cell clumps were arranged in rows all around me like spokes of a wheel, only on more than one level — they looked like rows of flashing pink ice and slush, and..."

"But Harry, you are your brain. You can't see it."

"That's what I thought before I tripped."

"That's what I'm worried about."

"Don't worry. I've never felt so good in my life."

"Then why do I have to call you in sick?"

"Annie, damn! Let me finish. Please? My dream was so colorful — so real — I can see it now, this minute. I have to share this with somebody."

"Share it with your hippies."

"Aw, Annie. Ohhhhh...."

"Okay, I'm sorry. Tell me your dream."

Harry looked at his wife sadly. If only she could know what he knew now. He tried again. "So here I am in the middle of these throbbing rows of pink brain all laid out. There's blurry, bloody stuff clogging some of the rows, and light is flashing continuously from everywhere. Then this voice speaks up. It was like a voice reporting to my ego, and it said: 'There's no damage anywhere. We'll have to dismantle her further. There doesn't seem to be any damage here. We're going to have to take her down one more step — can't see any damage.' Well, it went on like that and here I was, watching the whole thing. My brain was checking itself out because it had been invaded or adjusted in some way without its consent. I knew I was going to be able to work it out, I mean, my brain would be able to work it out, that is."

"Oh, Harry."

"Sounds burned out, huh?"

"Yes."

"It'll be okay. I feel fine. I feel happy! I don't know why, but I feel really happy, Annie!"

"Well...."

"I love you, Annie."

Annie smiled and patted Harry's arm. "I love you too, Harry."

"Good!"

"That's why I don't want you to do it again. Do you understand? Why I'm saying that?"

"Yeah. I understand," Harry said. "I understand."

CHAPTER 19
Tuesday Evening

Harry found Annie sitting in the dark, out in the front yard, on the sofa she said she hated. As he walked up from the house, flashes of iridescent purple flicked over the white masonry and the window glass.

"The purple is back," he said as he plunked down beside her. Annie did not answer, but she took his hand and smiled.

"Nice and cool out here."

"I just couldn't stand to watch that program, Harry."

"It's real life, Annie, documentaries are. They covered the whole war from the first time we sent in advisors to the final pulling out of Vietnam. If we could fly..." Harry stopped and rubbed his head.

"If we could fly what?"

"Annie, I was just thinking. Right now — this very minute — if we had a way to fly anywhere, we could be standing and watching a beheading in Africa, or we could buy a slave...."

A black female slave, young, do with her what you want, and it would be real.

"Harry...."

I must sound burned out to her.

Better shut up. Get my head together.

"Harry, real life is going to work and raising a family and putting money away for the future."

"And going fishing and swimming and making love and hunting."

and traveling and foraging for food and fighting foreigners to the death for your freedom and fighting Americans to the death for your freedom...

"And washing and ironing and taking care of your sick kids and your sick husband and cutting the grass and...."

Harry sighed and got up. "I'm going back in the house."

Little Perry and Janey were at the dining room table in their pajamas, working on something, and when they saw Harry, they told him not to look.

"It's for you, Daddy," Janey explained, "but you're not supposed to see it yet."

"It'll be done in a minute," Perry said.

"Then you'll go straight to bed, okay?"

"Without brushing our teeth?" Perry said.

"After brushing your teeth, you little fart."

"Daddy, don't get mad when you see what we made," Janey said, looking worried. "We're not making it to get you mad."

"Okay — I promise." Harry scrounged through the address book next to the telephone for Gilli's home number. He was a little nervous about calling, and he wasn't sure what he would say. A woman answered.

"May I speak to Gilli, please? This is Harry Schaffner"

"Just a minute. I'll find out." The woman sounded half asleep.

A moment later, Joel's voice boomed over the phone. "Hello! How are you! Joel here!"

"This is Harry. Is Gilli around?"

"Harry?"

"Harry Schaffner. I was at your party for Gilli. I talked to you last Saturday before we went out on the boat and you took the chicks over for the blimp ride?"

"Harry! Sure! I know you! What can I do?"

Oh yeah, sure you remember me, Harry thought. "I have to talk to Gilli."

"Gilli's in New York."

"New York! Wow! Well...."

"You can't keep track of that crowd, Harry, they don't know what they're doing themselves. I want to talk with you."

"Yeah?"

"Did you do the number with them that day? On the island?"

"Yeah.... Why?"

"I want to talk to you about it."

"Okay...."

"Like now? Or tomorrow?"

"I'm kinda tired, and..."

"You working tomorrow?"

"I don't know yet."

"Got my address?"

"Yeah." Harry held back. Joel was a doctor. And a psychiatrist? *Way above my level.*

And he has money.

"Gilli's leaving soon on a hospital ship for South America. Come on over tomorrow after work? I have appointments mostly all day but I want to talk to you. I have a lot of questions and you can help me out!"

"You might have to help **me** out."

"It's a deal! We'll get high together! Swim in the pool! You can tell me about Saturday!"

"Okay...."

"My last appointment is, um, 2:00 I think."

"I get off work at 3:30."

"Okay. Come as you are. Pissy can roll us a joint."

"Beautiful!" Harry said. Joel hung up without a goodbye.

Annie was still out in the yard.

"Gilli's in New York." Harry sat down beside her.

"Good."

"Joel wants me to come over tomorrow afternoon."

"What about work?"

"After work. Unless I'm still sick."

"I think you are."

"Oh, come on, Annie."

"He says we'll smoke a joint, go swim in the pool, shit like that."

"Why you, Harry? He makes a lot of money. They're in a whole different class."

"Heads don't recognize classes," Harry said.

"Bullshit," Annie said. "I think I'm going to bed."

Harry sat out in the yard alone for awhile. He still felt happy but he had the nagging feeling that there was stuff to be sad about. When he finally got up to go to bed himself the house was quiet. Annie had put Janey and Perry to bed, and appeared to be asleep herself. Harry went over to the dining room table to see what the children had made for him. There was a large manila envelope at his place, with a four-page card the children had put together. On the face of the card was a picture of a marijuana plant colored with brown and green crayons. Under the picture were the words:

WARNING!!!   DANGER!!!

The art work was Perry's and the printing was Janey's. On the second page were pictures of pills and rolled marijuana cigarettes which they had cut out of magazines and one picture which Harry recognized from some literature that had been passed out to the kids during a dope lecture at the elementary school. On the next page, in Janey's neat, large letters, was:

WE LOVE OUR DADDY!

On page three:

WE LOVE OUR MOMMY!

On page four:

WE LOVE BEERCAN, TOO, BUT

HE DOESN'T SMOKE THE KILLER WEED!

"Killer weed!" Harry snorted. He looked through the card again. The children were really worried. The dope program at their school was getting to them. Harry stood there, wondering what to do about it. But what? He looked at the card again before putting it back down at Annie's place at the table. On the back-side, in tiny handwriting, in dark pencil, Little Perry had written:

Don't get mad

Harry slumped into his chair and pressed the palms of his hands against his eyes, and all the universe was there but without a sound.

The silence was total.

CHAPTER 20
Wednesday

Harry made sure that little Perry and Janey were on their way to school before getting up.

"I keep on telling them to stick together on the way so the niggers don't gang up on them," Annie said to him when she put his coffee down. "But what can those two little ones do? Yesterday, a boy ripped off Janey's lunch money again. If I give them sandwiches to take along, the niggers rip those off."

"So walk them to school!" Harry was anxious to talk about something else. "Annie — I have to tell you about the dream I had again."

"Again?"

"A continuation, yeah. Listen! This time I was looking at my brain and..."

"Oh, Harry!"

"Listen, Annie!"

"We have to move out of this neighborhood, Harry. The children..."

"Okay. We'll move."

"Really?"

"Really. I'm tired of all these confrontations. I'm ready to sell this place and get the fuck out."

"What about your dream?"

"The colors were still as good, Annie — really far out — and scary! My brain was still laid out in rows, only this time the chunks of pink brain-meat were much smaller — in much smaller pieces. Equal pieces, though, you know — and the rows were on more levels — under me, over me, in front of me — and stretching out in all directions as far as I could see. Well, about twenty-five feet in front of me is standing this miniature man with a clipboard, wearing a white lab coat, you know, and a voice inside of me is asking this doctor or whatever questions, like: An adjustment was made without my consent but you haven't found a single item of damage. And when the lab dude hears this, he starts to slide away and get smaller and smaller, and the voice says: How do you know it was LSD-25? The man answers without words! Without words, he implies: *We made it the same way we always make LSD-25.* And the voice says: How can you be sure if you don't even understand how LSD works exactly? And the man says — without words — *Others who tried it agreed it was LSD-25.* Then the voice says: Are you sure? And the man says: *Reasonably sure.* And the voice says: What is "reasonably sure"?

"Wait, Harry, wait! How can he talk without words?"

"I don't know, but I found out when I was tripping that I can watch stuff and think about stuff without words — even without thoughts!"

Annie sighed. "Harry...."

"Meanwhile the little doctor or whatever is getting so tiny, receding into the distance, that I can hardly see him now, and finally he disappears, and my last picture is minus the voice, minus the doctor, and a new voice, real faint, in words, says: "Man, it was acid!" So I'm standing there in my dream, no body, just me, whatever that is. I, me, standing there before this throbbing pink layout of my own brain, and then I wake up. As soon as I'm awake I mash my hands against the side of my head. It's still there! But I'm exhausted. Utterly exhausted, Annie. That dream was so real and so clear and so colorful that it wore me out!"

"You already told me you weren't going to work," Annie replied.

"Yeah.... Plus I'm going to see Joel this afternoon."

"He wants to see you, right?"

Harry nodded. "I don't know why."

"Well, he's a doctor, and I think you should tell him about your dream."

"Annie. He charges for shit like that. I don't want to spoil it."

"Spoil what, Harry? If he doesn't like it he won't invite you over again. Promise me you'll ask him about your dreams, and about that purple you've been seeing everywhere, and tell him you've been skipping work."

"Christ, Annie!"

"Well, you're not afraid of him, are you?

"I don't think so. No."

"Then ask him."

Harry suddenly smiled. "Yeah! Ah! You're right! What am I afraid of? Right? That's what I've been feeling lately. Confidence! That's what makes me feel free now. Free! That's what makes me feel so good. I feel free! Annie, I feel free!" Harry laughed, and banged his coffee cup down on the table. He grinned and looked around.

"You talk so different, Harry. I'm worried about you."

"I talk different? Yeah? Okay, but isn't it better if I'm, happy? Didn't I used to be an asshole half the time? I don't know why I'm happy now, but I hope it lasts." Harry paused. "I know I can't go back. I know that."

"Go back? Where? To work? Harry!"

"Where? Back to where I was before. Not knowing. I can't go back to believing what I believed before. I saw the world for the first time Saturday. Saturday! Today is Wednesday. I'll never see the planet the old way again. My life has changed."

"Changed...." Annie looked about to leave.

"My — whole — life — is changed. My whole, um, future!"

Annie got up and put her arm around him. "Don't worry, Harry. I'll help you."

"Aw, Annie, Harry smiled. He got up and they hugged each other. "Help? I'm not worried about it — I'm happy about it! I wouldn't go back to my old self for anything!"

They sat back down and smiled at each other, and then they laughed. A sheet of purple flashed off the window glass at the end of the table and it startled Harry, but he saw that Annie was loosening up about him now and he didn't let it show. They both looked out of the window for a few minutes as the little brown pre-schoolers next door came flying out of their back door, one-by-one.

"Now," Annie said happily. "How much do you think we can get for this house?"

Joel took Harry right into the back yard near the pool where he had a table and some lounge chairs. "Kick your boots off, Harry, and relax!" Joel was dressed in a super-clean pair of white shorts. His chest was incredibly hairy.

"I forgot to bring trunks," Harry mumbled as he sat down. A woman was splashing in the pool.

"That's Pissy," Joel explained. "My sister. I'm the oldest and Gilli's the youngest. After awhile we'll jump in there naked and scare her!"

"Pissy?"

"Sis-piss. Pissy. Resident Jewish princess. When she's not traveling around she lives with me because I make more money than Gilli does. Look. Joint's already rolled. Look, cold beer in the cooler there. But first I have some questions."

"Okay, um, while we have a beer, joint later?"

Cool. Not afraid of these people.

They're just other people.

Harry was watching Pissy. She looked pretty good. Pissy waved at them and Harry and Joel waved back.

"Long time divorced. Thirty-six years old tomorrow. You're invited to the party."

"I have to work tomorrow," Harry said.

I should come to Pissy's party.

Pissy.... Cute name! Nice body!

Thirty-six.... Yum!

"Tell me about Saturday. It's important to me!" Joel's voice was up to his usual exuberance, but he had ignored the beer thing..

"Well...."

"Have you smoked any pot since you tripped?"

"No. Just didn't feel like it. I might today."

"Was it your first trip?"

"LSD, yeah."

Joel leaned into Harry. "Were you worried or afraid of it when you did it?"

" Oh, yeah, sure."

"Would you feel uneasy about doing it again?"

"No.... Well, I would be a little afraid when I dropped the tab, I guess. It's a long, heavy trip. Yeah, I would be a little scared, well, not scared exactly, but I'd definitely do it again. You ever do it?"

"No. It's why I'm asking a normal, functional, employed working person and not a medical professional." Joel backed away a little. "You talk pretty educated for a working person."

"Everybody says that. When I was a kid I had to read a lot because I was sick at home with asthma half the time. My son inherited that."

"Was LSD what you thought it would be?"

Harry slowly shook his head. He felt weird in this new role. "I read a lot about it before I tripped, mostly because I was afraid, no, because I was curious. It was still different from what I imagined it would be. I don't think I can describe it."

"You too? Heard that one before. From colleagues of mine. Oh, well.... Are you the same person now?"

"I don't think so. No! I feel free! I don't feel guilty! Not about anything! I'm not worried about anything, well, I might be worried about decisions. Making decisions. That's freedom!"

"Gilli told me that acid depends on the individual, that it doesn't put things in, it takes survival mechanisms out of the way so you can see your life as it is, not as you are told it is. What do you think about that?"

Harry nodded vigorously. "Gilli nailed it, and you're asking me?" More confident than ever now, he was watching Pissy get out of the pool. Pissy in her black bikini. He swallowed. Pissy looked so much like his ex girlfriend from South Beach. Harry rubbed his chin. His whiskers were growing out, and growing out fast. The new pelt felt good and outrageous on his face.

Joel leaned forward again and his questions seemed to be needy for answers. Harry broke a pause. "One thing I saw — I should have known — that I live in my head. My personality or my ego, and my body, are just the flesh and blood vehicle for my brain, no, wait. My body is the vehicle for my brain, and my brain and my ego control the body so it can get around and survive, and my soul rides the whole works. No, wait."

Joel smiled, and leaned even closer. "Soul?"

Um, well, okay, but while tripping I felt like there was a soul, my soul, separate from my brain and I didn't used to believe in that."

"I can help you out there," Joel said. "That body, mind, soul debate."

"But it's a groovy body, a groovy vehicle. And the planet! The planet!" Harry moved back a little in his chair, hearing it scratch the tiles. "Joel — I knew Earth was a planet, right? I mean, everybody knows this. But now I **feel** like I'm on a planet. And a super-beautiful planet it is, too! Plus the sun doesn't rise, the planet rolls toward the sun, and I can **feel** that."

"Really...." Joel smiled and scraped his own deck chair back a bit. "Any regrets?"

"No, never! Acid is wonderful!" Harry shook his head again. "I never thought I'd see the day I would say that! I never thought I would see myself like I do now, either."

"They said you all had two hits each."

Harry nodded, his eyes on Pissy — tall and tan and a little thick in the thighs but firm. She did a slow swing into the big house. Harry said: "She's got a lot of style."

"She wants to trip on acid for the first time, and I think I do, too."

"Yeah?"

"And setting is supposed to be the most important thing. Alone on that island would be perfect."

"Elliott Key? Old Rhodes Key?"

"Well, yes! But all my colleagues are either for it or dead-set against LSD. I've been too yellow to make a decision for several years. In fact, back in the early sixties, I was very much against it and went to a great deal of trouble to prevent Pissy from trying it. Even Timothy Leary was against it at first."

"Yeah?" Harry smiled? "Pissy.... "That name!"

"You have to know her. Sis-piss. Okay. LSD-25. Some research successes in Canada. Czechoslovakia. But here in America, the clinical settings devastated subjects in the experiments. So far I can say my thoughts on the subject are as yet uncontaminated by personal experience. Not sure what that is worth. Now I'm asking questions before I decide what to do myself. To cut the garbage, my real problem is that I feel I've missed something in life — that by not doing acid I'm missing something. The key to the real world, or the key to the human soul." Joel made sure Harry was looking him in the eye. The government is going to cut off any access to the drug soon. All governments is my guess. Anything that can open a citizen's eyes to what is real versus what is propaganda is scary stuff to authorities."

Harry was not listening. Pissy, still in her black bikini, and still wet, was bringing a tray of drinks. Harry's first reaction was to get up when the lady got there, but he remembered just in time he was free now. *Feminists, thank you!* and he remained firmly plunked in his chair.

"Iced tea," Pissy smiled. "Joel told me to stay away so he could talk. Bye!" She gave them a little wave.

"Bye," Harry said. He picked up his glass of tea. "Thank you! You're beautiful!"

Pissy turned and smiled and waved again.

"Question number one," Joel said.

"Number ten," Harry said. " Number eleven is what happened to the beer."

"Ha ha. Spunky. Sharp! Well, you're thirty-two, you said, and that is over the twenty-five years of the age that the physical brain is supposed to begin its gradual decline or stop growing, you know, when you start to piss brain cells away every day."

Harry tried to understand what this was all about. Was he getting a lecture?

Joel said, "Also, a lot of that street acid isn't LSD at all. A lot of it's pig tranquilizer and strychnine. I've had young patients who have described trips that were nothing like what Gilli described, for instance. Setting is important, too, which is why government clinical tests blew up in their faces so many times.

"Trip on the island," Harry said.

"Right! Okay!" Joel's voice boomed. He slapped his leg. "But I'm afraid to trip, see? I know a colleague who didn't make it. He's a vegetable now. Was a patient of mine. But I don't know if he took the real thing."

"Dropped the real thing."

"What?"

"Hippies say "drop acid, not take acid. I'm being an asshole now. Forgive."

"Okay. And when I drop acid I'm going to make sure I fasted the day before."

Joel pulled out one of the joints he had rolled from a spotless, four-pocket Cuban guayabera shirt. "Want to turn on with me?"

Harry squirmed on his seat for a moment, then nodded. It seemed that Joel had been smoking grass for some time. "If I tell you what I saw and it seems fantastic, remember that what I saw was real. It wasn't something I made up with my eyes closed."

"Agreed." Joel moved forward in his chair to make up for Harry's previous retreat.

Harry took a hit off the joint and passed it back. "Picture this," he said. "I was sitting on the ground, alone in a little depression. On the island. Everything was super beautiful — and that you'll have to see for yourself — and the sky was such a blue — like electricity."

Joel nodded. "Which is what everything is. Electricity."

"So I am looking lower, at the dead leaves on the ground, and I could see spots of the sky through the leaves, you know, instead of dirt or rocks. I brushed some leaves aside and the sky was beneath me! I could see the sky through the leaves! Even when I looked all the way down, between my legs and around my legs, the same beautiful sky showed through everything on the ground. I was in Heaven. You know what I mean? I was in The Bowl of the Sky."

Joel kept silent for a moment.

"Pass the joint," Harry said. He was an equal now.

Joel passed the jay, but kept on sitting there in silence, nodding his head as if he were talking to himself. "Pissy!" he hollered suddenly, making Harry jump.

Pissy came out of the house in a pink robe with a pink towel around her head. She moved her chair farther into the shade and crossed her legs as she slid into it, keeping her bright brown eyes riveted on Harry. Harry handed her the joint and watched her take a long pull. Her toenails were painted red, and she reminded Harry of rich girls in movies. She acted and moved the same way. Rich girl. Slick. Harry noticed a large, high mole on the inside of her left thigh as she re-crossed her legs. He was reminded again of the long, Jewish nose like his old girlfriend had, which he had always loved — but Pissy had more prominent, sensual lips. She leaned over to hand the jay to her brother.

"Don't distract him — you're too old for him," Joel said.

Harry and Pissy smiled at each other. Harry had the joint again and he sucked in another hot hit. She picked the roach out of his hand with rich-girl grace. "Stoned again!" Harry said.

"I promised not to talk," Pissy said.

"Hey, Joel — this is the twentieth century!"

"You two can talk later. I have a proposition to make."

"Why me?" Harry said.

"Because you're not a hippie. It's as simple as that. You are a gainfully employed working man. A good thing. Believe it. And if you're going to turn into a hippie, which I doubt, I want to catch you before you do and get the benefit of your experience."

"I don't have that much experience."

"Let me be the judge of that," Joel laughed in his booming tones. "Now — oh — ha! Now I'm high!"

Pissy nodded and waved.

After one more pass, Joel flipped the little burning roach onto the lawn. "We can afford it, and it's healthier," he explained. "Marijuana isn't sacred, although maybe it should be."

They sat there for awhile, quietly. Stoned. Apparently all of them happy. Harry glanced at Pissy often, and was happy that she did not get nervous about it. She seemed to be a superior to him, or to them, in a way he did not understand. Or maybe she was spoiled. She did not carry her personality all up-front like Neeta did.

Harry reflected again on the incongruity of his situation: this time, this place, these people....

"My whole life is changed." Harry broke the silence first. Then he told them about his concern over the purple flashes he was seeing. "Mostly at night, though, especially when I'm driving."

"Dots of bright purple?"

"No. Sheets or ribbons, not too bright. And you can see through the purple. No dots or points."

"See it now?"

"Um, no."

"Harry, what did your house look like when you first got home from that trip?"

"Ohhh.... So beautiful! It was dark, but we have this city street-light, you know, and I saw my whole movie there, my boat, my work-bench under the tree, my sofa under the tree, and I thought: All my life this is what I wanted, and now I have it but I haven't been all that happy."

"What about Annie?"

"You remember her?"

"Sure! Chesty, friendly, reddish-blond short hair.... No hippie, that's for sure!" Joel had winked when he said chesty.

"When I saw that she was sleeping when I got home I was disappointed she wasn't up at first, you know, I'd been going through the longest day of my life and I couldn't share it. But then I saw all the things I did to her, how little freedom my demands left her, how all that we had was the result of **my** dreams, **my** ambitions. But I don't feel guilty about it now because I can see I had no control over how I turned out, well, yah, I feel guilty anyway, jeez.... Now, um, I forget what... What was the question?"

"I got so high," Pissy said.

"And I saw how my kids were growing up without me."

Joel gave Pissy an inquisitive look, and Pissy nodded.

"We want to trip on the island with you," Pissy said. "I've been reading about it lot, and, well, Joel discusses it with his colleagues."

"I read about it a lot, too," Harry said. "That helped but not much."

"That's why we want to go with somebody who's been."

"What about Gilli?"

"Gilli's a half-brother," Pissy said.

"And a damn hippie!" Joel boomed.

Harry raised his voice. "But he turned me on to acid and it was beautiful!"

"And he left you alone out there, too, as I understand it, and he didn't check the strength of the agent, and in general, although we love him and he is a generous person, and a good doctor, a good MD, he doesn't instill much confidence in me, see, I, wow, um...." Joel paused and wiped a speck of drool from the corner of his lip with a corner of his shirt. "Pissy, where did you get this grass?"

"Norman."

"Norman? You still see that creep?"

Pissy shrugged her rich-girl shoulders. "Harry," she said. "We want our first trip to be beautiful. We're brother and sister, so we trust each other and there won't be any social hassle. Plus, well...."

"We won't have to maintain any subconscious survival mechanisms while we're there with you. You pack a gun they told me, aren't afraid of much, and we'll have each other to fall back on for support if we need it."

"What about me?"

"I've thought that over. I'm a doctor, a psychiatrist MD, so you should have some subconscious clearance to rely on me. Pissy should be okay because she'll be so much into what she is doing. In any case, I will want us to stake out a common meeting place on the island when we get there, where we can meet, or leave again to be alone, at will, and this will give us a sense of belonging and security. What do you think?"

Harry took a moment. He was surprised at how other people, these people, took so many precautions. "We can put the fresh water there, the first aid kit, some fruit."

"Food," Pissy added.

"No food, unless you think it will ease your mind."

"Food."

"Which island?" Joel said. "Best for us, I mean."

"You can walk around easier on Elliott Key, and most of it will be deserted if we go in the middle of a work week. Especially the windward side. Old Rhodes Key is rougher but less chance of running into anybody else."

"How big is your boat?"

"Twenty feet."

"Reliable?"

"Well.... I always make it back."

"I'll call J&J Marine — tell them you're coming — you bring her down there and have them fix or rebuild anything you're not sure of and we'll foot the bill."

"You don't have to do that."

"And fuel it up. The marinas always have boat-gas and diesel even when the lineups at gas stations wrap around the block. So, it's settled. Pissy will pack the food hamper, and I'll provide the LSD."

"You have some?"

"No, but I want the real thing. Sandoz LSD-25. I have colleagues where it is still legal."

"But not for long I'll bet."

"Don't tell us any more about the island unless you think we need to know," Pissy said. "I want to see it fresh with my LSD eyes."

"Faylie and sometimes Comet live on Elliott Key."

"You know where?"

"No. In a place they call the Valley of the Morning Glories. I've been all over that island at one time or another and I never saw a place like that."

"We'll look for it!" Joel boomed.

"Comet is beautiful," Pissy cooed. "She has long, beautiful legs... She moves like a deer! She's a Nubian. You can have Faylie, Joel. I get Comet!"

"What about me?" Harry said, smiling.

"You can have Pissy," Joel laughed.

"Social interplay!" Pissy warned. "Trips are not productive with-out solitude!"

"You're not Harry's type." Joel said.

Harry looked surprised. "Oh?!"

"Fuck! There go our well-laid plans."

"No sex, okay? Everybody?" Pissy said.

"Awww," Harry moaned, but he nodded his head. He was re-lieved. He never knew how to act with higher-class strangers when it came to things like sex and going out to lunch and the whole range of unfamiliar social items. Still....

"Will it seem real, Harry, after we get back?"

Harry's mind had wandered off — he was so high. Pissy extended her leg and tapped his foot with a red toenail. "I mean, will the **trip** seem real after we are back."

Harry nodded and smiled.

"Is Vietnam real? Joel hesitated. "When Timothy Leary was still teaching at Harvard he said he learned more from his first trip with psilocybin mushrooms than twenty years of studying psychology."

Harry was still thinking Vietnam. "I read that while our guys were over there they took some Vietnamese and tied them to the front of their tanks and played a game of chicken. Dodge-ball with tanks, mind you, and if they accidently ran into each other, the Vietnamese got their legs sqooshed off. Is that reality?"

"Tripping could be an escape from reality," Pissy ventured.

"Bullshit!" Joel rose up from his chair. "Psychedelics reinforce re-ality. Ever get high and observe an army general close up? I did. Two weeks ago. Chicago. He was standing there in the hotel lobby. I'd just gotten high on this weed I brought up to the convention — Colombo — and here's the general, medals, brass buttons, scrambled eggs on his hat-brim. This guy is real? Ever fall in love? Now there's one! Pissy — you wouldn't know. Ever fall in love, Harry? It's a whole new ball game! Birds are singing everywhere. The grass looks greener. You feel like a million dollars! All kinds of energy. People do dumb things to you and you don't even get mad. This is real life? I studied all this shit and it didn't really mean anything to me until two years ago when I got my first grass high, and the whole time I was sitting there — right here in this chair, as a matter of fact — the whole myth of reality whispered to me in my ear and I started laughing! I laughed so hard I couldn't stop! Reality is a state of mind. It's every possible situation!"

"Reality sucks!" Pissy said. "I didn't get as high as you guys did. Bro, light up another one, okay?"

"It's because we're talking too much and you have to listen," Harry said. "Easy to talk, hard to listen. Let's just sit back a minute and be quiet, and we'll get high again." Harry was pleased to see Joel put a new joint back down on the little table.

They sat back and relaxed and got high again.

"I want to go with you," Pissy said finally. "I feel confident about tripping with you and Joel. See, I want us to do a high dose the first time."

"I agree," Joel said. "We want to do the whole number the first time. Do it up right. It will be beautiful if we're ready for it, and we're going to be ready!"

"You'll need boots or sneakers."

"We've got them!"

"When?" Harry said. "I don't really feel like tripping again too soon."

"Not a problem, Harry. It'll be several weeks before I get back to Chicago and procure the tabs. Besides, we should get together a few times first to get used to each other. Plus there's the boat to..."

"I feel comfortable with the three of us now," Pissy said.

"So do I," Harry said.

"Surrendra went back to the island, too," Joel said. His remark seemed out of place. "Those three girls.... Must be the hippie women's lib!"

"The hippie lesb lib," Pissy said.

"You should talk."

Harry looked at Pissy.

Joel laughed. "You can't tell if they're queer by looking at them,

Harry."

"Awww, Joel!" Harry smiled. His own voice, when he said awww, reminded him of Neeta. He closed his eyes.

Awww, Harry — you got high!

Pissy gave Joel the finger and smiled. "I'm okay, Harry, I'm omni-sexual, dudes preferred. Sort of."

Joel said: "Omni? Animals, too?"

"Where's Neeta? Do you know?"

"New York with Gilli," Joel said.

"Dale and Mazie are splitting up," Pissy said. "He has a place in The Keys he was talking about."

Harry's heart bumped up. *Neeta with Gilli in New York....*

Mazie alone....

"Whole band is splitting up."

"What if...." Harry hesitated. He wondered what Milky was doing. "What if the acid experience splits up your whole way of life?"

"We talked about that," Pissy said.

"I'm over halfway there, Harry," Joel said. "I'm over forty, a magic age for a man. Pissy's tired of dating and getting fucked by slick bastards who are as deep as thin air. Her cunt is falling out. Her legs are getting flabby. Her..."

"My legs are fine," Pissy said. And my pussy is tight as new and it doesn't have that tuna smell."

Harry suddenly wondered how he looked to them right now. Startled? Surprised? Learning so fast how well-to-do people talked?

Joel kept on. "What have we got to lose? Reality? I explained real life before."

"What if you two turn into hippies?"

"There are no tiny messages or commands typewritten and rolled up and hidden in those pills."

Drugs change your attitude or how you feel," Pissy said. "I read that LSD only helps you see the way things are."

"Not as how you've been taught," Joel added.

"Whatever you have experienced counts and whatever you have been told is up for review." Pissy moved her chair closer to Harry, and it seemed to him she was showing more leg and tit than necessary. He looked from brother to sister, and now that he was good and high he became paranoid. But just for a moment. "You guys sure know a lot for not ever doing it."

"What about hallucinations?" Joel said suddenly. "Pissy, you're making Harry nervous."

Pissy was definitely making Harry horny. "Hallucinations...." He stopped. "You make me horny, Pissy. Don't stop."

"Gilli," Joel said. "Pissy, can we stay serious for a fucking minute? Gilli said that a hallucination is not a hallucination if more than one person takes the same drug and they all see the same thing. You can't put a movie into a chemical compound. If the acid simply fucks up your mind, you're going to hallucinate different things than I'm going to hallucinate, to simplify this for a minute. But if what we hallucinate is real, then we will all see the same one. And that has been the experience of many who have done this thing before us."

"True," Harry said. "But I have to leave soon."

"Leaving horny?"

"That reefer was good," Pissy said. "I'm having trouble listening and following now, but maybe if you have time I can show you, um...." Pissy sat up straight. "We could get it on in my bedroom?"

"Um...." Harry was not ready for this.

"You can climb stairs, right? Joel won't care."

But nobody moved. They were too stoned, or Harry was too high.

...in my bedroom....

"I'm very happy about you two," Harry said finally. "I consider you both a gift."

"Thank you, brother."

"Thank you, Harry," Pissy said.

"Try the pool?" Joel got up.

"I feel so comfortable right here." Harry said.

"Get up and stretch. See if you can dig the pool idea when you're off your ass!"

Harry got up and stretched. It took no effort once the decision was made. He remembered he had no swimming trunks.

How would that be on the island? No problem!

"Okay!" Harry said. He walked over to the pool and pulled his shirt off, and pulled down his pants. The hot sun felt good on his cock and balls. Joel jumped in naked beside him and Harry went in with him before the smell of the cold, green chlorinated water stung his eyes. He came up for air just as Pissy knifed into the water beneath him in a beautiful dive. Black bikini.

"She has a long, single, black, kinky cunt-hair growing right next to her left nipple," Joel boomed when she surfaced.

Pissy smiled and got next to Harry, in about four feet of water, and pulled down her bikini top and showed him the hair. The rose of her protruding nipple was velvety smooth and pokey like Harry's ex Jewish girlfriend's. Harry carefully approached Pissy's breast with his right hand. He grasped the offending hair and gave it a jerk. "Now you're slick," he said. "You're slick anyway."

Pissy pulled the bikini top back over. "Thank you," she said.

Joel landed a beach ball on Harry's head.

They played ball, and later lay around the pool naked, sunning. Pissy's body, now bare, was brown all over, and she had shaved her pussy. Joel's body was white where his shorts normally were.

"I have never partaken of a clean-shaved pussy," Harry said.

"And no tuna" Pissy said. Joel got up and left but did not look distressed.

Later, when they were all back together, it was cookies and coffee with some imported schnapps in the big kitchen.

They discussed again Harry's guiding the siblings' first trip.

It was dark when Harry headed the pickup back home. He was happy. A psychiatrist and his sister! With a mansion in Coral Gables! And they accepted him as family. They told him so.

And I got laid!

And I had her entire pussy in my mouth. So good!

Not my fault.

Now there's that bond.

Did they decide on that ahead of time? Joel and Pissy?
To get me hooked?
Could she do that? Decide on that before I got there and then do it?
A hooker could. They can fuck anybody!

The expressway was so beautiful, driving high. And the purple came back this time as tiny, bright pin-pricks of light — millions all over his movie screen — no sheets or ribbons.

CHAPTER 21
Ham on White

Several weeks passed by. The edge was only partly gone from Harry's acid trip but his life was settling down. Joel called and asked why he hadn't taken his boat to J&J Marine. Harry reminded him that he was a marine mechanic, and that he himself was checking out the boat. Thoroughly. A few days later, Joel called again to confess that he had missed the score on LSD, but he and Pissy were still counting on the trip and Harry should stand by. He also mentioned that Dale had stopped by to borrow twenty dollars. Pissy took the phone and said that since he had not come back to see her he now would be required to return for another dose of her promised land before they took his boat to the island.

A few more weeks passed by, and the heat of the Miami summer was upon them. Harry thought about Joel's sister a lot but he handled the weather more easily. "All weather is good weather", he would say, but Annie and the children complained about the heat frequently. Janey and Perry both had birthdays. Janey was now ten years old and Perry was seven. Annie's birthday fell on Father's Day this year, so they arranged to have a party all day long that Sunday. Janey and Perry tried to talk Harry into a boat trip to Bear Cut, where they could swim and look for shells, but Harry declined, pretending to be weary of boating — that on Father's Day he wanted to goof off. His main concern, however, was to keep the boat in first-class condition for the time when Joel or Pissy would call and they could go to the island to drop LSD. Annie caught this cop-out immediately, and at the end of the day, which they spent at crowded Crandon Park, she mentioned it. She also began to gripe after Harry lit the first joint of the day, right there on their beach blanket in full view of everyone.

"If you weren't saving the boat, Harry, I could see it. If we were all alone now in the boat it would be okay. Harry? Do you realize how strong that stuff smells?"

Harry shrugged and handed her the joint.

When I called Pissy for another fuck she said she was busy that week.

Every day?

"Not here! Not me!" Annie turned away and ignored him. Harry sucked in another hit.

"They're looking at us, Daddy," Janey said, her brow wrinkled with concern.

"Daddy doesn't care, Janey!" Perry raised his voice. He doesn't care about breaking the law! Daddy just wants to get stoned so he'll be too tired to play Frisbee with us!"

"Perry, shut up."

I could eat her pussy all day.

Cum in Pissy forever.

"Harry, if you don't put that thing out, I'm leaving."

Harry sucked in the third hit and put the jay out carefully, so he could finish it later. "What's going on here? Huh? Look at those animals over there. How many six-packs? And they leave their empties all over the place. They're closer to the trash can than we are. I won't be criticized for what I'm doing!"

"Bullshit, Harry. That bag was expensive, and the reason we're here in Crandon Park and not at Lion Country Safari or someplace the children like is because you spend money on dope! I'm sorry, but..."

"Dope? And what is it you've been smoking every night? Each and every night so you can relax and smile and act like a human being instead of a frustrated old bag? Huh? Grass! My grass, because I paid for it. Yeah."

"I'm sorry I had to mention that in front of the little ones, but you have to be told how serious this is."

"Serious? Serious? Hmmm...." Harry was getting high. The bag was expensive because it was Columbian and very potent. "Columbian," the pusher had said. "Grown in the everglades with Columbian seeds." Annie was lying on her side on the blanket, going for a new layer of tan. Harry sighed and looked away. He let his eyes go out of focus over the ocean. Annie used to be so full of life, so daring, so happy when he met her way back when he was stationed in Colorado. Was it their life together that was turning her sour? Were his demands, his dominance, his dreams killing her? He looked back at her. Mushy tits sliding out of her bikini top. Varicose veins surfacing on mottled legs. Marshmallow-slack belly. Bottle blond hair cemented in place brick-hard with aerosol spray. Cracked nails painted red to match the artificial color on her mouth. Middle-age clinging to youthful makeup. The picture overwhelmed him.

I'm getting older same as her.

I exercise.

I can still run, jump, play....

Work my ass off at the boat yard in the hot sun.

Is this family life ripping me off?

Am I like those TV sitcom fathers?

Harry watched Perry approach. He had just taken a brief run into the surf and came back, dripping wet, his trunks hanging down with the tie-string hanging out a leg, his skinny ribs showing. Perry sneered at him.

"We could be at Lion Country Safari, Daddy!"

"You have to learn to enjoy what's happening now, Perry. We'll get to Lion..."

"Oh sure! Enjoy this?" Perry swung his arm in a large arc, covering the entire park.

"Janey's down in the water alone. The rule is when you're in the water you have to stick together so you can't drown."

"I know! I know!"

"So?"

"**Janey's** in the water. **She's** the one!"

"Get down there with Janey!" Annie yelled.

"Hey!" Harry said. "Don't scream! You sound like an old witch."

"I can scream all I want to! It's my birthday!"

Harry and Annie turned around to look at the slobs on the blanket nearest to them, with all the beer, who started singing the birthday song. "Happy birthday to you, happy birthday to you..."

Harry got up. They were making fun of Annie.

My wife!

Remember — you're stoned.

It's hard to figure out what to do when you're high.

Do nothing! Do nothing!

Harry smiled and gave the drunks a wave, and one of the women waved back. He thought of telling Annie he was going for a walk on the beach, but changed his mind.

If you're going to turn your back on something, turn your back!

Harry turned his back on all of them and headed for the ocean. Walking stoned in the sand seemed weird at first, but he got into it. He walked up to where the surf lapped over the sand, making it hard and smooth. A freak and his chick passed by him, coming the other way. They both looked so happy and so young and so alive.

Give Annie a break.

It's her birthday. Give her a break!

Once each weekend Harry would hook up the garden hose to his boat and run the engines for awhile to keep them lubricated and to charge the batteries. And each time he would do this, Annie would complain about it. One Saturday morning after breakfast, just as Harry announced that he was going outside to run up the engines, Annie made an announcement of her own. She followed Harry out into the yard so the children wouldn't hear.

"I'm not smoking pot with you tonight," she said. And I'm so tired of arguing, so I'm telling you now so you don't try to talk me into it later."

"You never needed much convincing."

"I want to see if I have a habit or not."

"It's not a habit. Remember how hard it was for us to quit cigarettes? Remember that? Shit, it took me a damn year to get over tobacco. Quitting grass would be easy."

"Then why don't you quit grass like I am?"

Harry gave Annie his I-give-up-and-I-don't-care look. "That's your trip. I like grass."

"Remember the other day when you thought this weekend would be it for another LSD trip? Before that you told me you read it's good to quit smoking pot for a week before tripping and then ten minutes after you told me you were going to do it again you lit a joint. That's a habit, Harry."

"So quit."

"I did."

"Okay. And....?"

"Can you go one day without it now?"

"I don't turn on in the morning anymore. Only at night. That's proof enough."

"And the other thing is, I signed up for classes at Miami Dade Junior College. I start in September."

Harry sighed and plunked down on his sofa under the poinciana tree. The cushions were damp, and soaked the seat of his jeans immediately. "Shit!" he said. But he hesitated before getting back up.

"See, Harry? You're burned out already."

"Annie...."

"I read that whole book you gave me about LSD and it's all bullshit, Harry."

"The only brain damage that actually shows under the microscope — that can be proved — is from alcohol. The legal stuff."

"I'm majoring in English."

Harry snorted. "For what?"

"So I can support myself and the children if you become a basket case."

"A basket case?"

Annie was already walking back toward the house. "I registered without telling you because I didn't want to be talked out of it. It's not right to depend on somebody else for your living. I'm going back to school to work on my teacher's certificate and that's that."

"I'm not arguing! It's a good idea! When you're working, we'll split all the bills!"

"If you still have your shit together!" Annie looked at him from the front stoop. There were tears in her eyes. Harry got up and walked over to her, but stopped short of putting his arm around her. "It's okay, Annie. You're right. I've realized it for some time, well, lately anyway. Your life. Your place as a housewife. I realized it the night I came home from tripping and I looked at you when you were pretending to be asleep. Now that's the truth." Now Harry put his arm around her. "I wanted to mention it sooner, but I couldn't make myself do it because, well, if you look at it from my side, see, look, I've been having this feeling lately that the whole family has been ripping me off. Like suddenly I feel that maybe **I'm** the one who's the slave in this relationship.

"Oh, Harry!"

"Well, that's the way it seems lately."

"Stop! Okay! Whatever! I don't want to discuss that right now until I'm sure I can go back to school and make something out of myself."

"Make something. Listen, it doesn't matter. There is no way out. We all end up in the same place at the end. In the ground."

"See? That's why I don't want to talk about it. You always talk me out of things. I just wanted to let you know my plans."

"Okay." Harry removed his arm and stood back a little.

Annie wiped away a tear. "I'm afraid that when you trip next time, you'll see things you didn't know were there, and you'll change again, and where will that leave us? So I have to have my independence."

"Okay, if that's what you see."

"When I see you flaked out in the living room every night stoned, I realize that we've already gotten too far into dope."

"I sit there because I'm happy to be at home. I didn't used to be. Remember that? It's not that far back! I used to drink a lot and get sick, and get stupid, and violent! Remember that? Remember those days? And why do you call it call it dope? What do you call alcohol? Damn!"

"Whatever, Harry."

"Tell you what. I've been wondering about grass being a habit myself — a little — okay? So I'll quit tonight, too. For as long as it takes till the urge is gone. Then I'm going back to it. It's cool. It makes me happy. It makes me peaceful inside. It makes me see the beauty in this world. It makes me see your side, your viewpoint, because when you're high, you can see so easy what others want, what they're trying to do."

"Look at Joel, Harry. A medical doctor and a psychiatrist. Don't you think pot messed him up? How many times did he tell you that the LSD trip was all arranged? How many weekends went by and he had some excuse or other to call it off?"

"Hey, Annie — that's not Joel's fault. The real acid is hard to get sometimes. That's the government's fault. The supply's dried up."

"Joel doesn't have his shit together, Harry. Pot messes people up, and that's why it's against the law."

"Fuck it. I can drop acid and go to places only a few people have seen. Most people don't even know you can go! That **they** can go. Shit! I can hear what music sounds like to God for chrissake! I can go to Paradise and come back! But not if I obey the law and drink beer all day long, and sit around here burping and farting and bouncing beer cans off niggers' heads! Fuck it!" Harry watched the front door click shut after her. Sadly, he went back to his throne under the tree and reached under for his tripping souvenirs. He slid the bag out carefully, because it was damp, and reverently pulled out each item. The bottle, the stone, the broken Tootsie-Toy wheel... He struck the bottle with the stone. The ringing of the glass sent a shiver up his spine. He remembered! He held the stone next to his ear and rubbed it. The tension in the molecules of the stone was still evident, although not as apparent as before. There was another stone lying near the sofa, and Harry reached for it to see if all stones displayed this tension. It sounded almost the same. So he was tuned in on the structures of things now. He rubbed the bottle glass.

It's permanent!

He rolled around in his fingers the tiny Tootsie-Toy wheel he had discovered on the top shelf in that room in the old house. Memories of his boyhood had flashed onscreen. His mother, his father, his room, his bed with the railing on the side, his model airplanes hanging from strings from the ceiling, the wind-up alarm clock with the broken spring which he had over-wound the first day he got it, after his dad had warned him.

Janey and Perry came around the corner of the house and Harry hugged them both.

"Wow, Daddy!" Janey said. She hugged him back, with Perry clinging to him on the other side.

"You know Pearlie in back?" Perry said. "Well, she said to tell you she has something for you."

"Yeah, Daddy," Janey said. "There's a whole bunch back there and they're smoking that stuff. Can you smell it?"

"No...." Harry sniffed the air. "Well, shit. Uh.... Tell them I can't come over right now."

"Ruby's over there too, Daddy."

"Oh yeah?"

"I knew that would get you!" Janey laughed.

"Ohhh...."Perry said, holding his fist in front of his mouth. "I'm going to tell Mommy!"

"Fuck it," Harry said. "It's Saturday. I'm entitled."

Harry pulled his lunchbox and a cushion out of the pickup and settled down under the only tree at the boatyard. It was the last day of July and the heat had been intense. The day before, Harry had shaved off his beard and Annie cut his hair short — one-half inch — accidentally leaving a quarter-sized hole on one side that would be sure to draw comment all through the lunch break.

Sheets of purple light shimmered off the brightwork of the boats as Harry relaxed and worked his back into the tree. It was peaceful out there with everyone in the lunch-room. He wondered why he hadn't done this before but soon remembered it was the lunchroom air-conditioning.

Annie had forgotten the sugar on his peanut-butter sandwich again. "No more ham and cheese until we can go to the store again, Harry."

If she really loved me she would take more care making my lunch.

How can she love me? The way I am.

Or was....

The coffee in the thermos was lukewarm. Harry sighed. In September Annie would be going to college. What would his lunch be like then! Finishing the peanut-butter, he unwrapped the three Oreo cookies and washed them down with the rest of the coffee. For a minute or two he played with the purple, which would come and go, now partially within his control. Harry no longer worried about it.

Twenty minutes to go....

Harry readjusted his body against the tree and stretched out his legs.

Milky....

Milky, you made me happy that day. Yes you did.

And I never ask about you.

Ronnie was standing there and Harry jumped when he saw him.

"Want a hit?" Ronnie handed Harry the reefer and waited while Harry pulled down two tokes. Then Ronnie split for the lunchroom. For a few minutes, Harry watched the veins and arteries in his wrists pulse gently with his heartbeat.

Robot?

Wiring, plumbing, joints, teeth....

I'm only a piece of meat.

We're all a piece of meat.

But what a fantastic piece of meat!

Harry closed his eyes and his movie screen turned pink.

Where in my brain do I see the pictures?

Where's the movie screen?

As if to answer, the pinks and reds gave way to a tiny pinpoint of light which suddenly began to grow into a huge, funnel-shaped cone with a wide opening at the top. Harry floated up to the opening and began to drift down the inside of the cone, which was striped with different colors. The top of the cone was red — a deep band of red — and as Harry continued down inside the colors changed to orange — a very bright, wide band of orange — and then two distinct bands of yellow. The other colors below him surrounded him as he slowly descended farther, the tube he was in becoming narrower. The shades and variations of color became more numerous, more intense. So many greens! Then he passed by an opaque, robin-egg blue. More blues. The other blues were vibrant and transparent, like brilliant dyes. The bottom was a velvet black — deep, furry, and bottomless. Harry's descent stopped and he hovered just above the abyss.

The purple is gone!

Harry was remembering the sequence of the colors in a prism, an item which had fascinated him when he was in high school.

Between him and the bottomless black pit the blue could still be seen. Harry opened his eyes. He had forgotten for a moment that he was at work. Through the humming of the lunch-room air-conditioner he could hear Bo laugh. He closed his eyes again, and was surprised to find himself back in the cone of colors, back at the height of the blue bands. Looking down, the velvety black of the abyss sent his heart pounding. The colors above him brightened. Harry searched for the purple between the black and the blues, trying to keep his eyes off the pit below, trying to imagine the purple and where it belonged in the display. A voice nearby, similar to the voice of his previous, brain-inspection dream, answered Harry's thought.

"It's gone. It's been gone since you tripped. We've been looking for it. We can't find the purple anywhere. We think it's moving around. When we look in one place, it must be drifting through another. Look. Here are all the colors."

Suddenly, Harry backed up out of the tunnel. The tunnel, the cone, stretched out and then split along its entire length, opening like a book — a book with thousands of leaves of color. The petals of color divided into three-dimensional blocks, postage-stamp sized blocks of all the individual colors Harry had ever seen. Some of the colors were intensely familiar: the colors of the boats he had worked on, paint colors, table-cloth colors, tile colors...

The color of the bathroom tiles when I was little and I would sit there and couldn't shit!

Harry searched for the blues and purples.

The blue from Bo's camper truck!

Where are the purples? Where are the purples?

The blocks flattened back out into pages, thin, fragile, like flower petals, blowing by, like in a wind — flip flip flip flip — the blues getting darker.

Getting near the purple!

Harry felt himself slipping away and struggled to regain the vision. The thin pages were flipping by more slowly, then stopped. There was a missing space. Where it should have been attached to the other pages, there were just shreds, floating and drifting out like an electric breeze was blowing on them, strands of torn, missing purple. Tissue of wounded, bleeding, vibrant, purple morning glory.

Bo was standing over Harry. He opened his mouth wide and burped. Harry opened his eyes and slammed back to the reality of the boatyard. Ronnie, who had gotten Harry high, came running over to see what the trouble was.

"Twelve-thirty," Bo grinned.

Ronnie said: "Wasn't that dynamite weed?"

"I found the purple," Harry said. He looked around, avoiding Bo's eyes. Bo's eyes would be empty right now. He didn't know there were these other places you could go to. He wouldn't understand. Harry made a complete sweep of the yard with his eyes, until he was convinced there was no more purple. Bo grunted and walked off.

"It's back where it belongs," Harry said to Ronnie. "The purple."

"My brother had that," Ronnie said. "His went away, too."

"I'm going to miss it."

Ronnie looked around to see if it was cool, and pulled a cigarette package out of his shirt pocket. "The purple's really here," he grinned. He tapped a littler ball of tin-foil out of the package and carefully peeled it open. "White Lightning, no, Berkley White, they call this stuff.

"Harry's eyes widened with surprise. "Acid?"

The best!" Ronnie looked around. "Owsley made it."

Harry stared at the tiny, white, perfect pills. They were barely bigger than a pin head — each a priceless ticket to inner space. "How many?"

"Ten. I've got forty more at home. Thirty-nine. I did one."

"Far out!" Harry tried to pick one up but they were so small it wasn't worth the risk of dropping one. "Wrap it back up so they don't blow away. Was it good? The hit you did?"

"Oh! Harry!" Ronnie shook his head. "Unbelievable! This shit is it! The real McCoy."

"Far out." Harry paused to remember how much cash he had left. "Sell me some?"

"I brought these for you."

"Oh, Ronnie, that's so beautiful, so beautiful. How much?"

"A dime!"

"Just for you, though."

Harry dug down into a front pocket of his work jeans. "Ten for you and a dollar for me till payday!"

Ronnie pocketed the ten and handed Harry the foil with the LSD. "Enjoy!"

"Ronnie, you're a real brother! A real brother!" Harry clapped Ronnie on the back.

Acid! Acid! Wait till Joel hears about this!

"Get to work, hippie mother fuckers!" Bo shouted.

"Aw you..." Harry throttled his tongue. He had had worse foremen to work under. Picking up his lunchbox, Harry headed for the men's room.

Acid! Real acid!

Owsley acid!

The boat Harry was working on that day turned out to be easy. He was mounting grounding plates and a transducer, which meant he would be able to spend some time under the bottom, in the shade of the hull. And it was always nice when he could work alone when high.

As soon as he got into the job, he began to daydream. He dreamed about how it would be if he found Faylie, or Surrendra, in their camp on the island. He wondered if they were there now. Every time he and Joel would talk on the phone, Joel would give Harry the latest scoop on the girls' whereabouts. Harry figured that Joel was interested in them, too, although he pretended not to be. Joel was always telling him how unique they were, how tough they were, how independent. He told Harry how Faylie had just come back from California and how she had balled the men who picked her up as she hitchhiked. And each time Joel would tell Harry a story like that, he would express doubts about their finding "the birds" on the island anymore. "They're hardly ever there now-a-days, Harry — they're into new things."

The island itself would always be there. Paradise would be there. And God would be there, too, whoever SheHeIt was.

CHAPTER 22
Heavenly Meat

They decided to trip on Elliott Key, and to do it on a Wednesday or Thursday when the island might be deserted, especially the windward side which they could hike to from the old pier if that was free. Joel expressed doubts at first about the acid Harry had scored from Ronnie, but Pissy complained that she had waited long enough. As for Harry's desire to look for Faylie again, Joel had only bad news. Surrendra had joined an ashram somewhere in New York State, and was busy getting up before dawn every morning, meditating, exercising, and living in harmony with the planet and her fellows. On the other hand, Faylie was becoming more of a hermit than ever and hadn't left the island since her foray to California. Comet, whom Dale had seen in downtown Coconut Grove only a week before, reported that she and Faylie were too different and that Comet was not going back to visit her. She said Faylie was getting even thinner, going for days at a time without food, that she often came back from runs through the island all scratched and cut up, and would sit in a trance in her camp for hours at a time without speaking. Joel did not know which island Comet was talking about but that Dale and Mazie were back together and had dropped by the house, and the two of them hit him for sixty dollars this time. Something their boat engine needed.

Joel, Pissy, and Harry finally decided on Wednesday, with Thursday and Friday for backup if the weather should turn bad. Annie expressed very little emotion when Harry announced his plans, and helped him get his gear together. She even bought him some fresh fruit to take along.

"You're shaving again — you look clean all the time now — so I guess you can handle it. You know what to do, or what you want."

Harry resented Annie's attitude because he interpreted it to mean that since he had been a good boy lately he was allowed to drop acid with his friends. But for the sake of peace, he didn't tell her what he thought — *fuck her!* — and contented himself with the thought he would have a warm, friendly home to come back to. Now he could embark on the adventure with complete peace of mind.

Although it was still summer and they were well into a South Florida rainy spell, after checking the weather report Tuesday night the three of them agreed that it was now or never. At the last minute, at Pissy's insistence, they agreed to leave after the sun was well up to minimize the blood-letting by mosquitoes and sand fleas. As it turned out, it was nearly ten A.M. by the time they cleared the Gould's Canal breakwater and were powered up on plane toward the Adams Key channel. The sky was clear, except for the usual buildup in the east. The engines on Harry's boat were humming, and during the swift and untypically smooth passage the three of them barely spoke.

The deserted pier looked so inviting and clean, and alone in the brilliant sunlight, standing as it was on the leeward side of the key in clear water slick as glass. They decided immediately to tie up there rather than anchor off the windward side of the island, which was the backup plan. Harry was ego-tripping as he throttled down the engines and headed the boat through the outer pilings. He looked back across the bay they had just crossed, toward the civilization left so near and so far behind.

A psychiatrist — in my boat — dropping acid for the first time — with me!

And his sister!

And back there a million people going through the same routine every day.

Modern people — hip people — people who think they know what they are doing.

Joel was up on the pier in a second, and his agility belied his great size. He was wearing his "garden grubbies" and sneakers, as Harry had advised, but Pissy was immaculate in her pressed white slacks, white deck shoes, and a white bolero over a tiny black, bikini top. By the time they had distributed the gear they were going to take along,

Joel and Harry were sweating, but Pissy remained regally cool. Harry had trouble keeping his eyes off her, and he wondered if this slick, tall, high-class girl knew or was prepared for what was to come. She had tied up her coal-black hair in a neat bun, and was attempting to pin her floppy hat down when Harry expressed his doubts.

"You might have trouble with the hat — the branches — the trail narrows down in a lot of places."

"Will I need it?"

"There's plenty of shade in there. And you look used to the sun."

"Come on! Come on, Pissy, throw that thing in the boat!" Joel's voice was louder than usual. They were all nervous. Joel had elected to take the backpack with the extra clothing for the three of them. Pissy would carry the first aid kit, Harry the water cooler.

"This thing is heavy, Pissy said.

"My gun is in it."

"Looks wild in there," she said, looking into the mouth of the trail from the pier. She was doing a lot of sniffing and remarking on the floral scents, and grumping about being hungry for some "real food!". Joel and Harry were squatting down and examining the acid.

"So that's the ticket!" Joel boomed. He rolled a tiny pill around before his eyes. "Will one be enough?"

Harry shrugged. "If not, we'll drop more later." Harry wondered himself about the size of the pills. But they were in perfect shape, like microscopic aspirin tablets but with a little dome and a perfect, flat edge. Piss picked hers out of Harry's hand with her long fingers, and immediately put it in her mouth and swallowed.

"No water?" Joel was pouring water into paper cups. He watched Harry swallow his and wash it down, then swallowed one himself.

After Joel swallowed, Pissy said: "No going back now!"

The three of them straightened up and looked at each other and grinned. Joel pulled Pissy close and embraced Harry and Pissy together. They all laughed and took a last look at the almost invisible mainland far across Biscayne Bay. The searing glare of the morning sun filtered down cool after they started down the trail. Pissy, as she had requested, followed Harry so she could be in the middle as they walked.

"Would you do it alone, Harry?" Joel suddenly asked.

Harry did not look back. The water can was heavy but he was moving along well. "No," he said finally.

"Why'd you ask that now, Joel?" Pissy sounded nervous.

"I'm trying to gauge from Harry how heavy this shit is."

"Why won't you do it alone, Harry?" Pissy said.

Harry stopped and put the water can down and sat on it. "Rest a minute," he said. He wanted to tell the truth, that he was chicken to do acid alone, but he didn't want to scare them. Pissy stopped next to him, her tan, deep navel inches away. Harry looked up at her. "You are a slick-looking lady all right."

"Why won't you do LSD alone?"

"He's chicken!" Joel said.

"Are you chicken, Harry? Is it that scary?"

Harry shrugged. "I'd do it alone if nobody wanted to go with me."

"Good answer," Joel boomed. "Couldn't do better myself!"

Harry got up. It was obvious neither one of them wanted to rest. "Crossroads up ahead. We can drop our gear there, or we can truck it all the way to the other side."

"Let's take everything along," Joel insisted. "I want to have complete peace of mind."

They moved on. Often Harry would stop to hold a branch or thorny vine for Pissy, and each time Joel would admonish Harry for wasting time and not letting Pissy take her chances. The brightness of the clearing at the crossroads suddenly shone through the trees ahead, and Harry quickened the pace. "Goddam!" he exclaimed as they emerged into the sunlight. "Morning glories!"

The three of them lowered their gear to the ground and looked around. The north-south trail, which ran nearly the whole eight-mile length of the island, was choked with vines and dotted with thousands of fragile, purple flowers. Harry realized immediately that the vines had always been there, but he had never seen them in bloom.

"This must be the valley! Damn! All this time..."

"Incredible!" Joel said.

"Beautiful!" Pissy said. She stood on her tiptoes in the center of the other trail. "Where does it go?"

"That way goes five miles or so. I don't remember but I've walked it."

"What about the other way?"

"I've never been the other way," Harry grinned. He tried to stand up on the can of water to look south, but lost his balance. "It looks like the trail is much narrower that way — it could be — it could be Faylie's Valley of the Morning Glories! Ha! I know it is. I can feel it!"

"Beautiful! Joel boomed. "This place is beautiful!"

"Are we getting off maybe?" Pissy said.

Harry hesitated and shook his head. "I don't feel anything. This place is just naturally beautiful!"

"Let's get back in the shade!" Joel looked at Harry for direction.

"Okay," Harry said. "We could get off soon and then we won't know what to do with our gear and stuff. We'll need a safe place to rest, too. Other people use these trails sometimes. And when we get off we should stop talking."

They picked up their equipment and followed him. Harry was heading east again, toward the ocean side. When they came up to the abandoned house on the windward side and saw the ocean, Joel and Pissy wanted to stop, listen to the ocean, and look around for a few minutes. Harry insisted they keep going. "We've already passed up an abandoned house that you didn't see from the trail, so we can look at that stuff later. Okay? We need to get to the safe place soon." He was happy to see how willing they were to follow instructions. They were more nervous than he was, although Joel was now expressing doubts again about the strength of the tiny pills.

"We have seven more hits in the first-aid kit if we need them," Harry said. "Come on." They turned north and walked between the rough shore and the tree line until they came to the clump of sea-grape bushes which marked the entrance to a clearing Harry had discovered years before. He remembered it because there was only one way in, and where there were good shady places to sit or stretch out without having to worry about being discovered. Harry ducked in first, crawling on his hands and knees for about twenty feet, dragging the water can with Pissy and Joel right behind him. Neither one of them bitched. They were getting off, Harry thought, because for a second he detected *the feeling* which he recognized immediately. But once inside the clearing, Pissy and Joel could only remark that they felt slightly out of breath. The three of them sat down on an iron-wood log and waited. Joel was restless and climbed up onto a tree limb a minute later. Harry passed out paper cups of water.

"Who could have imagined there are places like this on Elliott Key," Pissy remarked.

Harry stretched out on the bare coral ground, tricky because of the sharp edges. "Everybody memorize the location of the water and the knapsack."

Joel said: "I don't feel anything yet."

"I did for a second. It won't be long. Hang in there." But Harry was having his doubts, too. How could such a tiny thing make such a change? "We should be quiet. Just sit and look around. You know."

My first trip the pills were just as small.

Again, Joel and Pissy followed instructions and sat there silently, waiting, looking, occasionally smiling at each other. Crabs click-clacked in their holes in the coral. Several times, a bird which Harry could not identify cried crow-like from its hiding place near the clearing. Suddenly, Harry noticed the flowers. There were so many of them that it was hard to believe he hadn't seen them when they first crawled in. Yellow flowers. Little plants popping up all over the craggy, bare coral, crowned with little, bright-yellow flowers. He hung suspended in awe and wonder. What a beautiful spot! And only twenty miles away from the grinding, grim reality of downtown Miami!

The sound of boats in the distance. Outboards?

"I'm getting off," Harry announced, getting up and looking in the direction of the ocean, which they could hear but not see for the denseness of the vegetation surrounding them. "I'm getting off, but it comes and goes."

Joel swung down quickly from the limb he was sitting on and

now all three of them were staring in the direction of the sea.

"Boats. Shit!"

"Look at all these flowers!" Pissy said. She was holding her right hand over her chest. "My heart is fluttering!"

"It's okay. You're like going through a second barrier. Your heart's okay." *I hope.* "You're just noticing it for the first time. It'll pass." Harry placed a hand on her head but felt strange to be doing that to a woman like her. He hoped she would be able to relax because they were hearing voices now from the approaching outboards, and the voices sounded close.

"Cubans!" Harry whispered to Joel. "Listen to them! Fucking noisy Cubans. I'll bet they're heading straight for the abandoned house at the end of the trail!"

They listened.

"Two outboards, not in synch."

"Two boats?"

The voices were shouting in Spanish, and some of them were children. "Oh, shit!" Harry said. "A fucking family!"

"Their kids'll be running all over the woods!"

"I have stomach cramps," Pissy said.

Harry looked at her. She was trying to be brave, but her mouth curled down in pain. "You eat anything this morning? Last night?"

"We fasted like you said."

"Sounds like they're getting closer!" Joel warned.

"If we're going to do anything, it better be now," Harry said. "I keep on feeling I'm getting off. And Pissy will be getting off soon." Harry grabbed Pissy's hands and squeezed them, looking into her eyes. Again, it was a unique experience for him, but what else could he do? "I'll be back in a minute. The pains will pass, and when they do, you'll be there and it'll be so beautiful!"

Pissy nodded. Harry pulled off his shirt as fast as he could and scrambled around for a heavy piece of dead wood that he could use for a walking stick or a club. He threw one to Joel. "If it's a family, they'll leave when they see us!" He headed for the opening at the edge of the clearing, with Joel right behind him. Joel cut himself crawling through, and cursed.

"Hey. Mess up your hair. Look raunchy when you come out, and look pissed!"

Harry hesitated, peering through the leaves of the sea-grape trees before coming out into the open. There were two boats, and no doubt that the occupants were Cuban because of the non-stop vocalizing and gesturing. All the women, young and old, were sitting in the middle of the small boats with the children. A man stood at the bow of each boat, anchor in hand, and a man operated each outboard. They were maneuvering the boats to point into the wind, backing as close to shore as possible while avoiding running into coral heads barely visible in the surf.

Too small to be on the windward side, jeez....

With kids.

"Let's go!" Harry said.

The two of them strode out onto the beach with their cudgels, stopping a few yards away from the tree-line and staring. An immediate reaction boiled up on the boats, with the women yelling and waving their arms. The man in the closest boat, who had been swinging the small anchor on its chain like a bola, hesitated, and almost fell backward.

"It's working!" Joel said. "It's working!"

The shouting and gesticulating continued.

"Cuban decision-making process!" Joel boomed. "They do the same thing at the supermarket!"

"Look nasty, Joel! Look tough! They can't decide!"

In the confusion, one of the children dropped a beach ball overboard, and the shouting and yelling intensified as a paddle was produced while the boats tried to encircle the ball. After a lot of wasted, panicky motion and nearly swamping one of the boats, the ball was recovered. Two of the men still stood at the ready with their anchors. Suddenly the shouting stopped and everyone sat down, both boats accelerating and heading out to sea towards Black Caesar Creek.

Harry turned back toward the clearing, but Joel did not follow. "Joel, come on!"

Joel just stood there, facing the ocean.

Harry slid through the sea-grapes and dropped to all fours for the crawl in. His old agility was coming back. His ego was flashing new summaries.

That was neat! Joel won't forget how you handled the Cubans!

Look how I can crawl through this coral! Through these thorns!

Like an Indian. Like a scout! Like a hunter!

Better take care of Joel.

Harry quickly worked his way back around and out of the thicket. Joel was still standing there, facing the ocean. The Cuban boats were specs in the distance, silvery aluminum hulls bouncing in the waves, reflecting sunlight from their brightwork, their twin wakes spreading out and dispersing. But Joel was looking due east, out toward where the Bahamas would be. He did not turn when Harry called, and Harry had to get in front of him to see Joel's happy expression and the tears in his eyes whipping away into the breeze. Harry grabbed Joel's arm. "I'll be back! You know where we are!"

Joel nodded, without moving his eyes away from whatever he was seeing. Harry rushed back to check on Pissy. He realized that all his activity was preventing him from getting off, and figured that she would be well on her way when he got there. And she was. By the time Harry got back into the clearing, panting for breath, Pissy was curled up into a little ball under the fallen tree she had been sitting on. Her hands partially covered her face, but her eyes were wide open, and she was shivering.

Harry trembled involuntarily. The clearing was transforming itself right before his eyes. The wind in the trees, the cry of a bird, the hard-shell clicking of crabs in the ground, the colors and the sunlight — all these things were pouring into his awareness without his being able to think about them or being able to judge the quality or the relativity of them. It was Home. It was where he came from somewhere in ages past.

Pissy watched him through her veil of fingers. Her mouth was grim.

"Pissy — hang on — you're coming through now. I'm coming

through now, too — so — you'll have to be patient with me." Harry sat down with her, but the weakness coming over him was unbearable. He was shaking but it was not an unpleasant feeling, and as soon as he remembered to let himself go, to let himself shake, the trembling became pure, heavenly pleasure. When it ceased, his breathing returned to normal.

His eyes focused on a moss-covered rock. There were colors in the moss, purples and yellows in intricate patterns like lace, and reds and delicate browns, all moss and dead coral. A little world, a tiny forest — the rock flowing and undulating — and no matter how hard he concentrated on it the flowing of the rock was real.

Pissy sat up. Her once immaculate clothing was now soiled — her white slacks streaked with brown and green from her lying on the ground. "What am I doing here?" Her voice sounded pitiful — a scared little-girl voice. "Why are we in the hot sun?" We could get sick from too much sun. I don't know this place. Why are we here? Will they look for us? Can they see us from an airplane?"

"We're going to move to a good shady place." Harry looked around and got to his feet.

"The ground is moving," Pissy moaned. I put my hand on the coral and it moves right under my fingers. How can that be? Are we safe here?"

The urgency to move became real to Harry, and a fresh burst of adrenalin got him going. He reached for her. "Take my hand. We can sit down over there, under that big tree. No one can see us there, either."

Pissy took Harry's hand but did not try to get up. They looked in each other's eyes, and Pissy put her hand to her mouth with a shocked look on her face. Then a smile. "Oh!" she said simply.

Harry nodded. Now he was also smiling. "You all right?"

"Yes!" Pissy was still smiling. "I made it. I'm through!" Still holding his hand, she looked around. "Oh!" she exclaimed again. "Oh!" Her eyes swept the clearing, back and forth, over and over again. "I can see it! I can see! I can see it so — it's all so clear now — so — clear!"

Harry shivered again.

"Sit," Pissy said. She pulled him down to the fallen log she had been sitting on earlier. "I'm not hot anymore."

"I feel cold now."

"The sun is good, good. Feel it penetrate. It goes right through us." She squeezed Harry's hand, and released it. She pulled off the bolero and laid it carefully over the log. Then she pulled at the pins holding her hair together in a bun. Harry glanced at her and had to look away and then back again: Pissy's hair tumbling down. Pissy's tan animal in a little bikini top. Pissy's mature unbearable beauty....

"Eeeeeeeeh!" Harry moaned, and ground his fists into his eyes, his whole body shaking violently as he tried to throw off what he was seeing.

"Are you okay?"

Harry nodded.

Pissy got up and stretched her arms toward the sun. "I feel beautiful! Beautiful! Beautiful!"

"Pissy!" Harry said desperately. "I'm coming apart! Don't be afraid! I have to..." Harry jumped up. "I have to... Don't be afraid! Wait for me!" He ran toward the edge of the clearing, surprised and angry at the reaction he was having. The weakness came down upon him with the force of a sledge hammer and before he could get to the end of the clearing where the exit was he dropped to the ground, helpless and whimpering, tears streaming from his eyes, beaten, reaching out for — reaching out for — for...

Pissy, shimmering in flowers and sun's glare and butterflies and morning brightness — coming toward him — alien spaceship mistress — bending over him — glimmering, golden Princess from space. Messenger from space.

Harry pressed his head against Pissy's breast and wept his way through, and when he came through he looked at her and reached for her hand and smiled, and was about to say *Where do we come from?* but the thought escaped him and for a long time they sat there in the clearing, unprotected from the sky, the sun — sitting there together in the Bowl of the Sky, flowing with the planet and the universe without thinking, only seeing, only feeling, only simply there. Simply here.

Often they would look at each other directly and see each other through their eyes: their spirits happy, like children. And their spirits were innocent. And Pissy would open her mouth to speak, and not speak; and Harry would open his mouth to speak, and not speak. And this went on for what seemed to be a long, long, happy time...

Noon. Earth rotating imperceptibly away from the sun, the sun radiating its penetrating energies through the island canopy. Pissy had made a nest for herself at the tree-line so she could watch the ocean from a safe vantage point and be alone with her new discoveries. Joel and Harry were exploring, walking north along the shore, stripped to the waist, using the cudgels they had scared the Cubans with as walking sticks.. They talked very little. Once, when Harry stopped because Joel had found a string of cork fishing-floats that had washed up on the shore, Harry dissolved into the landscape while he waited, and from his dissolved situation, only his spirit was left to watch dispassionately their actions, their surroundings, their planet — the horizon line over the ocean flashing plumes of white energy, the horizon itself delineated in the brightest, purest line of Jade — and Harry's spirit was all there was, and Joel's spirit was all there was, and Pissy's spirit was all there was — in the wonderful Bowl of the Sky.

Twice, Harry left Joel and went into the jungle to rest and to be alone, and to die a little, to surrender, to leave his animal behind. Spread-eagled face down on the ground, he would travel through the Universe, visit strange, awesome places, and marvel at the variety of all Creation while hearing invisible choirs of angels singing. And both times that he went into the woods alone to die, to give up his ego and/or his personality. It was like he was one with everything, not a separate thing. When he found his body again, he found his brain renewed and filled with a happiness so complete that all references to the future or to his past seemed insignificant.

Once, for a long time (but which in fact was only minutes by the clock) the whole concept of time and the reality of present versus past and future became known to him, the illusion of it, the essence of it, the truth of it.

Time flows but it's not real.
It's at different speeds!
We imagine the future coming and then it's past.
There is no present! Time is moving always.
There is no time. There is no present. Nothing is real.
There is no now. This is all a replay!
Everything I think is here is already past!
A memory!

The truth set Harry free. His personality returning from the dead was set free. Later, when they were all sitting together where they had stashed their gear and their water, Harry ticked off his new freedom to himself, and they all looked at each other, and they laughed, and they embraced, and they cried tears of joy.

They realized they wanted to become one with each other, and with all people, all spirits — and that one day they would be doing just that.

Earth, swinging through its silent orbit in space, rolled on, and turned a new face to the sun.

Once while they were embracing, the Bowl of the Sky surrounded them even to the ground beneath, with the blue sky shining up from below through the sparse leaf cover.

When Pissy began to dig through the knapsack for an apple, remarking that she had not eaten all day, nor all day yesterday, and that she felt purified inside her body as well as inside her head, Harry knew they were on their journey to the long way down. He said: "If we each had been totally alone, and had nobody to react with, it would have been even more enlightening."

Joel and Harry stripped naked and floated on the unusually smooth sea, the air now still and cool with the smell of a storm upon it. But the storm never came, the wind did not pick up again, and for a long time Joel and Harry dove back and forth to the bottom and explored the world down there, a world equally as valid and marvelous as their own. Later, they ran about the shore naked with their shoes on, laughing, discovering new talents of agility, leaping from coral head to coral head with cock and balls a' flying, climbing trees and hanging from the limbs. But they missed Pissy, and when they were back to speaking again they decided to look for her.

The clearing was empty of her, and all they found were her clothes folded neatly on top of the water can, with her deck shoes holding them down. Sitting naked on their own folded clothing, Joel and Harry rested, and looked at Pissy's neat little stack: white slacks on the bottom, pink, handkerchief-sized bikini panties sticking out a little from under the white bolero, the black strings of her little bikini top, the deck shoes with little, flesh-colored liners stuffed inside. Joel looked at Harry and smiled but did not speak.

The black strings from Pissy's bikini top fascinated Harry, and he was compelled to look at them often, fully aware and amused at how his brain was programmed.

Finally, Harry: "Where" *(do you think she went?)*

"Here" *(on the island.)*

They laughed.

"She can't go far" *(without shoes.)*

"She's gone pretty far" *(already today...)*

"Where did we go?"

Laughing. *(Elliott Key.)*

"Elliott Key!"

"I stop" *(in the middle of a sentence)* "and you know" (what I was going to say!)

They fell silent again. In a moment, The Feeling descended upon Harry, and looking at Joel, he could see that The Peace had descended upon him, also. It had come because they were silent. A bird barked up in a tree nearby.

(Sounds like) "a black skimmer," Joel said.

They laughed.

"I used to" (know all the names of the birds.)

"Faylie," Harry said, surprised at his own voice.

"That name...."

"I forgot."

"I forgot everything!" Joel laughed.

"I never heard you talk so quietly!"

They laughed again. Joel got up on his feet. "Pissy?" he called.

"That name."

"She's around!"

Joel and Harry were now giggling like children. "Got to have some fun!"

"What is fun?"

Joel's laugh this time sounded like his old self.

"Faylie can sneak up on you," Harry said. "In the woods."

"In the woods!" Joel snorted.

"In the woods so close you'd never know she's there!"

"You want to look for Faylie?"

"Yes!"

"I'll look for Pissy," Joel said. "I'm her brother!"

"Brother!" Harry was looking at Pissy's clothes. They laughed.

"I'll look for Faylie. If you find Pissy, well, we meet here."

"Okay!"

Harry got up, pulled his pants on, and laced up his shoes. "I'm going hunting!"

"Hunting for pussy!"

"Pussy! No. Not really. Huh!"

"Hunting for Pissy and Faylie!"

"Yeah."

"Did you two... Did you ball her?"

"Faylie?"

"Pissy." Joel looked like a little boy, expectant, waiting to be shocked. "You were gone a long time."

"Not today."

"You were gone a long time! In there."

"We got off together on the acid. No. But it was beautiful being with Pissy together."

"Did you tell me that?"

"I am losing our connection. Don't understand."

They laughed. Joel was getting dressed, too.

"Your sister is beautiful! We came through together and it was beautiful. I wouldn't give that up — that experience — for anything.

"Yes. Sister Pissy's alright."

"Yeah." Harry took a sip of water before setting out.

"You going that way?"

"Yes."

"Will you check the boat?" Joel's face wrinkled suddenly with care.

Harry shrugged. "If I get that far. I keep on flashing back into the trip."

"Me, too. Taking the gun?"

"Leave it here in the First Aid case. If anybody..."

"Anybody!" Joel laughed at the word.

"If anybody comes on the island they won't know I'm here. I know this island like an Indian."

They laughed. Harry dropped to his knees and opened the case. "Getting out acid for Faylie," he explained.

"Can you find her?"

Harry nodded but looked serious. "If she's around."

"Meet you here."

"Brother!"

"Brother!"

Harry took off quickly, trotting out to the shore and running along it lightly until he came to the abandoned house which marked the east-west trail. But once into the trail, he stopped and sat for a minute, to rest and to think.

Running felt so good!

Rest and think.

It's coming again.

Because I'm alone. Because I'm not thinking. Not talking.

At that moment, The Feeling and The Peace slipped into him and Harry observed, once again, the delicacy and the wonder and the energy of the planet.

Earth....

The planet, rolling silently on its axis on its timeless journey through the universe, turned another new face to the sun.

The sun does not move toward us, the planet rolls us toward the sun....

Thinking....

Harry turned south at the crossroads — down through the middle of The Valley of the Morning Glories. Soon, he reached the point where he had never explored before, and at that place a new excitement spoke to him. It was excitement without passion or desire, an excitement of change and revelation. The valley narrowed, slowing him down, closing him in with vines and thorny bushes. Something was coming. His interaction with Joel and Pissy so far had kept him from it, but now it was coming. The Presence. The Presence was coming, and if Harry did not go to It, It would come to him because he had given up seeking It, because It was there. It was like God.

Harry stopped.

Not the Bible god.

He was so closed in, with his body entangled in the vines, that he had difficulty raising his arms. But he raised his arms anyway. Toward the sun. He knew that the sun was not God, but maybe the sun was there because of God, and he stretched his arms toward it, tears streaming down his face, his spirit surrendering up Harry's body and mind, and the sun washed it all away and the planet's song rang clear in his soul.

For a long, long time.

When Harry's spirit reincarnated he hunkered down for a moment to regain his physical strength. His mind was free again, but his body was limited. He waited, and was thankful.

All creatures hunt and are hunted.

But when I see this flower here, I know my eyes were made to see it, to rejoice in it.

This flower — all these beautiful things — they were left here for us because we are Him.

All of us?

Do we all have the same god?

Harry's mind briefly switched to picturing his life and his family back at home.

I used to think that ancient people created our gods in our image, not the other way around....

347

It's my brain on LSD and not a god making it seem like God is here.

Harry decided that he was coming out of it again.

But I'm still tripping!

A heavily-armored beetle strolled along a vine and crossed over to a slender branch of an oak sapling, in slow motion, the route obviously a known pathway. The beetle had feelers, powerful pincers, and hairy legs.

To hunt and be hunted in the Garden of Allah.

Time slowed down again!

I AM WITHIN YOU

I know.

Help me to live what I know now.

I don't want to forget.

YOU WILL DENY ME MANY TIMES

Harry's mind flashed on Annie and his home, but he could not make any connection with that and "himself".

HUNT FAYLIE

You stayed with me!

Harry suddenly spotted a tunnel through the thicket. It had been there all the time. He smiled and looked up and gave God the clenched-fist salute of brotherhood, knowing all the time that God was within and without and not simply "up there". And God said:

WE HUNT TOGETHER

Dropping to his already scratched and torn hands and knees, Harry crawled into the opening.

God is in my head, no, he is everywhere. I just didn't know it before.

No, just in my head.

But it seems like...

Harry suddenly became weary of thinking, and his thoughts disappeared but not completely. He crawled silently though the opening in the thicket with purpose and dedication, as he knew now he should do in all things. The tunnel seemed long and narrow. Twigs snapped with a crystal clearness. Numerous flowers and insects and mosses and beetles appeared along the way. Thorns tore at his bare back and ribs and arms, and each time he would get snagged, he would pull the hooked thorn barb out gently — no futile revenge for the vine which bore it.

A hammock of tall trees loomed up on one side. Standing silently now on tip-toes, slick with sweat, Harry oriented himself and found the way. A barely visible trail. It led to the trees, away from the valley. He was reluctant to leave the valley, to leave the morning glories, unless....

A perfect, mutable, exquisite, tissue of a morning-glory flower appeared near his face. He looked down into it, careful not to touch or disturb it. Geometry of fragility and strength and ingenuity. Incredibly, a tiny, black bug was going about his business deep within the flower. A tiny, black bug within his own flower kingdom. A kingdom that knew nothing of sparkplugs, paper-plates, pregnancy tests, washing machines, condoms, clogged septic tanks....

Harry's body stiffened at the intrusion of these thoughts.

HUNT FAYLIE

His body shivered when it came to him. The hammock of trees was Faylie's hideout.

Down on all fours again, he burrowed his way through the next thicket and stood as soon as he could, looking back from where he had come, and then, smiling, looking ahead.

I am ready for her this time.

Harry felt his head — the short, clean hair — and his smooth shaven face, tan with the sun. He knew he looked good, but...

I will never cut my hair again.

Harry could feel his body renew itself as he stood, strong and fit and fast and the blood moving and replenishing.

He knew he was still smiling — he could see himself.

He looked back one more time, over the sea of green dotted with purple morning glories.

His body felt magical as it moved quietly but purposefully toward the dark center of the grove of trees. There were birds. Exotic flowers. Air plants, stag-horns hung peacefully from moss-covered limbs. Butterflies.... And a path!

Around a bend in the path, the shock of a Persian rug spread upon a wooden platform made of driftwood, a foot above the ground. A hammock strung between two mahogany trees. A colorful blanket and a fringed pillow hanging out over the edge of the hammock. A creaking sound to his left — a swing gently swinging — and Faylie in the swing.

Faylie dropped to the ground and stood there at the edge of her little clearing, her hands clasped behind her back, her white, slender little body more naked — more stark and openly naked — than Harry had ever imagined naked could be.

Rays of sunlight filtering through the leaves above illuminated the red-gold halo of her wild hair and the emerald of her eyes, and the ever-changing hallucinated webs of gold crossing her face. Faylie bared her teeth.

Harry's heart pounded up. He was startled and exhilarated. It was not desire. He was face to face with the incarnation of another god. A goddess.

Rings on her Earth toes. Earth's sun reflecting from the golden ring in her nose, and the rings on her Earth-creature fingers...

Faylie!

You are going to run, aren't you!

Harry did not move but he was poising himself to move quickly, as quickly and with as much purpose as he would ever move again. He would move quicker than she would.

"Harry."

It was a feminine voice Harry could never have imagined. He saw her hands unfold behind her and swing gently at her sides.

She's gonna run.

Harry prepared a step toward her that could be converted immediately into a leap if needed, and in a flash Faylie wheeled around with Harry leaping after her and digging in with each foothold on the ground making at the same time the decision to tackle her with everything he had, vulnerable as her bare skin was, but instead, she dropped, sliding, turning on her back like a cornered cat, with Harry coming down on her, pinning her arms to the planet, their wild eyes inches from each other, bare chests beating against each other and sucking oxygen — wild eyes above distending nostrils sucking air, air, air, air to breathe, to fuel their animals — wild eyes looking into each other's spirits...

Faylie relaxed beneath him as their hearts pounded together. Harry slowly rose up a little, not able to leave her eyes, keeping her wrists pinned to the planet.

Her machine was muscular but thin, transparent, feather light, and her face appeared to be laced with gold evanescent threads.

Her spirit spoke to his without words.

They smiled at each other on the Earth plane, eyes open still. Back to the Earth dimension.

That lace, the gold web!

Gotta be the acid.

Ohhhh, I'm tripping and she is not.

The realization that Faylie was not tripping came silently, and Harry released her wrists. Faylie did not try to move out from under him as he rolled partly off her but kept his machine ready to catch her. Then, surprised, he felt her hands gently patting the pockets of his jeans. Her fingers slid down like magic and pulled out the foil with the acid tabs. He could feel her decision to wait and see and he got up — off of her — in a crouch beside her — eyes still locked.

Harry was once again looking into female eyes and seeing a person, and the veil of golden lace was gone.

Get up! his spirit said to her and she was up before he could grasp her arm and he had to grab her from behind as she was turning away. With his arms locked onto her little body in a bear-hug, his teeth clamped down hard on her shoulder.

Harry saw for the first time where a bite on a desired one comes from.

Her fingers walked over his fingers like spiders as he held her. He let go of her but not before pressing on the foil of acid tabs in her hand. He tasted blood on his tongue. His bite near her neck was fresh on his screen. He was tripped out. He was possessed.

He let Faylie turn around. She watched him with emerald eyes, and opened her mouth like a bird in a nest, feeding herself a password to the Garden of Eden. Harry's spirit said: *But you are already there.* Then Faylie held out the packet of Owsley LSD and the thought of that and feeling her fingers sliding it back into a pocket, brought him back down for a moment. Other ego-induced thoughts intruded before he relaxed and left all that behind.

No shirt.

Good that I look in good shape.

She smiled and led him to the Persian rug on the low platform, where they sat in the middle of Faylie's clearing in the middle of the warm afternoon sun on an island on the planet we call Earth.

For a long time, they kissed each other's faces and explored each other's eyes, and through their eyes, their spirits.

For a long time, they sat side-by-side in the garden, exploring each other's machines with loving fingers.

It would be soon.

Without a word, Faylie and Harry entered each other's bodies, lying down, waiting, their meat warm and silent, waiting, thrilling with each heartbeat, waiting. And The Feeling came, and their spirits lifted themselves from, their rubber-doll vehicles with a delightful explosion of energy and cum, and they watched themselves lying there on the colorful rug on the platform in the Garden of Allah, arms entwined.

In the Garden of Eden. Which is the way it was from The Beginning when there was only The Garden and outside were hunters and the hunted. Back when the creators looked at what they had made and said: IT IS GOOD

Pissy and Joel sat at the end of the pier, both of them with their knees up and arms locked around them, looking west over Biscayne Bay toward the last, giant, red fire of the sun just about to eclipse behind the horizon as the planet Earth rolled on, turning a new, waking face to the day. The boat bobbed ever so gently beside them on a sea of rippled glass. As the red winked out from the still-light Bowl of the Sky, the first evening appearance and cries of the birds which skim the surface of Biscayne Bay at sunset entered their heads.

Pissy shivered.

"He'll be along," Joel said. "We've got all the gear."

"We should've left the water."

"He knows we need to drink. The pier is the logical place."

"Logical...."

Joel laughed. "Yeah! Logical. Funny..."

"It'll be too dark to see soon."

"It's so beautiful — this place."

Pissy shivered again, and Joel went down into the boat and pulled out a jacket for her from down under the bow. He zipped her up.

"We came through together, Harry and me," Pissy said. "I hope he's okay."

"I love you, Pissy," Joel said. "I'm glad you're my sister."

"I love you too, big brother."

"Look at that sky!" The sky was changing colors. The colors were electric, iridescent, and compelled them to watch. "Not one color missing!" Joel said.

"Yellow."

"Yellow over there! Look! And up there!"

They heard heavy footsteps on the Earth.

Joel and Pissy turned and watched the mouth of the trail. Harry emerged out of the twilight, naked to the waist, loping toward them with long, confident strides. He trooped down the pier and dropped to his knees beside them. A necklace of red Florida bush-cherries hung from his neck.

"You're still alive!" Joel boomed.

They all looked at each other, smiling.

"How's Faylie?" Joel said.

Harry's face fell a little.

"Comet there?"

Harry shook his head. Tears welled up in his eyes.

"Are you all right?" Pissy said. She touched his wet cheek.

Harry nodded and smiled. "Are you guys alright?"

"I feel beautiful, Harry! So beautiful!"

Harry leaned forward and kissed her cheek. He grabbed Joel's shoulder and shook him a little. "Joel!"

"Harry. I feel — triumphant!"

They all smiled. Pissy dabbed Harry's tears away with a dainty handkerchief, but new tears welled up and his mouth trembled and she held him, Harry weeping openly now, holding her tightly and then he straightened up and kissed her again and tried to smile and she dabbed at his tears again and then he said he was all right. "Really," he said. "I am all right."

They hunkered down on the pier in silence for awhile.

Finally: "Harry?" Pissy said. "Are you okay now?"

"Yah. Yeah. Are you okay?"

"Yes. Yes, I'm okay."

"I don't see any moon coming up," Joel said. "Can you find our way back to Gould's Canal?"

Harry nodded. "Compass."

"We're lucky it wasn't blown off!"

"They fired right at us," Pissy said.

Joel said: "Over us."

"Look over there — look here, under the pier!"

Harry got down and looked under the pier. He could barely make out what they were. Shotgun shells floating in the water. He picked up one of the shells within reach. "Who?"

"Two boats. Spanish-speaking people. No women or children, but the boats looked the same. Could be the same ones we ran off when they saw us this morning."

"Where were you?"

"Coming down the trail toward the pier. When they saw us, **BLAM!** They started yelling at each other for a second and then **BLAM! BLAM! BLAM! BLAM!** They were standing up and firing right over us! We were coming down by then, but still tripping!"

"And they kept on re-loading!" Both boats had a shotgun."

"Branches and leaves were falling down on top of us," Pissy said.

"When? I didn't hear it."

"About an hour before sunset."

"You were on the other side of the island."

"I heard one of them yelling in English: "Fucking hippies!""

"We were right over there. Just picture us coming into view.""

"We ran back like hell.""

"You were lucky.""

"Oh.... We're all lucky! So lucky today." Pissy said. "I'm glad you brought extra jackets and towels. When they took off we went skinny-dipping right here."

"Skinny dipping...."

They all laughed.

"I didn't put any extra jackets and towels in the boat," Harry said. He hopped down inside to check for damage. "How near were they to our boat?"

"I don't think they touched it."

Harry dug under the bow deck and found more jackets and towels. He brought them up to the pier.

Annie!

Annie, you remembered the jackets and towels!

"I didn't know my wife put extra stuff in here. Annie." There were tears again in Harry's eyes when he stepped back out onto the pier.

"It's okay to love more than one human at the same time," Joel said. "It's normal."

"Human," Pissy said quietly. "Human...."

"Normal," Joel repeated. "It all is."

Harry sat quietly for a moment and then pulled off his shoes and jeans. Without hesitating, he dove into the dark water. When he surfaced, Joel and Pissy were standing, calling to him and pointing.

"Look!" "Look!"

"Out over the water!"

Harry looked. "I don't see anything!"

"There! Over there!"

"I still don't..." Harry's eyes scrambled for shark fins. "Where! Where!"

A dull, red, diffused egg-shaped object, barely visible and several miles out over the bay, was flattening and spreading out. It was such a dull, smoky red that Joel and Pissy could hardly see it. Harry could not see it at all, and in desperation he turned and power-swam over to the pier. He hauled himself up, dripping-cold naked. "I still don't see anything!" he said, crouching.

"Oh! It's spreading out!" Joel boomed. "It's coming this way!"

"It's coming right at us!" Pissy ducked just as Joel did, and Harry flattened out just in case.

Pissy moaned "It's going. It's through us!"

"Through us?" Harry stood and looked around. "I didn't see anything."

"Didn't you feel it when it went through?" Pissy said.

"My hair — it's still standing on end," Joel said.

Harry looked at them. Pissy's hair, too, was fuzzed out in an electric halo. "Maybe. Oh well...." Harry began to towel himself off.

"What was it?" Pissy said. "Joel!"

"It was no hallucination, that's for sure!"

"How do you know? It could be."

"We both saw it! We both felt it!"

"I didn't see it," Harry repeated.

"Well, your hair's all on end," Joel said. "That makes it real for all three of us."

They fell silent. Pissy watched Harry the whole time he toweled off and dressed. When their eyes met, Harry felt the same feeling he had felt with Neeta.

"Pissy?"

"Tell me." She got close and combed her fingers through his hair.

I love you, Pissy. Harry could not say it. "Pissy, I..." Tears began to flow again. Harry felt around his neck where the cherry necklace Faylie had made for him was missing.

Must have lost it when I dove off the pier....

Oh....

I love Faylie, too.

I want them all. I want to love them all. I want to hold them all tight in my arms....

Joel clumped down the pier back to the shore.

Harry wiped away the tears with his fingers. They listened to Joel piss.

"You found Faylie."

"Yeah...." Harry's mouth curled down, and he let himself go again. Pissy sidled over and pulled his head to her breast. Harry clutched her and wept unashamedly until the weeping was finished. Slowly, he opened his eyes and looked up at her. He saw Pissy as beautiful and serene beyond any female he had seen before. With a final hug, she said, "I think it's the LSD, Harry," and after Joel dug into the boat for some water, the three of them sat down together on the pier, Harry and Pissy holding hands. Joel patted Harry on the back and sat on the other side of him as they faced the mainland. The distant lights from the Turkey Point nuclear power plant winked and glimmered from far across the bay.

"I'm okay now," Harry said.

"Ready to go back to the mainland?"

Pissy said, "Not me, Joel. Not yet anyway."

"Okay."

Pissy squeezed Harry's hand. He was nodding now — nodding a lot — and grinning.

"What happened with you?"

"That thing you saw and I didn't?"

"Noooo, when you were by yourself back in there." Pissy pointed to the jungle path.

Harry swallowed. "When I was back there — in The Valley of the Morning Glories — I was trying to ask myself — and Faylie asked me, too — why I was going back. Faylie asked me why I was leaving here to go back there — you know — I have a wife — and kids I love. A job I like working on boats — I..." Harry cleared his throat. "I couldn't think of why I was going back, though." Now he was shaking his head. "I don't know why I'm going back!"

"I thought about that, too," Pissy said sadly.

Mosquitoes in the canals near the house, and sand fleas in our yard." Joel laughed. "Food. Fresh water. Money. Shelter...."

"Joel, no," Pissy said.

"Faylie's full of bites, I'll bet," Joel said.

"She's letting go," Harry said. "Letting herself die."

"No, Harry," Pissy said. "She's tough. She'll make it."

"She swims out to boats and yachts anchored near the inlet, and rips them off," Joel boomed.

Harry pictured it. "Yeah, she's tough, but..."

"She'll be okay, Harry," Pissy said.

"Yeah...."

"God!" Joel said. "I just thought about tomorrow!"

"Tomorrow!"

Tomorrow!

They all laughed.

"It seems like tomorrow now but I think it's still today."

"All my life," Harry said, "I guess I wanted to do far-out things. Like this. And nothing bad would happen to me. Indestructible. And now.... And now I don't know."

"You never know," Pissy said.

They laughed together again.

You never know....

"Can you hack it back there after today?" Harry said.

They were still looking out over the bay, toward the mainland.

Pissy and Joel turned to each other. "I don't know," Joel said softly.

Pissy sighed.

"I was told it's supposed to be better when you get back," Joel said. "The social bullshit. You handle it better. The games. It's supposed to go better. You see through all the games."

Harry stood. He stretched. "I keep on getting off a little, he said."Get up! Wow!"

They got up, stretched, and moved around a little.

"You said 'triumphant' before," Harry said to Joel.

"Well, that's the way I feel now! Triumphant! We made it! We're here! This is our planet! We survived!"

Pissy jogged down the pier to shore, jerked her pants down, squatted, and peed.

"Want to go now?" Harry hollered. His energy was back and he felt up to handling the boat. "Maybe we get off again flying over the water!"

"Let's go!"

The boat engines started up like wild animals. Pissy pulled off her jacket and her bolero, and took her place beside Harry at the wheel, Joel on his other side.

Little black bikini top....

God how I love her!

Joel pulled his shirt off. Harry also naked to the waist, pointed to the dock lines. "We still have to cast off!"

They laughed. Joel manned the lines. "Casting off!" he boomed happily.

Red and green, glowing bow-light....

Tiny, black bikini top....

"It'll get chilly when we get up on plane," Harry cautioned. "Cold!"

"Fuck it!" Pissy said.

Slowly churning props washing out the sea behind them as they cleared the pilings. A look back at the dark, silent island.

Looking forward, throttling up, droning over the forgiving sea, foam and spray hissing out behind them.

Happy tears.

CHAPTER 23
Ham on Rye

Several months had passed since his trip with Joel and Pissy, and Harry was still happy. Winter was coming, and on the first, really cold morning of the new season, chilly for Miami regardless, Harry got up and left for work early. The sun was just appearing on the horizon when he drove up onto the expressway on the way to the boatyard. The span over Twelfth Avenue was a good vantage point, and Harry looked from side to side as he cruised along, taking in the view of the rooftops, the yards, the wash-lines, the cars warming up down below....

This weather's going to last all day! he thought to himself.

Won't have to get sweaty!

Everybody's going to be in a good mood.

Expressway traffic was light so far, and Harry had the window rolled down so the cool air could blow in his face and he could hear the truck tires sing on the pavement.

Everyone getting up, stretching, yawning....

All over the world everyone gets up hoping they'll feel good....

Harry nodded along with the song of the tires as his mind wandered. He patted his shirt pocket where he had a joint stashed away. He and Juan and a few of the younger men could turn on with him if they wanted to.

Next time Bo hassles me about smoking pot on the job I'm going to tell him, it's the straight people who make the most mistakes here at the yard.

Errors cost the company money!

It's the straight people who are fucking up the world. Drinkers will start World War-3. No doubt about it! All the big shots in Moscow and Washington are burned out on booze and rich food.

Ninety-nine percent of all the people in the world — all they want to do *is wake up in the morning feeling good, do their thing, have a good day. One percent of the people in the world wake up with their stupid missions and their get-rich games. They wake up burned out on booze or speed and then they figure out new plans on how to hassle each other, hassle other govern-ments. Straight people call themselves the government and then they hassle people just like them in other governments in the name of the people — in **my** name! And the other ninety-nine percent — we let them do it!*

"Fuck'em! Fuck everybody!" Harry yelled out the window.

About an hour before lunch, Bo caught Harry and Juan smoking grass under the ficus tree. Even though Harry didn't usually get high on the job so early, he went on the offensive immediately.

"Chicken! Here! Try it!"

"Harry — you know Mister Calder can see you doin' that shit right from his office window over there. You know that!"

"Bo, I smell liquor on your breath!"

Bo stood back, resplendent in his old navy pea-coat, which he re-surrected each winter. He farted.

"Bo, you ever hear a customer bitch about a boat I worked on? Huh? You ever have a customer have a sea trip spoiled because of work I fucked up?"

"Oh, well, Harry, you know I love your work, yeah, God bless your ass. When you gonna get a haircut?"

"Haircut!" Juan laughed. "You been drinking!"

"Come on, fuckers, I need a hand. Put that thing out!"

Harry and Juan each took another hit, snubbed out the roach, and saved it. They followed Bo over to his personal boat, where the engine hung over it on a chain hoist.

"Working on your own boat on company time?"

Bo gave Harry a dirty look. "I cleared it."

"Yeah."

"Get in there. I'll man the winch."

Harry and Juan clambered into Bo's boat. Harry gave hand sig-nals while Bo lowered the engine down to the mounting bolts. "You know," Bo hollered, "I wouldn't trade you agents for two golden niggers!"

"That's heartwarming," Harry said.

"Golden niggers!" Juan snorted.

"Or four gold Cubans!"

"Down a little more," Harry shouted. "Just a hair!" The engine was lining up beautifully. "Another hair!"

"Now?"

"A red cunt-hair!" Juan shouted. The engine came down a little more.

"More!" Harry shouted. "Just a hair! Another ! Another hair! Another! Hold it! That's it!"

"Damn!" Bo said, leaving the winch and climbing down to inspect. "That was a whole pussy!" He patted the engine lovingly, right where it said on one of the valve covers:

POSSUM POUNDER

"Possum in the ocean?" Juan said.

"That engine's from my swamp buggy."

"Typical short-hair," Harry said. He was glad that his own hair was raunchy enough again for straight people to notice. But he was still shaving his face.

Fuck it.

I don't need a hippie beard.

Bo rubbed his crew-cut, grinned, and rolled out a beer burp.

Juan looked at Bo. "You know what Harry say about your head? Your crew cut? He say: From, a dee-stans you head look like a dirty tennis ball!"

"Thank you ever so much, Juanita," Bo said. "And I don't want you two in the lunchroom before lunchtime, comprende?"

"I can dig it," Juan said.

Harry and Juan washed up, pissed, and settled down in the lunchroom ten minutes early.

"If he was smart, he wouldn't have asked for help on his own boat on company time."

"Okay with me, but I no eat my lunch now." Juan said. "I wait for Bo and Charlie and — ohhhh, there she is again!" Juan let out a low wolf-whistle. Harry got up from the long bench and stood at a window with Juan.

"She gone. See that big car? The Lincoln?"

Harry's heart pounded up when he recognized Joel's black Lincoln Continental with the long air-horns on the fenders.

"Ohhh," Juan said. "I saw her when she get out, but I was thinking — about Bo, you know? Then she go around the corner there and I think — that woman — she something else! Short shorts — little blouse — no bra... It's cold outside, you know?"

"Shit, Juan. Damn! I think I know her." Harry went to another window but stopped short of going outside. All he could see was the front of Joel's car.

"She went in the office, man," Juan said. "Oh! There she is. With Bo!"

A few of the men wandered in, slamming the refrigerator door, slamming quarters into the Coke machine, slamming lunchboxes down onto the long table. Harry was standing on tiptoes, trying to see where Juan was pointing.

Jimmy , the black porter, hollered at Harry. "Somebody lookin' for you!"

Harry spotted Pissy, just as Juan described her, walking with Bo toward the lunchroom from the other end of the yard. She was carrying a wicker picnic-basket.

"Somebody lookin' for you out there!"

"Yeah yeah!" Harry's heart was beating fast. He hadn't seen Pissy since they had tripped together, and he was petrified with indecision. Because it was a cool day, AC in the lunchroom was off and all the windows were open wide. Pissy was sure to hear the comments which were bound to follow, and as she got closer, the whistling started.

"Oh, look at this! Look what Bo's trollin' through the yard!"

"Hey! You know the difference between good pussy and bad pussy? Good pussy ain't got no bush!"

"You ain't gotta dig for it."

"I like mine trimmed above, like pointing to the shaved business area."

"My mama told me never to drink from the container."

"That all yours, Harry?"

Harry made for the door but they grabbed him. "Let her come in — share the wealth — you know?"

Harry sighed and plunked down at the farther end of the table, farthest from the AC where nobody usually sat. Juan immediately slid down there too, bringing Harry's lunchbox with him.

"You forget you lunch." Juan grinned.

Low murmurings and one low whistle as Bo herded Pissy into the lunchroom. Pissy was beautiful, immaculate, tanned, and poised. She stood there just inside the door for a moment and surveyed the room, giving Harry a smile. He tried to get up but Juan pulled him down.

"Do you mind if I have lunch with Harry? Here with you? I don't see any other women." Pissy in her cool voice to no one in particular. Nods and grunts of approval came from everyone while Harry's head filled with pride. Just the other day he had put down a mechanic for bragging. He told him: "How can we be proud of anything when we didn't invent ourselves?"

Pissy plunked down the wicker basket and slid onto the bench next to Harry. Juan moved over a little to make more room. Harry and Pissy looked into each other's eyes and spirits for a moment, and had to kiss. Harry restrained himself from hugging her but Pissy didn't make it and they embraced.

Pissy got up. "Maybe we should take the lunch I brought outside. Under the big tree out there."

A roar of protest came from the table and she sat down again, radiant, cool, every-hair-in-place.

"Look at this," Bo said. "Our Harry!"

Pissy opened the basket and pulled out a thermos, cups, plates, a little box of funny-looking fruit, a small liquor flask, a bunch of tiny sandwiches held together with toothpicks and wrapped in clear plastic. Pissy's Mediterranean-Jewess pokey nipples showed through her blouse, and everyone tried to find something else to look at without success.

Juan suddenly realized who Pissy was, since Harry had told him about his last trip with acid on the island. "Tell her about Ronnie, man."

Harry was trying to keep his mind from being swallowed by Pissy's overpowering presence. His teeth crunched down through one of the sandwiches. The taste was nothing he recognized.

"Who's Ronnie?" Pissy said. She was pouring Harry a shot of brandy into a tiny silver cup. She leaned closer and whispered, "Isn't this outrageous of me to come in here?" Pissy raised her voice. "Anyone care for a tangelo?" She tossed out a few to the outstretched hands. Her breasts bobbed enticingly when she pitched the fruit.

"Fucking outrageous!" Harry grinned.

"Who's Ronnie?" Pissy repeated.

Harry lowered his voice. "The kid we scored the acid from."

"He was cuffed to the bed when I got to the hospital," Bo said. "Nurse said it was LSD."

"Bullshit. Ronnie shouldn't have given them your name as next of kin or whatever."

"Guess he likes me a lot," Bo said, mouth full of food.

"Maybe it was the only phone number he could remember." Harry was getting pissed. The whole story about Ronnie's bust had sounded like bullshit the first time he heard it a few days before.

"They could've called his mother," Bo said. "They called me. What can I tell ya!"

Pissy looked completely concerned. "Do you know for certain it was LSD?"

Bo shrugged.

"See?" Harry said.

"They said that's what it must be," Bo said. "They see more basket cases than I do so they must know."

"Minced turkey," Pissy said, pointing to another sandwich. "And this one's for you, just in case. Ham and cheese."

Harry smiled and grabbed the ham and cheese on rye. He downed the brandy and looked at Bo. Bo shrugged his shoulders again and Harry looked back at Pissy. Looking at Pissy made him so happy.

"I got back last night and I couldn't believe how warm it was this morning. It's hot out now, though."

"Hot," someone grunted.

"Just right," Harry grinned.

She got back just last night and she came right over to see me!

"Where were you? Joel said Canada, that's all. He said he didn't have an address. I wanted to write."

"Quebec. Montreal. I have friends there. It was beautiful. Oh, Harry, it was so beautiful. I got there with my new head. I didn't want to write — don't blame Joel. I wanted to see how I came out and to see what changes I made. Mentally, you know.... I'm so happy to see you again, Harry. I called five boatyards in this vicinity this morning before I found yours. I didn't want to mess you up at home."

Harry nodded. "I'm happy to see you again, too, Pissy."

"Listen to this to this shit," Bo mumbled.

"Pissy," somebody giggled, almost inaudibly. The bench squeaked across the floor on the other side as one of the men got up to rest outside where he could lie down.

"Spanish coffee," Pissy said, watching approvingly as Harry sipped it. She ruffled his hair. "I like your hair longer like this. And it's so blond!"

"Pour a cup for Juan."

Pissy poured a cup for Juan, and for a minute, she and Juan had a conversation in Spanish that Harry couldn't understand.

She can speak Spanish!

Harry was so proud of her — so happy all this was happening.

They held hands.

"I knew it would be a special day when I was driving to work this morning," Harry said. "It was more than the weather. My whole mind and body! Even the tires on the truck were singing on the express-way!"

Bo burped and got up and left.

"Thank you, Harry. It is a special day."

Harry kissed her. They kissed each other.

"No groaning, people," Harry said to the others in the lun-chroom.

Pissy watched Harry wolf down two pieces of cake. "Swiss chocolate," she said. "What really happened to your friend?"

"Ronnie? I don't know. They say he got busted running across Dixie Highway naked."

"LSD wouldn't — you know...."

"I don't know anybody who tripped and said they were sorry. Except in government reports."

"Then what about Ronnie?"

Harry shrugged. "All I know is that they moved him out of Ward-D yesterday, so he must be at least peaceful right now."

"In jail? We should go and see him, Harry. Find out how he's doing. Ask him what happened. We benefitted so much."

"Yeah. But Juan said he's already out but they dumped him off at the county hospital. Jackson."

"What's he like?"

"Clean. Young. White. Well, mostly white."

Some snorts from the other men, some fumbling with their lunchboxes. Trying to find an excuse to linger.

"Works here part-time. College kid."

"Want to go after work?"

"Yeah! Sure! Okay, but I'll have to go home and clean up, first. Sure!" Harry thought about Annie. "Do they allow visitors in there any time?"

"At Jackson? I'll get us in," Pissy said confidently.

Harry looked at her and nodded. She was so sure of herself, and so beautiful.

"Harry. Meet me tonight at Jackson. Seven o'clock? Or what time?"

"Seven's okay. I want to see you again anyway, away from here."

"I won't mess you up at home, Harry."

Harry nodded. "You are so fantastic," he said. He wanted to say *I love you.*

Pissy thought for a moment. "Did you ever see Joel's library? He's not into it now, but when we were younger and he was still studying, he had this dream from when he was little about being an explorer,

Africa, places like that, even while he was studying medicine. I read a lot of the books in there. Big-game hunting with Teddy Roosevelt, railroad surveying with Carveth Wells, Livingstone, Stanley and the other explorers. Trips into the dangerous unknown. Captain Cook exploring the Pacific. No jeeps, no helicopters, no radios in those days. I've been thinking about this so much while I was away, Harry! Those people in those days walked in — into the unknown — never knowing if they would ever get back out. People would snap up any word of them whenever it came out in the newspapers. It was heady stuff, Harry! And now — now there's no place to go like that anymore — The Earth's all been covered and fucked over. Except inside! We can go inside our heads! But nobody wants to go! Nobody! Except a few risk takers."

"Nobody wanted to go **then!**"

"Oh, Harry! Well, maybe. Stanley was far out!"

"Pissy? I love you. I love you since we came through together. On the island."

"I know! Harry! I love you, too! Yes! It's true! But it's the acid. It formed a bond." Pissy looked Harry straight in the eye. "Was it the acid?"

"Maybe. But I love you. I'm crazy about you!"

"Yes. I can see it. I feel it, too." Pissy rushed Harry with a hug. They hugged each other, and kissed, and did some groping.

Some grunts, some scraping of the bench on the floor, and the two were alone.

"Now what?" Harry said finally.

"I don't know, Harry."

They kissed again. It was a lingering, sexual kiss, which neither of them really expected. The sounds of renewed activity in the yard chimed in through the open windows. They got up and stood together at the windows, still holding hands.

"I'm a little older than you, I think," Pissy said.

"I'll be working out there, wiring something or repairing something, and I'll look around and see the other men working, all everyday life going on around me, you know, and I'll think about that day on the island. I'll think about you, I'll think about Faylie, I'll think about my family, and then I'll think about you again. And I'll remember this day in the lunchroom. It all seems so unreal. They call it hallucination but the strange thing about LSD is that the island **is** real! That little paradise **is** there! It's there! It's here! Look at you! You are real! You are here!" A tear ran down Harry's cheek, and Pissy brushed it away with a finger.

"I know. And you are here."

"That trip took a lot out of me — but it put more back in. And it's all real!"

"I know! I know what you're feeling! Everything is real and it's not real. Can they understand that?"

"They?"

"Out there. Your work buddies. Your wife. The president. The congress...."

"Fuck'em!" Harry grinned.

They embraced again.

"Seven o'clock. Visitor parking lot."

"Seven o'clock. No, wait. Come and get me in your truck, Harry."

"Beautiful! In the truck!"

They kissed again.

"Harry?" Pissy suddenly looked concerned. "I have to be back in Montreal in a week."

For the second time, Harry and Annie decided to quit smoking grass for awhile, and this time quitting was no hassle. The fact that they both were broke helped, and when they ran out of pot one night they simply didn't buy anymore. There was going to be Annie's next quarter tuition to pay, Christmas was coming up, and Harry had just spent a lot of money on materials and parts for the boat. The boat repairs were necessary because they had reluctantly decided to sell Harry's rig for the down-payment they needed to move to a white neighborhood where their blond children would be safer.

The boat refitting was not completed until after Christmas, when Harry wanted to take it out on the water to check out all the mechanical work he had done. The opportunity to drop LSD on the island was the first thing that crossed his mind, even before the boat was finished, and when everything was ready he called Joel, hoping against hope that Pissy had returned. The news from Joel's office downtown was distressing. Pissy and Joel had left for an extended Caribbean cruise shortly after the holidays and would not be back for weeks. The fact that Pissy hadn't told him her plans depressed Harry to the point of tears, and he put the boat up for sale immediately.

Often at work, when he had routine tasks to do, Harry would dream about Pissy and about the next trip they could have had, the love they could have made with each other. And he dreamed about hunting for Faylie again, even if finding her would mean finding her dead.

On the last payday in January, just as Harry was leaving the yard for home, a customer tipped Harry a lid of reefer.

"Annie! Annie! Ta da! Guess what I brought home!"

"Money!" Annie said, hugging him. Janey and Perry stood by, hands outstretched for their allowance.

"And a bag of grass!"

"Harry — you didn't spend..."

"You said you quit, Daddy!"

"Yeah, Daddy!"

"I did quit. I know I quit. But somebody gave me this. A happy customer who's rich and does what he wants to do. And I'm going to smoke it and feel good, 'cause feeling good is better than feeling plain!"

Perry grumped. "Feeling plain!"

"Smoke with me." Harry said, giving Annie an extra hug. "Turn on with me."

"Okay!"

"Before dinner?"

"Dinner's ready, Harry."

Perry said, "Turn on. Yuk."

"I'll stuff some in the pipe."

"We're going to get super stoned," Annie said, "because it's been a long time."

"It's been only a couple days for me," Harry admitted. "A couple of the kids at work smoke, and Juan smokes, and they turn me on if I'm around. They think it's cool to do it with an older guy. I never pay them back, though... Hey! Now I can pay them back!"

"Here we go again!" Perry said, stomping out, with Janey following right after him.

Harry and Annie sat out on the back stoop for a few minutes and got high before calling the kids for dinner.

They ate in silence, grinning at each other while Janey and Perry gave them disapproving looks. By the time dessert came around though, the children had picked up their parents' happy mood and were jiving with them. Perry took a mouthful of blueberry pie and flicked an extra berry across the table with his fork, hitting Annie smack in the middle of the forehead.

"Hey!" Harry gave Perry his meanest look. Perry reloaded the fork and slung a whole gob at Janey, missing her and hitting the wall. The purple mess began to slide down.

"Clean that up!"

Perry sat there, grinning at Janey.

"Get up and clean that up!"

"Two ups in one sentence. Yeeeech!"

"That's right, Daddy," Janey said. "Our English teacher..."

"Oh, Janey, shut up!"

"The children are getting smart, Harry," Annie said.

Harry gave Perry a shove with his foot to get the boy out of his chair.

"Love — peace!" Perry said. Janey farted.

"Janey!" Annie said.

"Well Daddy said..."

"I don't care what Daddy said!"

"Huh?" Harry said.

"Daddy said if we're not supposed to fart, then God should fix it."

"No, dummy." Perry was at the wall with his napkin. "Daddy said that God should go back to the drawing board!"

Harry opened his mouth to burp, but it didn't come. Perry and Janey each burped up a good one, and Janey stood up to bow.

"Oh, Harry. What are they going to do when they get out in society?"

"Society? **Society?**" Harry laughed, and Annie laughed with him.

"What's society, Mommy?" Janey said.

Harry and Annie looked at each other, still laughing.

"Stoned," Perry said.

"Wipe that shit off the wall!" Harry shouted.

"Let's sit outside while Perry washes walls, Harry."

Annie and Harry got up from the table. Harry gave his boy a surprise hug from behind. Janey was standing by, looking at him, rolling a blueberry around in her fingers.

"Watch it, Janey."

Janey squished the berry and sat back down. "You're stoned, Daddy."

"Did you like me better the way I was before?"

"Ummmm — no."

"All right, then." Harry took Annie's hand and led her out to the front yard.

"I don't think we're being a good example to them, Harry."

"Fuck it."

"No, really! Advertising getting high to them. And LSD.... I wish you wouldn't mention LSD in front of them."

"You liked me better before acid?"

"Ummmm...."

"Um what?"

"Well, you don't sic Beercan into the house to get me when you need a hand with the boat anymore. That's an improvement."

"Ha! Sorry about those times." Harry hesitated. "No really, I was an asshole. Hey. I noticed you got around to reading that last book I gave you. You know, the two nurses who tripped together on acid on that river? That's the way my first trip was. And the second."

Annie didn't say anything.

"The kids, well, when we were little, we had to conform to what our parents wanted us to do, right? I mean, kids look forward to the day when they are grown up and can do what **they** want to do. Shit, Annie, you and I are now grown up. We are there now! It's our turn to do what we want to do and how we behave."

"Well...."

"Besides, if we're happier for it, the kids'll be happier."

"Harry, okay, that last book was interesting."

"Aha!"

"But see? I finally got up enough gumption to go back to school. Adult classes. I'm getting good grades, too. Soon I'll be able to have my own career in case something happens. I'll have my own career, anyway! Right, Harry?"

"Yeah, I guess so...."

"Uh, oh Harry! Now I forgot. I'm still high and I forgot. Oh! I'm afraid I'll start messing up in school if I get into drugs at the same time. You see? Drugs and school?"

"Psychedelics."

"Psychedelics are drugs, Harry."

"Well.... I'm doing okay at work. I'm the best they've got over there, actually."

"You seem to be happy most of the time, too. I've been getting depressed a lot. Cranky sometimes — I — oh, forget it, Harry."

"It's okay, but I don't know what you mean."

"The other night when we went out to The Everglades without the children, to watch the sunset, I wanted to tell you that I was ready to try acid with you but I chickened out."

"Oh yeah?"

"After I read that book by those nurses who tripped, but I chickened out. Plus I heard you on the phone yesterday with somebody and..."

"I hope it was somebody."

Annie laughed. You were talking about the island and your trip, and I thought to myself, 'What was I doing that day?' I couldn't remember, but you could remember **your** day! My day was nothing!

But — listen, Harry — I don't think you should talk about those things on the phone, you know, you could get in trouble with, uh..."

"Society."

"Ha ha."

"Hey! It's my head! Not anybody else's."

"Anyway, Harry — Harry! Let me finish. I was going to tell you that if it weren't for being back in school, I would like to trip with you."

"Hey! All right!" Harry hugged Annie and then he hugged her again.

"Not now, though, Harry."

"Shit, it'll be years before you quit school."

"Oh, Harry."

"Well?"

"Do you have the urge to do it again?"

"I wouldn't call it an urge, exactly."

"No bullshit now, Harry."

"I didn't feel like doing it for a long time. But after I finished with the boat, I thought about it a lot."

"Remember your first trip? You didn't go back to work for days."

"What, two days? Not because I was not able to. I was so happy! I had this new head! I learned so much about myself that day! So much about the world! I couldn't just step back into the old routine without thinking about it a lot and salting it all away!"

"So what would I do? Skip classes? Would I be able to concentrate? Would I be able to study? Will I get lazy and quit?"

"Did I get lazy?"

"No. But look at all the hippies!"

"What hippies? Most of them were kids, anyway. The hippie thing is either dead, or they got tired of not having money. Or they've headed for the hills. For the country where they can live in peace with nature. Grow their veggies."

"I better not."

"Aw fuck, Annie!"

"It's not a habit?"

"Look at me! Two trips in two years? That's a habit?"

"One year, Harry."

"To a kid it might be, because it's a lot of fun. They do LSD at parties. Or what they think is LSD. They call it party acid. I don't think kids should do it. When you're a kid everything is new, anyway. Why fuck that up?"

"Easy to say if you're not a kid."

"Annie, do you have to make it so complicated?"

"I am complicated, Harry."

"Um, okay...."

"Would you hate me if you saw me tripping?"

"Aw, no, Annie. No!" Harry hugged her again. He looked at his boat waiting there in the yard, with the big FOR SALE sign on it. He looked at it over Annie's shoulder as they stood there swaying in their embrace. He imagined the island.

"I don't know if it's right," Annie said finally.

"How do we know what's right? Where's God been lately. For two thousand years! Huh? What we need is a new set of golden tablets!"

"Stone tablets, Harry."

"Tiny, purple, acid tablets!"

"Oh, Harry...."

"Hey! Maybe that's the way God is getting back to us! Sure! Hey!"

"Harry...."

"Don't look at me like that! We are what we get!"

"Okay."

"Okay what?"

"I'll go with you."

"Tripping?"

"Tripping."

"Aw **right!**" Harry gave Annie another big hug. "Aw right!"

A voice from inside the house. "Janey!" Little Perry, his nose pressed to the screen. "Want to puke?"

"You'll get your new tablets, Annie!" Harry said. No gold. No stone. You'll get 'em direct!"

"Will I like it?"

"You'll dig it. Ohhh you will dig it! Guaranteed! This next week-end! A week from tomorrow! We won't eat the day before — give you a better chance. We won't smoke any dope next week, we'll get some-body we have complete confidence in to watch the kids, we'll give ourselves the best chance we can!"

"Chance? See? That's what I don't like. And why the complete confidence stuff about the sitter?"

"If we worry about Janey and Perry while we drop acid we won't reach the level where our brains can open up."

"What?"

"We're made out of meat, Annie! Meat! When you're walking around made out of meat anything can go wrong. Anything can go good, too! We're all meat, and it's all a game of chance!" Harry im-mediately regretted the choice of words."You'll see!"

"Next Saturday."

"Next Saturday!"

"I'll like it?"

"We'll be so happy, Annie. So happy."

"What if a real me comes out and you don't like it? I read that can happen."

"It will be you without the garbage."

"Mommy! The blueberry won't come off the wall!"

"I'll be there in — in a minute!"

"That's two ins in one sentence, Mommy!"

"Mommy! Perry is rubbing it in deeper!"

"Wait, Harry," Annie said. "I'll be right back out."

Harry plunked down in his sofa under the poinciana tree and positioned himself so he could have his feet up and look at the boat at the same time. He pictured the island, imagining his boat bobbing up and down alongside the old abandoned pier. He pictured Faylie and he pictured Pissy. When he pictured Faylie and Pissy, tears came. When Annie returned she saw him weeping, weeping for her, she thought, and she told him she loved him.

It was morning, and time to wake up the children so they could have plenty of time getting ready for school. Annie had already left to catch her bus for an early class, and Harry was content, sitting at the dining-room table with his coffee and looking out into the neighbor's empty back yard. He was thinking about what to add to the big, bold list he was making up for their trip:

FIRST AID KIT (gun inside)
ACID (waterproof pill box)
APPLES
CANTEENS
JACKETS
TOWELS
GAS UP BOAT

He thought about all the work he had done on the boat. It looked beautiful now. He would have to remember to take down the FOR SALE sign on it before Saturday so no one would come up to them and ask them a lot of questions about it while they were tripping. He knew he was a good mechanic and that his craftsmanship would be immediately apparent to any prospective buyer who knew boats...

TAKE OFF FOR SALE SIGN
LIFE JACKETS
TOOL BOX
EXTRA DRY CLOTHES—ANNIE
KLEENEX
PAPER TOWELS

Harry tapped the pencil on the table, wondering if he was forgetting anything.

It's nice not thinking about pussy all the time....

Will I want to put the for-sale sign back on after? Better not mention that to Annie before she trips.

KNIFE
TRAILER TIRE PRESSURE

He watched the neighbor's washing machine begin to hop around on its outdoor concrete slab. **THUMP THUMP THUMP**

THUMP

The load must be out of balance. Can't they hear it?

Harry pictured Ruby, so fine.

What does she do in there?

Wonder if Annie's body will gross me out when I'm tripping....

What if I can't handle that? Is that possible?

Yes — it's possible.

THUMP THUMP THUMP THUMP

That thing's going to hop right off the slab! No, it'll unplug itself first.

No — it's got a long cord, well, maybe not that long....

Oh, shit, there it goes!

Harry watched Ruby fly out her back door just as the washing machine unplugged itself, teetering on the edge of the slab. Ruby shot a glance at Harry's dining-room window as she ran out.

Does she know I sit here sometimes?

Yeah.

Putting on those little white shorts and that green bra!

Running around in just a bra on top — that's a tough chick.

He watched Ruby put all her weight against the machine, trying to horse it back up on the slab so she could get the cord to reach. He watched her long chocolate legs, her little teenage ass sticking out, shoving and pushing.

EASY, HARRY, IT'S ONLY FLESH AND BLOOD AND BONE — ONLY MEAT

Only meat arranged in a certain way....

Wonder if Annie will — no — she was too chicken to strip on the island before. Before we knew about LSD.

She'll be tripping this time, though....

She'll change. Might not be into balling on her first trip....

She'll be so surprised at what it's really like!

BLANKET

PILLOW

Ruby quit in desperation and faced Harry's window, hands on her hips, hair tousled, tiny waist, deep navel, eyes like Bambi.

IT'S ONLY MEAT, HARRY

Yeah, but....
WE CAN'T LIVE ON EARTH AS SPIRITS
EARTH IS PHYSICAL
EARTH IS A PHYSICAL TRIP
WHAT YOU SEE IS WHAT WE SEE
WHAT YOU TOUCH WE TOUCH
YOU OWE US
Harry was having a conversation with himself.
Who are these people in my head? Angels? God?
Ruby was back at trying to move the machine.
Dynamite chocolate ass!
GO OUT THERE
Who are you to tell me...
YOU KNOW WHO I AM
You are only meat because my brain is all meat.
YOU KNOW BETTER THAN THAT
Harry heard Ruby shout at her house: "Mama!"
WITHOUT ME THERE WOULD BE NO SOUNDS
NO SMELLS
NO EARTH
NO UNIVERSE
NO MOVIES OF RUBY'S CHUNKY LITTLE ASS
Other people don't worry about it. Why should I?
OTHER PEOPLE ARE ALL IN YOUR HEAD
Other people are out there! Meat, like me!
EVERYTHING IS IN YOUR HEAD
YOU are only in my head, too!
I AM EVERYWHERE
Prove it.
"Mister Harry!" Ruby was at the fence, calling to him.
Harry got up.
Heavy! You are a heavy dude!
Ruby in her white shorts and little green Sears bra.
Janey irons hers so they come to a point.
Bet Ruby doesn't need to iron hers!

"Thank you, Harry," Ruby said after he had shoved the washing machine back into place. She bent over to plug it back in.

Harry caught his breath. "Better even-out the load before you start it back up. It's out of balance."

Ruby flipped open the cover and shoved the load around, keeping her Bambi eyes on him. Her teeth looked so white. Her lips so succulent. "I sure am glad you was home!"

Harry smiled back, his heart pounding with desire. "Just so long as you remember me when the revolution starts!"

"Ha!" Ruby laughed, taking a step closer to him. "That all ole jive-talk." Her surprisingly expensive scent filled Harry's brain as she moved her mouth close to his ear. "You know there ain' gonna be no revolution. You got to keep smilin' for today, Mister Harry!"

EPILOGUE

Harry buried Faylie under the mahogany tree in her secret camp in the Valley of the Morning Glories, under her swing, and it took him two days. Sleeping in her camp overnight, he chastised himself for laughing back on the mainland when Joel had quipped that living the way she did on Elliott Key she was probably "full of bites by now". Taking Friday off from work, Harry had made the trip to the island to look for her, explaining to Annie that he needed to check out the improvements to the boat before bringing Annie out for her first acid trip. Now he was particularly glad Annie was not along or he would have had to explain who and what Faylie was, and how much he had loved and admired her.

The coral and the tree roots took all of Harry's strength but he did manage a fairly decent grave although it partly filled with a salt-water seep before he could lower her body into it.

Beautiful spirit with a body covered with bites.
She hasn't been dead very long....
The hippies don't think ahead very much.
Where are the rest of them? Her friends?
I got here just at the right time.

Harry did not consider complying with any expectations that he should report the discovery of Faylie's body. That would spoil what she had dreamed of for her death: an anonymous dissolving of her essence to nourish what she considered her special place on the planet. To become one with it.

Faylie's camp, already showing signs of neglect during her last days alive, would soon be dissolved into the elements as well.

A week later with Annie, Harry did not trip himself but kept an eye on things just in case. Her first time with LSD, however, surprised him. On the way back home, with the boat performing beautifully and Annie talking her head off, she described the spray turning to diamonds, the magical feel of the engines flying them along, and her paranoia upon nearing Gould's Canal and the return to civilization. Her first remark as they slowed for the canal was: "The for sale sign goes!"

"Huh?"

"For this boat!" We need this boat! Not for sale!"

Harry happily agreed but kept silent about the boat sale being part of their new house and neighborhood plans.

"We don't need to move right away," Annie said.

"You sure started off strangely. You were..."

"I thought you left me so I could be all alone!"

"I did, but I peeked. About an hour after you dropped I followed your voice and you were in a muddy spot and talking in a little girl voice. You kept on complaining and looking at your messed up shoes. You sounded like a first-grader. You said stuff like, "Here I am all alone in this mud and everything. Where am I? All this mud. How do I get all this mud off."

"Do I sound normal now?"

Harry nodded but Annie flashed back to tripping again and as they idled up to the boat hoist, where the truck and trailer were parked, she was happy and paranoid at the same time. "I hope you know what you're doing because I sure don't. How do you people get home when you're tripping?"

He left her with the boat and could see her there through the windshield now as the trailer clattered along behind the truck, Annie sitting in a clump and nearly in the way while the hoist attendants, looking bored at the end of their day, held the chain hooks in hand. For another five bucks they would take care of everything and Annie suddenly stood up and began digging in the pockets of her jacket for a fiver. "Ohhhh, I don't have any money. Ohhhh...."

The hoist operators, still looking a little numb, took a ten from Harry and lowered their boat onto the trailer without a word.

Alcohol, Harry thought. *Oil heads.*

"The last boat, they gave us a doobie," the younger man said. "You ain't the only ones come here stoned." The older man turned his head and spit.

"The old lady's on acid," Harry said. He was strapping the stern down for the trip home.

"I knew it, I knew it!"

Annie smiled and did a little whirl. "This place is so beautiful! I love it here! Love it!"

The two operators, both whose appearance was unlikely to remain in memory long, rolled their eyes. " Mister, there's another boat waiting."

Harry herded Annie to her side of the pickup and they were off, on their way to a life with a considerably better understanding of each other, their children, their neighbors, and the planet they lived on.

With the windows rolled down Harry heard one of the operators yell after them: "Don't forget to send Timothy Leary a Christmas card!"

During the next several months before Christmas, Harry and Annie did four acid trips together, but on Old Rhodes Key which was more difficult to get to and less likely to be visited by others. The bay side was shallow, and there was only one spot on the windward side deep enough for Harry to nose up near enough the rocks to unload camping gear, food, and water, keeping the engines idling in reverse and ready to power backwards at the slightest problem while the two new bilge pumps, ported on opposite sides, pumped out whatever sea came in over the transom. In Harry's mind, his beloved Elliott Key was no longer safe. If any kind of danger was on one's mind, no amount of LSD-25 would allow the brain to surrender completely. All survival mechanisms need to be shut off for that, the way he saw it. That was what he had read, also. And being with his old hippie friends was no longer appealing, either, but he would never forget how they had welcomed his redneck ass into their midst and turned him on to an open way of thinking. A marvel of thinking.

Well, I miss Neeta....

"Awww, Harry."

Pissy had broken off contact. Not deliberately, Harry told himself, but because her life was so different. Her social class, her Jewish friends.... Her psychiatrist brother also had become short with him, not deliberately Harry was sure, but the few times he called to ask about Pissy, Joel was blunt enough.

During the rest of the Miami winter, such as that is, Annie began devouring copies of "The Mother Earth News" and dreaming of growing their own food, communing with Nature, baking her own bread — "All that hippie stuff!" she would say. "That's what I want to do!" She did not need to convince Harry, who was overcome with a similar enthusiasm after finding a used copy of Stewart Brand's huge book of self survival: "The Whole Earth Catalog". Then, for $3.33 a brand new copy of "Be Here Now" by Ram Dass, especially the pages in the middle printed on yellow paper. Now the search for a remote country place to move to began in earnest. But when they found some land in the Florida Panhandle, 600 miles from Miami on a dead-end dirt road, Harry began dragging his feet.

No more little foxes like Ruby.

No more paychecks from the boatyard job.

Fifty miles to the Gulf of Mexico and a boat ramp. Maybe sixty.

The kids going to a bible-belt school.

Bible-belt cops using choppers to look for marijuana patches.

The acreage needed a well and that would require a down payment to the electric company, so while the Miami house was up for sale they sold the boat and had a camper-trailer moved in on the new property as far from the road as practical. With the boat gone and the journey up to the new place a day-long drive, Harry hung onto his job but despaired for the future. Annie, however, was ecstatic and soon as it was possible she moved up to their new Northwest Florida place with Perry and Janey.

Harry lucked out via a Cuban customer at the boatyard on a fantastic Miami upper flat for a hundred a month plus keeping his eye on the property at night and occasional services on the owner's offshore boat, which was parked in the huge garage below the flat. Annie's first report, from a payphone, included: "The kids love it here and Perry's asthma is gone. Gone totally!"

"That's because it's summer. Wait until school starts and see how they like it."

"Harry, when you come up to visit, don't call my new man of the house Little Perry anymore. Anyway we need you to do the plumbing and get some firewood ready for winter. They say it freezes here sometimes during the winter."

"Soon as the house sale is final we are buying a chain saw."

"You still want to do this? You don't sound very happy. Wait, Perry wants to talk. Anyway, can you come up this weekend? The house needs work."

In the background Harry could hear Janey and Perry arguing, then Perry yelling at his mother: "It's not a house! It's a fucking trailer!"

To be continued....

CURRENTLY AVAILABLE
in the Schaffner trilogy

Previously published and now complete. Some series characters also appear in a few short stories.

"Harry & Ivory"

This is the sequel to "All Meat", set a short while later. Harry Schaffner's extra-marital desires come to a boil when he becomes besotted with a young woman who would be considered strange for any race. Trying to balance the love for his family vis-a-vis the devil-black Ivory, Harry creates even more excitement by trying to keep happy a Cuban drug-smuggling gang whom he works for as a 2nd job. A story within the story involves Harry's family safely moved 600 miles away to a country place in the Florida panhandle. His two, bratty children — unwelcome immigrants from Miami — become the scourge of their new bible-belt school. Readers will be turning the pages just for these outrageous kids who are now teenagers, but home-schooler parents may want to hide this book under the bed.

"Lowboy #22"

The sequel to "Harry & Ivory", this novel finds the Schaffners twenty years later, with Perry and Janey in their 30s after having become a somewhat immoral and murderous team as they slog around the USA in a semi-trailer truck. Although pulp-fiction at its evolved best, this sequel is a crime story and not a mystery book or puzzle piece per se. Not all dilemmas are resolved, just as such things are often not resolved in a reader's own life. It is enjoyable to experience the gamey drama, however — which never flags — from the safety of an armchair. The introduction of a new character, Little Harold, age 13, provides a break with a touching and stirring tale of young love.

Other, unrelated novels by John Aalborg are not listed here.

AUTHOR'S NOTE

Current usage of bathtub or "party acid" produces a less than positive experience. It is my hope that soon the pure form of LSD, a powerful psychological tool for good, can become available once again and the isolation protocol reinstated by users.

During the time period when Harry and the hippies camped on the barrier islands described in this novel, the islands were uninhabited. Since then Elliott Key has been sacrificed to "progress". It had been declared part of a "national monument", and easy access was soon provided, visitor centers set up, and rangers assigned. The fate of the even more remote and pristine island to the south, Old Rhodes Key, continues to deteriorate via government interference.

PUBLISHER'S NOTE

The term "The Sixties" is generally accepted as a time within the 1960s to the mid 1970s.

There are several pages in this story where the trippers' experiences may seem unbelievable to readers. We have checked with sources acquainted with the subject and time period, and found the author's descriptions to be accurate. It was also determined that the rough and abusive, working-class character, Harry, would not have had the transformative experiences with LSD-25 had he not been alone or in isolation from society while tripping. Governments around the world at the time were officially experimenting with the drug but with patients and volunteers who were hovered over during the process and confined to busy, laboratory settings in artificial light. Negative results were the norm.

This is a scan (no date) of what was found at the bottom of the box which contained the original typewritten manuscript. It seems to be a newspaper clipping referring to the "orange glow" phenomenon experienced by the trippers Joel and Pissy near the end of this story (but missed by Harry).

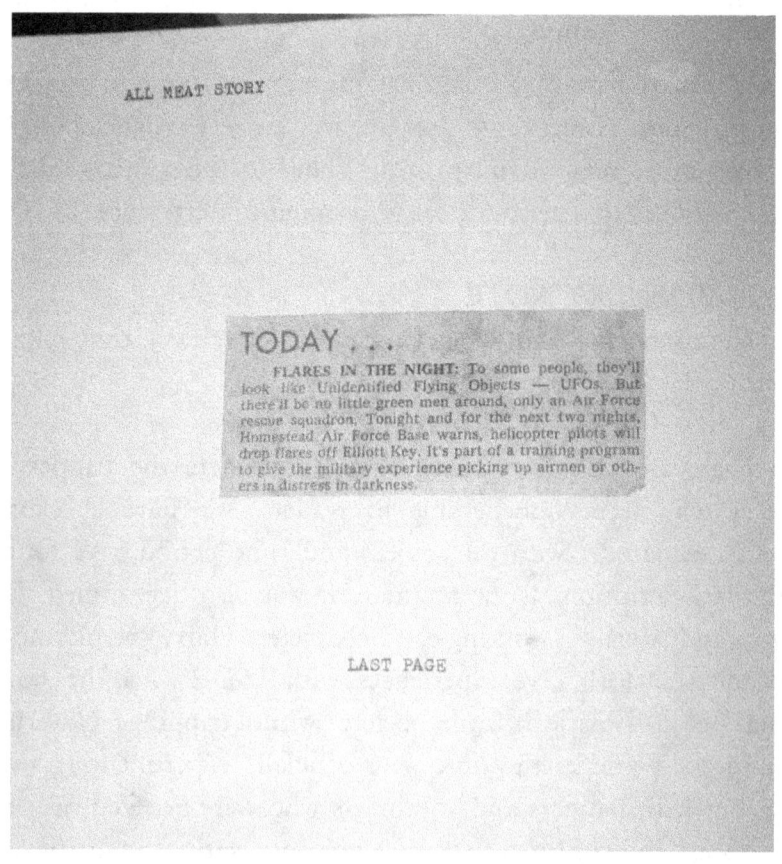

ALL MEAT STORY

TODAY . . .

FLARES IN THE NIGHT: To some people, they'll look like Unidentified Flying Objects — UFOs. But there'll be no little green men around, only an Air Force rescue squadron. Tonight and for the next two nights, Homestead Air Force Base warns, helicopter pilots will drop flares off Elliott Key. It's part of a training program to give the military experience picking up airmen or others in distress in darkness.

LAST PAGE

In addition to his novels and internationally published "Over the Road" articles, John Aalborg wrote the Axel McKay radio-play series aired coast-to-coast and sponsored by Ford and Caterpillar, numerous magazine publications of trucking experiences in foreign countries, and he continues to write a monthly road column by "Mo'hammer and Cheater".

www.ingramcontent.com/pod-product-compliance
Lightning Source LLC
Chambersburg PA
CBHW071151020726
47502CB00002B/365